Born and brought u[...] began her career in [...] years before becomi[...] into the world of jou[...] 'proper job' as Books and Fiction Editor on *Woman's Own* magazine in 1990, she has written features and fiction for various newspapers and magazines. Her first novel, *Real Women*, has been adapted into a 3 part BBC television series. She lives in North London with her husband and four daughters.

Also by Susan Oudot

REAL WOMEN

Virtual Love

SUSAN OUDOT

POCKET
BOOKS

LONDON · SYDNEY · NEW YORK · TOKYO · SINGAPORE · TORONTO

First published in Great Britain by Simon & Schuster, 1997
This edition first published in 1998 by Pocket Books
An imprint of Simon & Schuster Ltd
A Viacom Company

Simon & Schuster Ltd
West Garden Place
Kendal Street
London
W2 2AQ

Simon & Schuster Australia
Sydney

A CIP catalogue record for this book is available from the British
Library.

ISBN 0-671-85470 4

1 3 5 7 9 10 8 6 4 2

Printed and bound in Great Britain by Cox & Wyman Ltd, Reading,
Berkshire

For Daisy and Percy Oudot
with love and gratitude

– *April* –

The ambulance screeched to a halt at the end of the narrow West End lane, directly opposite the glass-fronted offices of Virt-E-Go PLC, its blue light flashing. It was mid-afternoon and a small crowd of shoppers and office workers stopped to watch as the green-uniformed medics jumped down and ran round the back of the vehicle, throwing open the doors and taking a stretcher and a bag of medical equipment from inside.

'Make way!' one of the medics cried as the two ran inside the building, past a bemused-looking janitor, who looked up from his mop and bucket at the clamour. The medics paused, taking in the fact that the solitary lift at the far end of the marble-floored reception area was stacked wall to wall with packing cases, then ran over to the stairway, to the right of the main reception desk.

'Third floor!' Carol, the receptionist, a tiny, neat-looking woman in her thirties, called after them, her dark-curled head popping up over the counter, but she was too late. They had already disappeared around the turn of the stairs.

Up on the third floor, a young woman – her voluptuous, full-formed figure squeezed tightly into a simple black dress – strained forward on her toes, peering out of the window at the flashing light of the ambulance down below.

From the far side of the hallway, Bob Guppy, Virt-E-Go's balding, middle-aged Marketing Manager called over to her, one hand raking distractedly through his thinning hair, a VR helmet dangling from the other. 'Chastity? Where in God's name are they? The poor bastard will be dead before they get here!'

'It's okay,' the girl said soothingly, turning from the window, the sound of hurried footsteps coming from the stairs nearby. 'They're on their way.'

'Thank bloody Christ!' Guppy said, and disappeared back through the plastic flaps that covered the doorway to the laboratory.

There was the smell of burning rubber in the air, while from the lab itself came the hiss and fizz of a machine electrically shorting. From time to time a low groan could be heard – the deep, incoherent sound of a man in intense pain.

Coming to the head of the steps, the two medics stopped dead, staring at the sight that met their eyes. Chastity Lloyd stared back at them from wide green eyes that were capped with long dark lashes, then made an impatient gesture at them.

'Well?' she said, her voice betraying strong working-class origins. 'Ain't you gonna help him?'

The reminder brought them back to sudden life. With a nod, the two ran past her and through the flaps. Chastity waited a moment, hearing them noisily clear their throats as they took in the scene, then she click-clacked across the hall and into the lab.

Nobushi Fukuada was where they'd left him, curled up like a spiked hedgehog on the floor beside the machine, his wide Japanese face creased with pain as he clutched his manhood. Apart from an expensive watch which doubled as a TV and fax-modem, he was completely naked.

The two medics were kneeling either side of him, trying to persuade him to remove his hands from the afflicted area so they could assess the damage, but Mr Fukuada seemed most reluctant. And who could blame him? His plain dark business suit hung on a hanger to the right, like a badge of corporate respectability, while just beyond him the machine sparked and hissed, chattering to itself from time to time, like some alien kitchen appliance that had been partly dismantled. The hoselike attachment – which reminded Chastity of a cross between a small vacuum cleaner accessory and the moist dark muzzle of a seal – hung limply now, a wisp of smoke rising from its mouth.

The sensory pads were scattered here and there across the laboratory floor, wires trailing where Mr Fukuada had torn them from his body in his agony. To her untrained eyes they looked like strange, alien tadpoles.

To the left of this scene, the twins – William and Benjamin – looked on sympathetically, their hands, she noted, positioned over their own crotches, as if the accident had triggered some deep, primal response in them. Their normally pristine white lab coats were smoke-blackened and stained, their faces black, but for the white rings round their eyes where the goggles had been.

'*Chas-tity*!' Bob Guppy hissed from the far side of the room, the way he broke her name into two distinct parts irritating her as always. '*Chas-tity*!'

She looked across. Her boss was clutching the handset of a phone to his chest and staring at her with desperate, pleading eyes. Sighing inwardly, she went across to him.

'Yes, what is it?'

'I can't get him!' he answered, almost doubling up in his anxiety.

'Can't get *who*?'

'Sir James!' he answered, almost apoplectic now. 'That bloody bitch Patricia won't let me speak to him! She says the board meeting's already started and he's not to be disturbed. Explain to her, will you, before I say something I might live to regret. I'll see what's happening with the Jap.'

Chastity put her hand out for the phone. 'Leave it with me,' she said calmly. 'I'll sort it out.'

Taking the handset, she waited a moment, watching as Guppy crossed the lab floor, gingerly skirting the sparking machine, the medics and the groaning, naked man, then put it to her ear, speaking into the receiver, her voice matter-of-fact, as if she were ordering sandwiches from the greasy spoon café on the corner.

'Patricia? . . . Yeah, it's Chastity. We've got a bit of a problem down here . . . Yeah, Sir James *will* have to know . . . Well, I suppose it *can* wait till he's finished his speech . . . Yeah. Okay. I'll do what I can. Bye.'

She put the phone down, then looked across again. Bob Guppy was standing in front of the twins, glaring at them angrily, but they simply shrugged, as if it were all a total mystery to them. Closer to hand, the medics had finally succeeded in persuading Mr Fukuada to remove his hands. As his toasted testicles came briefly into sight, the previously impeccably restrained man – surely a credit to his race? – let out an anguished cry.

'Ahhh . . . my baws! My framin' baws!'

Sir James Grant moved his half-spectacles a little way up his nose, straightened the corners of his typed speech, then, clearing his throat, looked up at the others gathered about the massive oak-topped table in the penthouse boardroom.

'Gentlemen,' he began, oblivious, it seemed, of the fact that his secretary, Patricia, sat directly to his right, 'we come finally to the main business of this meeting, the Chairman's annual report.'

Beside Sir James, his son, Charles – twenty-five years old and bearing an uncanny resemblance to his namesake, Hugh Grant – glanced up at his father shyly, then combed his thick, dark hair back from his brow with the fingers of his left hand. It was the first time Patricia had seen the lad out of either school uniform or cricket flannels and he looked distinctly uncomfortable, despite the fact that he was born to wear the beautiful Savile Row suit he had put on for the day.

As Sir James struggled through his speech, Patricia looked about her, thankful that such meetings happened only twice a year.

Next to young Charles, resplendent in navy pinstripe and flamboyant red braces, was Sir Alex Littlejohn, Tory MP for Appleby in Cumbria. 'Odious Alex', as she liked to think of him, spent as little time as he could in Appleby, preferring to lounge away his days at the Garrick or some other club.

Next to Littlejohn was one of Virt-E-Go's own, the Finance Director, Roger Appleyard. Patricia didn't like Roger, but she had grudgingly to admit that he was damn good at his job, and his optimistic budget forecasts were always the high point of a fairly dismal occasion. Roger adored figures. Unfortunately, the figures he loved best were too often of the curved and fleshy variety.

Looking over onto the other side of the table, Patricia's eyes fell upon the woeful sight of Hadfield and Morrissey – 'Tweedle Dum' and 'Tweedle Dee', as they were known in the office. Minor gentry, the two were Old Etonian cronies of Sir James and seemed to come as a job lot. In ten years she had never seen one of them without the other being there, nor had she heard either of them utter more than a gruff 'Hear, hear!' to one of Sir James's suggestions.

Last, and most definitely least, was Jimmy Harbottle, Director of Operations, who ran Virt-E-Go's manufacturing complex in Croydon. He sat there with his arms folded before him, staring at Sir James through thick pebble glasses, his poorly knotted red tie making him look for all the world like an overgrown schoolboy. Apart from board meetings one never saw the man.

What a crew! she thought, her usual dismay worsened by the fact that she didn't know what was going on down in the labs. No wonder British industry is in decline!

'And furthermore . . .' Sir James was saying, scanning the typed sheet in front of him with a bemused expression, 'despite running at a small operational loss for the past three years, the prospects for Virt-E-Go have never been

brighter, and, in view of the Japanese deal, I am delighted
. . .' He paused and gave everyone a beaming smile. '. . .
Yes, *delighted*, to announce a one-hundred-and-fifty-per-
cent-increase in directors' fees for the coming tax year.'

'Jolly good show!' Sir Alex bellowed.

Sir James nodded, then looked back at the sheet,
frowning deeply as he tried to find his place again.

'And, and . . .'

Patricia leaned across and placed her finger on the line
he was looking for, then sat back again.

'Furthermore,' he said, nodding to himself, as if he'd
known where he was all the while, 'this new foreign
investment will allow us to increase the research budget
for our Virtuous Reality project—'

'Virtual,' she said quietly, correcting him, but Sir
James ploughed on oblivious of her.

'—by a whopping six hundred thousand pounds. A
significant figure, as I'm sure you'll all agree.'

But still less than they pay themselves, Patricia thought
wearily.

'Finally,' Sir James said, looking down at his son,
then pushing his notes aside, 'finally, gentlemen, let me
announce that, after sticking on eleven for these past five
years, I have decided to make a strenuous effort to reduce
my golf handicap.'

'And about bloody time!' Sir Alex Littlejohn called out
boisterously.

'In view of which,' Sir James continued, grinning now,
'I shall have precious little time to steer this small ship
of ours through the great oceans of commerce.'

Patricia groaned inwardly, wishing that Sir James
would stick to the typed script.

'Pardon?' Hadfield asked, jerking awake. 'Did someone order coffee?'

'He said he's retiring,' Sir Alex said.

'Well, damn good,' Morrissey said, sitting up. 'You've neglected your swing far too long, James.'

'That's by the by,' Sir James said. 'Charles here will be taking over as Chairman. That is, if you gentlemen all agree?'

'Hear, hear!' rang out from all sides.

'Good, then—'

The sudden, muffled bleep of a mobile phone sounded in the room. Roger Appleyard felt inside his jacket, a sheepish look on his face, then clicked the phone open and put it to his ear, conscious of Sir James glaring at him from the far side of the table.

'Oh, it's you,' he said. Then, in a desperate whisper, 'Can't it wait?'

'Wife, is it?' Sir Alex said, eyeing the Finance Director with an innate disdain.

'Urgent call, sir,' Appleyard said, looking across at Sir James as he snapped the phone shut and slipped it away. 'If you gentlemen would excuse me a moment . . .'

'Go on,' Sir James said. 'But don't be too long, Roger. We're all waiting to hear that financial plan of yours.'

'Of course, sir. I'll be two shakes.' And with that he clambered from his seat and hurried from the room.

Looking through the glass panel of the door, Roger let his eyes roam down the length of Louise's seemingly endless legs. She was sitting on the far side of the room, perched on the edge of her desk. One sheer black leg crossed the other at the knee, the darker band of her stocking tops just visible before disappearing provocatively beneath the hem of a leather skirt that stretched across her thighs. Instinctively, Roger smacked his lips.

'What's up?' he asked, poking his head round the door.

'Nothing . . . yet,' Louise giggled, sliding her bottom down the edge of the desk so that her skirt rose a fraction higher, giving Roger the eyeful she'd intended, before running her hands down the sides of the ruched-up garment.

Roger glanced along the corridor, then furtively entered the room, clicking the door shut behind him. 'Don't muck around, Louise. You know I'm in the middle of a big meeting.'

'Oh, a *big meeting*,' she mimicked, mocking his air of self-importance.

'Yes, and it's important.'

'So *I'm* not important now, then?' she said petulantly, staring up at him through mascara-caked lashes.

Knowing exactly which avenue this particular little exchange was likely to lead down, Roger groaned inwardly. Oh, fucking great, he thought. This is just what I need.

'Aw, come on Louise. Don't start. You know what the old man's like,' he said, with more good humour than he felt. 'I have to get back in there.'

'Well, you'd better go then. Go on. Pee off back to your important meeting.' And, turning away, Louise walked round to the other side of her desk and sat down, busying herself with the piles of paperwork spread out before her. With her back to him, he could see how her long dark hair curled over the lightly tanned flesh of her back.

Turning to go, Roger caught sight through the glass panel of their receptionist pushing a trolley laden with tea and cakes along the corridor towards the boardroom, the green china cups clinking in their saucers as the wheels rattled through the thick pile carpet. Great, he thought. It'll be a good twenty minutes before they start up again. He looked back into the office. Louise had her nose in an accounts folder, still resolutely refusing to acknowledge his presence. Allowing himself a smile, he wandered back over, perching himself on the corner of her desk.

'So,' he said, reaching across and taking one of the long, dark curls of her hair between his thumb and forefinger, gently pulling it straight before wrapping the fine, soft strands around his finger. 'What was so urgent?' he asked gently.

'It doesn't matter now,' she replied, refusing to look at him.

'Louise,' he said, pulling on the thin rope of hair to turn her face towards him. 'It *does* matter. What did you want?' He allowed the long dark curl to fall from his hand, watching it spiral into a ringlet. 'Come on, Lulu,' he cajoled, stroking her cheek with his finger.

Allowing her lips to form into a smile, she tilted her face to look up at him. 'If you must know, I wanted to check that you'd booked a table for tonight or if you wanted me to do it.'

'*Tonight?*' Roger's face was blank but even as the word escaped his lips he knew he was in trouble. The fan was on and a large chunk of Fison's was heading straight for it.

Louise's eyes narrowed. Reaching up she pushed his

hand away. 'Yes! *Tonight*! We were supposed to be going out for a meal. Remember?'

'Oh, Christ, Louise,' he said, suddenly recalling the row they'd had, followed by the promise. 'I'm really really sorry. I forgot all about it.'

She leaned back, tensed, like a tigress about to leap at its prey. 'Well, thanks very bloody much. Nice to know I'm so important to you. You know, Roger, it would be nice if just for once you organised this so-called affair instead of leaving everything to me.'

'Louise, I—'

'Don't start grovelling. *I'll* do it. And just to teach you a lesson I'm going to book somewhere *really* expensive.'

'Louise, you don't—'

'Don't complain, Roger, I know you put it down on expenses anyway. The Ivy. Yeah, I'll book the Ivy, for seven. That'll give us time to go on afterwards.' And she gave a coy little grin.

'Louise!' he said, rather more loudly than he'd intended. 'What I'm trying to say is . . .' He hesitated like a suicide on a cliff edge who's just changed his mind.

'Yes?' she asked, slowly, deliberately.

His voice was tiny. 'What I'm trying to tell you . . . is that I can't make it. Not tonight.'

Her face changed, a mixture of hurt and anger distorting her features so that she suddenly looked much older than her thirty years.

'What do you *mean*, you can't make it!' Her voice boomed in that tiny room.

'It's just that Harriet—'

'Oh, I just *knew* it'd be something to do with your

13

bloody daughter!' she spat, her look of venom cast toward the bespectacled grinning face of the offending fourteen-year-old as it peered from the elaborate, gilt frame on Roger's desk.

Ignoring the reprimand, Roger pressed on. 'It's just that Harriet's singing in the choir tonight and—'

'*Again*! That bleeding child of yours gives more concerts than Pavarotti!'

'And she wants me to be there.' The confession ended, Roger felt a brief moment of relief. 'And you know what Jane's like. She'll make my life a bloody misery if I miss it.'

'Yeah, well, maybe your wife's got more sense than I give her credit for. Maybe *I* should make your life a bloody misery, then *I* might get *my* way a bit more often.'

'What are you talking about?' he said, pulling her round on the swivel chair so that she came to rest between his legs, facing his chest. He laughed softly. 'You already make my life a misery.'

Gently he reached down, taking her face between his hands, making her look at him.

'Come on, Lulu,' he coaxed. 'You know I'm crazy about you.'

Her eyes opened wider. She wanted to be convinced, *wanted* to believe what he said.

'You know I'd rather be with you, Lulu,' he said, gently stroking her earlobes and the soft, delicate skin down the sides of her neck.

'Would you, Rog? Really?'

'Really,' he whispered, leaning down to breathe the word softly into the shell of her ear, and as his lips brushed the side of her face he heard her whimper and smiled triumphantly.

He felt her slender hand close over his and then the warm moistness of her mouth as she placed his fingers, one at a time, between her teeth, holding each one there, as she ran her tongue provocatively around the tip.

The telltale bulge at Roger's crotch brought a satisfied smile to Louise's lips as they closed over the forefinger of his left hand. He remained perched on the corner of the desk, his eyes closed as if in prayer, his face lifted to the ceiling, like a waxwork with a stiffy. The sound of the boardroom door opening and closing brought him to.

Roger glanced over his shoulder towards the door, then back down at Louise, her red lips parted, her hands now resting on his thighs.

'What colour underwear have you got on?'

'Guess,' she replied huskily, reaching up to undo the top button of her blouse.

'Black,' he said, smiling.

Louise giggled and threw back her head so that her mane of dark curls tumbled down her back and her breasts were thrust forward invitingly. Like magnets to iron filings, Roger's hands instinctively reached forward, fumbling over the remaining buttons finally to reveal Louise's ample breasts encased within the delicate black lace.

Roger's intake of breath was audible.

'Oh, Lulu,' he whimpered, lifting out each side of her blouse as though drawing open a pair of curtains, then gazing down at the swell of her breasts as they quickly rose and fell with each breath. Then, like a diver taking a last gasp of air before submerging, he buried his face between the soft folds of Louise's bosom, his tongue lost in the depths of her impressive cleavage.

'I'm wearing stockings,' she whispered, running a hand through Roger's thinning but imaginatively distributed brown hair, and taking hold of his hand she guided it a short way up her skirt, his nail catching on the sheer nylon before finding the warm flesh of her thigh. Roger groaned.

'Take them off,' he said urgently, running a thumb along the crotch of her thin black panties.

Louise giggled as she lifted her bottom and wriggled the tiny garment into something resembling a pair of swimming goggles before kicking them under the desk. She moved her hands slowly up the crease of her boss's trousers until they finally came to rest over his fly.

'Does Roger's todger want to come out to play?' she cooed in a little-girly voice, taking up the metal zip tag between her finger and thumb and teasing it down over the now considerable hardness inside his pants.

'Quick! Over here!' he said urgently, pulling her up from her seat and across to his desk, out of sight of prying eyes. As she looped her arms around his neck Roger guided his unresisting secretary down onto the teak desktop, her long legs dangling down over the side like a rag doll's.

'You do love me, don't you, Roger?' she breathed, pulling her skirt up around her waist.

'You know I do, Lulu,' he sighed, dropping his trousers around his knees.

She smiled, briefly satisfied. 'And you *are* going to tell your wife about us, aren't you?'

Roger nodded as he dropped his head towards Louise's erect nipples rising through the lace of her bra.

'Soon?'

Receiving no response, she persisted. 'Roger! When are you going to tell your wife?'

'Soon,' he mumbled, covering her mouth with his own. 'Christ! *Soon*. I promise. Soon.'

Cupping her buttocks with his hands, Roger pulled Louise towards him, the tails of his shirt tickling the inside of her thighs as they draped like a circus tent over the erect pole of his penis.

'Oh, Roger,' she moaned as he thrust towards her.

'Oh, Lulu,' he gasped, the sight of her partially clad body inflaming his lust, quickening the rhythm of his thrusting hips until, in that final burst of passion, Louise's prostrate body was sent sailing along the polished desktop.

Their passion spent they both lay there a moment, Louise's backbone crushed against the unforgiving wooden surface while Roger lay on top of her, panting noisily into her ear. Lifting her arm above her head she reached down to remove the uncomfortably hard object that had wedged itself behind her other ear. And as Louise held it aloft Jane Appleyard's smug features beamed down on her from inside the silver-plated photograph frame.

'Fucking bitch!' screamed Louise and threw it across the room.

'What are you *doing*? Do you want to get us caught?' Roger Appleyard cried in a fierce whisper as he hurriedly extricated himself from her and tugged up his Y-fronts.

'That would never do, would it? Caught with your trousers down – well and truly.'

'Louise,' he cajoled. 'Lulu. Not now, babe. The time and the place. You know that. The time and the place.'

'Yes, but it's never the time nor the bloody place, is it?' Her face hardened. 'I'm warning you, Roger Appleyard, you'd better bloody well tell her and soon . . . or *I* will!'

'I will. Honest I will, Lulu. Scout's honour,' he said, straightening his tie. 'Now be a good girl and tidy yourself up while I get back in there.' And, patting her knee, he beat a hasty retreat to the door.

'You know, Louise,' he said turning back to her, his hand on the handle, 'you don't seem to realise how much pressure I'm under.'

As she listened to the door click shut behind him she whispered under her breath, 'Not as much bloody pressure as you're gonna be under soon, my darling little ferret.'

Roger Appleyard sheepishly re-entered the boardroom, quietly closing the door behind him. Loud chatter filled the air and those around the long, oval table leaned towards one another, engrossed in serious discussion. At the far end Patricia laid her hand on Sir James's shoulder and when he looked up she nodded towards the door, indicating Roger's return. He had begun to make his first tentative steps towards reclaiming his vacated seat but stopped in his tracks when, following their Chairman's gaze, everybody stopped talking and Sir James's deep voice boomed across the silent room.

'Well, Roger?'

'Sir?'

'What are you going to do about this bloody mess?'

'Mess?'

'Yes, *mess*! What the bloody hell else would you call it?'

Shit! he thought. The old man must've heard everything. The intercom! She must have had her bloody arse on the intercom!

'It's not what you think, sir,' he blustered. 'It's er . . .'

'What do you mean, it's not what I think?'

'Well, things aren't always how they appear, are they, sir? I mean, look at you and Patricia, sir. I mean, some people might think—'

'What are you drivelling on about, man? Either the Jap's burned his balls or he hasn't!'

'Jap? Burned his balls?'

Enjoying Roger's discomfort Sir Alex Littlejohn tilted his chair back to rest precariously on the two back legs, undid the button on the jacket of his pinstripe suit and hooked the width of his red braces over each of his thumbs before flexing them back and forth.

'Yes, old boy,' he smirked, more amused than concerned in spite of the disastrous implications. 'Didn't you know? Seems our major backer has just charred his chipolata, deep-fried his dick, sautéed his sausage—'

'Yes, yes, yes, Alex. Thank you very much. I think we get the picture.'

Sir James only tolerated Alex Littlejohn because of past favours and the fact that he'd prevented him being blackballed by the Garrick in years past, before he'd received his own knighthood. How the odious man had managed to hold on to his seat remained a mystery even to the most ardent Tory supporter.

Roger's face was a picture of uncomprehending misery. 'I'm sorry, I don't . . .'

19

'Read this!' Patricia said wearily, thrusting a sheet of paper into his chest before moving past him to answer the ringing telephone. She didn't have much time for Roger Appleyard – not since she'd seen him sneaking into his ex-assistant's hotel room after a sales conference a few years ago. A couple of weeks later she'd been forced to ask the poor girl to leave when Roger had complained that her work wasn't up to scratch. Personally, however, she had little doubt that the wretched man had been after only one thing, and efficiency wasn't it.

'Oh, fuck,' Roger muttered.

'Yes, fuckety, fuckety, fuck, eh?' said Littlejohn, clearly amused by the whole appalling incident. 'You know, I knew a chap once, he—'

'The lawyers have just arrived, Sir James,' Patricia interrupted, dropping the handset back onto the telephone, ignoring the look of tense annoyance on Littlejohn's face. If ever there was a man who liked the sound of his own voice it was Sir Alex Littlejohn.

Sir James nodded. 'That was quick,' he said with faint amusement as he indicated to Charles that he should move further down the table to make way for them. 'They've obviously got the whiff of an expensive law suit in their nostrils. Parasitic bastards!'

There was a concurrent murmur and nodding of heads at the shared recollection of expensive divorce settlements.

'You'd better get in that girl of yours, Appleyard. Linda—'

'Louise,' Patricia corrected.

'Louise. Yes. She can minute the meeting while Pat goes off to see what's happening with the Japanese bod.'

20

'Mr Fukuada,' Patricia said.

Roger made to get up but Patricia laid a hand firmly on his shoulder as she glided past. 'Don't worry, I'll get her,' she said, adding quietly, 'It'll be a hell of a lot quicker.'

'Shit!' Roger mouthed silently, nervously rubbing a finger up and down the side of his twitching nose. 'Oh, shit!'

McTaggart paced up and down the floor of the lab like an expectant father, distractedly raking what remained of his hair with his right hand.

'They'll sue us!' he wailed. 'The Japs will sue us and then we'll *all* be out of a job!'

'Don't overheat, man!' William said, from where he knelt beside the machine, delicately unscrewing one of the limblike attachments. 'With what we know we could walk into any job in Silicon Valley tomorrow!'

McTaggart turned to face the twins. 'That may be true for you two,' he whined, genuinely distressed, 'but what about me?' He had exchanged contracts on a new flat only a week ago and now the prospect of almost immediate unemployment stared him in the face. 'Besides, I don't want to go to America. In fact, I hate America! It's full of madmen with guns!'

'Hey, chill out, man. America's cool,' Benjamin said, blowing into the hoselike mouth of the machine, then wiping round the rim with a finger. 'And with a CV like yours . . .'

William's eyes met Benjamin's and the twins exchanged a smile of perfect understanding. Brian McTaggart was nominally Head of Research and Development at Virt-E-Go, but the advanced technicalities of the job were now well beyond him and he knew it. He felt like a parent whose knowledge has been superseded by that of his children, as his role in the development of the company's top-secret project had now become one of encouraging and supporting the twins, in the hope that some time in the future he would bask in the reflected glory. At best McTaggart was little more than an office manager. Bill and Ben were the real stars and they and everyone else at Virt-E-Go knew it. That's why they were paid four times what their 'boss' took home.

'I think I've found our culprit,' Benjamin said, stooping to pick up something between the thumb and forefinger of his left hand.

'What is it?' McTaggart said, rushing across. 'A shirt button? A netsuke?'

Both Bill and Ben looked up at that. Neither of them had ever heard of the tiny carved-ivory pieces.

'No,' Benjamin said, placing the tiny object in McTaggart's open palm. 'It's a fly. A *Sarcophaga carnaria*, unless I'm very much mistaken. A flesh fly, as they're known. Must've hatched in there.'

McTaggart threw the offending item down, then shuddered. '*That*? That caused the short?'

'That and a couple of dozen like it. Fishermen use the grubs.'

William looked up and grinned. 'Seems like poor old Fukuada caught more on the end of his dick than he bargained for!'

The twins chuckled and did a high-five, but McTaggart remained morose.

'So who's responsible?'

The twins shrugged. As with all of their gestures it was like watching a highly polished and much-practised dance team. At times their every gesture was so alike it made even those who knew them double-take to check that they'd seen what they *thought* they'd seen.

'Brian?'

McTaggart turned. His assistant, Cynthia – she refused the title of secretary – had stepped through the clear plastic flaps.

'Yes?'

She walked across to him, pushing dark wire-framed spectacles up the length of her nose as she stepped over the discarded machinery, her long woollen skirt stretched across her calves. Her dark brown hair was pulled back and tied in a ponytail at the nape of her neck, short, frizzy curls framing her pale round face.

'I wondered whether you'd found out just what happened yet.'

He nodded distractedly. 'It seems some flies got caught in the mechanism.'

She laughed. 'Flies! Are you serious?'

'Ah-ha.'

'Unbelievable!' she said, coming across to accept the tiny fly William held out to her. She stared down at the inert black speck, amazed that such a small thing could wreak so much damage, as an image of poor Nobushi Fukuada flashed before her eyes. Shaking her head, she handed the insect back to William.

'This isn't getting us anywhere,' McTaggart said, wringing his hands. 'Unless we are able to come up with some explanation as to how the things got in there. Unless we're able to smooth things over, we're out of a job.'

Despite the seriousness of the situation, the twins couldn't resist smiling to one another.

'What if the Jap decides to sue you personally?' William said suddenly. 'I mean, as Head of R and D . . .'

McTaggart placed his clammy palms together and raised his eyes heavenward in silent prayer.

Cynthia looked to the twins and pulled a face as they fought to contain their laughter.

'Hey, Brian, don't worry, man,' Benjamin said reassuringly, raising the hoselike contraption in the air. 'You never know. It might've destroyed the evidence altogether!'

'Oh, no,' McTaggart wailed, a hand dropping automatically over his baggy crotch.

The phone rang.

McTaggart glanced across to the workbench on which it stood, as if at an apparition, then slowly went across and tentatively lifted the receiver.

'Y-yes?'

The others watched as he came to attention, his head nodding to the words they couldn't hear.

'Yes, Sir James. Of course, Sir James. At once, Sir James.'

'So?' Cynthia asked, turning her attention on the twins. 'The answer's flies, is it?'

'Maybe,' the twins said as one.

Cynthia frowned deeply. 'But you said—'

'Oh, they caused the short,' William said. 'But that shouldn't have made the system overload. The backup's failed. And the lubrication feed—'

'—didn't work,' Benjamin finished for him.

Cynthia shrugged. 'I don't follow you. I thought—'

'Well, it's like this,' Benjamin said. 'One of the problems we've been having all along was keeping the attachment moist. We've tried all kinds of solutions, from a regulated oil feed to a mini radiator, and we thought we'd licked it . . .'

'So to speak,' William interjected.

'But when poor old Fukuada put it to the test, it just didn't work at all.' Benjamin made a pained face. 'It must have been like rogering a thick sheet of sandpaper!'

'I see,' Cynthia said, wincing at the thought.

Across from them, McTaggart finished the call and slumped into a chair. Sweat beaded his brow. Seeing it, Cynthia went over to his jacket, where it hung on its peg, and, reaching into the inside pocket, removed a bottle of pills.

'You don't look well, Brian,' she said, a moment later, handing him a glass of water and two of the tiny red and yellow capsules. 'You really ought to go home.'

'I can't,' he groaned. 'Sir James says he wants a full report on his desk by tomorrow morning, or he'll have my B-A-L-L-S.'

'That's as may be,' she said, encouraging him to swallow first one and then the other pill and wash them down. 'But you'll be no good to anyone if you go having a heart attack, will you? You know what your doctor said. So get on home. The twins and I can do the report. I'll type it up nice and neat and bring it round for you to sign at home.'

McTaggart stared up at his assistant with a mixture

of relief and adoration. 'Would you? Oh, Cynthia, you really are an angel.'

'A veritable saint,' she said. 'Now go home and rest. I'll phone you if there are any further developments, okay?'

'You promise?' he said, setting the glass down and easing himself up out of the chair. 'If Sir James—'

'I *promise.*'

When he was gone, she went over and stood beside the machine, watching the twins strip it down and begin to reassemble it once more. She had seen them do it a dozen, maybe fifteen times in all, but she never tired of watching them at work. She loved the cold clarity of machines. Loved their simple efficiency.

Cynthia shivered. Yes, and their brutality.

Patricia buried her face in the extravagant bouquet of flowers and breathed in deeply, the heady fragrance masking the smell of disinfectant pervading the hospital corridor. She had phoned more than a dozen specialist florists before finding one that stocked this particular species of native Japanese orchid, and had ordered the lot to be delivered to Virt-E-Go's offices at once. The startling purple and white blooms, with their single speckled petal stretching out like wings on either side, resembled a collection of exotic butterflies as they danced within the cellophane wrapping, drawing appreciative looks from fellow visitors.

Following the signs, Patricia finally stopped outside the private room where Nobushi Fukuada had been placed. Pressing her ear to the door she could make out a high-pitched muddle of Japanese voices from within and raised her eyes to heaven, wondering why she always got the bum jobs. Several times her knuckles almost touched the wooden door, her hesitation borne from the knowledge that, inevitably, she would bear the brunt of the poor man's anger. But, never one to shirk her responsibilities, she took a deep breath, then rapped her knuckles firmly against the door.

Inside the room the chattering stopped abruptly. A single voice called out resonantly. 'Come!'

Forcing her mouth into a fixed smile – sincere and sympathetic – Patricia eased the door open. The tiny room was packed to the corners with besuited Japanese, evoking memories of a TV programme she'd once seen about Tokyo in the rush hour. All heads were turned in her direction, their startlingly Oriental faces staring out at her.

'Er, hello,' she ventured. 'My name is Patricia Hampton. I've come to see Mr Fukuada.'

Their faces were blank, unsmiling.

'From Virt-E-Go.'

A collective 'Ahhh' filled the room as a couple of dozen faces broke into a welcoming smile and the press of bodies parted like the Red Sea, revealing not the Promised Land but a grinning Nobushi Fukuada resplendent atop his bed. He was propped up against a mountain of crisp, white pillows. Patricia was struck by the smoothness of his naked torso and, as her eyes were drawn to the area of his injury, she could feel her face redden and the beginnings of a hot flush taking hold. Encircling his hips and running down over his private parts, the white bandage gave the patient an appropriate sumolike appearance, his thin bony legs crossed beneath him.

'Mr Fuku—' she started, her head tilted sympathetically to one side, her voice apologetic.

'Miss Hampton,' he interrupted, dropping his dictating machine onto the bed beside him and enthusiastically extending a hand.

'I am so sorry. *We* are so sorry,' she began, forcing herself to look into his small, jet-black eyes and offering the flowers.

'Prease. No need,' he said, handing the flowers to a young man standing by the bed and indicating the chair at his bedside.

Excusing herself several times, Patricia eased her way round the bed and took up her seat, sinking down into the green vinyl-covered armchair so that her eyes were unavoidably level with the poor man's injured pride. Forcing herself to look away she glanced up at the rows of smiling faces and was suddenly struck by the absurdity of the situation, imagining how surreal the scene must look. All those suits surrounding a near-naked man and a middle-aged secretary with a penchant for short blokes and who hadn't had sex for two years! It was bizarre!

'Mr Fukuada, we just want you to know how *incredibly* sorry we are about this appalling incident. Sir James—'

'Ah, Sir Jame. I must speak wiv him,' he said enthusiastically, reaching for the telephone.

Knowing full well that the Chairman would steer well clear of any kind of conversation until fully briefed by his lawyers, Patricia moved into her best PA mode.

'I'm sorry, but Sir James is tied up right now. He's leading a full inquiry into how something as . . . as *dreadful* as this could possibly have happened. He insisted on personally seeing to the matter straight away, so I'm afraid he can't be reached.'

'Ah,' Fukuada said, returning the receiver to the cradle. 'Nerer mine. Prease. Convey to Sir Jame how derighted I am wiv machine and—'

'*Derighted*? I mean, delighted?' Patricia asked incredulously, her forehead furrowed in confusion.

'Absorutely. Brirriant machine. Very powerful. Maybe *too* powerful,' he joked patting his bandage.

'But Mr Fukuada. Your . . . your . . .' Patricia nodded towards his groin.

'Ah yes,' he said, smiling down at the bulky pad. 'But machine provide two good thing. Sex and pain. Powerful combination, neh?' And on that note the room broke into spontaneous applause.

'Now, Miss Patricia, you tell Sir Jame we have deal. Five mirrion, as agreed.'

The unfortunate incident with the machine proved a rich vein of jokes amongst the staff and when, three days later, they were gathered in the Champion to celebrate Chastity's eighteenth birthday, it gave way to a relentless stream, most of them in the worst possible taste.

'Here, I've got one for you,' said Roger Appleyard, who was standing at the bar with a handful of his male colleagues. Taking a swig of his Scotch and dry, he raised his voice so that the women, sitting a dozen feet away at a table, could hear. 'What does a Japanese bloke with burnt balls have for his dinner?'

The women, other than Louise, feigned disinterest while the men shook their heads, smiling expectantly.

'Raw tush-i!' He looked from one to the other. 'Get it? Raw tush. Sushi. Raw tush-i.'

A groan went up. Bob Guppy chuckled, then reached across the bar for his pint of bitter. Lifting the glass mug to his mouth he downed a third of it in one go, then wiped the back of his hand across his mouth to remove the froth from his upper lip.

'I'll tell you what,' he said. 'It's a wonder the little fucker's hair didn't stand on end the way that current shot up his arse. I reckon he had enough electricity in him to shit a set of fairy lights!'

Roger roared at the thought of it, then passed his hand through the air creating an imaginary banner. 'I can see it now. Virt-E-Go Illuminations!'

'Better than bleedin' Blackpool,' laughed Bob Guppy, swallowing another mouthful of beer. 'Still, you've got to hand it to the Japs. They're tough little bastards!'

There was a murmur of admiration as they recalled the image of Nobushi Fukuada clutching his singed testicles and with almost military synchronisation each of them placed a reassuring hand over his genitals.

Catching Roger's eye, Louise gave a provocative nod towards his crotch, whereupon he made a grabbing motion over his balls and gave her a knowing wink. The high-pitched giggle that followed drew the attention of all those around her as Roger turned back to face the bar.

'You on a promise tonight?' Bob Guppy laughed, glancing across at Louise and running his tongue over his upper lip.

'Could be, Bob old man, could be,' he said, pushing out his chest.

Bob Guppy shook his head. 'I don't know how you do it, you jammy bastard. Either you've got a fucking big dick or else she needs glasses.'

'You're only jealous,' Roger replied, feeling rather pleased with himself.

'Too bloody right I am! The last time I had any red hot nookie I had a full head of hair!' And, as happened any time anyone mentioned the word hair, he ran a hand over his smooth, shiny pate.

'Maxine still not keen?' Roger had met Bob's wife only once and had decided she could have rented out her 'box' as a freezer unit.

Bob laughed, surprisingly with more amusement than bitterness. 'Nah. You know, asking Maxine if she wants sex is like asking an anorexic if she'd like a nice plate of tripe and onions.'

'Or a nice big portion of spotted dick, eh?' Roger suggested, nudging his colleague knowingly.

'Excuse me, Roger,' said Brian McTaggart, who until now had stood silently nursing his half-pint of lager. 'I don't wish to pry, but am I right to infer that you and Louise are . . . well, that you're having . . .'

Enjoying the other man's discomfort, Roger Appleyard stood there grinning inanely while McTaggart struggled for the appropriate phrase. 'Oooh, Brian,' he said finally, before breaking into song: 'If you knew Lulu like I know Lulu . . .'

'Oh, oh, oh what a girl,' added Bob Guppy, and the two men joined together in deep-bellied macho laughter while Brian McTaggart looked on in utter bewilderment.

'It's a song, Brian,' Roger explained, as though talking to a child.

'Aah,' McTaggart replied, nodding, as though he now understood perfectly. As a bachelor Brian McTaggart possessed somewhat limited experience of the opposite sex, in spite of the fact that he was now forty-seven. And, though he appeared to be fascinated with the dynamics of relationships, his interest was purely academic, a gathering of information which would then be fed back into the development of what he hoped would be the ultimate love machine.

'I'll tell you what, Brian me old mate,' Bob Guppy announced, placing a brotherly arm around his colleague's dandruff-laden shoulder and winking across at Roger Appleyard. 'I think you're getting too stressed out over this project. I reckon that in the interests of Virt-E-Go you wanna hop in a cab up to King's Cross and get your leg over with some gorgeous little lovely. I'll tell you what – you could even put it down on expenses as research. What d'you think, Roger?'

'As your Financial Director, I don't have a problem with that,' Roger replied straight-faced. 'We could put it down as R and D. Rogering and dodgering!'

McTaggart made a face of tired amusement. He was used to this kind of ribbing from his two workmates when they were on the sauce and knew from experience it was best not to rise to the bait. 'Ha, ha, ha. Very amusing. Very original.'

Taking away his arm, Guppy gestured towards where William and Benjamin, heads locked together, were discussing the finer points of subatomic theory and superstrings. 'Yes, and while you're at it, you could take Bill and Ben with you. Sad bastards!'

The two boys looked up, aware that Bob's voice was raised.

'I said,' he said, turning to toast them with his half-empty glass, 'you're a couple of sad bastards.'

The brothers roared with laughter and slapped each other's hands in mid-air before hastily fumbling to undo their shirt buttons. Beneath the brushed-cotton plaid shirts – one in blue, the other in red – they wore identical white teeshirts. Across their narrow chests was emblazoned the slogan 'Glad to be Sad'.

Roger and Bob shook their heads in amused disbelief while Brian McTaggart looked on with bemused incomprehension.

'Why would anyone want to wear a teeshirt like that,' he enquired of the others.

''Cos they're a couple of bleedin' oddballs,' Bob replied, draining his glass and placing the empty mug on the bar.

'Talking of oddballs, Brian. How's Madam Cyn shaping up?'

'She was shaping up very nicely when I followed her tight little arse up the elevator on the tube this morning.' Bob Guppy chipped in.

'Madam Cyn?' Brian McTaggart furrowed his brow in genuine puzzlement.

'Yeah. Cynthia. Madam Cyn.'

McTaggart gave a brief smile. 'I must say, sin isn't something I would necessarily have associated with Cynthia. She seems a rather serious young woman. Very professional. Very helpful.'

'Yeah, well we can all do with a helping hand,' said Bob, looking across to catch the barmaid's eye.

'No, Brian me old mate,' Roger confided, pushing his empty glass along the bar towards Bob. 'Take it from me. Under that prim exterior lies an unexploded time bomb of pent-up passion. It's just a question of waiting for it to go off.'

Failing to attract the barmaid's attention Bob turned back to join in the conversation. 'And you know what they say?' he said, without awaiting a response. 'The quiet ones are always the worst. In fact I bet you a pound to a penny she's the sort who doesn't wear any knickers.'

Brian McTaggart cleared his throat and took a sip from the warm, flat lager in his glass. 'I bow to your greater knowledge, Bob,' he said, braving it out and trying to control the shakiness in his voice.

'Now little Chastity on the other hand,' Bob said, resting both elbows on the bar and looking over at the women sitting round the table. 'Chastity looks like pure fucking jailbait, but I bet that underneath it all she's just an old-fashioned girl looking for a bit of romance.'

'You've *got* to be joking!' Roger said, slapping the other man's back and turning to face the table of women. 'She's positively gagging for it! Nah, Bob me old mucker, I'm surprised at you. You should've scored there by now.'

'I know what I'm doing, don't you worry. Young girls like Chastity can't be rushed.'

'The young ones are the worst,' Roger countered. 'No, you mark my words, Robert. If you make a move on that one you'll get your end away, no problem.'

'Actually,' Brian said, feeling that at last he had something to contribute to the conversation, 'research shows that women reach their peak of sexual desire at the age of forty-three.'

'Forty-three! There you go, Bob,' Roger laughed, slapping his back once more. 'You want to make a move on Patricia instead. According to Brian she's ripe for it. Though you'd probably need to get her pissed first. Mind you,' he added, looking across at her, 'you'd probably need to get *yourself* pissed first.'

'Patricia is a very capable woman,' Brian said, coming to her defence. 'She carries big responsibilities.'

'Yeah, but has she got big tits?' Bob Guppy countered, laughing heartily as his elbow slipped off the edge of the bar.

'My dear Brian,' Roger said patronisingly, placing a protective arm around his shoulder, 'I'm afraid you haven't quite got the hang of this nookie lark. You see, the idea is to have rampant sex. As much of it as possible. Not to have philosophical conversations about the meaning of life, or whatever. If I want to do *that* I can go home to my wife . . .'

'Yeah, I can't imagine you having many discussions on the meaning of life with our Louise,' said Bob, amused by the thought.

Roger Appleyard smiled as he recalled their last sexual encounter over the office desk a couple of days before. 'Louise,' he called over. 'Bob was wondering if you wanted to have a discussion about the meaning of life?'

Louise raised her eyes to the ceiling. 'Daft bugger,' she said good-naturedly before turning back to the other women.

'That's my kind of girl!' Roger said with affection. 'In fact,' he added, turning to Brian McTaggart, 'I'd have thought that Louise was the perfect female type for the Old Banger. A good face, a damn good body, perfect understanding of what a man needs, and a genuine desire to please. What more could a man ask for?'

Brian glanced across at Louise with a flicker of pity in his eyes before he spoke. 'You really should do a test run for us, Roger. I'm sure we'd find your insights extremely valuable.'

Roger bridled a little at what he took for criticism. 'As you well know, Brian, I was going to have a go myself.'

'Really?' Bob Guppy stared at his colleague in amazement.

'Absolutely,' Roger answered. 'Anything for the firm, that's what I say.'

'So why didn't you?' Guppy asked.

It was McTaggart who answered. 'Because Mr Fukuada got there first.'

'And a bloody good job, too,' Roger said, wincing at the thought that it might have been him and not Fukuada in the hospital.

'So are you going to have a go when it's fixed?' Guppy asked, perhaps a shade too keenly for Roger's liking.

'Nah,' Roger said, staring at his empty glass. 'I'm a bit too fond of the old crown jewels to risk that, I'm afraid. I'll wait now till they've found another couple of mugs to try it out first. In fact,' he said, glancing over at the twins, 'I don't know why we don't use those two as test fodder. I don't suppose they have any other use for their todgers.'

'Don't they ever stop?' Bob Guppy asked, watching the two brothers as they scribbled on scraps of paper and gesticulated enthusiastically. 'Oi!' he called across to them. 'D'you two want a drink? A glass of hydrochloric acid or something?'

The young men looked up and grinned. Pushing the scraps of paper into their pockets they edged up the bar towards their colleagues in an attempt at being sociable.

'A bottle of Bud please, Bo, my man,' William replied.

Already knowing the answer, Bob turned to Benjamin. 'Ditto.'

'I was just saying to Brian,' Roger smirked, 'that you two would make good test pilots for the Old Banger when the alterations have been made.'

'Hey, no prob, Rog. It's gonna be faaaan-tastic, that little beauty,' William enthused, 'the Rolls-Royce of sex simulators.'

'Yeah, we've already worked out ways of incorporating Japan's requirements,' said Benjamin.

'It'll take a couple of weeks,' William said. 'But once we've got all the bugs out of the system—'

'No pun intended.' Ben chipped in.

'—then we'll be in possession of one hot doozie of a simulator.'

'Well, knowing what old Fukuada got off on I'll be buggered if *I'll* get on the machine,' Roger announced.

'You're probably right there,' Bob Guppy chuckled, handing Roger a fresh drink. 'No, I'm with Roger. I want to see a few more test runs before I'll give it a go.'

'Well,' Benjamin announced, standing straight. 'I'm willing to put my balls where my mouth is!'

'Putting your balls where your mouth is might make you a bit more interesting to talk to,' Roger teased.

'Actually,' Brian McTaggart announced, initiating a

fresh turn in the conversation, 'the actual sex isn't the problem. The main challenge we have with the project is in making the experience seem real.'

'You mean you're going to give the machine a headache every time somebody wants to use it?' Bob Guppy said, laughing uneasily.

'If that's what turns you on,' William said, with a twinkle in his eyes. 'But Brian's right. It ain't the *stim*-ulation, it's the *sim*-ulation we've got problems with.'

'Yeah,' Benjamin added. 'It's getting people to believe they're not just screwing a machine.'

Roger laughed. 'I'd have thought that it was bleedin' obvious that that's *exactly* what they're doing!' He took a sip of his Scotch. 'It must be just like fucking an old Electrolux!'

'So why did you volunteer your services, then?' Bob Guppy asked, winking at the others.

'As I said,' Roger answered, donning a serious expression. 'Anything for the firm. But my comment stands. However you try to wrap things up, we're still marketing what is, in essence, a glorified wanking machine!'

'Ah, but that's just the point,' McTaggart said with real feeling, warming to his subject. 'We've got to somehow overcome our machine being perceived as just a technological version of a blow-up doll.'

'Well, isn't it?' Bob Guppy asked, playing Devil's Advocate. 'That's going to be one of our biggest selling points, surely?'

'No,' McTaggart said vehemently. 'I think you're wrong. People don't just want sex. They want romance. They want—'

'Not to burn their nuts to a frazzle, for a start!' Roger said, turning to order himself yet another Scotch.

'I think Brian's right,' Benjamin said, glancing at his twin for confirmation. 'If it's just gonna be a sex machine, then . . . well, what's the point? You might as well just go and buy it down at King's Cross, or—'

'Paddington,' Roger chipped in knowingly.

'Right,' William took up. 'Because this machine ain't gonna be cheap.'

'Even so,' Roger said, turning to hand Bob Guppy the tray with the girls' drinks on. '*Romance*? I ask you!'

'Yes, romance, damn it!' McTaggart said, a slight edge creeping into his voice. 'If this thing's going to work, it can't just be a sex machine – an Old Banger as you and Bob call it – it needs to be a love machine. It needs to care for its user.'

'Now you are talking bollocks,' Roger said. 'Whoever heard of a machine that *cared* for you? What's it going to do, stroke your back after you've come and whisper sweet nothings in your ear?'

'Hey, that's a great idea!' William said, looking to his brother, the twins nodding at each other like mirror images. 'Maybe we could make the machine come first – you know, pamper the male ego a bit.'

'Now I've heard every-fucking-thing!' Roger said, shaking his head. 'And I suppose it'll get out a Kleenex and give you a good wipe-down, too!'

'Too tacky,' Benjamin said. 'We were thinking more along the lines of some kind of chemically induced afterglow.'

'After—' Bob Guppy spat his beer back into the jug. 'And this program that you're planning to write – how are you going to go about making Joe Public believe in all this tosh?'

'Black-box theory,' William answered confidently.

'Sensory deprivation,' Ben added.

'You see,' McTaggart took up, 'we don't just stimulate the body, we also stimulate the mind. We tell a story.'

'It's *jack-a-bloody-nory*!' Roger said, with a guffaw.

'More like *Penthouse*, actually,' William said. 'You know. Boy meets girl.'

'Boy shags girl,' Roger threw in.

'Girl tells wife,' Guppy added, causing Roger to glance at him strangely.

'Yes,' McTaggart said, nodding his head exaggeratedly, 'though not perhaps that *particular* scenario. It'll be more like a simple love story.'

'Mills and bloody Boon, I bet,' Roger said with a sigh.

'With sex,' Ben said, grinning, as if he relished the challenge.

'And the Japs?' Bob Guppy asked.

'Special storylines,' Bill said, 'just for their market.'

'Horses for courses,' said Ben.

'And Slappers for the Jappers?' Bob Guppy suggested, and the laughter rang out once more, carrying across to where the women sat in the corner.

It was an open secret around the office that Roger Appleyard and Louise Baines were having an affair. Louise had replaced the poor unfortunate Michelle, who, seduced by Roger's promises of promotion in return for a quick fumble over the fax machine, had been disposed of when it was payback time. Louise was an altogether different and more amenable proposition. Having followed in Michelle's ill-fated footsteps as a temp she was only too pleased to be taken onto the permanent staff. Fortunately for her boss, that was where her ambitions ended. Or to put it another way, as far as Louise *had* ambitions, they were of an altogether more personal nature.

It was six months ago, her back pressed against the side wall of the lift, her arm extended over Roger's heaving shoulder so that her fingertip rested upon the 'Door Close' button, that Louise had first broached the subject. As Roger pulled away and slumped against the wall beside her, reaching down to do up his fly, Louise had nuzzled into his neck and uttered the words that every adulterous male must anticipate with a combination of inevitability and dread.

'You will leave your wife for me, won't you?'

Of course, he said. He loved her, didn't he? So of course he would leave his wife. It was just that right then wasn't a good time, what with Harriet and Edward still at school and all that. But he would tell his wife. Soon. Yes, of course he meant it. And like a silly cow Louise swallowed it – along with everything else – lock, stock and barrel.

'I don't know what they find so amusing,' Louise said, turning round in her seat to face the others. 'But it's good to see them enjoying themselves, ain't it?'

Patricia glared across at the bar hoping to catch Roger Appleyard's eye, but he had turned away to talk to Brian McTaggart. Appleyard was a shit of the first order and totally beneath contempt, yet in spite of her feelings she could see the obvious physical attractions of the man.

Cynthia was looking down into her glass, not wishing to meet Louise's smiling face, amazed by the idiocy of the woman. If a man ever dared to treat her the way that Roger treated Louise, she vowed that she'd give his pubes a short back and sides, use his balls as a pair of earrings and throw his dick in the shredder!

'Is Roger going to leave his wife, d'you think, Louise?' Chastity asked matter-of-factly, unintentionally forcing Louise onto the defensive.

'Well . . . yes, of course he is. He's promised me.'

'Has he said when?' she persisted.

There was no malice in Chastity's enquiry, merely a desire to clarify the situation in her own mind.

'No. Not an actual date, as such. But he's promised to tell her. Soon.'

Chastity nodded as if she understood things perfectly now. 'And have you met his wife and kids?'

Patricia and Cynthia shifted uncomfortably in their seats, embarrassed by the bluntness of the questions, but an unhealthy curiosity kept them from interrupting Chastity, and they listened with obvious fascination to Louise's account of the dragon wife and manipulative kids whom she'd seen only once, quite by chance one weekend, out with Roger in a pub by the river.

'But don't you ever feel guilty?' Chastity asked with genuine interest.

'No,' Louise responded quickly. 'No, I don't.'

'But what about his kids?'

'What they don't know can't hurt them, that's how I see it,' Louise responded, a touch too flippantly, perhaps.

'But they will know, won't they? If he leaves his wife, I mean.'

The welcome arrival of Bob Guppy with the overdue tray of fresh drinks saved Louise any further embarrassment.

'Here we are, ladies,' he announced, placing the tray in the middle of the table. 'I think I've remembered correctly,' he said, distributing the glasses. And as he placed the large goblet of gin and tonic before Chastity, he rested a, clammy hand on her shoulder, squeezing his fingers over her soft, bare flesh. 'There's a double in there, birthday girl,' he whispered in her ear, the smell of his warm beery breath on her face making her wince.

Forcing herself to smile up her thanks, she felt him pat her familiarly on the upper arm before returning to the bar.

'What a creep!' Cynthia hissed when he was barely out of earshot.

'Who?' Louise asked, looking about her.

'Guppy, of course!'

'Why?' Louise asked in genuine bewilderment.

'Surely you can see. The way he's always touching and stroking . . .' And she pushed out her tongue in an expression of disgust. 'The oily git!'

'Ah,' Louise said, casting a fond eye towards the group of men. 'He's only being friendly. There's no harm in it.'

If there was one thing Louise couldn't abide it was these bloody so-called feminists: all small tits, dungarees and no sense of humour! How else was a bloke supposed to show his appreciation if he wasn't allowed to touch?

'Being friendly's one thing,' said Chastity, glancing over her shoulder towards the bar, 'but thinking you can have a grope whenever you like is another. I feel like Jacques Cousteau sometimes.'

'Jacques Cousteau?' the other three said as one, all equally bemused.

'Yeah,' Chastity said, straight-faced. 'It's like working with a bleedin' octopus!'

Louise giggled and gave the younger girl a friendly nudge.

'You could always put in a complaint, you know,' Patricia said, introducing a serious note into the conversation.

'Who to?'

'Sir James,' she replied automatically. 'Although I suppose it'll be Charles now.' She nodded to herself thoughtfully. 'Yes. I could have a word with Charles, if you like. But only if you want to make an official complaint. You know, of sexual harassment.'

Chastity wrinkled her nose. 'What's the point? Nah,' she added a moment later, reaching for her glass. 'I can handle old Guppy. Anyway, the poor sod'd probably drop dead of a heart attack if he ever did get lucky.'

All four women laughed out loud, eliciting looks from the bar.

'Not that it'll be with me,' Chastity assured them.

'Nor anything with only two legs,' Cynthia added in a moment of uncharacteristic humour, causing Louise to squeal with delight.

Her laughter was infectious and, as the other women joined in the joke, Patricia skirted her way round the table and across to the ladies'. While she was gone, Louise took the opportunity to give the others a potted history of her colleague's life, not saying that most of it had been gleaned second-hand from post-coital gossip with Roger Appleyard. According to Roger, Patricia's recent divorce was a result of her frigidity. It seemed that her husband had been unable to bear the imposed celibacy. Two years it was since they'd had it off. Two whole years!

'Really?' asked Chastity, wide-eyed.

'Guide's honour,' Louise said, her face carrying a look of gained wisdom as if she, at least, had learned a lesson from the sorry tale.

'So what's he like then, Pat?' Chastity asked, swiftly changing the subject as the older woman returned to the table.

Patricia bristled slightly. Sir James was the only person in the company who used that familiar abbreviation of her name. This time, however, she let it pass. 'What's *who* like?'

'Charles. What's he like? Looks a bit of a dish to me.'

'Bit of a drip, you mean,' Louise added.

Patricia tilted her head to one side and thought a moment, trying to think of Charles without comparing him to his father.

'He's a nice enough chap, I suppose.'

'Nice! Yuk!' said Louise, pretending to vomit onto the table.

'He's not married, is he?' Chastity asked.

Patricia shook her head. 'No. But he is engaged.'

'Oh.'

The table fell silent once again.

'*They're* an odd couple,' Chastity said after a moment, nodding across to William and Benjamin as they stood, heads touching, deep in conversation. 'D'you think they've got girlfriends?'

Louise spat her drink back into her glass at the absurdity of the suggestion. 'The only love interest those two have got in their lives is in that bloody machine. You know, they're even sleeping in the lab now.'

'Really?' Cynthia said, looking across to where they stood. 'What, all night?'

'Yeah,' Louise laughed and shook her head. 'Bleedin' mad if you ask me.'

'It's nice to see people get involved in their work,' Patricia said pointedly. 'There's precious little dedication to be found these days. In fact that's what I find so admirable about Brian, his current illness aside. I suppose it must have something to do with being creative.'

'Roger's creative with the accounts,' Louise said. 'Especially double entry!' And she laughed loudly at her own joke.

'He don't look the creative sort, does he?' Chastity observed, squinting slightly as she studied McTaggart. The others followed her gaze and solemnly shook their heads in agreement. Looking much older than his forty-seven years, he stood incongruously cupping his glass of lager, accepted under protest from the insistent Bob Guppy. Everything about his appearance was just slightly wrong: the knot on his tie was too large, the waistcoat he wore looked like it had been knitted by an elderly aunt and there was dried food on his lapel. Even the black, rectangular glasses he wore looked out of place on his aquiline features, resting heavily across his long, thin nose, giving him the appearance of being weighed down by all of the world's woes.

'Poor sod,' Louise commiserated.

'I think he's really nice,' said Chastity defensively.

'The ugly ones always are,' Louise sighed. 'They have to be.'

'One thing you will learn as you get older, Louise, is that you can't judge a book by its cover,' Patricia said, lifting the glass of vodka and tonic to her lips.

'What's that, then? You reckon our Brian's a bit of a dark horse, do you?'

'What I'm saying,' Patricia sighed with a trace of exasperation, 'is that people are not always what they seem.'

Looking doubtful Louise turned to Cynthia. 'Well, you should know, Cyn. What d'you reckon? Do you think Brian dresses up in women's suspenders and hangs from chandeliers?'

'I have no idea!' Cynthia replied, amazed that they could be having this discussion about boring old Brian McTaggart. 'And who cares if he does?' she went on. 'Anyway, I thought we were talking about whether or not he was creative.'

'Well, I don't know about you but that's *my* idea of being creative!' Louise hooted, and in spite of themselves the others had to smile at the incorrigible creature.

The Virt-E-Go building was in darkness apart from a night-light in the reception area and three brightly lit windows on the second floor. Cynthia stood there a moment, staring up at them, then, taking the duplicate key from her handbag, she went across to the solid-glass front door.

With Louise slinking off a couple of minutes after Roger Appleyard, Cynthia had quickly made her own excuses and left. By that time, William and Benjamin had been long gone and she knew they'd have headed straight back to the lab. After the 'accident', Brian McTaggart had taken a couple of days' sick leave, whereupon responsibility for the project had been placed temporarily on Cynthia's young but eager shoulders.

Locking the front door behind her, she took the lift up to the second floor. The noise hit her as she stepped from the lift, intensifying as she pushed through the big plastic flaps across the entrance to the lab. Bill and Ben were so engrossed in their work, reconnecting wires and inserting microchips, that they were unaware of Cynthia entering the room. Music from the CD in the corner of the lab attacked every fibre as the air pulsated with the heavy rock sound of Nine Inch Nails, so that, even when she cleared her throat they didn't look up, their heads bobbing up and down to the beat of the music.

She took two paces towards them, then shouted. 'Hi!'

The twins jumped up as one, banging heads, shocked by the unexpected intrusion.

'Hey, like, we didn't hear you come in,' William called, regaining his composure, his gangly limbs bending awkwardly like those of a drunken giraffe.

'I'm not surprised,' she yelled back, nodding her head towards the CD player.

Benjamin reached across and clicked it off, smiling apologetically. The silence was almost physical. 'Hey, how did you get in?' he asked. 'I thought this place was supposed to be secure.'

'Don't worry,' she smiled, holding the keys out to show them, 'your secrets are safe with me. I'm just curious, that's all. I'm so busy running around most of the time. And I just love being involved in the actual mechanics of the project. I thought you wouldn't mind.'

The boys looked at each other, then gave an uncertain shrug.

'And I'm absolutely fascinated by the work you're doing for the Japanese programs,' she said earnestly, looking from one to the other, her eyes widening behind the round wire frames of her glasses. 'But if you'd prefer me to leave . . .'

'No . . .'

'. . . it's cool,' they responded quickly, and made a space for her at the bench.

'So what exactly are you doing?' she asked, peering about at the complex tangle of wires and components that covered the workbench.

'It's a nervous system,' Bill began.

'For the machine,' Ben added. 'Nothing so complex as the human nervous system, naturally, but—'

'Why do we need it?' she asked, interrupting him, staring directly into his eyes in a manner that clearly disconcerted him.

'For the feedback,' Bill said, rescuing his twin, whose mouth seemed to have stopped functioning. 'Like the human nerves, these wires carry messages back from the core program. Those messages stimulate the pads attached to the body and provide the sensation of pleasure or—'

'—pain,' Ben said, finally freeing his eyes from Cynthia's and looking away, a slight colour appearing at his cheeks.

'So it's not just goggles and gloves, like other VR units?'

'That's right,' Bill said, picking up what looked like

the stippled pad from the back of a table-tennis bat. 'We use lots of these little pressure pads. They contract or expand according to the program. Using them we can make it feel as if you're being stroked . . .'

'. . . or squeezed . . .'

'. . . or pinched . . .'

'. . . or kissed . . .'

Cynthia gave a little shiver. 'Really?'

'Well . . .' Bill hesitated. 'In theory, anyway. Getting it to work just how we want is the difficult bit.'

'But you'll get there?'

'Sure,' both twins said, as one, nodding their heads vigorously.

'And how about the vulva?'

'The . . .' Bill swallowed nervously. 'You mean the attachment?'

She laughed. 'Is that what you call it?'

The twins looked to each other, then looked back at Cynthia and shook their heads sheepishly.

'So what precisely *do* you call it. In secret, I mean. When no one else is around.'

For once the twins looked to each other, each clearly wanting the other to take charge.

'You do have a pet name for it, I assume,' Cynthia went on, moving away from the workbench and walking over to the machine, then crouching beside the nozzle of the attachment.

'Sure,' Ben said finally. 'But it's . . . well, kinda personal.'

'But you can tell me, boys, surely? After all, I'm part of the team.'

'But you're . . .'

'I'm what?' she said, looking to Bill, who had begun the sentence. 'A woman? So? Surely that's a good thing? I can advise you. Give you hints on things. Things that a man wouldn't know about. Things that could improve this until it's' – her eyes lit – 'until it's the best damn sex machine anyone ever made!'

The twins stared at Cynthia, astonished. They had never guessed.

'You want to help with the development?' Ben began hesitantly.

'Sure,' she said, standing again and facing them. 'Why, does that bother you boys?'

'No, no . . .' Bill said, glancing at Ben. 'It's just . . .'

'Embarrassing?'

'Kind of,' Ben said, looking down at his feet. For once Bill didn't do the same.

'Then let's be scientific about it, eh?' Cynthia said, walking across and donning a white lab coat, then pulling on a pair of surgical gloves. 'Let's see this as an exercise in problem solving, yes?'

'Sure,' both twins answered, but the same hesitancy was still there in their voices.

'Now, you said the other day that you were having problems with the lubrication system. Maybe we should start with that. That's a common enough problem, and maybe I can come up with an idea or two you boys haven't thought of . . .'

Louise listened to the front door close one floor below. Moments later the sound drifted up of a car door slamming shut, followed immediately by the unmistakable purr of Roger's engine. Laying in bed, propped up on one arm,

Louise imagined him adjusting the crotch of his trousers, which she'd noticed he always did out of habit, and smiled to herself. She waited for the inevitable revving followed by the squeal of rubber against tarmac as he pulled away too quickly, off into the late-night traffic. Only then did she allow herself to slump back against the pillows.

Reaching across to the bedside cabinet she flicked open the packet of cigarettes and pulled one out. Reaching up, she wiped the back of her other hand across her mouth, smudging the remains of her lipstick along her knuckles, before pushing the cigarette between her teeth and lighting it. She drew deeply so that the tip glowed brightly in the darkened room, filling her veins with calming, dulling nicotine.

This was the worst time — the time she hated most. Certainly it was the time when she hated him a little. How often had she begged him to stay the night, just for once, wanting nothing more than to wake up beside him in the morning, for him to bring her a cup of tea? Louise sighed. She just wanted to be allowed to pretend sometimes. She knew it wasn't real life: *this* was real life — her lying awake in the middle of the night, unable to sleep. Thinking.

But Roger was firm about it. No matter the hour, he had to go home. Even if he arrived back at three in the morning, he was able to come up with a plausible excuse. Yet he felt that even *his* luck would run out if he had to explain away whole nights to his wife. At the thought of Jane Appleyard, Louise bristled. She took a long drag on her cigarette and stubbed it out with an unnecessary degree of force, grinding it into the saucer.

Rolling over onto her stomach, she buried her face in the soft pillow, filling her nostrils with the smell of Roger's aftershave and sweat, uncertain even in her own mind whether she did it for comfort or punishment. It seemed to her that most relationships were a combination of the two. Certainly her parents' was; except that her mother had ended up taking far more punishment than comfort from her philandering father. At least Roger loved her.

Louise glanced across at the clock: 1.30. With a clear road, Roger was probably halfway home by now. She imagined him lying in bed next to his wife, and, even as the words 'frigid bitch' formed in her head, she could see in her mind's eye Jane Appleyard's smug features as she rolled over to mould her body to Roger's, her arm encircling his waist proprietorially. Louise shook her head to dislodge the taunting image.

The sound of a baby crying filtered through the thin wall that divided Louise's bedroom from the flat next door. She lay on her back listening to the catlike, unrelenting wail of the young child and smiled fondly as she pictured its tiny, crumpled face. Gradually the noise increased in volume, becoming more angry, more insistent, in spite of its parents' soothing words. She could hear them, too, their voices raised to compete with the infant's screams, and Louise thought wistfully of the two of them sitting on the edge of the bed, taking it in turns to nurse the baby, the two adults united in a battle of wills with their tiny creation. She could hear the tiredness and irritation in their voices and silently chastised them for their impatience. Then came their audible relief as the baby finally quietened, its screams subsiding to a bearable grizzle until Louise could hear nothing at all. She imagined the three of them huddled together in bed and smiled, but there was a sadness behind her eyes.

The same thing had happened the night before. When she had bumped into the husband that morning Louise had commented on how tired he looked. He'd apologised about the baby even though she'd said there was no need. Then he'd said that she looked a bit tired as well and he'd grinned, a knowing look in his eyes. It was only then she realised that, if she could hear what went on in his bedroom, then he could undoubtedly hear what went on in hers. He was saying something about popping in for coffee sometime but in her embarrassment Louise had already fled halfway down the stairs.

The silence now was broken only by the occasional passing vehicle. Louise closed her eyes, willing herself to find some peace of mind, but sleep would not embrace her. Reaching across to the cabinet, she fumbled inside the top drawer before pulling out a small, brown bottle of pills. Tipping two of the white tablets into her palm, she screwed the lid back on before dropping them onto her tongue and swallowing them down. Content that sleep would soon follow, she closed her eyes. She must look forward to tomorrow. After all, tomorrow was another day.

Patricia's breath caught in her throat as she entered the Chairman's office, staring at the young man at the window. Charles Grant was so like a younger version of his father that she had thought herself back twenty years, when she had first come to work for Sir James.

Charles stood with his back to her, looking out

through the penthouse window on to the Square below. His hands clasped together on his back, his feet a step apart, he stood in solitary silence, staring out at the grey, cloud-filled sky.

As the only son of Sir James and Lady Grant, Charles had always been conscious that he would one day inherit the family firm, but in truth he had little or no interest in assuming Sir James's mantle and becoming a player in the world of big business.

In fact, Charles Grant's ambitions stretched little further than the boundary of the cricket pitch on the family's country estate where, every other Sunday between May and September, he could be found leading his motley team of old schoolfriends and local men to proud victory or, as was more frequently the case, to noble defeat as they battled against teams from neighbouring villages. His main preoccupation between each match was the upkeep of that hallowed pitch and the condition of the wicket, which he personally attended – along with Atkins, the family's faithful old retainer – in order to produce the perfect surface off which his celebrated spinners could rebound with varying degrees of accuracy.

The sound of the door closing made Charles jump, and turning quickly he looked about him, as though he had been woken from a dream and wasn't quite sure of his whereabouts. Seeing Patricia on the far side of the room, he gave a brief, forced smile as reality dawned, then turned back to the window.

'Good morning, Mr Charles,' Patricia said brightly, walking over to his large mahogany desk and placing a tray of opened correspondence on the green leather inlaid surface.

'Morning, Patricia,' he replied quietly without turning round.

She had already prepared the paperwork, placing each letter in order of importance in readiness for the session which, when Sir James was in charge, had begun the day. This had been the time when they would catch up with each other and where she would capture her Chairman's interest with tasty morsels of gossip picked up from around the building. When Sir James was at the helm, there hadn't been much going on that the old man hadn't known about.

She waited a moment or two, then, when Charles made no sign of turning back, asked, 'Shall I get you some coffee before we start, Mr Charles?'

'No!'

Patricia had already turned away, making for the door. But at Charles's abrupt reply, she bristled and stopped in her tracks, her hand tensed over the doorknob. A pink flush rose her neck.

'Sorry. No thank you,' Charles said more softly, turning back.

Walking over to the desk he took the top letter from the tray and stared disinterestedly at its content before allowing it to float back to lie at an angle across the pile of papers. Dropping down heavily into his father's massive, padded, leather chair, he placed his elbows on the desk and stared down into the open diary. Names and times of meetings were written over both pages in Patricia's neat hand. Sighing, he pushed his hand through his short dark hair and leaned back in the chair.

'Would you like me to take you through the meetings we've arranged for you, Mr Charles?' Patricia offered with regained enthusiasm, hurrying back across the room towards the desk. 'Your father suggested—'

'Is it absolutely necessary to take the bat up straight away?' he interrupted, looking up at her imploringly. 'Do I really need to have so many meetings?'

Patricia smiled down fondly at the young man. She could remember the first time she had met him, nearly fifteen years ago, although it didn't seem so long. His mother had brought him into town to buy a uniform in readiness for his move to senior school after the summer break and they had called into the office to whisk Sir James off for lunch. Patricia could recall the reluctant eleven-year-old modelling the blazer and straw boater for his father, and just how big they had seemed on his tiny frame.

Now that young boy was in charge of the company his father had built, and the role he was expected to fill hung as heavily on him as that uniform had all those years ago. Patricia gave a smile of encouragement. It was her job to be supportive, to be his crutch; that's what Sir James had told her as he'd placed his arm around her shoulder during their tearful farewell. 'Look after the boy, Pat,' he'd said. 'He's going to need you.'

'Would you like me to reschedule, Mr Charles?' she said kindly.

He smiled gratefully, his shoulders drooping with relief. 'And Patricia,' he said, closing the diary and handing it across to her. 'Could we drop the Mister? Just Charles would do fine.'

She smiled, holding the diary close to her chest, feeling a genuine pleasure at this offer of familiarity. 'Your father always called me Pat,' she responded, a slight coyness in her voice.

Charles looked into his lap a moment, his face a mask of solemnity when finally he glanced up at her. 'I'm not my father,' he said quietly, almost apologetically.

'I know,' she said, the consoling tone of her voice full of pity rather than the scorn he had expected. 'I know.'

They exchanged a brief smile.

'Shall I get us that coffee now?' she said, wrinkling her nose.

'Yes,' he said. 'Good show, Pat.'

Chastity Lloyd was a surprising girl. At her tender age and with her model-girl looks it would have been reasonable to assume that the breadth of her interests did not extend beyond the content of the pop charts and the latest street fashion. It was an assumption that was, in actual fact, pretty wide of the mark. Perhaps because she had been raised in an urban environment, still living on the fifth floor of the block of flats where she'd been born, she had developed a passionate interest in conservation and a fascination for country pursuits. In the light of which, assuming responsibility for the office plants was, for her, a pleasure rather than a chore.

Several weeks earlier Chastity had planted half-a-dozen small cuttings from the prodigious spider plant that hung in the corner of the office from a white macramé pot-holder, arranging them in a row of small terracotta pots along the windowsill in Bob Guppy's office. The warm dry air pumped from the heating system running along the wall below had a tendency to absorb any moisture, so, to ensure healthy growth,

Chastity included the tending and watering of her beloved plants as another part of her daily office routine.

Looking out onto the Square below, Chastity stood mesmerised by the bright green leaves of the massive chestnut tree. She was about to turn away when her eye was suddenly caught by the figure of a young man leaving the front of the building. She watched as he crossed the narrow road to a turquoise sports car parked alongside the fence surrounding the Square's gardens. She recognised him at once. The appointment of Charles Grant as head of Virt-E-Go had caused quite a stir, not to mention considerable resentment amongst many of the older, more experienced managers, and whilst to most he remained an enigma, to those with most to lose he was seen as a bit of a joke, and a sick one at that. Chastity had been prepared to make up her own mind about him rather than accept Bob Guppy's jaundiced view, and had been disappointed when he had cancelled the staff meeting he'd been scheduled to address that morning.

Charles Grant looked like a man in a hurry as he quickly slid into the seat of the car and zoomed away, round the Square and off, out of sight. As she stared after the vehicle, Chastity felt a hand on her arm and Bob Guppy's unmistakable breath on her neck. Her body tensed, but if he noticed it didn't seem to bother him and he ran his hand up over the rise of her shoulder.

'This won't do, my little dreamer,' he said in mock chastisement, his body within a hair's breadth of hers as he stood behind her.

She made a sound feigning amusement as her mind swiftly assessed the situation and made a snap decision that if this groping went much further she'd have no option but to do what any self-respecting girl with an ounce of common sense would do and knee him in the goolies.

Leaning further into her so that Chastity could feel the stiffness of his penis against her back, Bob Guppy allowed his hand to drop down the girl's side and come to rest on her slim hip.

Her fists clenched and her teeth grinding, Chastity had made a forty-five degree turn, her knee rising to position, when Patricia's voice called out from across the office.

'Would you mind if I borrow Chastity for a few minutes?' she said, in a tone that made it clear she did not require Bob Guppy's consent.

'Yes . . . Yes, of course,' he replied shakily, swiftly dropping his hand to his side. 'Go on, Chastity, off you go,' he said, the pitch of his voice higher than usual. 'No problem, Patricia. None at all.'

'Good!' she replied from the corridor as she led the way into the lift. They travelled up in silence and, on reaching the penthouse, Chastity followed Patricia into Charles's empty office, closing the door behind them.

There was something about this girl that attracted Patricia, and that she found disquieting. It was nothing sexual, she was sure of that. She had never been attracted to any woman in that way. Even so, there was something . . . *special* about Chastity.

'Take a seat,' Patricia said, indicating the one she herself normally occupied across from Sir James, and she walked round the huge wooden desk to sit where Charles had sat only minutes before. 'What was all that about?'

'It's nothing I can't handle,' Chastity assured her,

the look on her face belying the confidence of her tone.

'I just want you to know that if he goes too far, if he oversteps the mark, you must feel you can come to me.'

'It'll be okay,' Chastity said, giving the briefest of smiles. And having regained her composure she went on, 'I wouldn't mind if he wasn't so *old*. Gawd, he must be even older than my dad!' And she wrinkled her nose in disgust.

This time it was Patricia's turn to smile. 'Well, as long as you're sure,' she said, moving round the desk. 'Listen, he'll be going off to the management lunch soon, so if I were you I'd stay here for ten minutes or so. Water the plants for me. Maybe Guppy'll have cooled down a bit by the time he gets back.'

Chastity had never been in the Chairman's office before. Patricia had always been very protective of Sir James, so that even senior management had had restricted access to him, with almost every request and decision being channelled through her. The room was far grander than those lower down the block. Full-length glass windows stretched along one side, leading out onto a narrow terrace overlooking the Square. Inside, it was sparsely but expensively furnished, with antique-leather upholstery, Turkish rugs and imposing oil paintings in huge gilt frames, the most intimidating of which was one of Sir James looking out across the room from its position above the Chairman's seat.

As she might had she been left alone in a stranger's home, Chastity found herself with time to browse and to examine various personal items that she would otherwise have merely glanced at out of fear of being thought

rude or intrusive. Disappointingly, the three framed
photographs on Charles Grant's desk did nothing to
assuage Chastity's curiosity over the family's country
home nor the fiancée Patricia had hinted at. Instead
there was one of Charles in full cricket gear, his bat
tucked underneath his arm, another of Charles in his
hunting pink upon the back of a handsome grey gelding,
raising a toast with a glass of sherry, and the third —
bearing a greeting from his mother across the bottom
— was a picture of his parents taken a good fifteen or
twenty years before.

Smiling to herself Chastity replaced the photographs
and made her way to the adjoining kitchen.

He's got a nice face, she thought, as she filled a white
china cup from the tap, staring at herself in the mirror,
but maybe a bit too posh.

She pouted at her image, then tilted her head slightly,
her eyes thoughtful as she wondered what Charles would
make of her, wondered if he'd even notice her. Then,
making a face at herself, she took the cup back into the
office and began to water the plants.

The phone in Patricia's office was ringing urgently when
she returned from looking after Chastity. She crossed the
room quickly and sat behind her desk, composing herself
a moment before she picked up the receiver.

'Yes?'

'Patricia?' a panicky little voice addressed her. 'It's
Carol. In reception.'

'Yes, Carol, what is it?'

'We've a visitor. A Detective Inspector Holly. He's
demanding to look around the offices.'

'I see.' Patricia paused, wondering if any kind of report had been made to the police about the incident. No one at the hospital had mentioned anything, and as far as she knew, no one here in the offices had been on to the authorities, but there was always the possibility that Fukuada's office may have said something. She decided that the best policy was to deny all knowledge. 'Keep him down there,' she said. 'I'm on my way.'

Detective Inspector Richard Holly was a wholly unimposing creature. With his shabby mac and his uncombed greying hair, he might have seemed like some cross between Columbo and Morse, except that his blue eyes were less disconcerting than Columbo's, and his voice – its coarseness undeniably rooted in the East End of London – lacked the suave sophistication of Morse.

The truth was that, until recently, Holly had been a simple detective on the Bow force, responsible for investigating robberies. Six months ago he had got his first big break, and, along with promotion to DI, had been given charge of an important undercover job, trying to break up a drugs ring. A four-month investigation, involving three dozen men and two other forces – one of them a special squad from Amsterdam – had ended in total farce, when Holly, thinking he was speaking to one of his own men 'inside' the gang, had tipped the villains off on the phone. Half a million of Her Majesty's money and half a ton of marijuana had gone down the Swanee, along with Holly's career.

Holly's 'reward' was to be given command of the new and hastily formed TVS, the Technological Vice Squad. Deemed a total backwater by his superiors, who were only reacting to a Commons sub-committee resolution handed on to them by the Commissioner, the TVS was one of those makeshift measures the authorities sometimes indulge in when they don't know what the hell they ought *really* to be doing. Accordingly, Holly was given a grand total of three men and a pair of offices in the basement of a shoe factory in Wembley. Moreover, because of budget cuts, the newly formed TVS was allowed the use of two second-hand wordprocessors, two desks, four chairs, one filing cabinet and the occasional use of a typist named Doreen.

It was, as even Holly had to admit, a wholly inauspicious start for the fledgling department, particularly as its concerns lay at what his superiors had termed 'the cutting edge of modern crime'.

But Holly was keen. Keen to resurrect his career and make his name. Keen to wipe the blot of shame from his record and begin once more to mount the golden ladder that led to the rank of Chief Constable.

Seeing Patricia appear from the lift, he pulled his ID from his pocket and held it out to her.

'Detective Inspector Holly, I'm here—'

'Have you an appointment?'

Holly bristled, taking against the woman instantly. 'No, I haven't. I'm here—'

'I don't care *why* you're here,' Patricia said, walking up to him and raising herself to her full height so that she stood a couple of inches taller than the man she so clearly looked down upon. 'We are a very busy organisation, Inspector. Now, if you would like to call for an appointment—'

'Now just a bloody minute—'

'Or perhaps when you've learned some manners.'

'*Manners*?' The word came out sounding suspiciously like 'mah-nahs'.

'Yes,' Patricia said firmly. 'We are a prestigious limited company, quoted on the Stock Exchange, and incorporated thirty years ago, and until this morning we have had an outstanding relationship with our local constabulary. Sir James Grant, our Chairman . . .' – corrected herself – 'our *ex*-Chairman, is a personal friend of your Commissioner.'

'That's as may be—' Holly began, but Patricia was not about to let him get the upper hand.

'So, if you would return to your office and telephone us, I'll see whether I can arrange for you to come in and see the new Chairman the week after next.'

'The week . . .' Holly looked close to apoplexy. 'Now look here, woman!'

'Mrs Hampton,' Patricia said with a firmness that brooked no argument. 'Patricia Hampton, personal assistant to Charles Grant, Chairman of Virt-E-Go. Now if you would excuse me, Inspector, I happen to be very busy.'

And with that she turned her back on him and returned to the lift, not even deigning to look at him as the doors slowly closed.

Holly stood there a moment, halfway between rage and bewilderment. Then, with a parting glare at Carol, who still cowered behind her desk, he pushed out through the glass doors, and headed for the nearest tube.

Back in her office, Patricia sat again, staring into space. Something would have to be done. Holly would be back. She had seen that in his face. Worse, she hadn't, in her panic, actually found out what the man wanted. And it was important to know why he had turned up out of the blue. Was it something to do with Fukuada's accident, or had someone tipped him off?

The Project was supposed to be absolutely top secret, but with pissheads like Bob Guppy and philanderers like Appleyard in the company, it was a wonder that the *Sun* wasn't serialising what they were up to in their third-floor labs.

'Sir James . . .' she said quietly, realising that the key to things was in what she'd said to Holly. Sir James played golf with the Chief Constable. If they needed to know what Detective Inspector Holly was up to, Sir James was the person to find out.

Patricia swallowed, then, taking up the phone, she began to dial Sir James's home number.

Patricia stood at the supermarket checkout cursing the woman at the front of the queue. It was beyond her why housewives with kids, who had all day to shop, had to do it in the evening when busy people like her were trying to whiz through after a hard day's work.

She looked on as the woman loaded interminable bags of food into her trolley, surrounding the disgruntled toddler who stood there, finally forcing him into one corner. In protest he tipped his tube of Smarties over the side of the trolley, spilling the multicoloured sweets along the aisle only to be seized upon by other bored youngsters grateful for relief from this weekly tedium. At the sight of his sweets being devoured, the imprisoned toddler screamed uncontrollably until his embarrassed mother – tiny baby strapped to her breast – handed him another tube of Smarties from one of the plastic bags, warning him that if he carried on there'd be trouble.

With vague interest Patricia wondered what the trouble might be, but as the woman looked apologetically at her along the conveyer belt she decided it probably wouldn't be anything particularly spectacular. No, by the look of her, the woman wasn't likely to give the spoilt little brat a smack across the backside, which is what *she'd* be tempted to do if he carried on being such a pain.

It was at times like these that Patricia told herself she was grateful for her solitary status. Having only herself to please, nobody else to worry about or cater to. She could watch what she liked on telly, go to bed when she wanted; there was no one to wait up for or worry about.

The woman took her receipt and credit card from the checkout girl, even as the baby at her bosom stirred. The woman smiled at the sound, bent her head and kissed the soft fuzz of dark hair on its tiny head. The toddler in the trolley had quietened now and was busy pulling pieces off the end of the baguette and stuffing them in his mouth. His mother laughed and ruffled his hair. 'Come on, let's go and see if Daddy's home yet,' she said, squatting down to receive a soggy piece of bread from his grubby fist before pushing the trolley towards the exit.

Patricia smiled and shuffled forward, pushing her wire basket on another pace with her foot.

A young couple, both in smart pinstripe suits, passed through quickly. Patricia noted with interest the sparse content of their basket: a bottle of champagne, some smoked salmon, a lemon, salad, brown bread and two family-sized cartons of thick whipping cream. They packed the shopping away swiftly, falling into each other and giggling helplessly as they walked away from the checkout, so that Patricia found herself smiling again.

The contents of her own basket were far more mundane. A small loaf, a carton of milk, two apples, two frozen complete-meals-in-one, a small box of tea bags and her little indulgence: a packet of chocolate digestives. It had taken her a long while to shop so efficiently for herself. For months after her husband had left she would find herself buying the same amount of food she had before: filling the fridge with meat that would eventually go off and end up in the rubbish; large crusty loaves that would turn green in the bread bin or be fed to the birds in the Square on her way to work. Now she had things down to a fine art: only two days' worth of food bought at a time and only what *she* needed. In spite of her moans, at least the supermarket provided somewhere to go between work and home.

Having pushed the last forkful of lasagne into her mouth, Patricia lifted the tray from her knees and placed it on the floor at her feet. Reaching under the coffee table for the TV magazine, she flicked through the pages, glanced down the four columns of listings, wrinkling her nose in distaste at what was on offer. Directing the remote control towards the television screen, she muted the sound, and the sports section of the ten o'clock news played out before her in welcome silence.

She had never shared her husband's love of sport, had never been able to understand his passion for football; and on occasions, certainly, she'd resented it. She'd always said that if a man was passionate about another woman then at least it would be understandable, but twenty-two men, a ball and a bloke with a whistle! Once the pain of his rejection had passed she had often mused over what he must have thought hearing her say those words. How he must have laughed at the bloody irony of it!

Sometimes Patricia would think back to the night when, finally, she could not deny his infidelity any longer. She would drag from her memory that awful journey to where the woman lived, the feeling of inevitability turning the corner into her street and seeing his car parked not outside the stadium where his favourite team were playing that evening but right there outside her house. Unable to stop herself she had walked up to the front gate and had peered through the window. The sight of them sitting there on the sofa – holding hands, laughing, cuddling like lovesick teenagers – pierced her like a shard of glass, entering her skin and shattering into tiny pieces, flooding her whole body with an unbelievable, excruciating pain. But still she stood there, unable to look away until, suddenly, her husband had looked round. In a split second their eyes had met, and then she ran.

Patricia felt down the side of the armchair for her book and opened it at her place. Glancing up at the silent TV screen she watched a moment as a group of burly footballers jostled in the goalmouth waiting for a corner kick to be taken. She looked down at her watch. It was only 10.40. She'd read for a bit. Wait till she felt tired enough to go to bed – tired enough not to be tormented by the cold wide emptiness of the sheets, or plagued by the loneliness she felt each night. She reached across for the packet of chocolate digestives, then found her place halfway down the page.

> '*Eh! what it is to touch thee!*' *he said, as his finger caressed the delicate, warm, secret skin of her waist and hips. He put his face down and rubbed his cheek against her belly and against her thighs again and again . . .*

Patricia sighed, then, reaching for another digestive, read on.

A week later, Chastity sat poised with notepad and pen, awaiting Bob Guppy's instructions. The evening before, he had been called into the young Chairman's office and given the brief to put together a marketing strategy for Virt-E-Go's newest product, the VR sex simulator. Now that the Japanese were on board, mass production of the machine was no longer a fantasy, and within six months could be a fully functional reality. But while that was good news, in that it meant they kept their jobs, it also meant that the stakes were much higher than any of them had imagined possible when work had begun on the project a year earlier. The importance of its successful launch into the marketplace was crucial. And that was Bob Guppy's problem.

Pacing back and forth behind his desk he racked his brain for some small seed of inspiration that would set him off on the right track.

'When did you say this meeting was?' he asked nervously, glancing at Chastity and running his fingers through imaginary locks of his hair.

'Ten days,' she answered, looking at the date of the project-planning meeting written in bold figures across the top of her pad. 'Friday week.'

Guppy took a sip of lukewarm coffee then looked imploringly across the table at Chastity.

'What the hell do I know about mechanical sex machines?'

The query made Chastity want to laugh, but she merely shrugged her shoulders, uncrossed her legs, then crossed them again.

'Toasters – great! Kettles – brilliant! Electric deep-fat fucking fryers – the dog's bollocks! But a sex machine!' Bob Guppy rested his hands on the desk, hung his head and shook it in despair. 'I tell you, Chastity, this is a whole new ball game!'

Affecting a cough the young woman covered her mouth.

'I mean to say,' he went on obliviously, 'we're not talking traditional outlets here, are we? We're not talking a nice buffet launch at the Savoy to the likes of Curry's and Dixon's with a complimentary sample to take home to the missus, are we?'

He glanced across and Chastity shook her head in agreement.

'I haven't even told the wife you know. About the machine, I mean,' he added, seeing Chastity's quizzical look.

'Why not?'

This time it was Guppy's turn to shrug. 'I dunno really. I suppose I guess she'd think I was shagging some page-three bird all day long.'

You should be so lucky! thought Chastity, looking

across at the paunch hanging over his suit trousers. Keeping all trace of amusement from her voice, she asked, 'Why would she think that?'

'I don't mean *actual* shagging,' he explained, a little shakily. 'I mean, you know, on the machine. The tart they've used looks like one of them page-three girls – all big tits and blonde hair.' His eyes dropped down momentarily to Chastity's breasts before he forced them away, looking down with feigned fascination into the cold dregs of his coffee cup.

'Well? What're you gonna do, then?'

'What?' he said, looking up, his mind a million miles away in a parallel universe.

'About the marketing plan. What're you gonna do about it? You've gotta do something, haven't you?'

Bob Guppy let out a heavy sigh and slumped down into his chair. 'Chastity, sweetheart, I haven't got a bleedin' clue what I'm going to do,' he said, resting a hand on the rise of his protruding stomach, unconsciously patting it with the affection of a pregnant mother. 'In fact it'd be true to say that if it were a straightforward choice between a night of unbridled passion with a bevy of *Baywatch* babes and a magic formula for marketing this fucking thing – no pun intended – Miss Anderson and her mates would just have to live with the disappointment. That's how desperate I am!'

And, as Bob Guppy sat with his jowls resting in his hands, elbows perched on the edge of the desk, he did indeed look a desperate man, a man devoid of all imagination. He had been comfortable with the mundane, household equipment English Electrical Goods Limited had traditionally produced before the change of name and emphasis twelve months back. To him the latest double sandwich maker for thick-sliced bread and extra fillings was much more than just a machine: it was a beautiful work of art. Present him with the latest dry/steam super-duper crease-cutting flat iron with added extras and detachable lead and he could wax lyrical for hours – but sex simulators were something entirely different. This was something that he couldn't quite get to grips with.

Chastity could almost feel sorry for Bob Guppy as he sat there, an expression of pathetic incompetence pervading his crumpled features.

'What about an agency?' she said suddenly.

He opened one eye, raised one eyebrow, and looked across at her.

'What?'

'What about getting in one of them agencies? You know, like that Saatchi's or whatever they're called.'

Bob Guppy let out a loud, derisory laugh and sat up in his chair to resume his position of superiority.

'Don't be ridiculous! We haven't got a budget for that kind of expenditure. Not yet anyway. Saatchi's!' he said, smiling indulgently at Chastity as though amused by the innocent utterings of a young child.

'Well, I didn't actually mean Saatchi's,' she said, controlling her irritation, 'but, you know, somebody like that. And anyway, I thought you only had to pay them if you took them on. What about if you get a load of them to pitch for the job just to get yourself a few ideas of how you can market the new machine. You know, a bit like having your own think tank.'

Chastity watched Guppy as the idea took hold on the

small mass of grey matter floating in his skull. She smiled with satisfaction as her solution to his problems dawned across his features so that his furrowed brow smoothed out, his jaw tightened and his lips took an upward turn, revealing a set of square, yellowing teeth as his mouth curved into a smile.

'Chastity, my sweet,' he announced, jumping to his feet, 'you are an angel in disguise! An absolute twenty-four-carat bloody angel! Why didn't I think of that?'

Chastity held her tongue and smiled sweetly.

'Right!' he said, with renewed vigour, banging the desk with his fist. 'Get a list of some of the top people and arrange appointments. We'll get them to come in for a briefing — got to be careful who we involve, though. Secrecy and all that.'

'I'll get the lawyers to draw up a confidentiality agreement, shall I?' Chastity offered, already writing the instruction on her pad.

'Good idea! Yeah, great idea! Right!' he said, his enthusiasm and relief palpable in equal quantities. 'So you get that done, get some appointments lined up and we're up and running. Up and bloody running!' And with that he threw his pen into his empty 'out' tray, sank down into his chair and placed his feet on the desk, a self-satisfied smile splitting his none-too-pleasant features.

Bob Guppy's eyes followed Chastity as she made her way to the door, jotting notes on her pad as she went.

'Chastity,' he called after her. 'Well done!'

'That's all right,' she said, smiling over her shoulder. 'I've got it all in hand.'

And she made her way out into the corridor, not

hearing the soft groan that left Bob Guppy's quivering lips.

Even as Chastity strolled down the corridor and into her tiny cubby-hole of an office, Patricia was standing in the labs looking on as William and Benjamin lifted a huge curved sheet of thick see-through plastic up onto the top of what looked to her eyes like a cross between a bath and a coffin.

'What in God's name is that?' she asked, as the sheet clicked into place.

'It keeps out any extraneous sound,' Bill said, removing the gloves he'd put on to move the sheet.

'And the inside acts as a kind of TV set,' Ben added, his own gloves having been removed at precisely the same moment as his brother's. 'We plan to project images onto the surface.'

'But I thought . . .' Patricia frowned. 'What about the lounger you used to have?'

'A stopgap,' Bill said.

'Until this arrived,' Ben added.

'So this . . .' she hesitated. 'This is what the user will be put in to experience the program?'

'You got it,' Ben said, patting the side of the machine fondly. 'Ain't it a beauty?'

'But it looks like a coffin.'

The twins took a step back and stared at it thoughtfully.

'A little, perhaps,' Ben said.

'But what it really is,' Bill said, smiling once more, 'is a state-of-the-art immersion tank.'

'But they'll go stark staring bonkers in there!'

'No,' Bill said confidently. 'They'll only be in there for half an hour – an hour at most. That's not long enough to go mad. Besides, they'll be having a whale of a time. I'd say that once they're in they won't want to come out!'

'Hmm,' Patricia said. That was what she was afraid of. 'Don't you think we should have a meeting about this, boys?'

'Why?' Ben asked, as if he couldn't conceive of any reason why it needed discussing. 'You want this thing ready, don't you?'

'Yes,' she said hesitantly.

'Then trust us,' Bill said, standing beside his twin, the two of them grinning back at her. 'We know what we're doing.'

'Okay,' she said doubtfully, making a mental note to raise the matter with Charles the next time she spoke to him. 'However, there's another matter I need to talk to you about.'

'Fire away,' Ben said.

'Yeah, like shoot,' Bill added.

Patricia looked about her briefly, noting the dozen or so variously sized and shaped dildos that rested on the workbench – part of the twins' recent attempt to begin a female version of the program – then looked back at them.

'We had a visit from the police a week ago.'

'The fuzz?' Bill looked to Ben.

'Man, that's heavy,' Ben said, nodding. 'What did they want?'

'They wanted to poke their noses into our affairs, that's what they wanted. It seems there's a new department called TVS – the Technological Vice Squad. They've been given the job of looking into the whole shadowy question of sex and virtual reality.'

'Wow!' Bill said, his eyes lighting up. 'The techno-fuzz.'

'Well, whatever you want to call them, the problem is this. While I've arranged for the commander of this unit – a Detective Inspector Holly – to come in and visit us next week, it's conceivable than he may just pay us a visit before then.'

'You mean, like, get a warrant?' Bill asked.

Patricia nodded.

'Heavy,' Ben said.

'So what I want to know is this. How quickly, and how thoroughly, can you disguise all of this?'

The twins looked to each other and laughed. 'Like, hide the dildos, you mean?'

Patricia cleared the tickle from her throat, then nodded.

'Five minutes,' Ben answered. 'All we have to do is drop the attachments into the water tank.'

'And the machine itself?'

'Is an immersion machine,' Bill said. 'For meditational purposes only.'

At which the twins began to giggle in that high-pitched way they had.

'Good,' Pat said, looking across at the workbench again, her eyes dwelling perhaps overlong on the biggest of the attachments laid out on the surface. 'Then I'll leave you to it.'

'Any time,' they both said, turning back to the machine.

Back in her office, Patricia sat for a long time, deep

in thought. The police were a nuisance, there was no doubting it, but this was an aspect of things that they hadn't really given enough thought to. They had both the know-how and the backing to create the world's first fully functional sex machine. But was it legal?

Until a week or so ago it had all been hypothetical, but now things had changed. Now they had to deal with real problems in the real world. For a start it would be useful to discover just what the legal situation was in respect of sex toys, and whether what they were doing counted as such. If it was classified as just a super-glorified dildo, then maybe there was no problem. But what if it came under some other category? Some category that broke an ancient statute, maybe, or could be deemed – heaven help them! – pornographic? What then?

It was best to find out. Best to know the precise situation before they went any further or spent any more of the Japanese money.

– May –

Charles laid an arm along the top of the stable door and, reaching into the satin-lined pocket of his hacking jacket, pulled out a fluff-covered mint which he offered up to the eager mouth within. Patting the horse's soft pink muzzle, he laughed as the animal showed its impressive set of tombstone teeth, a plume of hot breath rising on the cold air.

His earliest memory was of being on the back of a horse, or a pony to be more precise — a tiny Welsh cob his father had bought him for his fourth birthday. Jamie. How he had loved that pony! Every day his nanny had taken him along to the field or stable to visit and, if conditions were good, he had been allowed on Jamie's back, with nanny or old Atkins walking ahead with the lead rope.

Even now he could clearly recall how, at the age of seven, he had been sent away to boarding school, and the miserable journey to Berkshire throughout which his soft, damp cheek had remained pressed against the car window, tears silently falling over his thick dark lashes. Nanny had assumed he was sad to leave his parents, of course; he could remember her reassuring him, squeezing his tiny hand, reminding him that the holidays weren't far away. But the tears were not for his family: they were for his best friend, Jamie.

It was only the thought of seeing his pony again that had got him through that first term and enabled him to cope with a barbaric system that allowed strangers to take in other people's children, often with as little concern for their emotional wellbeing as the parent who placed them there, but strangers nevertheless. Tears were shed in the privacy of his own bed, his face buried in the pillow to muffle the sound of his crying.

Looking back on it now, he felt sure his father hadn't meant to be cruel. It was just that he hadn't understood. His mother had written a short note before the end of term informing Charles of the arrangements for his journey home by train, along with other boarders, and hinting at a surprise he had in store. Nothing could have prepared him for the shock of discovering that this so-called surprise was that Jamie had been sold on and a younger, bigger pony bought in his place. He had felt the pain as though he had been stabbed in the heart, the loss as tangible as the amputation of a limb. And he had never even got to say goodbye. All he could think about was his beautiful little Jamie being pushed into the horsebox and shipped off to somewhere he didn't know, believing that Charles didn't love him or care about him.

The imposter, as he saw the feisty bay gelding that had replaced Jamie, was put out to field, and, when Charles steadfastly refused to acknowledge him, he was given his daily exercise by the jockey-sized Atkins. The boy would watch critically as the old man trotted him round the

menage, determined not to admire any of his obvious
qualities. But, with the remarkable healing ability that
only the young possess, Charles's broken heart appeared
to mend by the beginning of the second week – though
who could know of the scars that remained beneath the
surface? – and he was persuaded out to the field to cast
a critical eye over Bobbin. And so began his second love
affair. He kept the pony still, in spite of its now being
too old and too small for him to ride.

Every morning he would walk over to the back field
and Bobbin would trot lazily over to the gate to greet him,
and there the two of them would stand, the pony's head
nuzzling into Charles's neck as he talked to the animal
about his problems and what was going on in his life.
In truth, he had shared every worry he had ever had
with Bobbin.

Nowadays his daily companion on the hills and marshes
was a handsome grey gelding called Jester, affectionately
known as Jessop, and peering into the stable Charles
watched as Michael, the young Irish groom, prepared
him for the morning's exercise. His soft voice, with its
lilting Dublin accent, was there all the while, reassuring
the gelding, as the young man picked out his hooves,
scraping the mud and straw from the grooves inside the
shoes, tapping the metal pick against his thigh to shake
free the clumps of muck which trickled down his dirty
jeans and onto the straw-covered stable floor.

Becoming restless now and anxious to be out there,
galloping across the soft damp earth, Jester whinnied and,
stepping back, jostled Michael against the stable wall.

'There, there, boy,' Charles soothed, reaching in and
stroking a hand down the length of his face, over the

dark, dappled coat that gave him such a distinctive look. 'Not long now, my beauty. There's a good boy.'

Giving him a final brush down, Michael threw the numnah over his back, buckled the girth and placed the gleaming black leather saddle upon his unresisting back. Knowing the routine, Jester readily accepted the hard metal bit into his mouth, noisily neighing with excitement and anticipation as the tack was fastened.

Out on the yard Michael handed over the reins to Charles while he pulled down the stirrups, adjusting the straps to the correct length for his master's long legs.

'There you are, sir. Ah, he's a handsome lad, so he is,' he said, patting the gelding's neck affectionately, grateful for the opportunity to work with such quality stock. As an Irishman he knew a good horse when he saw one.

'He most certainly is,' Charles agreed, nuzzling into the horse's face, breathing in that familiar smell.

The sublimity of the moment was shattered by the shrill sound of Davina Bottomley-Crewe's voice cutting across the silent courtyard as she made her way towards them along the path from the house. Beside her, yapping at her heels, was a recently acquired black Labrador puppy, as essential an accessory for any self-respecting country gel as a pair of green wellies or a Gucci headscarf.

Lady Davina had been a part of Charles's life for almost as long as poor old Jamie. Their families owned neighbouring estates and delighted in the prospect of a merging of their considerable holdings with the eventual marriage of the young people. In his darker moments during the prolonged engagement, Charles often mused that his and Davina's prospective fate was not so much an *arranged* marriage as an *assumed* marriage.

Charles peeped out from behind the horse's head to see Davina striding through the gateway, her short and – one might say without being *too* unkind – substantial frame presenting a formidable sight as it stomped determinedly across the gravel.

'Dee!' he called, moving round in front of the horse. 'How nice to see you! I'm just off for a hack, I'm afraid,' and he patted Jester's soft neck, running a gloved hand down the length of his silken mane.

'Yes, I know you are, silly,' she said, reaching down to attach the lead to the tiny collar around the dog's throat.

'Well, what's up, then, old thing? You popped over to have brekkers with Ma or something?'

'Charlie, you really are the most hopeless boy, you know,' she said indulgently, her arm at full stretch as she reached up and ruffled his already dishevelled hair. 'Don't you remember asking me to join you for a ride?'

Charles felt sure he would've remembered if he'd asked the Lady Davina to do *that*.

His blank expression left her in little doubt. 'You don't remember, do you?' she said petulantly. 'You really are the most useless chump, Charles. Tuesday night?' she prompted. 'Over the phone?'

It was only then that Charles realised what any attentive fiancé should have noticed the moment he set eyes upon his partner-to-be, and that was that Davina was dressed in full riding garb – brown check hacking jacket, beige jodhpurs and knee-length leather boots, a soft, brown cashmere scarf tied around her neck to keep out the morning chill. And thinking back to Tuesday night he recalled with a sudden attack of guilt the excuse he had made to get out of their planned visit to the opera and the appeasement of a shared hack later in the week.

'Sorry, old thing,' he apologised, his anticipated pleasure in the morning's ride diminishing with each uttered syllable.

'Never mind. I'm here now.' Looking down on Michael, who sat on his haunches fussing over the puppy, she turned back to Charles. 'I've left my hat in the car. I'll send the boy round to fetch it then we can be off.'

'Right! Fine! Michael would you mind . . .' began Charles.

'Of course he doesn't mind,' she interrupted, meeting the young groom's eyes with a challenging stare. 'And when you're back you can tack up Connie.'

Charles had hoped to spend his time out on the hills giving some thought to the meeting with Bob Guppy planned for that afternoon. Since taking over as Chairman he had had a fax machine, an Apple Mac and a special computer modem installed in the house in order to give office staff access to him when he wasn't there. And occasionally, when a meeting was absolutely necessary, he would arrange for it to take place at his home, which satisfied his desire to remain in the country and seemed to meet with the approval of those involved, who welcomed the opportunity to get away from the office and the noise of the city.

He understood from Patricia that Guppy had prepared a working document with his ideas for the marketing of the new and as yet top-secret project and had requested a meeting with Charles to go over it before preparing a more detailed proposal for approval by the Japanese. Charles wasn't sure what use he could be – he knew as much about marketing sex machines as he did about ironing shirts – but there was something else he wanted to speak about with Bob Guppy, and that was the real reason he had agreed to see him.

On several occasions when he had been forced to work at the office, Charles had noticed a young girl there – a beautiful little filly with a bit of a spring in her step. But it wasn't until they had literally fallen into each other's arms – she walking into the lift as he was walking out – that he had been totally captivated. Her wide green eyes had stared up at him as he'd held her shoulders, and if he closed his eyes and breathed deeply he could still recapture the beautiful fragrance that had filled his nostrils as they had stood there for those few brief moments. The papers she had been carrying had scattered along the corridor and, as they both instinctively bent down to gather them up, their faces had almost touched; the memory of her sweet breath on his cheek had caused a flutter inside him.

Charles had been thinking about her ever since. He could be in the middle of something and suddenly an image of her face would come into his mind, or he would find himself struggling to recall the sound of her voice, with its strange accent. All in all it had become profoundly disturbing and Charles had decided that Guppy was the person to talk to. To what avail he wasn't quite sure, but as her boss he seemed to be the right man.

'Charlie?' Davina called over her shoulder, pulling on

the right rein to guide the striking bay mare off the woodland path and into a clearing. 'Charlie!' she called, a note of impatience in her shrill voice. 'Have you been listening to a word I've said?'

Charles drew up beside her, a look of bewilderment on his face.

Davina gave an exasperated, exaggerated sigh. 'I said, Jeremy is getting a crowd together for the cricket on Saturday and has asked us along.'

'Thought you didn't like cricket, Dee.'

'Yes, well, I don't . . . much. But this is *the* cricket match of the season, Jeremy says. *Everyone* will be there. And you *love* cricket. Besides, Clarissa's invited everyone back to the Manor afterwards for dinner. She says it'll just be an informal affair but you know what *she's* like!'

Charles knew precisely what she was like and groaned at the thought of having to suffer another wretched dinner party with the same set of Right Honourables and Ladies-in-waiting that were his social group.

'Not sure I can, I'm afraid, Dee. Not this Saturday,' he said, turning Jester back onto the path and leading the way through the last stretch of woodland.

'Why not?' she said, with an air of indignation, kicking the horse on with rather too much force so that she threw back her head and threatened to bolt. But Davina held tightly to the reins, pulling hard on the bit to regain control.

'Well, it's, um, work, you see, Dee.'

'Work!' she said incredulously. It wasn't something she associated with Charles, nor, indeed, with many within her acquaintance. 'What do you mean, *work*?'

'I have to go into the office. A special project we're working on.'

'What? On a Saturday?'

''Fraid so, old thing. Can't be helped, unfortunately.' And with that Charles squeezed his thigh gently against the horse's side and man and beast broke into trot.

Within seconds Davina was by his side, her voice more shrill than ever as she breathlessly harangued Charles on the upbeat of the trot.

'Well, really, Charles! I think it's a pretty bloody poor show! What am I going to tell Jeremy?'

'Tell him the truth. He'll understand.'

'Huh! Well, what about Clarissa's?'

'What about Clarissa's?'

'There's no reason you can't come on for dinner, is there? Or are you *working*?'

'Better not count on me, Dee. The meeting might go on rather late. Probably best if I cry off this time.' Charles felt rather proud of himself as they emerged from the woods onto the rise of the hill. He really felt he was coming to master the art of persuasive excuse making and although he realised his release was likely to be temporary, it was nevertheless most agreeable.

'Well, I hope you're pleased with yourself, Charles!' she said, trotting up alongside him. 'You seem determined to make me look a complete and utter fool. I suppose you know I shall be the only one there without an escort. It really is *too* much!'

With that she gave her horse one almighty kick with her formidable legs. Charles watched as the horse broke into a gallop and Davina's rump and Connie's flying tail disappeared over the hill.

'Dee!' was all Charles could think to yell, before he cantered off in hot pursuit, his crop cracking across Jester's hindquarters as he pushed him into a gallop. But Connie now had the devil in her and, with Davina crouching low in her saddle, she flew down the wet grassy hillside towards the familiar landmark tower rising from the folly behind Charles's home. Lacking in both the indignation and determination of his fellow beast, Jester failed to gain on her and, as horse and rider rose to clear the roadside hedge encircling the estate, Charles was unseated and thrown along the length of the hedge, landing with a thump.

Charles grew conscious of the muffled sound of voices, close and yet unclear, as he lay prostrate on the damp ground. He willed his eyelids to open but they lay as heavy as sandbags over his sockets and remained determinedly closed. He could feel a cool hand on his cheek and another at his chest, hastily unbuttoning his jacket, followed by more conversation, close and yet indecipherable. Straining to understand the meaning of the words, Charles lay shrouded with a strange feeling of serenity as he awaited his fate, conscious only of the fingers that continued to stroke his cheek and smooth his brow.

Battling through the fog in his head, an image slowly formed of Davina disappearing over the hilltop holding on for dear life to Connie's long neck as the horse descended at full gallop. Feeling his lips curl into a half-smile, Charles allowed himself a moment to enjoy the memory. But the soft hand on his face would not allow him to dwell on it and out of a sense of loyalty

– or was it fear in his vulnerable position? – he allowed his mouth to slacken into a downwards curve.

He remembered being asked to wriggle his toes and to move his legs, then the sound of sudden, relieved laughter. Charles felt a hand behind his neck, lifting his head onto something soft, and was aware of a familiar fragrance as a wisp of hair fell across his face. The thought that Davina was so concerned for his wellbeing was surprisingly moving, and indeed wholly unexpected.

Gradually, Charles's head cleared and the weights over his eyes grew lighter until he was able to flutter and finally open them. The brightness of the white, cloud-filled sky immediately forced them closed again. Squinting against the light he tried to focus on the faces that peered down into his. And at that moment an image came into his mind. It was of an angel with the wide, innocent face of Chastity, her dark lashes closing over huge green pools like a portcullis across a watery gateway as she smiled down upon him reassuringly. For one glorious moment he thought he had died and gone to heaven only to be brought back to reality by the obscene sound of Bob Guppy's voice and beery breath on his face.

'You're all right, sir. An ambulance is on its way. You just lay still now.'

Charles continued to stare up into the face of the woman beside him. She was no angel, at least not in the biblical sense, but Chastity Lloyd had rendered him speechless. She smiled down at him and he was conscious once again of her slender fingers gently playing over his face, combing the damp hair away from his forehead, and only one thought was in his head. He was in love.

*   *   *

Davina looked on with a mixture of annoyance and envy as Chastity slowly ran her tongue over the back of the chocolate-covered spoon before placing it on the plate that minutes before had contained her second helping of truffle torte with double cream. To her left Bob Guppy watched with barely concealed lust as she dabbed demurely at her mouth with the starched damask napkin, while to her right Charles felt as self-conscious as if he were watching a blue movie flanked by members of the local Women's Institute, and fidgeted uncomfortably in his seat, his lips parting slightly as he followed the dark chocolate on its enviable journey over those delicious pink lips and into Chastity's warm, moist mouth.

Chastity placed the napkin on the table and sat back in the broad, mahogany chair, oblivious of the effect she was having on her three fellow diners. Looking round the table she smiled at each of them and, catching their looks, anxiously ran her tongue over her top row of teeth and into the corners of her mouth.

Charles had been unaware of Guppy's intention to bring his young assistant along to their meeting. Feeling a bit shaken after his riding accident, Charles had decided to postpone their talks until the next morning. It had been Guppy's suggestion that he and Chastity stay at the local pub for the night, but Charles wouldn't hear of it. He insisted that they remain at Maltby House as his guests. Davina felt she required no formal invitation to remain there, and so, with Sir James and Lady Grant away for the evening, the four of them had the house to themselves.

The meal had passed amidst an acceptably unembarrassing level of general chit-chat, predominantly instigated by Bob Guppy, who talked endlessly, and in a largely uninformed manner, about agriculture and EC policy, a subject close to the heart of Davina, who expected to inherit the proceeds from that very industry some time in the future.

With an obvious depth of feeling that quite surprised Charles, Davina was vehement in her condemnation of 'those blighters in Brussels' who she felt were determined to decimate her family's considerable fortune. This led nicely into a tirade against the government, which, she declared, was squeezing people like her to death, and all to finance council tenants and all those ruddy single mothers – a pointed look in Chastity's direction – who bred like rabbits and then used their screaming brats to sponge off the state.

Into her stride now, Davina broadened her theme to encompass the unemployed, the homeless and those who expected free health care on the NHS whenever they just happened to be ill. She conceded that a nominal standard of free education had to be maintained, if only to train people up for working in shops and so on. After all, one didn't want to be waited on by somebody who couldn't string two words together, did one?

Chastity listened in bemused silence to the verbal garbage spilling from Davina's thin lips, marvelling at how Charles Grant could find anything about her remotely attractive. She glanced at him now and then, as he sat back in his chair, a glass of claret in his hand, listening to the rantings of his fiancée, and could only guess at what he was really thinking. He seemed so . . . *nice*.

'Coffee, everyone?' Davina offered, barely pausing for

breath from her lamentations over how one couldn't go
to the theatre these days without falling over beggars at
every turn. 'Shall we take it in the blue room, Charles?'
she asked, but before he could answer she called across
the room to the housekeeper's retreating back.

'Coffee in the blue room, Mrs Webb.' The order was
acknowledged by a brief nod of the older woman's
lacquered curls as she left the room. Rising from the
table, Davina led the way out into the wood-panelled
hallway, Bob Guppy at her short, sensible heels.

Chastity felt suddenly nervous finding herself alone
with Charles Grant for the first time that day. Glancing
up through heavy lashes, she stole a sideways look along
the table, surprised and a little embarrassed to find him
staring at her, an unreadable expression on his face. She
looked away, staring down at her hands where they lay
in her lap. Not having expected to stay overnight, she
still wore the same black dress she had arrived in that
afternoon, except she had removed the white teeshirt she
had worn beneath the shoestring pinafore, revealing her
pale silky shoulders. Goosebumps began to spread along
her arms and up her neck.

'Are you feeling better now?' she said suddenly, looking
up at him.

'Sorry? Oh . . . yes, thanks. Much better.'

'Me and Bob were really worried when we found you.'

'Were you?' he asked eagerly, barely conscious of her
flawed syntax.

Chastity nodded, revealing her pearl-white teeth in
a charming smile. 'You're not kidding. Bob thought
you'd had it!'

'Had it?'

'Yeah. He thought you'd kicked it. You know, lights out! I was about to give you the kiss of life . . .'

Charles's mind reeled at the thought of those luscious lips covering his own, her sweet breath filling his mouth, swelling his lungs, and hastily dropped his napkin over his lap.

'But then we saw your chest go up and down and we knew you were all right.'

Charles watched, mesmerised by the movement of her mouth as she formed each word, and silently cursed that taken breath. If only he could have lain still a moment longer! Yet even as he teetered on the edge, seeing clearly in his mind that mouth descending to meet his own, the shrill sound of Davina calling them from a far-off room destroyed the moment's reverie as effectively as if she had doused him with a bucket of ice-cold water.

Chastity frowned, as if deeply puzzled by something. 'Is she . . . I mean, is Davina *really* your fiancée?'

Charles smiled indulgently. 'Well, it's our parents, you see. They feel. Well, they seem to have decided—'

'But you are engaged?'

Charles nodded forlornly.

'And d'you love her? I mean, you must do if you're marrying her!'

Mesmerised by those startling green eyes, Charles opened his mouth to speak, the words sticking in his throat as he caught sight of Davina standing in the doorway, drumming her fingers over the heavy brass door knob.

'We're waiting!' she said bluntly, then turned away, defying Charles to ignore her a second time.

*   *   *

95

The only time Chastity had been inside a house the size of this was when she'd been on educational outings with the school, to some stately home or other. She hadn't been aware of even *knowing* someone who owned a place this size and until today had considered a semi-detached or a nice bungalow the epitome of grandeur.

Indeed, the blue room itself – named after the china-blue ceiling, so Charles informed them – was big enough to contain not only her mum and dad's flat, but the flats above and below as well. A dozen huge paintings hung about the panelled walls, showing rural scenes of hunting, shooting and other such activities. A number of massive leather chairs rested on a thick-piled, powder-blue carpet that was the size of a duck pond. Most impressive, however, was the fireplace, whose surrounds reminded Chastity of a grand, arched entrance. You could have driven her dad's van through it with plenty of room to spare!

She and Bob Guppy sat in separate chairs on one side of the massive fireplace, while Davina and Charles sat on the other, a good ten or twelve paces distant, the engaged couple sharing a chaise longue. Drinks were brought by the long-suffering Mrs Webb – double brandies in huge, balloon-shaped glasses – and once again Davina warmed to her favourite subject: to those odious state scroungers.

Several brandies later Bob Guppy was the first to be taken to his room, being a little the worse for wear. In mid-conversation his mouth had stopped working, his chin had dropped onto his chest and loud snores had issued from his flaring nostrils, incongruously echoing round the elegant drawing room. Having guided him to his bed, removed his shoes and loosened his tie, Charles returned to the blue room where he had left the ladies enjoying a final nightcap, only to be greeted by a stony silence.

The women sat facing each other across that huge expanse of carpet, each cradling her crystal balloon of brandy. As Charles entered, Chastity looked up imploringly. Like a sleepwalker drawn to a cliff edge, he felt himself pulled across the room towards her until the sound of Davina, clearing her throat and patting the space on the sofa beside her, diverted him from his chosen path.

But, before his backside could sink into the soft upholstery, Chastity had risen to her feet, a vision before him as she smoothed the clinging black dress down the length of her divine torso.

'I'd better get to bed myself,' she said, bending forward to place the empty glass on the table before her.

In the moment of silence that followed, Davina looked up at Charles, who stood in open-mouthed admiration of the young woman before him. Pursing her lips, she gave a sharp tap against his ankle, which he rubbed at absent-mindedly while his eyes remained firmly fixed on Chastity.

'I'll show you to your room.'

'No!' Davina said firmly, jumping to her feet and standing between them, a full head's height lower than the other two. '*I'll* show her!' And casting a disdainful look in her fiancé's direction she marched off towards the door. 'This way,' she called to Chastity over her shoulder.

'Goodnight, Chastity.'

The sound of her name curling over his tongue was as sweet as nectar.

'Night, night,' she said, following Davina through the door and closing it behind her. The thickness of the old oak-panelled door muffled the sigh that escaped Charles's lips and kept it from her ears so that she followed in Davina's wake ignorant of the quivering mass of manhood she had abandoned on the other side.

As she sat at the large mahogany dressing table, Chastity could hear Charles and Davina talking in the corridor outside. Tiptoeing to the door, she pressed her ear against the heavy, polished wood. She had to strain at first to make out what was being said, but all became clearer as Davina's voice rose to an offensively excited shriek. Chastity covered her mouth to stifle the sound of her giggles.

There were slurred accusations and reproaches. She listened in silent fascination as Davina berated Charles over his lack of interest in her, his lack of sex drive, and then she heard the word 'trollop' rise above the rest and wondered whether it was for her benefit. She could hear Charles attempting to quieten and placate her, but all to no avail. Finally she heard footsteps disappear along the long, polished corridor, the sound of a door closing in the distance, closely followed by another.

Chastity folded her clothes and placed them on the gold-brocade armchair by the window. Pulling aside the heavy curtains, she stood there, naked, looking out onto the moonlit fields and gardens, the deep line of woodland dark and mysterious in the distance. It was like something from another age, and standing there the young woman could imagine herself as a character from *Brideshead*

Revisited or *Lady Chatterley's Lover*, which she'd seen on the telly. It was all so beautiful, so unspoilt. And all of it such a far cry from what she was used to.

Across the bottom of the bed lay a crisp white shirt. Holding it before her, Chastity smiled at the long tails and the starchiness of it, imagining many similar garments hanging on rails in Charles's room along the corridor. She pulled it over her head, and it fell almost to her knees. Wrapping the cool cotton fabric about her she held it close to her body and closed her eyes, burying her face in the folds gathered in her fist and held to her mouth and nose, breathing in its freshness.

She reached into her handbag and pulled out a clean pair of knickers – something her mum had always drummed into her: you never know what life has in store, so be prepared – and placed them with her clothes for the morning. Unzipping her make-up bag she removed a collapsible toothbrush and mini tube of toothpaste.

It was long past midnight and she had drunk far more than she was used to; even so, Chastity did not feel in the least like sleeping. She lay on top of the heavily embroidered bedcover, staring up into the pleated canopy over the four-poster bed, still bemused by her presence there. It seemed incredible to her that people could sleep like this all the time; that people still lived like this, with an apparent acceptance of this luxury as being somehow normal.

The sudden, brief knock at the door made her jump.

'Who is it?' she called softly, sliding her legs off the side of the bed and stepping onto the silk rug.

There was no answer. Once again there was a sharp, insistent knock.

Chastity had her suspicions and, tiptoeing over to the door, she took hold of the massive brass doorknob in her hand and held it tightly.

'Bob? Bob, is that you?' There was no answer. ''Cos if it is I'm telling you I'm not interested. I'm not that kind of girl. So just go back to bed.' She waited, the room still and silent but for the sound of her own soft breathing. 'Go on, now,' she added, sensing him there still.

Moments later she heard the faint sound of a door closing and she slumped against the wall with relief, sliding down until her bottom came to rest on the floor. 'Dirty old git!' she said quietly, a shudder of disgust running through her body as she imagined Bob Guppy pawing at her, his small beady eyes hungry for the sight of her young flesh.

Charles Grant stood inside his room, his back pressed against the door, his chest quickly rising and falling with each short breath. What *had* he been thinking of? What on earth was he proposing to say to the girl supposing she *had* let him in? His mind reeled at the uncharacteristic bravado that had led him to Chastity's door in the first place, had forced his knuckles against the unrelenting wood but had finally failed him just as swiftly as it had found him when the time had come to speak.

Instead she had mistaken him for Bob Guppy. *Bob Guppy*! The thought both amused and appalled him. And over and over in his mind he replayed her words, the recollection of her haunting voice sending a shiver of delight through his receptive body.

Bob Guppy woke abruptly. The room in which he lay

was in total darkness. His mouth, which gaped open in the manner of the fish that was his namesake, was as dry as a camel's armpit, while his tongue felt like a clump of swollen sponge stuck to the parched roof of his mouth. With an audible smack he pulled it free, peering out into the dark through half-lidded eyes.

Where the hell am I?

Trying to get his bearings, he attempted to raise his head from the pillow on which it rested, but the effort was too much, the weight too great. With a groan, he allowed his eyes to fall closed and his head to slump the few inches back onto the soft mound of duck feather cushions.

Where in fuck's name am I?

His head spun mercilessly as he tried to recall the events of the evening, but he was thwarted by a sudden and overwhelming desire to empty the contents of his stomach over the side of the bed.

The loo was still flushing as Bob Guppy struggled to the sink, still on his knees. Reaching up to the basin like some latterday Toulouse Lautrec, he fumbled for the glass, filled it with water, then rinsed out his mouth, belching loudly into the cold silence, filling the cool air with his foul-smelling breath.

'Aah, that's better!' he said, slumping back against the toilet bowl.

As the events of the evening crept back into his consciousness, he began to edit them, selecting those he wished to preserve. Unsurprisingly, most of these involved young Chastity. Chastity crossing her legs. Chastity popping food into her mouth. Chastity . . .

Guppy grinned. The set-up was better than he could

ever have hoped for. When he'd suggested that she accompany him on the trip, he had it in mind that they might stop off at a hotel on the way home, have a meal, a few drinks and – well, Bob's your uncle, so to speak! Never in his wildest dreams could he have anticipated spending the whole night under the same roof as the object of his all-consuming desire. It was clearly fate. This was an opportunity not to be missed!

The corridor was in almost complete darkness, the subdued glimmer from a lamp in the hall below filtering up through the balustrade, casting the faintest of shadows over the walls. Tiptoeing out onto the cool, tiled floor, Bob Guppy wedged his tongue into the corner of his mouth as he concentrated on the task ahead. The chequered floor swam before him like a floating chessboard, constantly moving like a liquid force before his narrowed eyes.

Pressing his face to the door jamb, he hissed Chastity's name into the crack, tapping his knuckles lightly against the wood at the same time, wincing as the sound reverberated through his head. Then, taking the doorknob in his hand, he tried the door handle. It gave! A broad smile of satisfaction split his features as the door eased back. Bob Guppy gave a quick look over his shoulder, gently pushed the door and slid quietly into the darkened room.

Bob Guppy screwed up his eyes against the bright morning sunlight flooding in through the open casement window. Rolling onto his back he gave a huge sigh as he stared up into a pink canopy of extravagantly gathered fabric.

Beside him his lover lay face down beneath the crisp white sheet, her head buried in the pillow at the edge of the king-size bed. Reaching across he laid a hand proprietorially on the curve of her hip, squeezing it gently as she stirred beneath his touch, and was almost immediately aware of the tingling sensation in his aching groin.

Last night had been unbelievably, unimaginably brilliant. Never in his wildest dreams – well, maybe in his *wildest* dreams but never in his waking moments – had he dared hope for passion like that! That a girl less than half his age should welcome *him* into her bed, and should do to him the things that she'd done so eagerly, so enthusiastically ... well, it was what happened to the rich and famous, not to humble salesmen with bald heads.

He was about to turn to her, to mould his body to hers and proudly press his stiff penis into the curve of her back, when he heard noises from the corridor outside: footsteps and the rattle of bone china.

Desperate not to be discovered, Guppy slipped from the bed and into his trousers, which lay discarded on the floor. Casting around for his shirt he caught sight of it draped over the arm of a chair. He quickly grabbed at it and was pulling it on when the full horror of the situation smacked him between the eyes.

On the chair from which he'd removed his crumpled shirt sat a pile of neatly folded garments. Bob Guppy looked from the chair to the bed and back again, hoping to see something that might contradict what he now feared to be the truth. Then he saw the dress hanging on the outside of the huge mahogany wardrobe and –

with a gut-wrenching sense of awfulness – knew that it was true.

A soft, feminine moan drifted up to him from the nest of tangled bedclothes.

Guppy looked on in horror as an arm was raised, the tired limb pushing away the effects of sleep as it stretched into the morning air. Leaving his shirt buttons for later, he hastily pulled up the zip of his fly. There was a sharp intake of breath, followed by a stifled shriek. Looking down, he saw the painful truth. The tip of his limp penis had caught in the metal jaws of his trouser zip. Tears filling his eyes, he waddled towards the door as quickly as he dared, stopping only to check that the corridor was clear before, half limping, he headed for the safety of his own room.

Chastity stood at the window brushing her hair and looking out across the endless green of the Maltby Estate. There was not a single building to be seen in the whole of that landscape. In the hazy morning sunlight the smudge of distant woodland faded into the skyline. Turning from the view, she put the hairbrush down, then slowly shook her head in wonder. So much land. And all of it Sir James's. It was hard to believe in this day and age.

From below came the unmistakable sound of hooves on cobblestones. Returning to the window, she craned her neck round, trying to see where the noise was coming from. Her cheek pressed against the cold window pane, she could just see, out of the corner of her eye, the grey horse as it emerged through the arched gateway from the stable block, plumes of warm breath rising from its mouth as it strained against the bit, pulling at the lead rein in the young groom's hand. A moment later Charles skipped down the stone steps leading from the house, pulling on his riding gloves as he walked towards his mount. Chastity stood back a little and watched from behind the edge of the drapes as he greeted the horse, stroking its neck and mane, and feeding it some titbit from the pocket of his hacking jacket. So gentle he seemed. So unlike that harridan of a fiancée.

Chastity turned from the window, knowing she must hurry. Pushing her feet into her shoes, she wrapped herself in her long woollen jacket and quickly made her way downstairs and out to where horse and rider stood, her pace slowing as she emerged onto the stone steps.

Hearing the house door creak open, Charles looked up, then watched appreciatively as Chastity's long legs, encased in sheer black stockings, descended the steps, the hem of her dress stretching across an expanse of thigh as she came towards him. He cleared his throat and busied himself with the horse's mane, aware of the groom standing goggle-eyed beside him.

'That'll be all, thanks, Michael.'

The young man stood rooted to the spot, his hand tightening on the rein.

'Thank you, Michael,' Charles said more insistently, catching his eye as the groom reluctantly glanced towards him. 'That will be all.'

'But sir—'

'I can manage,' he said, taking the rein from his hand and giving the smallest of nods to indicate that Michael should bugger off back to the stable.

'Good morning,' Charles called as Chastity came closer.

'Hello,' she beamed, reaching up to stroke the horse's muzzle.

'Morning, miss.'

They both turned to see Michael walking backwards towards the stable, a stupid grin across his face.

'Thank you, Michael,' Charles called over his shoulder, irritated by, yet admiring of, the young man's confidence.

'I think you have an admirer,' he said, turning back to Chastity.

'Really?' she giggled, her eyes piercing him. 'Who's that, then?'

Charles could feel the colour travel up through his body until his head throbbed with the weight of blood that had flooded it. Clearing his throat he busied himself with the horse, throwing the reins over the animal's head, then reaching up to adjust the stirrups.

'He's beautiful,' Chastity said.

Charles's eyes followed her slender white hand as it ran down the length of the horse's neck, the hairs on the back of his own neck standing on end as he watched the gleaming grey coat submit to her touch.

'I bet he's a real good jumper . . .'

'Yes. Terrific.'

'Do you show him? You should, you know. He's got the look of a champion, this one.'

Charles pushed out his chest with paternal pride. 'Are you interested in horses?' he asked, a mixture of hope and barely disguised surprise in his voice.

'Yeah. I love them. My uncle runs one of them city farms over in East London. I used to spend all my free time over there when I was a kid. I've been riding since I was five.'

'In London? *Really*?'

Chastity nodded, amused by his obvious delight at this piece of news.

'I don't suppose you'd like to come out with me? On a hack I mean.'

Charles forced his hands into tight fists, willing the blood to sink back to his boots.

Chastity giggled and looked down at her legs.

'Oh, yes, stupid me,' Charles said, his brow furrowed in annoyance with himself. 'Perhaps . . .'

'Another time?'

Charles's body visibly slumped with relief and a delightful squeal of pleasure could be heard in his voice in spite of his attempts to appear cool, calm and collected. 'Yes. Another time. I'd like that.'

'Yeah,' she said, kissing the side of the horse's face. 'So would I.'

Bob Guppy's usually healthy appetite had completely deserted him as he sat alone at the long mahogany breakfast table nursing a cup of strong black coffee and wondering how on earth he had come to have shagged the Chairman's fiancée. Try as he might, all he could recall was being welcomed into a warm bed and into the soft, unresisting arms of a woman, followed by snatches of hungry, frenetic sexual activity. The kind you can feel in your bones for days afterwards! To be honest, he could remember nothing beyond the fourth after-dinner brandy and had no inkling of how he had come to be in her bed. His only clear memory was the slow realisation, not an hour since, that he had just engaged in a night of unrelenting rumpy-pumpy with the bloody boss's bird. A sense of dread descending once more, Guppy refilled his coffee cup, forcing the dark, bitter liquid down his throat.

For several minutes he sat with his head in his hands, his eyes closed, willing his memory into focus, forcing himself to battle through the fog of alcohol-induced amnesia, but the pictures that danced before his eyes were those of limbs entwined in intimate embrace, breasts dangling pendulously over his hungry, upturned face and expanses of warm, soft flesh writhing beneath his eager, exploring hands. The tip of his penis began to throb as it became engorged with blood, but a sudden stab of pain doused his growing passion as effectively as if he'd used his dick to stir a Scotch and dry on the rocks.

What'll I do? he asked himself, groaning inwardly. What in God's name should I do? And what if Charles finds out . . . ?

The sound of Davina's voice floating in from the hallway as she called to the housekeeper filled Bob with renewed terror and trepidation. His cock was now as limp as a leaf of month-old lettuce, curled into inoffensive submission. Hastily he reached for the coffee pot and poured himself another dose of caffeine.

'Good morning,' Davina said cheerily, picking up the *Daily Telegraph* from the sideboard before sitting down in the chair opposite.

As though rigor mortis had set in, he sat with the white china cup resting against his bottom lip, then slowly raised his eyes over the rim, fearing the worst. An unexpected smile beamed back at him from a face that seemed somehow . . . transformed. Davina looked different. Gone was the knotted tightness that had lined her brow; gone the dour expression of thin-lipped resentment. It was as though a light had been lit inside her, its glow emanating from every pore, and as she beamed across at Bob Guppy he felt an overwhelming sense of relief, his body slumping involuntarily into the chair.

Forcing a brief, apprehensive smile, he took a sip of coffee and wondered, not for the first time in his life, about the unpredictability of the female sex.

'Did you sleep well?' Davina enquired, shaking the newspaper open to its full width so that her short arms were at full stretch.

Bob beamed a smile across the table, his head tilting slightly as he gave a knowing wink.

Davina stared a moment, confounded by the man's vulgar response but deciding the effort of repeating the inane question was too much in her delicate, morning-after-the-night-before condition. Instead she turned the page to Births and Marriages.

'And how did you . . . *sleep*?' Bob Guppy asked, a self-satisfied grin slicing across his features.

'Eh?' she grunted, dropping the paper down to below nose level.

'I said, and how did you, er, *sleep*?' And, as far as he was able in a seated position, Bob Guppy swaggered as the last word left his lips.

'Well,' she answered, the hint of a furrow threatening to invade her broad forehead. 'Very well, thanks.' And without further comment she held up the newspaper to cover the embarrassment that had brought a faint pink flush to her usually pale, lifeless complexion.

She had been annoyed with Charles last night; the way he'd ogled that bloody girl all evening. No wonder she'd had too much to drink. That, of course, had been his excuse for not wanting to go to bed with her. There was always an excuse. Which was why she'd been surprised, considering the row they'd had, to be woken from the depths of heavy sleep by a warm hand cupping her breast, moist fingertips tweaking at her nipple. The delicious sensation of being nudged onto her front and mounted from the back had taken her *completely* by surprise, but it was an experience she was now eager to repeat. The newspaper rustled in her hands as a shiver of delight ran through her body.

The only embarrassing thing about the episode was that the oik sitting opposite had obviously heard. In the throes of passion, she'd thrown caution to the wind, but now it had to be faced: Guppy had been sleeping in the room next to hers; he must have heard everything – hence the wink, hence the crude enquiry about how well she'd slept. He had no doubt enjoyed himself hugely listening through the wall to the vigorous lovemaking going on. Some men, she knew, got their kicks that way. Last night Charles had been like a desperate, hungry animal, and she had been only too happy to meet that need. But damn it, she wasn't going to let Bob Guppy spoil things!

With a determined motion, Davina folded the paper and set it down beside the white china bowl. Then, with a smile at the odious Guppy, she reached across and took a firm, round grapefruit from the crystal bowl.

'And how did *you* sleep, Mr Guppy?'

Charles sat behind the massive oak desk in his father's

library, shifting uncomfortably in his chair and trying to look businesslike. Across from him, Guppy fumbled in his briefcase, trying to find the report.

'It's here somewhere,' Guppy said, sifting through the piles of paper. He glanced up apologetically, not quite meeting Charles's eyes. 'Sorry,' he mumbled.

'You sure you haven't left it in your room?' Chastity asked, from where she sat by the window, notebook in lap, her long legs crossed at the knee.

Guppy stopped a moment, thinking, then shook his head. 'No. It was here. I know it was.' He searched again, then looked up with a grin of triumph. 'There! What did I say?'

Charles smiled patiently.

'So?' Chastity said, tapping her freshly sharpened pencil against the edge of the pad. 'Shall we get going?'

The two men looked to her, like errant schoolboys, and nodded.

Setting the briefcase beside his chair, Guppy quickly sat down and, clearing his throat, began to read.

'The first question we asked ourselves was this. Who is the machine aimed at?'

He paused, looking to Charles, who blinked, then shrugged. 'I, er . . . adults?'

'Yes,' Guppy said patronisingly. 'That's right. But what *kind* of adults?'

'Frustrated ones?' Chastity chipped in with a giggle, making both men stare at her, surprised.

'Demographics,' Guppy said into the silence.

Charles's fixed smile grew thin. 'Demo . . . ?'

'. . . graphics,' Chastity finished for him. 'Your age, your earnings. The newspaper you read.'

'Thank you,' Guppy said, smoothing one hand over the top sheet of the report. 'If you don't mind, Miss Lloyd . . .'

'Sorry,' she said, smiling brightly. 'I just thought that Mr . . . that Charles should know.'

'Yes, yes,' Guppy said, the faintest trace of exasperation in his voice. 'As I was saying, it's all a matter of demographics. Of accurately calculating just who we are aiming our marketing *at*. If we can get that bit right, then we can make sure that not a penny's wasted – that our resources are targeted at precisely the right part of the market.'

'I see,' Charles said, looking slightly blank. 'And what part of the market *is* that?'

Guppy grinned, pleased that he'd taken Chastity's advice and gone fishing for ideas among the agencies. He turned the page and, running his finger down the columns, came to the results of the poll he'd had commissioned.

'Our ideal buyer is as follows,' he said, smiling confidently. 'Aged thirty-five to fifty. Taking home a salary of thirty thousand plus. Male . . .'

'*Male*?' Chastity queried.

Guppy looked to his assistant.

'But she's got a point, surely?' Charles said, staring at his hands where they were folded on the desk. 'Surely women would . . . well . . .'

'Not interested,' Guppy said. 'Our preliminary studies show that our primary market is almost one hundred per cent male.'

'Four million dildos.'

'*What!*' Both men turned as one, staring at Chastity in shocked surprise.

'It was in *Cosmopolitan* last month,' she said, looking down. 'That's the total number of dildos sold in the western hemisphere in the last twelve months.'

'*Really?*' Charles asked, a definite flush at his cheeks.

'But this . . .' Guppy swallowed, the thought of those four million sales obviously too much for him. 'This is different, surely.'

'Why?' Chastity asked, resting her pencil on her pad and leaning forward. 'As my mum always says, it takes two to tango. So why not a version for women?'

Guppy made to interrupt her, but she pressed on, raising her voice slightly. 'Look, I know I typed all this up, Bob, but I've been thinking. Running it all through my head. And it just doesn't make sense.'

'*Sense?*' Guppy's voice had an edge of panic to it now.

'I mean, like what you said about it being only for the well off.'

'Well, that's obvious,' Guppy said, glad for the opportunity to turn the conversation back to the straight and narrow. 'The machine itself is going to cost a minimum of three thousand. It's not a Sony Walkman, you know. And the software . . .' He laughed. 'A hundred pounds a time, *if* we're lucky.'

'I know that,' Chastity said calmly, 'but you're assuming that our machines are going to be bought just by individuals, like exercise bikes. But what if we open up a chain of salons? You know, like Dream Parlours. Somewhere *anyone* can go. A bit like a video shop, only you stay to see the film.'

Charles and Guppy stared at her in astonishment.

'Brilliant!' Charles said after a moment. 'Dream Parlours. Absolutely brilliant!'

'Oh, it wasn't *my* idea,' Chastity said, beaming first at Charles, then at an ever so slightly miffed Bob Guppy. 'It was something Bob said in the car coming up that put it in my head.'

'Something *I* said?' Guppy said, mystified.

'Yeah. You were telling me about that club in Amsterdam you and Roger went to . . .'

'Yes, yes, of course,' Guppy said hurriedly. 'But Charles is right. It is a very good idea.' And as if to emphasise the point, he theatrically dropped the report onto the floor beside him. 'If I might make a suggestion, Charles?'

Charles nodded, his eyes never leaving Chastity. 'Go on.'

'What if we were to commission a new report? Something along the lines Chastity has suggested.'

'Yes . . . yes, excellent,' Charles said, as Chastity looked up from her pad and met his eyes. 'See to it, will you, Bob? See to it at once. You can use the fax in my office if you like.'

Halfway down the great sweep of stairs that led to the entrance hall, Chastity stopped and, pointing up at the massive canvas on the wall to her left, asked Charles who it was.

'That's the first Sir James. He built this house, back in the early nineteenth century.'

Chastity looked from the portrait to Charles, then smiled. 'You're very like him, you know.'

'Yes,' Charles said, with the slightest embarrassment. 'So everyone says.'

'And he was the first of the Grants?'

Charles laughed softly. 'No, not the first. But the first to be knighted, certainly. He made his fortune in the Napoleonic Wars.'

'Was he a hero, then?'

'No, he was a draper, actually. The government gave him an order for a hundred thousand uniforms. Made the family fortune.'

Chastity walked on. Charles hesitated, then walked after her, conscious of a sudden thoughtfulness there. He had just caught up with her again, when she turned, directing those startlingly green eyes at him once more.

'I guess it's always like that, isn't it?'

'Pardon?' Those eyes robbed him of thought. It was like staring into two deep pools of forgetfulness.

'With nobs.' She laughed. 'Aristocrats, I mean. There had to be a time when we were all equal. You know. When they were no different to anyone else. Just . . . well, *people*.'

Charles tried to follow what she was saying, but the idea seemed a little on the radical side. No divisions? He couldn't for the life of him imagine it. But the last thing he wanted was to argue with her.

'Maybe,' he said, finally.

'Nah,' Chastity said. 'There's no maybes about it. I mean, there wasn't no *Lord* Adam and *Lady* Eve, was there?'

'I . . . I guess not.'

'There you go, then. It's like sin, isn't it? It wasn't there to start with, but somewhere along the way it crept in, while no one was watching.'

Charles gave a bemused nod. It was certainly an original idea, and not one he'd come across at Eton.

But none of this was why he'd sent Guppy on ahead. 'Er . . . I was just wondering about that hack.'

'Yeah?' Chastity's eyes seemed to widen even further. Staring into them Charles felt his head swim.

'I . . . I . . . well, I wondered if we might set a date?'

'All right.'

'I mean, you don't have to decide right now, but . . .' Then he realised what she had said. He grinned at her. 'Great! Terrific! I'll arrange something, shall I?'

Chastity beamed back at him. 'Whatever you say.'

Charles stood at the window of the downstairs study, watching as the silver-grey Sierra made a one-hundred-and-eighty-degree turn on the gravel, then sped out onto the long, narrow road that led to the gate half a mile away, his eyes never leaving the slender figure in black, sitting in the passenger seat.

As the car disappeared between the trees, he sighed heavily, then turned from the window, not knowing what to do with himself. It was as if the light had suddenly gone out of his life. While she was still there, he could still fool himself that life was good, but now she was gone . . .

He moaned quietly. What a mess! What a damned, awful mess!

Walking over to the corner of the great, book-lined room, Charles slumped down into the huge, green leather chair. He was still slouched there, staring into space, when Davina came in, carrying a laden tea tray.

'Charlie? Chazzie-Waz? What's up?'

He looked up slowly, barely recognising her.

Davina hurried across and, setting the tray down on the low table by Charles's side, knelt and put her hand on his brow. He tensed, unused to any kind of physical contact with his fiancée, then relaxed, surprised by the unexpected tenderness of her touch.

'There,' she said, almost cooing at him. 'That's better, isn't it?'

'Davina?' he began.

'Yes, my darling?'

Charles blinked. *Darling?* When had she ever called him darling when they weren't in company? Besides, hadn't they rowed last night? Or was he confusing it with all the other times she'd got drunk and made advances to him?

'I . . . I have something to say to you, Davina.'

Her fingers slowed their repetitive motion across his brow, then she withdrew her hand altogether and knelt back. 'What is it, darling?' she asked, smiling broadly at him, her face – now that he actually looked at it – somehow different. He frowned, trying to understand it. Had she used different make-up? Was her hair done differently? He just couldn't make it out.

'About last night . . .'

Davina giggled. No, there was no mistake. She actually giggled. Charles stared at her, shocked. If she had said a four-letter word in front of the local vicar he would not have been more surprised.

'Are you all right?' he asked.

'I'm amazed you even ask,' she said, reaching down to take his hand, for all the world like a lovesick schoolgirl. 'And *about* last night. It was the most wonderful night of my life, and without wanting to be indelicate, any time you want to repeat the experience, Charles, you just go ahead. You don't need my permission.'

Charles stared at her, mouth slightly open, certain now that he was asleep and dreaming, for if he wasn't mistaken she had as good as said that she didn't mind if he invited Chastity back again.

'I was thinking we might go . . . *riding*.'

Something strange seemed to happen to Davina at the mention of the word. Apart from the faint blush that slowly mottled her neck and cheeks, her face seemed to go . . . well, all *silly*. Like a six-year-old who's just been told a rude joke.

She quivered. Charles *saw* her quiver. And then she nodded. 'Yes,' she said. 'Whatever you say, Charlie. *Whatever* you say.'

Charles frowned, trying to recollect when he'd last heard those words, then, indicating past Davina at the tray, asked, 'Well, old girl, how about some tea?'

As the Sierra sped between the pillared wrought-iron gates that signalled the boundary to the Maltby Estate, Chastity slumped into the upholstered seat, allowing herself to relax. Pressing back against the headrest, she briefly closed her eyes. When she had gone to work for Virt-E-Go she had never imagined that she'd get the chance to travel, let alone get to stay somewhere as grand as Maltby House, and as the boss's guest at that!

She was glad she hadn't known beforehand that they were going to stay overnight, otherwise she'd have agonised over what to wear, what to talk about and which bits of cutlery to use. As it happened she felt she'd managed not to make a complete fool of herself. Maybe she shouldn't have accepted Charles's offer of a second helping of the chocolate dessert when everyone else had refused, but it had been so delicious, and he had seemed genuinely pleased that she was enjoying it.

Men like Charles were a mystery to Chastity. From her early teens she had grown used to dealing with the attention of boys from school and from the estate where she lived, but there had never been anyone special – no one who had treated her like a lady, or with respect. Most of them had been younger versions of Bob Guppy: crude, shallow and unpolished; quick to praise her, but just as quick to bad-mouth her – *slag, prick-teaser, frigid bitch* – when they didn't get what they wanted.

Some might have been hardened, even embittered by the experience, but Chastity had weathered all of it rather well and had emerged not merely stronger but also with a remarkable sense of her own self-worth. It was that same strong sense of self that had allowed her not to be overawed by Charles and his family's estate. Even so, she was still intrigued by the young 'Master'. He had been so . . . different.

Chastity jumped as she felt a hand brush across her thigh. Her eyes flicked open, glaring at Bob Guppy.

'If you pull that lever there,' Guppy said, his cheek twitching as he reached across her and indicated a lever on the far side of her seat, 'you can go into recline. Have a little snooze.'

'I'm all right, thanks,' she replied, smoothing out the wrinkles in her dress and pulling it down towards her knees.

'Course you are. Course you are,' he said, smiling at her reflection in the windscreen, with just the briefest of glances down at her long stockinged legs, which, he felt, parted suggestively at the knee and seemed to fill the car. He sighed deeply.

'Well,' he said finally, 'I thought this morning went rather well.'

'Mmm.'

'I think I can say without fear of contradiction that Charles was quite impressed with my . . . with the, er, marketing proposal.'

'Yeah! He really liked my idea about the Dream Parlours, didn't he?' she said with pride, recalling Charles's enthusiastic response.

'Don't you worry your pretty little head,' Guppy said, turning to look at her so that Chastity became a little concerned about the safety of his driving. 'I'll take care of you, my little lovely. You know, you're just the ticket for this job. You're bright, keen, and you know when to give due credit.'

Chastity looked down and smiled tightly. So that was it, was it? If she kept coming up with the ideas and giving Bob Guppy the credit for them, all would be well. And if not?

'Yes,' Guppy went on, turning his attention back to the road, much to Chastity's relief, 'we could be a good little partnership, you and me. And when it comes to bonus time, I'll make sure there's a little something in your pay packet, you can be sure.'

'Ta,' she said, but in her mind she kept seeing Charles, leaning forward in his chair, nodding and smiling encouragingly as she put forward her idea, and then his praise, his enthusiasm; such wide-eyed, unselfish delight. No one had ever made her feel as important as she'd felt at that moment, and she knew that, if Bob Guppy hadn't been there in the room, she would have got up, walked across to Charles and kissed him for making her feel that way.

A tiny shiver went through her, bringing her back to the moment, to the slight judder of the car beneath her, and to Bob Guppy's voice droning on and on.

It had gone well. It had gone very well, considering. And the sex. Bleeding hell, now that he thought about it, the sex had been bloody brilliant.

Bob Guppy stretched his neck, then grinned, letting the car glide at a steady eighty-five down the fast lane of the M4, Chastity asleep beside him in the passenger seat.

Maybe Davina knew, after all, that it had been he who'd come to her in the night. Maybe that was what all that stuff was about at breakfast. Who knew with these toffs? They were hard to fathom. She must have known it wasn't Charles. Surely she'd be able to tell the difference between a boy and a real man? No, now that he'd had a chance to think about it, he was *sure* Davina knew. And if that was the case the question now was, how did he go about organising a return match? Because he couldn't leave it at that, could he? Jeeze! The things they'd done! The incredible, sordid things they'd done! His balls still ached, as though they'd had the blood squeezed out of them. But what the hell! It had been worth it.

Suddenly conscious of Chastity beside him, Guppy glanced at her, then carefully adjusted his trousers.

Comfortable again, he leaned across and put the radio on low, then sat back, trying to sort things out in his head.

He knew for a fact that Charles didn't like coming up to London for meetings, so, if he could get him to agree to a few more strategy meetings at Maltby House, then maybe he could set something up with Davina. The only trouble with that was that it was unlikely that Charles would invite him to stay over, and they couldn't count on his falling off his horse every time they visited.

Guppy frowned, racking his brains, trying to come up with a reason for staying over, then, looking up into the mirror, he broke into a smile.

Chastity! Chastity was the key. Hadn't he seen Charles feasting his eyes on her all night? And at the meeting . . . why, the boy was all but drooling every time he looked at her.

Yes, and who could blame him? Look at her. Like a bleeding angel she was. Bob Guppy sighed, then looked back at the road. One of these days, he swore to himself, pushing down on the accelerator, the speedometer needle swinging past ninety. One of these fucking days!

~ *June* ~

Roger jumped in his seat as the office door swung open. He had been staring intently at his computer screen, almost frowning with concentration, but at the sound of the door opening he had sat up, mouth open, as if someone had stuck him with a pin.

Louise giggled.

'Christ, Louise!' he said, his hands fiddling nervously with the knot of his tie, his blushing face looking strained as he struggled to regain his composure. 'Can't you knock?'

Louise giggled all the more. 'You're a bit edgy, ain't you? You got some porn channel on the Internet or something?'

'Edgy! I'm not edgy!' he said, nudging the screen round just a touch. 'You startled me, that's all.'

Louise straightened provocatively and took a step towards him, one eyebrow raised suggestively. 'It's executive stress, that's what it is. What you need is a nice long massage with some of my special oil. That'd do the trick.'

For a second or two the lines on Roger's face briefly

disappeared as he contemplated this most attractive proposal, but at the sound of a telephone ringing in the next office they reappeared, so that his face resembled a ball of crumpled paper.

'Poor baby,' Louise commiserated, closing the door, then making her way across the office to where her boss sat hunched in his chair. Yet as she advanced his eyes glanced nervously at the screen, one hand reaching across to tap a sequence of keys. Louise had a brief glimpse of a heading – 'RA SUND' – before the columns of words and figures turned blue, that solid block of colour interrupted only by the occasional appearance of the computer's logo as it floated across the screen.

Louise raised her eyebrows, then reached down and ran her fingers through his hair.

Like a child, Roger nuzzled into her comforting warmth, his face buried in the soft fabric stretched across the gentle swell of her abdomen. She ran her hand delicately down the back of his head onto his neck and could feel his hot breath through her skirt as he sighed deeply, his shoulders slumping into her thighs. Tilting his face to look up at her he strained to smile.

'D'you fancy a quick one?'

'Roger!' she said, tapping his nose like a naughty puppy.

'Not that! A drink I mean, you daft cow. We could nip to the pub for lunch.'

'Oh, bloody hell!'

'What?' he said, sliding back on his castors so that he held her by the hips at arm's length.

'That's what I came in to tell you.'

'What?'

'About lunch.'

'What about lunch?'

'It's Mr Fukuada. He's turned up early for his appointment, and both Brian and Patricia are at lunch.'

'Oh, shit!' he said, jumping up out of his chair and smoothing his hair with one hand as he dragged his jacket from the back of the chair with the other. 'Where have you left him?'

'In reception,' Louise replied indistinctly, her hand still clasped across her mouth. 'Shall I fetch him?'

'No!' Roger snapped. 'I'll get him and take him up to the lab. You give Bill and Ben a bell and make sure everything's ready and then arrange for some tea or someth—'

The final word was cut off abruptly as the door slammed shut behind him.

'Well, thanks for telling me, Louise,' she muttered to herself, staring at the door, slightly angered by his abruptness. Then, determined not to be put in a bad mood by it, she picked up the handset and dialled the extension for the lab.

Settling into Roger's chair, she leaned forward, one elbow on the desk as the ringing sounded in her ear.

The ringing stopped. 'Howdy doodly-do,' a voice answered on the other end.

'Bill?'

'It's Ben, actually.'

'Panic stations: Mr Fukuada's in the building. Roger's throwing a bit of a wobbly. He wants to make sure you've got everything ready.'

'Well,' Ben hesitated, 'I guess—'

'Good. They'll be up in a minute.'

Replacing the handset, Louise gripped the edge of the desk and pushed herself backwards in the swivel chair. She was about to set off for the penthouse kitchen in search of the best china when her eye was caught once more by the blue screen. Glancing across at the closed door, she hesitated, then skated the chair back to the desk and, drawing the keyboard towards her, tapped at it, bringing up the menu.

Her eyes scanned the list of files intently, her face almost as serious as Roger's had been earlier, then she smiled, her fingers already typing in the word.

RA SUND

God knew what it meant, but from that look of surprise on Rog's face, it had to mean something. Yeah, and it was just like Rog to give something important a boring name. Those entries in his diary, for instance. 'Dentist' they read, but the only serious drilling that had been going on those Saturday mornings was in her flat in Harlesden.

It made her wonder if his wife ever looked at Roger's teeth.

Louise waited, humming an old Madonna song to herself as the screen filled with columns of figures. For a moment she couldn't make head or tail of it, then she sat back, making a little sound of surprise, her mouth dropping open.

'Bloody hell!' she said quietly, sitting forward in the chair. 'Roger Appleyard, you *have* been a naughty boy now, haven't you?'

As the doors hissed aside, Roger's arm emerged from the lift ahead of the rest of him and remained stiffly horizontal as he strode across the reception area, giving the impression that he was being pulled towards Nobushi Fukuada by an invisible wire.

'I am *so* sorry to have kept you waiting,' he oozed apologetically. 'I was tied up, I'm afraid.' And, catching the twinkle of interest in the other man's small, dark eyes, Roger blustered quickly on. 'With business. I mean I was tied up with business.'

'Ah, yes, I unnerstan',' Mr Fukuada said, his mouth stretching upwards in a broad grin so that his face was suddenly filled with two gleaming rows of huge white teeth. With surprising strength he gripped and shook Roger's hand, bowing his head in formal greeting. 'Where Miss Pah-tricia?' he said, staring past Roger's shoulder expectantly.

'Ah, yes, Miss Patricia. She'll be . . . ahem . . . joining us shortly, along with Mr Grant.'

Freeing his hand from that vicelike grip, Roger stepped aside, his head tilted slightly, his arm held out again, this time to indicate that Mr Fukuada should lead the way into the lift. 'Shall we?'

As the doors hissed shut and the lift juddered into life, Roger looked up with feigned fascination at the six numbers indicating floor levels as they slowly laboured up the shaft. As the number two lit up he struggled to break the silence that had engulfed them in that tiny space.

'I . . . ahem . . . I trust you have fully recovered from the earlier unfortunate incident, Mr Fukuada. I really can't tell you how sorry we all were . . .'

'No sorry. No probrem. Skin graft work brirriantly. Erryfin' good as new. Better than new! It's rike a trophy. I show women and they say to me, "What happen to you, Nobi?" and I say, "Big metal machine fry my nuts!" Work rike a charm. They want to play nursey nursey, neh?' And he threw his head back, laughing heartily at his good fortune.

Roger smiled and nodded as if with perfect understanding, resisting the temptation to place a comforting hand over his own nuts, which were not so much *al dente* at that moment but more akin to his dear mother's overcooked cabbage: soggy and limp.

'Ah, here we are,' he said enthusiastically, his relief obvious as the lift jolted to a halt and the doors slid open. 'After you, Mr Fukuada.'

William and Benjamin never took lunch breaks as such: a Pot Noodle, a can of Coke – regular, not diet – and a Mars bar, hurriedly consumed whilst hunched over the computer for a shared game of Ultimate Doom, was their daily diet and relaxation rolled into one.

Having been forewarned of Fukuada's early arrival, they had, with considerable reluctance, curtailed their daily dose of Doom, and now awaited their sponsor's presence, only too well aware of the importance of impressing him with the refinements they had made to the new prototype. A good deal of work had been done since Fukuada's earlier, ill-fated trial run. As well as making numerous technical adjustments, the boys had put a lot of effort into developing the machine to meet the Japanese market's particular demands. Both knew this could be the crunch.

Standing proudly beside their machine – their hurriedly donned white lab coats covering the logos splashed across the teeshirts they wore beneath – the twins bowed their heads as Mr Fukuada entered, walking past Roger as he held open the heavy, security-operated outer door.

'Greetings!' they said in unison. Raising their eyes briefly, and seeing Fukuada's head bowed before them, they bowed again. Tentatively they raised their heads once again, to find that Mr Fukuada was already examining the machine, looking closely at its various components, running his small, delicate hand down the length of the synthetic bodysuit, his fingers squeaking against the smooth rubber.

'So there it is,' Bill said nervously, running through the sales patter he and Ben had agreed upon earlier. 'The Mark Five. Slicker, wetter, hornier. It quite literally knocks the pants off anything else on the market!'

'So?' Fukuada said, allowing the hoselike extension to fall from his hand. 'What reports you get from trials of new prototype?'

'Well, we . . .' Benjamin began, glancing sideways to meet his brother's eye.

William in turn cast an anxious look over the businessman's head towards a nervous-looking Finance Director.

'Well, you see,' William said, 'the thing is . . .'

Roger stepped forward, standing alongside the much shorter Fukuada. 'What our technicians *mean* is that they have only just finished working on the refinements to the prototype in readiness for our meeting today, so *unfortunately* there hasn't yet been an opportunity to test-run the machine.'

Roger made eye contact with the twins, the three of them exchanging looks that agreed they would all go along with this line.

'What, not yet been *tested* by anybody?' Fukuada queried.

There was a brief flicker of panic in Roger's eyes. 'If we'd had just a little more time . . .' he began to explain, fearing the other man's anger, but before he could get any further, Nobushi Fukuada's jacket was hanging on the back of the chair, his socks were tucked inside his small, neat shoes and his trousers were round his ankles . . .

Cutting his speed as he approached the Square, Charles glanced to his right then turned left into the one-way system that would take him round the gardens to Virt-E-Go's offices. Through the trees his eye was caught by blue flashing lights and as he followed the road round he realised, to his horror, that the fire engine was parked smack in front of his building. Firefighters stood casually on the steps talking to one another, their yellow helmets pushed back on their heads, their jackets hanging unbuttoned over their teeshirts. Rushing across from his hastily parked car, Charles pushed between then with uncharacteristic assertiveness.

'What's happened? What's going on?'

The men looked from one to another.

'Could I ask who you are, sir?' one of them asked, his uniform slightly different from the others.

'Charles Grant. I work here. I mean, I'm the Chairman of this company. What in God's name has happened?'

'Ah,' replied the man, placing a gloved hand on Charles's shoulder and guiding him inside, to the reception area. 'Well, Mr Grant, it's nothing to worry about. There was a small fire caused by a faulty piece of electrical equipment. We were called out, but two of your young ladies had already dealt with the problem by the time we arrived.'

'Faulty electrical equipment?'

'Mmm. I believe that's what it was. I haven't actually *seen* it myself, but it's certainly caused a stir among my men.'

'Nobody was hurt were they?' Charles asked anxiously, watching the blue lights of the ambulance silently flashing through the plate-glass door.

'Not as far as I know. But you'd best have a word with the medics. There was a chap they had to have a look at, I believe.'

Charles could sense the repressed laughter of the firefighter through his straight-faced politeness, which only served to fuel his dread of the horror that may have befallen his colleague.

'Yes. Yes, I shall,' Charles blustered, looking around him for a paramedic. 'Of course. And thank you. Thank you very much.'

The firefighter nodded, then went out to join his team in the street. Charles was only vaguely aware of their laughter as he looked desperately around for someone in a green medic's uniform. He had just picked up the telephone on the reception desk, meaning to summon Patricia, when he felt a hand on his shoulder.

Turning, Charles found himself looking down upon what he at first assumed was a vagrant. A grey, crumpled face emerged from the top of a shabby raincoat that had certainly seen better days. The top button was missing so that the coat came together only at the waist, revealing an oversized, loosely knotted tie which in turn disappeared beneath a navy V-neck jumper with little telltale food marks on the ribbing.

'Look, go bother someone else,' Charles said, the handset still in his clenched fist. 'I haven't *got* any change.'

'Charles Grant?'

Charles blinked. 'Yes?'

The man reached inside his coat and pulled out a small black credit-card case which he flicked open and held up before Charles's face. 'Detective Inspector Holly,' he announced, in case Charles was unable to read. 'TVS. Special Investigations.'

'Ah . . . Yes. *Detective*. I thought . . .' Charles put the phone down, then turned to face him again. 'How exactly can I help you, Detective?'

'Well, Mr Grant. You can help me by explaining what the hell's been going on here.'

'Well, I can't I'm afraid . . .'

Holly straightened up, like a dog who's just spotted another dog on his patch. 'I have to warn you, Mr Grant—'

'No, no, what I mean is, I can't tell you much because I don't know what's happened myself. Not yet, anyway. I've only just arrived. Haven't even been upstairs yet, I'm afraid. But I'm sure my secretary will be able to enlighten us both if you'll give me a moment.' And, smiling his most charming smile, he turned away, reaching across to tap Patricia's extension into the handset.

'No!' Detective Holly said, rather louder than he'd intended.

Charles turned and stared at the man. Maybe he *was*

a vagrant after all. Maybe he'd found the ID card in the street. '*No?*'

'What I mean, sir, is . . . well, let's just have a little chat, eh? Find out what's been happening. Then, perhaps, we can go up and find Miss, er, Hampton.'

'Oh, you *know* Mrs Hampton?'

Holly gave a brief nod. 'Now Mr Grant,' he said, his tone a little friendlier than before, 'let's take a seat a moment and perhaps you could tell me about this *machine*. You know, the one that caused the fire. The fireman told me it was rather, er, *unusual*.'

'Unusual? Er, yes, I suppose it is,' Charles said, ignoring Holly's offer of a seat, desperate now to get upstairs where he could find out the state of play.

'What is it used for, exactly?'

'Used for?'

'Yes. The machine. What's it actually used for exactly?'

'Well, it's a state-of-the-art interactive machine,' Charles said matter-of-factly, still peering through the glass door in search of a paramedic.

'Aha! An interactive machine! I knew it!' Holly said, smiling triumphantly, a broad grin revealing a gappy smile.

Charles looked at him with complete bemusement, a moment that was curtailed by the emergence of Patricia from the lift.

'Charles! Thank goodness!' she called, striding towards him.

'Patricia!' he called back, rising out of his seat to meet her. 'What's going on?'

She made to speak but, catching sight of the detective,

caught herself, pursing her lips while she gathered her thoughts. Her eyes glanced over Holly dismissively before turning back to Charles.

'There was a problem in the lab.'

'Yes, yes,' Charles responded anxiously. 'I know that. But is everybody okay?'

'Yes, fine.' She laid her hand on Charles's arm, taking a handful of suit cloth in her clenched fist and gently but firmly pulling him towards her. 'Let's go upstairs and—'

'Er, just a moment Miss, er, Hampton.'

'Yes?' Patricia said in a superior voice. 'What is it?'

'I have a few questions I'd like to ask.'

'Can't this wait?' she said, attempting once again to lead Charles away, towards the lift.

'No, I'm afraid it can't!' Holly snapped, grabbing hold of Charles's other arm so that the three were locked in a ludicrous tug-o'-war with the bewildered, besuited chairman.

Patricia exhaled a loud sigh, then released Charles's arm and turned to face her shabby opponent.

'Okay. How can we help you, Detective?' she said with exaggerated geniality.

'Oh, Mr Grant has helped me quite a bit already, actually.'

'I have?' Charles said, wondering if he'd missed something.

Patricia, meanwhile, looked on with a feeling of dread welling up inside her bosom.

'Yes,' Holly said, with what was almost a smirk on his face. 'Young Mr Grant here was just telling me about your machine. Interactive, he said it was.'

'Oh?'

'Yes, indeed,' he said triumphantly. 'In fact, I think I'd like to take a look at this machine.'

'Yes, by all—'

'No!' Patricia interrupted, laying her hand on Charles's arm to allay his protests. 'I'm afraid that won't be possible.'

'Oh?' Holly's brow wrinkled deeply. 'Might I ask why not?'

'Because now is not a convenient time, Detective. Some of my staff have been very upset by the incident. In any case there's a good deal of mess to deal with. So no, I'm afraid that now is not at all convenient.'

Charles smiled. This woman was indeed formidable! He was lost in admiration.

'I'm afraid that your *convenience* is not my problem,' Holly said, trying to match her determination with his own. He offered a disingenuous smile, then took a step towards the lift.

'Have you a search warrant, Detective?'

Holly stopped dead. 'I beg pardon?'

'I said, have you a search warrant?'

'A search warrant? You must be joking!'

'No, I'm not joking, Detective. I think you'll find that if you wish to come onto our premises and examine items of our property you'll need to be in possession of a proper search warrant. So I repeat, *have you a search warrant*?'

There was nothing Holly hated more than a smart-arsed woman. Nothing! Except maybe Welsh men. His cheek started to twitch uncontrollably as he fought to contain the anger he felt, the feeling of utter humiliation at the hands of this stiff-necked bluestocking.

'This won't be the end of the matter!' he hissed, wagging a stubby finger just millimetres from her face. 'You mark my words!' And as he turned his back on the two of them he called out with as much dignity as he could muster, 'You just wait. I'll be back!'

Patricia could not suppress a smile as she watched him leave. 'Who the hell does he think he is?' she said, turning to Charles. 'Arnold Schwarzenegger?'

Though all the picture windows had been opened wide, the pungent smell of burning rubber still hung in the air as Patricia and Charles pushed through the plastic flaps that covered the doorway into the laboratory. The bodysuit lay in a heap on the floor surrounded by a pool of water, like a deep-sea diver's suit, the hoselike extension partly melted, the end of it scorched and crispy.

'Oh, my God!' Charles exclaimed, fearing the worst. He stepped closer, intending to inspect the damage, then turned to Patricia, struck by a sudden thought. 'Has somebody phoned Mr Fukuada? We really ought to put him off.'

'Too rate, Mr Gwant!'

The startled young Chairman spun on his heels to see his dishevelled backer sitting on a chair, his shirt tails dangling over his bare thighs, his thin, smooth legs hanging like two scrawny drumsticks of boiled chicken.

There was a moment's silence while the full horror of the situation broke into Charles Grant's consciousness, at which point he rushed towards the ill-fated Fukuada with genuine concern.

'My dear chap . . .'

'Prease!' Fukuada responded, holding up his hands to fend off any physical contact with the young man.

'Yes! Yes, of course,' Charles muttered, dropping his arms self-consciously to his side.

'Mr Fukuada has had a bit of a shock,' Patricia explained. 'Quite literally.' Her eyes widened as if to impart some special coded message that Charles should understand.

'It wasn't our fault,' Brian McTaggart said shakily, wringing his hands as he stepped up next to Charles. 'The machine performed perfectly, but there was a short in the damn feed cable.'

'Where the power comes in,' Patricia explained hastily, noting the total absence of understanding in Charles's face. 'It's Korean-made,' she added, as if that made things better.

'I see,' Charles said, as if he really did.

There was the *fwup-wup* sound of someone coming through the plastic flaps. All heads turned to see Bob Guppy standing there. Smiling sheepishly, he sidled up to Roger Appleyard, his beery breath warm in Roger's ear as he whispered, 'What the fuck's going on?'

'You've heard the expression, "nearly dropped a goolie"?' Roger whispered back, tilting his head towards the smaller man.

'Yeah?'

'Well, old Fukuada very nearly dropped two!'

'*Shit!*'

'Yeah,' Roger confided, 'another couple of seconds and Fukuada wouldn't have been able to fuck at all.'

'*Bloody hell!*'

Both men turned, looking across at the unfortunate

victim, who had risen from his chair and was attempting to remain composed despite looking faintly ludicrous.

'Accident no one's fawt,' Fukuada said, narrowing his already narrow eyes as his scantily clad figure confronted Charles's besuited form directly.

'Well, of course . . .' Charles began.

'But machine no good enough.'

'No good?' Charles looked about him, bewildered, seeking enlightenment from someone on his staff, but the sensation of Mr Fukuada's hand tapping his chest with a delicate kung-fu poke forced his attention back to the smaller man.

'Machine need refinement,' Fukuada said decisively. 'Need better programming.'

The twins looked to each other, horrified.

'Machine need rot of work be suitable for Japanese market. I send over video material. If programming not changed to suit us, no deal.'

'But Mr Fukuada,' Roger began, a certain unctuousness slipping into his voice, as it always did at such moments.

Fukuada turned, glowering at him. 'You want fry bawrs of customers, Mr Appu-rard, then you buy hot-fat noodle cooker. Much more efficient. But you want sex-machine – give customers prenty jorries – you risten to expert, *right*?'

'Right!' seven voices said as one.

'Good,' Mr Fukuada said flatly, gesturing for Cynthia to bring him his suit. 'You do as Nobi say or no deal. You unnerstan'? No deal.'

The video was on Charles's desk within the hour, courtesy of Mr Fukuada's personal courier.

'Well?' Patricia asked impatiently, when Charles had sat there for almost ten whole minutes, staring silently at the unmarked black cassette.

He looked up, startled. 'Sorry, Patricia. I . . . I guess we'd better see what Mr Fukuada wants.'

'All the staff?'

'Pardon?'

'You want all the staff to see it, or just the senior management?'

Charles shrugged. 'Everyone that's involved with the project, I suppose. It's best if we have as much input as possible. Team effort and all that.'

He didn't know whether it sounded a convincing reason or not; all he knew was that, if everyone was there, then Chastity would be there, and despite the morning's events it was Chastity he had been thinking about for those ten minutes, not the dilemma of whether Mr Fukuada would withdraw his backing or not.

'I'll get everyone to come up to the penthouse at once,' Patricia said, scooping up the video and hurrying from the room before he could change his mind.

'Fine,' Charles mumbled, but the truth was he barely heard what she said. He was thinking of Chastity again – he couldn't *stop* thinking of her. Closing his eyes, he could see her push yet another piece of chocolate truffle torte between those budlike red lips, and groaned.

Standing, he went over to the door. 'Duty calls,' he said, buttoning his jacket, as if about to report to the Duty Master at his Prep school. Then, resolved to make the best of things, he hurried from the room.

Despite the fact that they would be watching a video and

not a proper real of film, Charles had insisted they draw
the curtains along the glass window panels lining the
penthouse boardroom and turn out the lights, plunging
the room into cinema-like darkness. His rationale – that it
would hide any embarrassment on the part of the ladies –
was somewhat dubious in view of the invited audience.

'Any chance of a little drinkie?' Bob Guppy called to
Patricia from his seat at the back of the room.

'I don't really think this is an occasion for celebration,
do you? There's a lot riding on this video.'

'A lot *of* riding,' Guppy whispered out of the corner
of his mouth to a solemn-looking Roger Appleyard, who
stared with uncharacteristic seriousness at the blank
screen that dominated the wall behind the Chairman's
desk.

William and Benjamin sat in the middle row, flanked
by Brian McTaggart and Cynthia, while Charles was on
his own at the very front watching glumly as Patricia
busied herself with the television and video controls.

At the sound of the door opening all heads turned in
time to see Louise entering – make-up freshly applied, lips
glistening in the half-light – followed by Chastity. Louise
squeezed between the rows of chairs, almost falling into
Bob Guppy's lap as she eased herself into the seat beside
Roger, her hand resting unashamedly on his thigh until
in all decency he felt compelled to remove it.

Out of the corner of her eye Chastity could see Bob
Guppy patting the seat beside him, and with heavy
heart she had taken a half-step in that direction when
Patricia's voice called out to her, her words thrown
across to Chastity like a rope to a drowning woman:
'Why don't you come and sit here, down the front,

dear?' and the older woman nodded to indicate the seat beside Charles.

Chastity gave a smile that barely concealed both her relief and her delight, taking care to avoid Bob Guppy's look of disappointment. The thought of sitting through this video – and goodness knows what *that* held in store! – would have been purgatory had she also had to contend with Bob Guppy's twitchy hands and hot breath into the bargain.

She sat down without looking at Charles, yet, as Patricia pressed the play button and switched off the Anglepoise lamp, Chastity was conscious of their closeness, of how near his leg was to hers, of the rhythm of his breathing, of the way he cupped his hands in his lap, and she felt a weird sensation flutter through her body.

'Who's got the popcorn?' Bob Guppy called, recovering his air of joviality as a countdown sequence of Japanese symbols flashed on the screen.

'You won't be interested in popcorn once this starts if it's anything like I think it's going to be,' Roger said gloomily.

'*Really*?' The thought of food and drink was immediately banished from Guppy's mind as the last symbol disappeared from the screen and the film jumped into flickering, dimly lit life.

'What the hell is *that*?' Bob Guppy said after a moment as everyone in the room struggled to comprehend just what it was they were staring at.

It looked as though a juggler had stacked three flesh-pink spheres in a kind of triangle on the screen; only the top sphere – at the apex – joggled about quite a bit, while the other two seemed to be pushed sideways in a regular, rhythmic fashion.

After a further moment or two, Roger gasped. 'My God!' he said, in a tiny, strangled voice. 'He's rimming her!'

'*What*?' Guppy said, eager for enlightenment.

'The bald little bugger in the middle! Look! He's got his tongue—'

The camera angle changed abruptly. The whole room gasped. If the last sequence had been vague – abstract in a peculiarly perverse way – this next shot was simply perverse.

'Bloody hell!' Louise said, stifling a giggle. 'We ought to have him in the post room with a tongue like that!'

'Actually, the Japanese are very *keen* stamp collectors,' McTaggart threw in.

'Well, I don't think *he's* interested in Stanley Gibbons,' Roger said, leaning forward, *his* interest – among other things – mounting.

As the camera slowly zoomed out, they could see that the woman was bound, her hands lashed to one bamboo pole, her feet to another.

The room fell silent. On the screen the film ran on, ruthlessly, relentlessly explicit, leaving nothing to the imagination.

'Christ!' Bob Guppy said finally. 'It's a bleedin' cross between *Fanny Hill* and "Endurance"!'

Several heads nodded in stunned agreement, but the two heads at the front remained resolutely still. Chastity had never read Cleland's erotic eighteenth-century classic, whilst Charles was under the misapprehension that 'Endurance' was a film about long-distance walking and couldn't, therefore, make the connection with what he was looking at, in all its glorious colour.

From time to time the assembled heads tilted sideways with an almost comic synchronicity as each of them struggled with the complexities of the actors' physical contortions, brows furrowing and eyes narrowing as revulsion fought with fascination.

There was a good deal of throat clearing and fidgeting throughout, particularly from the middle row where, by the end of the film, the twins had edged closer together so that they almost appeared to be joined at the hip and shoulder.

As the action on screen abruptly ended, the credits swiftly rolled. Drums rolled and cymbals clashed over a lot of frenetic wailing that, one guessed, was typical Japanese traditional music. As it ended, Patricia rose from her seat and, without saying a word, switched off the video recorder, ejecting the tape.

Turning, she flicked on the lights. At once everyone stirred in their seat, but no one, it seemed, wanted to make eye contact.

'I think perhaps we could do with that drink now,' she said, looking to Charles for approval. But Charles seemed in a trance. He continued to sit in stunned silence staring at the grey, lifeless screen.

'Bob!' she called across the room, taking charge. 'Would you mind getting some wine from the fridge? There's beer in there as well, if anyone wants it.'

Roger and Louise sat side by side drawing deeply on their cigarettes, the effect of the nicotine beginning to calm their shattered nerves.

'Well!' Bob Guppy said, returning with two bottles of

good burgundy and a couple of cans of lager. 'That was a bloody eye-opener!'

'How the other half live, eh?' Brian McTaggart observed, attempting to conceal his alarm.

'*Live*?' William queried. 'That guy looked as though he was about to strangle her!'

'Yeah!' Benjamin added. 'From the inside!'

Chastity winced. She refused to meet Bob Guppy's eye as he handed her a glass of wine. Her mind swam with a confusion of images and in one of the more ghastly pictures Bob Guppy's head had superimposed itself onto the leather-clad body of the small, Japanese actor who had played the part of the sadistic jailer.

Stealing a sideways glance at Charles she was touched by the telltale pink flush that peeped above the crisp line of his white shirt collar. She could almost feel his embarrassment, could see just how awkward he was, and her heart went out to him as he rose, the typical Englishman, to address his assembled workforce.

'Well!' he said, giving a brief, nervous laugh and placing his hands together as though in readiness for prayer. 'That was, well, um, that was ... *interesting.*' He sniffed. 'Yes,' he continued after a moment, pleased with himself for getting thus far, 'that was *jolly* interesting.'

'It was certainly that,' Roger muttered, staring down into his lager.

'I, um . . .' Charles looked about him, his smile pained. 'Has anybody got any, um, comments?'

There was a moment's silence before Bob Guppy stood up. Pushing his hands into his trouser pockets he rested back on his heels.

'Good man, Bob. First at the crease,' Charles encouraged.

'Well, it's a non-bloody-starter, I reckon,' Guppy began. 'I mean, I'm no prude or anything, but it was pretty bloody hot, you've got to admit. We'd never get it past the censors.'

There were murmurings from around the room, heads nodded vigorously.

'Get it up in front of that lot of tight-arsed buggers and I don't know about X-rating – it'll be given a triple-bloody-Z certificate. I don't know about you lot but I reckon I've aged ten years watching that film! Anybody clocking that with a dodgy ticker and we'll find ourselves being done for manslaughter.'

'I think you're missing the plot,' Roger said quietly.

'Eh? What d'you mean, "Missing the plot"?'

'Well, it's not actually as though we have any option. You heard Fukuada. We *have* to incorporate some of this . . . *stuff* in our programming, or it's no deal.'

'And how d'you propose we manage that *and* get it past the censors?'

'I'm not saying I have the answer to that,' Roger answered wearily. 'All I'm saying is that if we don't come into line then Fukuada's going to pull the plug.'

'Is there a possibility that we could try to attract another backer?' McTaggart ventured hopefully, the prospect of having to simulate the kind of sex he'd seen today filling him with a good deal more than horror.

'Get real, Brian! The project almost collapsed before Fukuada came on the scene. We need his money, it's as simple as that.'

'Perhaps if we were to moderate it a little,' Charles

suggested. 'A sort of compromise with our Japanese friends.'

'You saw Fukuada,' Roger responded, shaking his head. 'He didn't really look in the mood for compromise, did he?'

Charles shook his head forlornly, struck suddenly by the thought of his father's fury should the deal collapse. 'We just *have* to make it work!'

Roger nodded in agreement. 'Absolutely! We *need* that money.'

'Yes, but how is it to be done?' Brian McTaggart said, draining the glass of wine in his hand.

'I thought that's what we paid *you* for,' Bob Guppy sniped quietly, lifting his glass of lager to his mouth.

Like a schoolmistress bringing her unruly pupils to order, Patricia went across and stood beside Charles, putting her hands up and raising her voice to carry over the sudden hubbub.

'This is presupposing that we can actually adapt this kind of material to our programme,' she said, looking towards William and Benjamin. 'The question as to whether we can give Mr Fukuada what he wants rather depends on whether it's possible to simulate this kind of material.'

'Everything's *possible*,' William said uncomfortably.

'Good,' Patricia said, smiling now that they were actually getting somewhere. 'So, supposing there was no censorship problem, you would be able to come up with something similar for our machine?'

Benjamin shrugged. 'I don't see why not.'

'Providing we had some direction,' his brother added quickly.

'*Direction*?' queried Bob Guppy. 'Who d'you two think you are? The bleedin' Attenboroughs!'

William gave him a dismissive glance before turning back to Patricia. 'It's just that this is a whole new ball game, if you get my drift. This is pure S and M. To stage it right we'd need some input.'

'In-and-out-put more like!' Bob Guppy said, and gave a lewd snort into his beer glass.

'Christ Almighty! It's like being in a soddin' *Carry On* film having a conversation with you, Bob Guppy!'

The words left Chastity's lips before she could stop herself. As the flush stampeded up her body and over her face, she dropped her head, willing the floor to open up and swallow her. She could feel everyone's eyes boring through her.

It seemed like an eternity, but there could have been no more than two or three seconds of silence before Charles burst out laughing, which started off everybody else until the whole lot of them – with one exception – had broad smiles across their faces.

As the laughter died, Cynthia spoke up from the back. 'Maybe there *is* a solution.'

All heads turned eagerly towards her.

'Well?' Patricia prompted.

Cynthia stood, taking off her glasses and chewing on the end of them briefly before she spoke. 'If what we've just seen is typical, then I think we can presume that they don't have a censorship problem in Japan with this type of hard-core material. If that's the case, then what's stopping us producing one program specifically for the Japanese market to satisfy our backers and a softer program for our home and export markets?'

'Spot on!' Charles exclaimed, clapping his hands together.

'Yes! Brilliant!' Roger added, his face suddenly lit up. 'The girl's a bloody genius!'

Cynthia sat again, basking in her moment of glory, balking only when Bob Guppy attempted to squeeze his tongue between her pursed lips as he leaned forward to add his congratulations to those of his colleagues. Barely able to conceal her revulsion she almost spat into her lap as she all but head-butted him away.

Sidling up between Roger and Louise, Guppy leaned in conspiratorially. 'I thought she'd be bloody gagging for it after watching that video, what with the plonk and everything!'

'She'd need a couple of *cases* of wine before she'd let you anywhere near her, Bob!' Louise responded with sisterly solidarity.

Guppy brushed aside the insult like a cow swishing its tail at a fly. 'Unlike you, eh, Louise? I bet it got you going didn't it? I bet our Roger's in for a bit of a treat tonight, eh?'

'Actually we do that sort of thing all the time,' she said, keeping a straight face. 'Doesn't everyone?'

Guppy's cheek twitched involuntarily. 'Well, me old mate,' he said, slapping Roger Appleyard on the back, 'if you ever get tired of her just let me know.'

Louise waited for Roger to speak. 'Roger?' she wailed finally, when no gallant reprimand was forthcoming, when the man who professed to love her failed to threaten to punch this odious creature's teeth down his fucking throat.

'No offence, Louise,' Bob Guppy said, backing away,

holding up his hands in mock surrender. God! Women were so bloody touchy!

Over on the other side of the room the others were huddled together now, deciding on how best to proceed, the shock they'd been feeling beginning to pass, replaced by a shared mood of cautious optimism. But there was still the question of how to produce an authentic package for their friends overseas.

'It may be a question of hiring the services of a specialist,' said Brian McTaggart.

'A *specialist*?' queried Charles with endearing naivety.

'Yes, a specialist,' Patricia confirmed. 'Good idea, Brian. Perhaps we could leave that to you and the boys?' And she smiled across at the three of them as they sat staring over as her, looking suddenly less confident than they had only a moment earlier.

'Perhaps *I* can help.'

Once again all heads turned to Cynthia.

'It's just that I have this friend . . .'

They looked from one to the other. In a flash this one simple statement had totally transformed the way they saw Cynthia. Suddenly she was no longer the staid, bespectacled bluestocking. Suddenly she was one hell of an interesting woman, even if it was only by association.

'Well done, Cynthia!' Charles said, making to pat her on the shoulder and then thinking better of it. 'Perhaps you could, er, liaise with Brian and the twins?'

Cynthia beamed a winning smile across to the three men as they sat still gobsmacked by what they considered to be a revelation.

'It'll be a pleasure,' Cynthia said, her smile unwavering. 'A real pleasure.'

Cynthia gripped the edge of the bathroom sink and leaned forward, staring into the black-edged mirror. Removing her glasses she placed them on the bamboo table beside her, then reached up to unclip the coil of hair piled on the crown of her head. Falling around her face, the soft, brown waves cascaded over her cheeks and shoulders, her look instantly and unutterably transformed by that one simple act. Gone was the studious, serious persona known to her colleagues at Virt-E-Go. Reflected in the mirror was a Cynthia that none of them would recognise – a deeper, more passionate person that she herself barely recognised.

Kicking her clothes to one side, Cynthia stepped into the shower, her feet suddenly cold on the white ceramic floor. Pressing the power button, she held her face up to meet the full force of the shockingly hot spray, welcoming its warmth as it splashed into her eyes and mouth and down over her body, each powerful jet of steaming water stabbing her like a needle, yet if she felt the pain she did not wince or draw away.

Blindly reaching up she felt the bulbous shower head and pushed it to one side, diverting the spray away from her so that it hissed against the tiled side of the cubicle. Resting her back against the opposite wall, oblivious now to its sharp coldness, she ran her fingers through the heavy, sodden bangs of dark hair, pushing it back, away from her face. Mesmerised by the water as it hit the wall, rebounding onto the dark coils of her pubis and down over her parted legs, Cynthia was transfixed, helpless to move as the warm liquid caressed her hips, her thighs, like a lover, its spent force coursing down the walls of her tingling skin.

The sound of the doorbell was like an alarm, intrusive and unwelcome as she stood there, her eyes closed, her mouth fallen open, her whole body tensed. She was so close. So *close*. For a moment longer she fought to deny the doorbell, to force it from her consciousness and surrender to that pure, physical sensation.

It rang again, jolting her back from the edge.

She felt dejected, her arm heavy as it reached up to kill the power. Stepping from the shower, she swiftly wrapped her hair in a white towel and her body in the flimsy black kimono that hung behind the door.

As she walked along the hallway, the tatami mats scratched at her bare feet. Glancing across at the clock on the black lacquer bookshelf, she was surprised by how late it was. In spite of the hour, the two men who stood on her doorstep were expected, and, as Cynthia pulled open the door, they bowed low.

'*Kon-nichi-wa*, Cynthia.'

'*Kon-nichi-wa*,' she answered, returning their bow and maintaining it as they moved past her into the flat.

Cynthia turned, a small sigh escaping her, then, straightening up, she closed the door and went inside again.

'*Nomimono wa ikaga desuka, shinshi?*'

From the window of her darkened office Patricia watched William and Benjamin as they strode across the empty Square, their heads almost touching as they walked, their legs moving in perfect time. She could imagine them travelling back together, locked in conversation, and then, later on, at home, content in each other's company, communicating with a perfect understanding. If that was sad, as Roger and the others claimed, then she didn't know what they'd call her life. As she watched them turn the corner of the street, she sighed heavily.

On the floor below the offices were in eerie darkness as Patricia made her way along the dimly lit corridor, the muted night-lights casting shadows along the walls as she walked silently through. Outside the lab she stopped, her pulse quickening at the thought of what she was about to do, then, with a feeling of compulsion, she punched the security code into the digital mechanism on the wall and, glancing about her, pushed open the heavy doors.

The orange glow from the street lamps below filtered up through the long glass windows, bathing the room in an eerie amber tint. Walking over to the windows, Patricia closed the narrow Venetian blinds, then reached across to flick on one of the stainless steel Anglepoise lamps. At once the room looked different. The concentrated light reflected off the white laminate worktop and onto the bizarre contraption in the middle of the room, upon which all of their hopes were pinned.

The steel frame held something that looked a little like a heavy-duty tailor's dummy, the whole thing hanging lifelessly from a metal clip-and-pulley system. A wide leather strap with a series of holes punched along it was fitted over each shoulder and attached to a bandeau-style strip of leather which ran across the chest and met in the middle of the back. Over each nipple was placed a tiny black plastic box, to which wires were attached, while around the waist ran another leather strap, with a third belted low, around the hips. The two strips were joined by a piece of padded leather running down over the abdomen, wires spewing from all sides and connecting elsewhere on this elaborate contraption. But the *pièce de résistance* – the object that immediately drew the eye – dangled from the lower belt. A black leather sheath, exactly a foot in length, hung between the imaginary metal thighs of the dummy, like a stallion's engorged penis, a single black wire attached to the nipple-like button at its tip, a whole host of small sensor pads placed intermittently along its long, tubular surface.

Patricia moved towards it slowly, cautiously, almost as though she expected it to spring to life at any moment. She walked around it, examining it as if it were a fine piece of sculpture. Then, gingerly, almost fearfully, she reached up and touched the shoulder straps, her finger tracing the circumference of each hole as she ran it up its length. Slipping her hand down to cup the compact nipple sensor she felt a definite erotic surge, the smell and feel of the smooth leather surface beneath her fingertips curiously sensual, in spite of its hardness and angularity. She closed her eyes.

Dropping to her knees, Patricia tipped her head slightly to one side, examining the tiny buckles at the waist and hip straps that secured the machine to the dummy. Fanning out her hands, she reached up and placed them over the metal abdomen, her little fingers tucked up inside the higher belt as her thumbs ran over the smooth leather pad running down to the lower strap. Then, closing her eyes once again, she allowed her hands to feel their way down, over the length of the phallic casing, her grip tightening as one hand closed above the other, her excitement so heightened by its touch that she could almost imagine the pulse of blood in her head and chest to be somehow transposed to that dark phallus she held within her grasp.

She had to try it. Had to.

Going across, she locked the door, leaving the key in the lock. Then, with a tiny self-conscious shiver, she began to undress, letting her clothes fall onto the floor beside her. Naked, she went across to the VR suit again, smoothing her hands across its leather surfaces until she could wait no longer.

Patricia had seen the twins do this many times before. They had been fully dressed, of course, but the routine was the same. Squinting at the keyboard, she tapped in the command instructions and saw the RUN programme begin to activate. Reaching across, she flicked through the box file on the desk beside the main computer, then retrieved the disc marked 'Chartres'.

Turning, Patricia looked over at the shelf in the corner. Five headsets rested in a row between the metal struts. Going across, she reached up and brought down the one marked 'female'.

The RUN programme finished. The machine bleeped twice. She leaned across, slipping the silver disc onto the sliding tray of the CD-ROM drive, then moved back. There was a faint buzzing sound and then the indicator panel flashed green.

'Good,' Patricia murmured to herself as she pulled the helmet over her short blonde hair, pressing the coils flat to her head.

Next was the suit.

It was not easy sliding the suit up over the dummy's

torso on her own, but eventually she managed it. Getting into it was another thing, however. Both Bill and Ben had twenty-eight-inch waists; hers was a good thirty-two. Nonetheless, a moment later she was inside it, struggling with the straps at the hip and waist to make the thing more comfortable.

That done, she began to connect the thing up.

Tugging the bunch of wires up over her shoulders, she carefully attached them to the appropriate pads on the suit and helmet.

Finished, she straightened up. The tug of the wires all about her naked body made her feel strange, amazingly *sexy*.

Reaching across, she tapped in the command word – CATHEDRAL – then stood back, an excited anticipation making her flesh tingle and stand up in goosebumps. For the briefest moment she stood there, staring at her reflection in the dark screen of the computer, then, with a tiny shiver, she pulled down the visor on the helmet as the program kicked in.

'Have we *got* to watch this, Mum?' Chastity asked, fidgeting in the corner of the sofa, unable to settle to the latest episode of *Dynasty* on UK Gold.

Faith Lloyd glanced across at her daughter – her fingers not missing a stitch, her size-eight needles click-click-clicking like a berserk mantis – then looked back at the screen, half squinting through her glasses. 'Yes, we have.'

Chastity sighed. 'I wouldn't mind, only you've seen it once already.'

'I know,' her mother said, her eyes never leaving the

TV. 'But that was years ago. I've forgotten most of what happened. Now for gawd's sake leave me in peace to watch the bloody thing, will you? Christ knows I don't ask much.'

Chastity shook her head in disbelief, watching her mother hang on to every word uttered by the glitzy fantasy figures that peopled her favourite soap, until, unnoticed, she slipped from the room, hoping to find a moment's peace in her bedroom.

The look of the room had barely changed since Chastity had been a little girl: one pink floral duvet-and-curtain set had been replaced by another; otherwise the only acknowledgement of her passage from childhood into womanhood was that the small Goldilocks night-light she'd had as a youngster had given way to a more sophisticated brass Anglepoise lamp, while the Winnie the Pooh clock had been replaced by a digital clock radio. A menagerie of cuddly toys, a fluffy hangdog nightdress case and the white cat-shaped hot-water bottle remained as comforting reminders of a cosy, uneventful childhood. Of safety and simple parental love.

Lying on her bed, Chastity held the TV remote, flicking uninterestedly through the terrestrial channels before settling on one. Cutting the volume, she stared vacantly at the TV, her mind a million miles away from the images flickering on the screen before her.

After the day's events, the evening had proved to be something of a disappointment. Having overcome her initial embarrassment at having to sit through the Japanese video, Chastity had found herself unexpectedly aroused by what she saw, her body responding in spite of her mental revulsion. The on-screen sex and the romantic fantasies that filled her head had combined in a powerful cocktail that had made her feel more than a little unsettled as she sat beside Charles Grant, his leg only a whisper from her own, the sleeve of his jacket brushing her skin as it rested beside her arm.

The confusion of emotions as the lights were switched on had rendered her almost speechless, so that, when Charles had asked if she would like a lift home, she had muttered something about getting the bus before the question had properly registered. Her mouth had worked on automatic, and, almost before she had had time to realise just what she'd said, Charles was picking up his briefcase and calling his farewells over his shoulder as he left the room.

She played out the scenario over and over again in her mind, each time shaking her head in disbelief at her own stupidity.

'You silly cow!' she chastised herself, each time she thought of how the evening might have ended. 'You blew it! You *really* blew it!'

Staring once again at the silent screen, Chastity sighed, then reached over to the bedside table for the market research file from Pop-U-Samp. Before this latest intervention by their Japanese backers, they had commissioned a survey on the most common sexual fantasies and activities of the good old British public. She had intended to begin reviewing it this morning, before Mr Fukuada's latest accident, but there hadn't been a moment since. Now, having missed out on a possible evening in Charles's company, she decided she might as well catch up on some work.

Plumping up a couple of pillows behind her, Chastity

slit open the sealed packet with a bright red fingernail and pulled out the thick folder of questionnaires. There was an eight-page typed summary on top of the stack of anonymous sheets. Setting the bulk of paper down beside her, she took the summary and began to read, her eyes opening in wide disbelief as she consumed each page, slowly at first, and then more eagerly, the researchers' findings doing nothing to quell the frustration that gripped her body like a vice so that she sat there as taut as an overstrung violin, the strings threatening to snap at any moment. It needed just one more turn of the pin.

'Bloody hell!' was all she could whisper as she turned the final page. Was that *really* what people got up to in the privacy of their own homes? She looked about her, trying to regain some sense of normality, yet after what she'd read the innocence of her room seemed strange, almost perverse, its dominant pink the badge of her naivety.

If *that* was what people got up to . . .

She whistled, long and low, then, setting the summary down, picked up the first of the questionnaires, a sense of feverish curiosity gripping her. It was going to be a long night.

Returning from the bathroom, Cynthia paused in the doorway to take in the sight that met her eyes. The two Japanese were where she'd left then, naked, kneeling with their heads down, their hands and feet securely shackled, their pale white buttocks stuck up in the air beside each other like the knuckles of a giant's fist.

Cynthia smiled to herself, then swished the cane

through the air. Both pairs of buttocks trembled with anticipation.

'*Onegai shimasu!*' the two men said, almost as one. *Please!*

Again the cane swished through the air, this time landing on the left-hand pair of cheeks. There was a tiny groan, then:

'*Domo arigato, gozaimashita!*'

A swish. The cane whacked down upon the right-hand pair of buttocks. A groan, then:

'*Domo arigato, gozaimashita!*'

'Good boys,' she said softly, drawing the cane softly across the upjutting flesh, like a schoolboy running a stick across the school railings. '*Honto ni tanoshikatta desu.*'

She had indeed enjoyed herself. Much more than usual. That video they'd watched earlier at Virt-E-Go had triggered something in her. Tonight she'd gone just a little further than she'd ever gone before, and they had loved it, had lapped it up, eager for more.

It was a lesson.

But now she was tired. If she was to be any use at work tomorrow, she would have to send them home.

Going across, she took the tiny key down from its peg on the wall, then went back and, kneeling between them, began to unlock their shackles. As each head came up, there was a deep and intense gratitude in the eyes that she had never noticed before.

'That was good,' Hamamato said in his jerky English.

'Velly good,' Okata added, giving her a little nod of respect. '*Tottemo i desu.*'

'I like it, too,' she said, smiling at them both. 'But now I must go to bed, understand? *Toko.*'

The two men looked to each other, then back to Cynthia.

'You want us come too?' Hamamato asked.

She laughed, surprised. Though she had known the two men for almost six months now, they had never actually slept together. For a moment she considered the idea, then shook her head. '*Domo arigato. Osoku narimashita.*'

Thank you, but it's getting late.

'Next time, huh?' Okata said.

'Maybe,' she answered, standing up and adjusting her breasts where they rested in their cut-away cups. 'Maybe.'

'Charlie!'

Lady Davina's voice squealed high and loud in an attempt to get Charles's attention as he bent over the steering wheel of his father's Rolls, his eyes staring blankly at the road ahead.

'Charlie! Have you heard a single word I've said?'

She didn't mean to punch his arm quite as hard as she did, but Charles did quite well, considering. He'd swerved, certainly, but he didn't actually hit the cab, and it really wasn't right for that dreadful cabbie to go on like that.

'I say, Dee,' Charles said, holding his hand up apologetically to the taxi driver, who responded by sticking his own hand out of the window, his thumb and middle finger forming a definite 'O' shape, shaking it up and down in a very suggestive manner. Charles pretended not to see, concentrating on the traffic up ahead as they approached Piccadilly Circus.

'What the hell was that for?' he said, reaching across to rub the spot where she had punched him.

'I'm sorry Charles,' she said with total insincerity, 'but it really is *too* bad, you know.'

'What is?'

'You know *exactly* what I'm talking about.'

'I'm sorry Davina,' he said, risking a small laugh. 'I may be a little dim' — Davina raised her eyebrows — 'but I really haven't the foggiest idea what you're talking about.'

'Well that just makes it even worse!'

Charles sighed heavily.

There was a moment's silence as they weaved in and out of the traffic in Haymarket. As they pulled up at the lights Charles tapped impatiently on the steering wheel. Davina stared at him a moment, then huffed loudly.

'If you *really* have no idea what I'm talking about, then I *suppose* I shall have to tell you.'

Charles turned to look at her. 'If you would.'

'Well the truth of the matter is, Charlie,' she said, half turning in her seat to face him, 'I'm feeling bloody neglected, I don't mind telling you. You never call me. You *never* want to take me out—'

'But Dee—'

'Don't interrupt, Charles! You're always too busy. You've always got something you've got to do.'

'It's called work, Davina!'

'We all *work*, Charles.'

'Well, no, actually we don't *all* work. *I* work. The people I work with work. But *you* don't work, Davina.'

A hurt tone crept into Lady Davina's voice. 'Charles! How can you say that?'

'Because it's true.'

Davina shook her head in disbelief. '*Nobody* works harder than I do. There's the hunt. And then there's my charity work. Not to mention doing flowers for the church. Really, Charles, I don't know how you can say such things!'

Pulling across St James's, Charles turned left up a side street which brought them alongside the Ritz. As the Rolls braked sharply, Davina was pulled forward in her seat before crashing back against the headrest.

'I'm not sure what you want, Davina. I've brought you out this evening. We're here, aren't we?'

'Yes, but only because I phoned to remind you. If Patricia hadn't managed to catch you before you left the building you'd be at home right now.'

Reluctantly Charles had to admit to himself that there was an element of truth in what she said. Certainly he had not remembered their date that evening and he would most certainly not have turned up had Pat not caught up with him and reminded him. But home had most certainly *not* been his destination.

The truth was, his only thought had been to get out of the building and into a bar where he could get as drunk as a skunk.

Sitting through the video with Chastity beside him had been sheer torture. He had watched distractedly as the actors pranced around on screen, his body reacting involuntarily, instinctively, his hands poised strategically in his lap to cover any possibility of embarrassment. Yet all the while his thoughts were with Chastity, so close that he could almost feel the warmth of her body, could almost taste the sweet breath from her parted lips. He had not been prepared for her rejection. When he had offered her a lift he had hoped she would say yes and that they could have gone off together for a quiet drink, or a meal maybe, but he had obviously misread the signals. Charles shook his head, mystified – not for the first time – by the opposite sex.

'And it's no good you shaking your head, Charles. You know I'm speaking the truth. It really is a damn poor show. I mean, what would Rupert and Camilla have thought if I'd turned up at the engagement on my own? Besides, I thought we might stay over. You know, hire a room and—'

'Listen, old thing. I really don't feel quite the ticket.'

'Charlie!'

'Sorry, Dee. I really am feeling a bit queasy. I wouldn't like to spoil it for you.'

'But—'

'Really, Dee. I think it would be best.'

Davina made to speak just as the doorman opened the passenger door.

'Look!' Charles said, waving at two of the guests as they approached the car. 'There's Clarissa and George. Hi, you two! I wonder if you'd do me a tremendous favour? Not feeling too good, see. Bit of a dodgy tum,' he said, patting his abdomen. 'Could Dee tag along with you chaps? Brill!'

Davina's eyes narrowed as she threw him a look that should have sent him hurtling towards damnation, her mouth curving into the sweetest smile as she turned to greet her new companions.

'Yes, poor Charlie . . .' she agreed as she eased out of the car to join her friends, slamming the door behind her even as Charles revved the Rolls, then sped out into the evening traffic.

Louise sank back into the soft upholstery of Roger's Rover, her hand gently caressing the smooth leather. Through the tinted window she could see Roger in the shadows by the pub doorway, his mobile phone to one ear and his hand pressed against the other to shut out the noise of traffic.

Sometimes she wondered what she saw in him. Oh, he was still attractive and he wasn't backward when it came to putting his hand in his pocket, but he did have the distinct disadvantage of being married.

Louise watched him as he strode across the car park, in darkness but for the occasional glare from headlamps, furtively looking about him as he slipped into the car beside her.

'What did she say?' Louise asked casually as he slumped back into the seat.

'Nothing.'

'What excuse did you give?'

'Working late.'

Louise shook her head at his lack of imagination. 'She must wonder why you're not filthy bloody rich the amount of overtime you put in,' she giggled, nuzzling into Roger's neck.

'I look after her,' he said defensively, closing his eyes and tilting his head towards her.

'What, like you look after me, you mean?' she whispered huskily and gently ran her hand down Roger's chest, bringing it to rest over his crotch. She smiled as she felt his penis twitch beneath her touch.

'Ooh,' he groaned. 'Aah.'

Louise undid the fly of his trousers and slid her manicured fingers into the gap.

'Push the seats back, Rog,' she whispered into his ear, her teeth nibbling at the lobe.

Fumbling down the side of the chair, Roger pushed a lever, sending both seats into recline, and Louise quickly sat astride him, her skirt rising up her thighs to reveal dark stocking tops. He pulled at the buttons of her blouse, sending two of them flying off in opposite directions in his eagerness.

'God, I love your tits!' he croaked, reaching up to hold one of her ample bosoms in each hand, her erect nipples hard against his palms.

Responding, Louise bent forward so that her breasts hung pendulously on either side of his face, and as he squeezed them together the warm flesh moulded around his cheeks so that Roger looked as though he might drown in the heavenly folds.

'What colour knickers have you got on?' he panted.

'Guess.'

'Black?'

Louise shook her head.

'White?'

Again, she shook her head, smiling, her hips gyrating as she moved above him.

'I dunno. I give up.'

Slowly, provocatively Louise eased her skirt up over her thighs and hips. Roger raised his head to look, and, at the sight of Louise's pubic hair framed by dark suspender straps splayed across his white shirt front, he groaned.

'Oh God! Quick!' he said, pushing his trousers down about his knees. 'Quick! Shove it in! I think I'm coming!'

Entering the final statistic onto the computer, Chastity pressed EDIT and sat back in her chair, relieved to have finished. After a restless night she had turned up early for work, keen to get the results onto disk before Bob Guppy arrived. She couldn't bear the thought of his standing over her shoulder commenting on every entry she made. As it turned out, she needn't have hurried.

'Morning, Chastity,' Patricia said brightly, beaming broadly as she popped her head round the office door.

'Morning,' Chastity replied, bemused by the unusually cheery greeting.

'Bob in?'

'No. Sorry, Patricia. He phoned in. Says he's decided to spend a couple of days out in the field. See some retailers. Test the water.'

'Oh, bother!' she said, her annoyance evident.

'Anything I can help with?'

'Well, actually, you probably could,' Patricia said, stepping into the office and closing the door behind her. 'In view of last night's decision to originate two separate software programs I need to gather costings from all departments so that Charles can have a meeting with Roger.'

'Today?'

'What?'

'Today?' Chastity repeated. 'Are they having the meeting today?'

'Oh, no. Charles won't be in the office today. In fact he sounded quite out of sorts when he phoned earlier. No. I've arranged the meeting for tomorrow.'

'Ah.'

'Yes, well. In Bob Guppy's absence perhaps you could come up with a few facts and figures. I'm sure there's little you don't know, anyway.'

'Well, I could probably—'

'If you could manage to stay behind for an hour or two this evening, maybe we could work through them. You'll get overtime, of course.'

Chastity smiled. 'Yeah, sure,' she said. 'No problem.'

'Terr-ific!' Patricia said and turned on her heels, looking over her shoulder to Chastity only when she reached the door, the chrome handle firmly in her grip.

'By the way, how's Guppy behaving himself these days?'

Chastity shrugged.

'Because, if he really starts to pester you, you must let me know.'

Chastity looked up at her through heavy eyelids. 'Actually, he was a bit of a pain when we stayed overnight at Sir James's place the other week.'

'Oh?'

'It was after we'd all gone to bed.'

'Yes?' Patricia said, coming back across.

'He came knocking at my door. He was a right nuisance. Wanted me to let him in.'

'And did you?' Patricia was perched on the edge of the desk now, leaning forward conspiratorially.

'Course not!' Chastity responded, amazed that she could even ask the question.

'So what did he say?'

Chastity thought for a moment. 'Well, he didn't say anything, actually. He just knocked.'

'Oh,' Patricia said, a trace of disappointment in her voice. 'Well, if there's any more of it you be sure to let me know.' And patting Chastity reassuringly on the hand she made her way back to the door, an unusual lightness to her step.

That night, sitting in the corner of the wine bar, Patricia went through the figures Chastity had put together, then, removing her glasses, looked across the table and beamed.

'Great! These are just the ticket!'

She raised her wine glass, then, noting that Chastity's was empty, reached across and poured her another.

'What's up?' she asked, sensing that the younger woman was a bit subdued. 'Is something worrying you?'

Chastity looked down into her glass, then, wrinkling her nose into a frown, shrugged. 'I dunno, I . . .'

'Are you thinking about the film?'

Chastity hesitated, then gave a tiny nod. 'A bit much, wasn't it?'

Patricia put her hand over Chastity's. 'You didn't like it, then?'

Chastity raised her eyes, meeting Pat's, and gave an apologetic smile. 'Trouble is, I actually think I *did*.'

'And that bothers you?' Chastity nodded. 'It's how some people are,' Patricia said.

'Don't I know it.'

It was Patricia's turn to frown. 'What do you mean?'

'That survey we commissioned. I read through it last night. Talk about an eye-opener!'

Patricia leaned forward, fascinated. 'Really?'

'Yeah, it said that we Brits are a nation of pervs and sex-maniacs!'

'Hmmm . . .' Patricia downed her wine and poured another, turning to signal to the waiter to bring another bottle. 'And what in particular gave you that impression?'

'Well, the section on rubber for a start!'

Patricia reached out, almost as if to put a hand over Chastity's mouth. The words had come out loud and people at nearby tables had looked up, startled.

'*Rubber*?' Patricia almost whispered, withdrawing her hand.

'It made me think,' Chastity went on, nodding to herself. 'I mean, as you get older, as a girl you know that if you wear the right kind of clothes you can . . . you know, turn a man on. If you want to, that is. But that stuff on the film, it's like going back to being a kid again, don't you think, all that dressing up? Doctors and nurses and all that. Only for grown-ups.'

Patricia hesitated, then nodded. 'I . . . er . . . Look, d'you mind if I ask you something, Chastity?'

Chastity shrugged. 'I s'pose not.'

'Well . . . does it worry you, what we're doing?'

Chastity laughed. 'Well, I knew we weren't helping to find a cure for cancer!'

'So it doesn't?'

'Nah, not really. I mean, if it helps a few people find a little happiness, where's the harm? Even so . . .' She giggled. 'I don't think I'd like me mum to know exactly what we're doing.'

'You think she'd disapprove?'

'Disapprove? I dunno about that. I s'pose I'd just feel a bit funny about her knowing that I'm working for a company that makes *sex* machines.' Chastity laughed.

'She's been nagging me about bringing home some free samples. You know, a kettle or a sandwich maker or something. She'd get a bloody shock, wouldn't she?'

Patricia grinned. 'You never know, maybe she'd prefer it.'

'Nah,' Chastity said, without thinking, 'she's too old.'

The two women were silent a moment, then Patricia spoke again.

'Who do you think is going to use the machine? I mean, what *kind* of people?'

Chastity shrugged. 'I dunno. Lonely people, for a start. People who're looking for something they just can't get in real life.'

Patricia looked down, the slightest flush at her neck now. 'So you see it mainly as a kind of therapy machine?'

'Nah. Not really. I mean, they're only going to get sex from it.'

'And you don't think that that's the answer.'

Chastity shook her head.

Patricia laughed. 'So what *is* the answer?'

'Love, maybe?'

'Ah, yes, love. But what if you can't find love?'

Chastity looked away. 'I dunno. But sex can't solve everything, can it?'

Patricia studied Chastity a while, then, sensing that they might not be quite so close, quite so intimate again, asked what was in her mind. 'So what is it you want from life?'

'Want?'

'Yes. You know, what are your personal ambitions? Because I look at you and I find myself wishing I was

eighteen again. I wish I had all of the freshness and
energy I had at eighteen, but knew what I know
now.' She laughed. 'I tell you, I'd not make the same
mistakes again.'

'Mistakes?'

'Yes, with men. And you're right, Chastity. The
answer isn't sex. But sex *is* a problem. At least, it is
for most people. It kind of . . . well, gets in the way
of things. Complicates them. So maybe our machine is
a good thing. Maybe that's its task – to simplify the
problem of sex.'

Chastity considered that a moment, then wrinkled her
nose up again. 'So do you reckon it'll ever replace real
relationships?'

Patricia shrugged, then shook her head. 'So tell me,
what *do* you want from life?'

Chastity had opened her mouth, about to answer,
when someone hissed at them across the wine bar.

'*Patricia! Chastity! You gotta come! Quick!*'

The two women turned, staring at Bill's wide-eyed
face peering round the doorway.

'What is it?' Patricia said, getting up and going across
to him. 'Is someone ill?'

'Worse than that,' Bill said, breathlessly. 'It's the
police! We've been raided! They've been there an hour
already. I only managed to get away because I said I was
gonna pee myself if they didn't let me go to the loo!'

Patricia's eyes flared with anger. 'Holly! He must have
waited till I left!' She downed the dregs of her wine,
then stood, looking at Bill again. 'Did you do what we
agreed?'

'Yeah.'

'Good. Then let's get back there and sort that man out!'

'Ahah!' Detective Inspector Holly said as Patricia burst into the labs, Chastity and Bill in close pursuit, 'I see we have company!'

Holly's men – two plain-clothes policemen, even shabbier in attire than he was – glanced up from their work, then ducked down again, returning to their task of filling boxes with anything they could lay their hands on.

'I hope you've got a good reason for bursting in on us like this,' Patricia said, going over to Holly and thrusting her face into his.

'Oh, don't you worry,' he answered smugly, thrusting a folded document at her. 'I've got a warrant.'

'I wasn't talking about a *warrant*,' Patricia said, brushing his arm aside. 'I was talking about a complaint of police harassment of a legitimate business concern.'

'Now, now,' Holly said, the smug smile barely dented by Patricia's outburst. 'Let's just wait and see what we come up with before we start talking about *complaints*. Because, if we find what I *think* we're going to find, then I don't think that any of you will be in a position to complain.'

Bill and Ben looked to Patricia, but she seemed as solid as a slab of stone. 'You can look all you bloody well like, Inspector, but you won't *find* anything, because there's nothing to find.'

'No? Then what about this?' Taking a computer disk from his pocket, Holly showed it to her, without allowing her to touch it. 'See the label?'

'So?' Patricia said defiantly.

Holly tilted it so that he could read it aloud. 'Sex Mark Vee-Eye.'

'Six,' Ben corrected him. 'That's six in roman numerals.'

'I know,' Holly said, a little flustered by the correction. Then, recovering himself, 'Okay. How do I play this? You want to show me, or do I have to arrest you all and take you down the station?'

The twins looked to Patricia, who nodded.

'Here,' Ben said, stepping up and offering Holly a VR helmet, 'this goes on your head.'

'And this,' Bill said, offering the Inspector a VR glove, 'goes on your hand.'

Holly frowned. 'Is that it?'

Patricia glanced down, smiling now.

Chastity, looking on from the doorway, frowned, wondering where the special suit had gone. Only last night it had hung there in all its glory – complete with its unmistakable black rubber appendage. But now there was no sign of it. Surely they hadn't had time to dismantle it.

'We link you up here,' Bill was saying, attaching a bunch of wires that trailed from Holly's helmet to the computer. 'And here,' Ben added, linking the glove to the helmet by yet another bunch of wires.

'And then,' Bill said, 'we slip the disk into the slot.'

Holly tensed as the program began to run. For a full minute he stood there, hunched slightly, the helmet over his eyes, staring into nowhere. Then, with a little shudder of disgust, he tore the helmet off.

'Enough!' he said. 'What the hell am I watching?'

'Chartres,' Patricia answered, smiling politely now.

'You should have tried the glove, Inspector. It's completely interactive. The tour of the cathedral comes in eight different languages and you can decide which way you want to go round the place. If you want—'

But Holly clearly *didn't* want. Turning to his men, he gestured impatiently at them, then turned back, almost snarling into Patricia's smiling face. 'You think you're clever, don't you? You think you can give us the runaround. But I'll nail you. You have my promise on that. And when I do . . .'

'Oooh,' Patricia said, as if he'd just promised her a weekend of fantastic sex, 'I can't wait.'

Holly drew himself up straight, gave a little shudder of indignation, then wagged his finger at her again as his men trooped out, their filled boxes clutched to their chests. 'I'll be back.'

'Of course,' Patricia said urbanely, as if dealing with a difficult client. 'And Inspector . . . ?'

Holly, who had turned to leave, now turned back. '*What?*'

'If you could have a detailed list of everything you've taken on Mr Grant's desk by tomorrow morning, I'll take the matter no further.'

'If I could *what?*'

She stepped up to him again. 'I understand that the Commissioner is dining at Sir James's tomorrow night, and it would be nice to be able to tell Sir James that the matter has been *resolved*. So if you wouldn't mind . . .'

Holly's face, which had slowly turned beetroot red with anger, now exploded with rage. 'Like bloody hell I will!'

Patricia smiled. 'As you wish, Inspector. Now good day, or should I say . . . *au revoir*.'

'So where is it?' Chastity asked as soon as the police had left the building. 'Where have you hidden it?'

Bill grinned. 'We didn't hide it. It's here.'

'Where?'

Ben indicated various bits and pieces lying about on benches all around him. 'Here,' he said. 'We dismantled it last night, after the latest trial. Patricia asked us to.'

Chastity turned to Pat. 'Are you psychic or something?'

Pat smiled. 'Just a precaution. I thought it needed a good clean. I mean, we don't want anyone catching anything!'

Chastity stared at her a moment, then burst out laughing. 'And there was I thinking you'd worked out some special scheme between you all!'

Pat's smile faded. 'No. But we will now. Because I've an inkling that we'll be seeing a lot more of Inspector Holly.'

– July –

— July —

Roger Appleyard strode into the spacious kitchen of his family home and made a beeline for the television set. To groans of disapproval from his two teenage children, he switched channels from *The Big Breakfast* to the BBC news programme, turning down the volume so that the newsreader's sober voice was little more than a distant, background murmur. The youngsters turned their attention to the books that lay open beside their cereal bowls, while Roger turned his to the slices of lightly buttered brown toast his wife had placed on a blue china plate before him.

Jane Appleyard was a formidable woman who ran her home with, if not military precision, then certainly with the kind of organisational skills that would have been the envy of any ambitious PA. In her domain there was a place for everything and everything was in its place. There was a time for everything too: the first wash load in by 7.30 a.m. so that it was dried and folded away by lunchtime; the car washed every Friday on her way back from the supermarket; the kids' supper on the table by 5.45 p.m. so that it was cleared away before Roger returned from the office.

Alongside this rigorous schedule, Jane organised a succession of people who 'did'. There was the gardener on Tuesdays, the cleaner on Mondays and Thursdays (Friday, too, if they had a dinner party planned), the window cleaner every other Wednesday morning, the pool man every Wednesday afternoon during the months of May through to October, and her wonderful odd-job man as and when required. Within this remarkable schedule, she managed to fit in three sessions a week with her personal trainer and, in particularly *stressful* periods, a couple of visits a week to her therapist.

'What time shall I expect you home this evening?' she enquired, wiping a damp cloth over the gleaming chrome toaster.

'Not sure,' Roger replied without looking up from his paper. 'I'll probably have to work late.'

'Again?' she groaned.

Roger sighed. 'I know, I know. But there's nothing I can do about it. If you're in a position of responsibility . . .' This was such a familiar conversation that Roger felt no need to expound further.

'Well, give me a ring. So I know what to do about dinner.'

'Mmm. Sure,' he said, turning to the back page of his newspaper to catch up on the sports news.

'How many shirts will you need for the weekend?' Jane asked, turning her attention to the kettle.

'Better pack four, to be on the safe side.'

'Do you *have* to go Friday night, Rog?' she said,

discarding the cloth. Stepping across to stand behind her husband, she placed her cool, damp fingers around the back of his neck and began gently to massage the knotted muscles between his shoulder blades, causing Roger to tilt his head back a little and close his eyes.

'Couldn't you drive up early on Saturday morning?'

''Fraid not, sweetheart. The conference starts bright and early. I don't want to turn up knackered, or get caught up in traffic, do I?'

'I guess not,' she agreed reluctantly, removing her hands from inside Roger's shirt collar and retrieving the dishcloth from the worktop.

Adjusting his tie, Roger glanced across at the TV, noting with vague interest an item on some disaster or other: buildings had been totally destroyed and the reporter stood amidst the ruins and rubble, the wind blowing thick dust across his face so that he found it difficult to speak. Realising the time, and eager to beat the worst of the rush hour, Roger downed the last of his coffee and, folding his newspaper into quarters, he stood up from the breakfast table. Reaching across, he ruffled the hair of his thirteen-year-old son, Rodney, and lightly tapped the head of his slightly older daughter, neither of them acknowledging the familiar farewell gesture with anything more than an irritated movement of the head away from his touch.

'Right! I'm off, then!' he announced.

Jane stepped across and pecked him on the cheek. 'Bye, darling. See you later,' she said, reaching a manicured hand up to wipe at the faint pink lipstick mark she had left there. Looking over his shoulder at the bowed heads of their offspring, she called, 'Say goodbye to your father, kids.'

'Bye, Dad,' they responded automatically without bothering to look up from the pages of their respective books.

'Bye,' Roger answered, and with that he stepped out of the house and walked along the drive towards his gleaming red Rover.

The thought of three days of unrestrained sex with Louise was perhaps the reason for the added pressure on Roger's accelerator that morning. As he sailed along the fast lane of the motorway into London, he congratulated himself on coming up with the rather convenient conference that would afford them three days away together. A smile played across his lips.

If his wife knew about this latest infidelity, Roger was unaware of it. There was never a hint of suspicion in her voice nor rebuke over the amount of time he spent away from home. In Jane Appleyard Roger did, indeed, consider himself blessed.

On the other hand Louise, he felt, could prove an altogether more difficult proposition. It was obvious she expected more from their affair than rumpy-pumpy followed by a quick drink in the Champion or a curry up the Indian. Louise was a romantic. At heart, he knew, she was a wife. And he already had one of those. For the moment, however, Roger preferred to dwell on the more positive aspects of their relationship. Immediately an image of his secretary's ample bosom flashed into his mind, causing his foot to press a little harder on the unresisting pedal. Checking his speed, Roger reached down and flicked on the car radio, the muted strains of some vaguely familiar song oozing from the expensive sound system.

There was something about illicit sex, Roger had decided some time ago, that gave it a definite edge over marital nookie. Indeed, he prided himself on the fact that he was able to keep two healthy women satisfied simultaneously, as it were, and at times he had felt that even three would not have been an impossible task, given the right woman. Certainly he had felt tempted. There was something about little uptight Cynthia – with her glasses and sensible shoes – that brought out a missionary zeal in him. He'd known women like her before: they were just gagging for some bloke to come along and pull the hairpins out of their bun and rip off their tights, releasing them from their self-imposed celibacy.

But the focus of Roger's current fantasy shone upon Chastity. All that soft, young flesh and wide-eyed innocence was irresistible, so that the urge to convey her from naive adolescent into knowing – and unresisting – womanhood became as compelling and appealing as an ice-cold pint of lager on a hot afternoon. Roger licked his lips in anticipation.

The sequence of notes signalling the start of the eight o'clock news broke into Roger's consciousness. Automatically he leaned forward, turning up the volume.

'The death toll from the Osaka earthquake has now reached the six hundred mark and rescuers say that it is likely to double as they begin the task of clearing the financial district . . .'

Roger's mouth fell open in shock. So *that* was what he'd glimpsed on the TV earlier.

'. . . the damage to Japan's economy is estimated to be in excess of ten billion dollars, and . . .'

The words became a blur. Looking in his mirror, Roger slowed the car, then signalled to pull into the left-hand lane, his heart pounding. As the lay-by approached, he slewed the car into it and stamped down on the brake.

Leaning forward, Roger turned the volume up, his whole body curled in an almost foetal position, his right-hand thumbnail jammed into his mouth as he listened to the woeful tidings.

'Oh shit!' he murmured. 'Oh shit. Oh, fucking bollocks!'

Osaka. It was the home of Sumikana, their Japanese backers!

'Louise! Get hold of Fukuada at the Tokyo office!' Roger yelled, even before he'd fully entered the room.

Throwing his briefcase onto a chair he strode over to his desk and picked up the telephone, tapping in Patricia's extension number. Looking across he saw Louise still standing in the middle of the floor.

'Move it, will you! This is urgent!' Then, aware for the first time of the piece of flimsy paper she held between her thumb and index finger, and seeing the knowing look on her face, he added, 'What's that?'

'Good morning would be nice,' she said, shaking it in the air, teasing him, like a child with a bag of sweets.

'Oh, for God's sake don't piss about, Louise!' he said angrily. 'We've got a major problem with Japan!'

Turning his attention temporarily back to the telephone he allowed two more unanswered rings, then slammed down the handset. 'Shit!'

'I *know* we've got a problem,' Louise replied, sauntering over to his desk and placing the fax down before him. 'This came through from Sumikana's Tokyo office.'

Roger read it voraciously, then groaned. 'Oh, fuck!' he said through clenched teeth, reaching for the telephone again. 'Fuck, fuck, fuck!'

'What *exactly* does it mean?' Louise asked, picking up the piece of paper and reading it through once again.

'Exactly what it says,' Roger shouted impatiently. 'The fucking Tokyo stock market has crashed! It's gone into free fall and unless we're really sodding lucky the cash for our machine's gone with it!'

Roger drummed his fingers on the desk while he waited for Patricia to answer the phone.

Louise frowned. 'But it says here that they've only frozen the finance until further notice,' she said, reading from the fax.

'My dear Louise, at this very moment the office of our financial saviour is lying beneath a million tons of smouldering rubble. I'm only guessing here, you understand, but my hunch is that our hopes of getting cash out of them now are buried so much further than that, that in the next few hours they'll probably emerge in Melbourne!'

Louise's face held a look of total non-comprehension.

Exasperated by the lack of response at the other end, Roger dropped the phone and made for the door.

'What time are we leaving tomorrow?' Louise called after him.

The bizarre *non sequitur* had a surprising effect on Roger. He turned, a brief laugh of incredulity escaping his lips.

'You *what*?'

'What time do you want to leave for the conference?'

'Conference!' Roger shook his head, dumbfounded. 'I'm very sorry, Louise, but we'll have to knock that one on the head. I can't go gallivanting off for a dirty weekend when we're about to be thrown into the fucking shredder!' He took a long breath, then. 'I don't think you understand just how disastrous this news is!'

Marching over to where her boss stood and with uncharacteristic assertiveness, Louise pushed the door shut so that Roger looked down with astonishment at his hand, still formed into a ball, which only moments before had tightly gripped the brass handle.

'No, Roger,' she said, glaring up at him, 'it's *you* who doesn't understand! If we don't go away this weekend, then that's it!'

'Louise . . .' he implored.

'I mean it, Roger. We hardly ever spend time together. You're always rushing off to that frigid bitch of a wife. No, I've made my mind up. This is make-or-break time.'

'Please, Lulu. Not *now*. You don't understand . . .'

'No, *you* don't understand. I've had enough of always having to stand in line. Of never coming first. A little hiccup like this Tokyo business and—'

'A little hiccup!' Roger's voice had risen a couple of octaves. 'The livelihood of every person at Virt-E-Go is about to float up the Swanee and you think it's a "hiccup"?'

As the realisation of what Roger had said dawned on her, the tightness across Louise's features relaxed so that her look was all contrition when next she spoke.

'It's just that I was really looking forward to it. That's

all. Spending all night with you. Waking up next to you . . .'

Sighing inwardly, Roger took her by the shoulders and drew her close to him.

'Yeah, so was I, sweetheart,' he said, his voice softer now as he fought to stay calm. 'In fact I was thinking about what I was going to do to you as I was driving in this morning.'

Louise punched him playfully on the back and wriggled against him.

'Nearly made me crash.'

She giggled and the warmth of her breath penetrated the thin fabric of his shirt, forcing the tiny hairs on the back of his neck to stand on end. In spite of himself, Roger ran his hands down her sides until he could feel the soft flesh of her thighs.

'What colour knickers have you got on?' he whispered into her hair, all thought of Eastern tragedies temporarily forgotten.

'Guess,' she said.

Roger pushed his hand beneath the hem of her skirt and ran his palm up, over her hips, hooking his thumb over the elasticated band of her panties.

'White,' he hissed, his breathing more rapid now.

Louise giggled.

Inching them down over her buttocks so that the thin strip of fabric encircled her thighs like a giant garter, Roger quivered slightly as he ran his hands over Louise's warm naked flesh. With practised ease, she wriggled from side to side until her panties worked their way down her legs and fell around her ankles. Kicking them to one side, she fell back against the door and, reaching down to undo his fly, she pulled Roger to her, wrapping her legs about him.

Neither of them was aware of pressure being exerted on the other side of the door, nor of the handle being turned to no effect. In fact it wasn't until Patricia's high-pitched voice, demanding to know why the door wouldn't open, filtered through the door jamb that either was aware of another presence.

'Shit!' Roger hastily retrieved his trousers, straightened his tie and wiped the sweat from his furrowed brow, while Louise tucked in her teeshirt and stuffed her knickers in the pocket of her skirt.

'Hold on a minute, Pat,' Roger panted. 'We've been shifting furniture about and there's something against the door. Just a tick.'

Clearing his throat as loudly as he could, Roger attempted to turn the key silently to unlock the door, and, as the Chairman's PA entered the unaltered room, he was quick to take up the offensive.

'I tried to get hold of you earlier,' he said, moving behind his desk.

Patricia made a point of scanning the room with an exaggerated movement of her head before taking up the seat opposite him.

'I was in the boardroom. I've been trying to get hold of Charles.'

'You know the score then?'

'Of course. I passed the fax on to Louise.'

Roger glared across at Louise who stared resolutely at her computer screen.

'But what you haven't seen,' Patricia added, handing across a sheet of fax paper, 'is this.'

Roger's eyes flitted across the few lines of communication.

'Shit!'

'Precisely!' Patricia agreed. 'It's official now. We've lost our backing.'

Roger stared back at her woefully, like a child who has just learned that school isn't breaking for summer after all. 'So what are we going to do?'

Patricia stood determinedly. 'Well, for a start we're going to call a meeting.'

'A meeting?' Roger wailed. 'What good will that do?'

Patricia narrowed her eyes. 'Who knows? But it's better than playing Chicken Licken and waiting for the sky to fall.'

The assembled workforce gathered round the board-room table with the common look of condemned prisoners. The atmosphere was one of despondency as they awaited Charles's arrival, their low murmurings reflecting shared concerns for their future employment following the Japanese disaster.

'I bumped into a bloke I know at the rugby club the other week,' Bob Guppy confided miserably. 'He's been out of work for five years now. Five years! And he's a couple of years younger than me. Nah, I tell you, once you're past forty you're on the scrap heap!'

Brian McTaggart's cheek twitched involuntarily. 'Surely it depends what field one's in, Bob?'

'Not these days. We're living in ageist times. Employers are looking for whizz-kids. Bright young things with lots of energy and plenty to say for themselves. Experience counts for nothing these days, Brian, I'm telling you.'

McTaggart began to wring his hands. He seemed almost on the verge of tears. 'Oh dear,' he whined. 'Oh dear, oh dear . . .'

'You'd be saying a lot worse than "oh dear" if you had to go home and break the news to your wife that she can't have the conservatory extension you promised her. My life'll be bloody hell.'

'But it's not as if you can help it, is it?' Chastity offered from across the other side of the table. 'I mean, the Japanese thing's not *your* fault, is it?'

'You try telling *her* that!'

At the head of the table, Patricia threw the handset down and huffed loudly. 'That's all we need!' All heads turned towards her expectantly.

'What?' Roger said.

'That was the equipment hire company,' she said quietly. 'It seems they've gotten wind of the situation. They're demanding the return of all their machinery unless we settle our account immediately.'

'Bloody vultures! It didn't take them long, did it?' Roger hissed. 'Well, we can't pay them. Without the money from the Japs . . .'

There was a long silence in which the whole gathering sat, shocked, contemplating their predicament, praying for someone – anyone – to come up with an answer.

The sound of the door opening interrupted the almost religious quiet of the boardroom, as Charles Grant made his breathless entrance.

'I'm sorry,' he said, looking about him apologetically. 'Traffic and all that, you know . . .'

At a gesture from Patricia, Louise moved around the table, pouring fresh coffee, while Patricia herself took their young Chairman to one side and apprised him of the recent development regarding the equipment.

'What is the sum we need to allow us to keep the equipment, Roger?' he asked, looking to his Finance Director.

Quickly glancing at the figures on the ledger before him, Roger frowned. 'Not good, I'm afraid. Thirty-six thousand pounds.'

Like spectators in a slow-motion tennis match, heads turned to Charles in anticipation.

'Right!' Charles announced with uncharacteristic decisiveness. 'Let's deal with one problem at a time.' And with that he took his chequebook from his briefcase, wrote in the figure and signed it, before passing it across the table.

'Fill in the details, would you, Roger?'

Roger looked at the cheque then across at Charles. 'But this is your personal account.'

'Never mind that. Let's get on with the business at hand. What are we going to do about the Japanese situation? Any ideas?' Charles looked around the room at the sea of vacant faces, unaware that the question had not yet registered while each of them considered the gesture he had just made with a combination of envy and relief.

A half-hour of fruitless discussion had taken place before, unwittingly, William came up with a possible solution to their problem.

'Well,' he said, sitting back, 'why don't we try to sell the idea in Silicon Valley?'

Charles, who had been listening without comment, now sat forward. 'Actually, I've an old school chum over there. A guy called Toby Eastman. By all accounts he's something of a big cheese in the VR biz,' he announced casually.

Patricia and Roger made eye contact.

'Mmm,' Charles went on in somewhat distracted fashion, aware of Chastity smiling across at him. 'We were at Eton together. In fact, he's played for my cricket team a couple of times. Damn fine bowler, actually. Not so good out in the field. We usually stick him out on the boundary where he can do no harm, but—'

'Yes,' Patricia said, interrupting him gently, coming to sit at his elbow. 'But what exactly does he do in Silicon Valley?'

'Do?' Charles turned to look at Pat. 'Well, actually he's top bod of a company called Binary Infinity.'

'Bi-Fi?' Benjamin asked, staring goggle-eyed at his chairman as if he had never seen him before that moment. 'He's *president* of Bi-Fi?'

'I think that's what he sometimes calls it, yes,' Charles said hesitantly.

'Wow!' Benjamin cried enthusiastically. 'Bi-Fi! That's cool!'

'Yeah, that's really really cool man!' William agreed, his face sharing the awe that was on his brother's at the mention of the name.

Charles's smile spread across his face, like a child who suddenly realises he has amused his elders. 'You've heard of them then?'

'Absolutely!' Brian McTaggart enthused, keen to appear as informed as his two assistants. 'They're rapidly becoming one of the most innovative organisations in the Valley.'

'Yeah! They're hot!' William elucidated, nodding with an enthusiasm that would not have been out of place in a Warner Brothers cartoon. 'Everything they do is cutting edge!'

'Then maybe I should give old Tobe a ring?'

All round the table heads nodded enthusiastically.

Without a thought to the time difference between London and California, Charles punched in the long string of digits that would connect him to Toby Eastman, his erstwhile school chum and fellow cricketer. Considering the hour on the West Coast, the man could not have been more helpful.

'Of course, old boy,' Toby said, ending the conversation, which barely seemed to have touched on the subject, ranging as it did from rugby and cricket through to the fate of old school chums, 'it's no bother at all.'

As Charles put down the handset, a dozen expectant faces stared at him.

'*Well*?' Patricia said, unable to contain herself a moment longer. 'What did he say?'

Charles looked down shyly. 'He says he knows just the people. New company started up last year. Says they're looking for exciting new projects. He'll phone them first thing tomorrow morning, his time, and arrange an introduction.'

Across the table from Charles, Roger made a whooping sound. Charles looked up at him, surprised, then looked to Patricia again. 'I'll give you Toby's number. He says we're to ring, ten o'clock his time.'

The staff discussion that followed was far more vocal

than any that had taken place earlier that morning as each member came up with what they hoped were persuasive arguments why they should be amongst the team to fly out to America. Roger's inclusion was automatic, but, despite a half-hearted plea on Louise's behalf, it was felt that on this occasion he would have to make do without her helping hand.

The exclusion of Brian McTaggart was handled with aplomb and diplomacy by Patricia. It was frightening to contemplate their socially inept Head of Research and Development let loose on America, and with just the right degree of flattery she and Charles persuaded him that his talents would be best employed in the laboratory getting the project back on track. His momentary relief was tainted with resentment as they went on to announce that Cynthia should perhaps accompany Roger and Bob and be on hand should they require some technical backup out in the field.

The twins had been as excited by the prospect of a visit to Silicon Valley as a ten-year-old would be by a trip to Disneyworld, but in the end they had to be placated with the promise that, should it prove necessary, they would be flown over to join the core team.

It seemed sensible for Bob Guppy as head of Sales and Marketing to go along, a decision he received with a mixture of excitement and apprehension. He hadn't quite managed to get his head round the workings of this sex machine contraption and, in view of the seriousness of their current situation, he didn't want to make a cock-up of the whole thing.

Charles felt that, like the twins, he should also remain on standby in case his presence should be required. He assured Roger and Bob that should it prove necessary for him to put in an appearance – do a bit of the old public-school, English-aristocrat act – he'd be on the next plane out. He was wise enough to know where his strengths lay and realised that he would be of little practical help in securing finance, with his limited understanding of the finer details of the sex machine and how it actually worked.

However, it was his decision that Patricia should accompany the two men to organise the schedule and ensure that the whole thing ran smoothly. Her response was a pained, tight-lipped smile that barely concealed the panic she felt at that moment. She had always enjoyed flying; indeed, on her annual jaunt abroad with her neighbour, Pamela – for her ex-husband would have no truck with foreigners – the flights there and back were often the highlight of the holiday. Until the journey from hell four summers ago which had taken her from Heathrow to Lanzarote, where an engine had given out, forcing them to land on some God-forsaken strip of bumpy tarmac in Northern Spain. Since that day her feet had never left the reassuringly solid turf of England.

The meeting began to disperse. Had she not been so preoccupied, Patricia might have been aware of the way Charles's eyes, wide with admiration, followed Chastity from the room. Rising out of his seat, he made to go after her, to remind her about his invitation to join him for a ride, but Patricia, with more force than she'd intended, pushed him back into his seat.

'Charles. I need to speak with you.'

Cynthia slammed the door behind her, then, throwing

the tickets down on the hall table, stomped through to her bedroom.

'What a bloody pain!' she said, staring at herself in the full-length mirror as she unbuttoned her jacket and let it slip onto the floor. 'Why do these things always happen at the most inconvenient times?' But she knew that this was too good a chance for her to pass up – a real opportunity for her to show what she was made of.

But she would have to make phone calls, put people off, rearrange her already hectic schedule. It was all a total bloody nuisance.

Then again, America might be fun.

Cynthia took a moment to gather her thoughts, even as her fingers slowly unbuttoned her blouse. LA was supposed to have a good S and M scene. One of the best, she'd heard. The thing was, how did she get an intro into that world in the few days she was out there?

Peeling off her tights, she slipped from her briefs, then turned from the mirror, heading for the shower, but before she could get even halfway across the room there was a sudden, furious knocking at the front door.

Cynthia turned, startled. She was expecting no one tonight. 'Who the hell . . . ?'

Crossing the room quickly, she pulled on her black kimono, then hurried out into the passageway. There was a shadow against the glass panel of the front door. She hesitated, then made her way towards it, yet even as she did she heard a strange, small sound from the landing outside.

Peeking through the spy-hole, she looked up in blank surprise.

What was *he* doing here? She had thought he was in Osaka, under several tons of rubble!

Pulling the door open, she stared in astonishment at the sight that met her eyes. Nobushi Fukuada was half slouched against the wall, his normally wall-like face creased in pain, tears pouring down his cheeks.

'Nobushi!' she said, taking his shoulders, shocked by the sight of the devastation in his eyes. 'What is it?'

'Aw gone!' he answered, staring up at her like a bewildered schoolboy. 'Erry-fing gone, Cee-fee-a! Ground shake and Fukuada fucked!'

'Jesus!' she said. Then, knowing she could not leave him out there on the landing, she drew him gently inside and closed the door again.

'Come on,' she said, leading him through into the room where he had been so often before – the room where she had first mentioned to him, even as he had knelt stark naked before her, about the Project – then on through into her bedroom. 'You'll stay with me tonight, Nobushi. You'll be safe here.'

He turned to her, bowing low, his hands pressed together. '*Domo arigato*, Cee-fee-a.' Then, with a sad, sweet smile, he added, 'You good pal. Fukuada not forget.'

As the huge jets of the British Airways 747 roared into life, slowing the jumbo as it hurtled down the tarmac, Chastity heaved a huge sigh of relief. She hated flying, and most of all she hated landing. But now she was down, and safe, and all was well again. For the moment.

She glanced to her right. In the huge bedlike Club World seats beside her, Bob Guppy and Roger Appleyard slept on under their courtesy blankets, half drunk, oblivious of the fact that they had landed in San Francisco.

It was 3.15 p.m. local time, which meant that it was 1.15 in the morning back home. It certainly felt like it.

Looking out through the tiny port-hole window to her left, she could see that it was warm outside, not a cloud in that piercingly blue sky. Back in London it had been raining heavily when they left, the clouds over Heathrow packed like insulation in a loft. But this – *this* was an entirely different world.

For the first time, Chastity felt a real buzz of excitement pass through her. San Francisco! She was actually in San Francisco!

Looking across, she smiled shyly at Cynthia. She was glad Cynthia had come. The thought of being alone with Roger, Bob *and* Brian McTaggart in a strange country had filled her with dread. But thankfully Brian was still on British soil, and Cynthia, she knew, had been to America before. Cynthia knew the ropes.

Leaning across the gangway, she gave Roger a little nudge, speaking to him in a hissing whisper.

'Roger! We're here!'

Roger looked up, startled. 'What's that, Lu?'

Chastity looked away, embarrassed.

'Pleasant dreams?' she murmured.

'What?' Roger said. He looked about him like Rip Van Winkle, then: 'We're here? Already?'

'No,' Cynthia murmured audibly. 'We're in Chicago, arsehole. You and Bob drank the bar dry, so they had to set down to take on new supplies.'

'What?' Roger said again, slurring his words. 'What'd you say?'

Cynthia turned, facing him. 'I said you'd better sober up. Charles's chum is supposed to be meeting us in the airport lobby.'

Roger shuddered. He looked about him, then shook his head. 'Christ!' he said. 'I feel like shit.'

'You look like it, too,' Cynthia said, folding her copy of the *Guardian* and slipping it into her bag. Like Chastity, she had barely touched an alcoholic drink on the way out. 'But don't worry, Mr Finance. Just smile sweetly and I'll do all the talking.'

As if to confirm that this was probably good policy, Bob Guppy took that moment to wake. Snorting like a walrus, he sat bolt upright.

'Special accessories . . .' he said. Then, with a startled look that mimicked Roger's, he added, 'Shit! Are we here already?'

Chastity felt her heart sink. The whole venture was doomed from the outset, and all because these overgrown schoolboys couldn't control themselves.

She looked down, feeling sorry for Charles. Not only had he paid out of his own pocket to keep things running back home, he had signed a personal cheque to cover all their expenses while they were out here in the USA. Over twelve thousand they had budgeted, and Roger and Bob seemed determined to blow it all at the first hurdle.

'Cynthia's right,' she said, in a low voice. 'You really ought to let her do the talking. One whiff of your breath, Rog, and they'll put us back on the plane home, without even so much as a "hello, how are you?"'

Roger turned on her aggressively. 'So you're in charge

now are you, Miss Chastity? Had a promotion I haven't heard about?'

'No, but—'

'But nothing,' Roger said abruptly. 'I'm the most senior member of management here and *I* do the talking, okay?'

Chastity looked past Roger at Cynthia, a weary hopelessness in her eyes, but Cynthia just shrugged and mouthed a single word.

Wanker.

As it happened, Toby Eastman wasn't waiting for them in the airport lobby. Instead, as they came through customs and immigration, pushing luggage trolleys stacked high with suitcases and bags of equipment for the demonstrations, a tall, crop-haired man in a dark suit and wearing sunglasses hailed them from the far side of the barrier. In one hand he held a sign that read 'VIRT-E-GO', in the other a walkie-talkie. He looked, Chastity thought, like a bodyguard, or someone from the CIA.

'Welcome,' he said in a broad Southern States drawl. 'Mr Eastman sends his apologies. He's in a meeting. But if you'd come with me, I'll take you to your hotel. Mr Eastman and his associate will meet you there just as soon as they can.'

Chastity looked to Cynthia and heaved another huge sigh of relief.

'Thanks,' Cynthia said, glaring a warning at Roger. 'It'd be nice to freshen up.'

The 'bodyguard' – he said his name was Manley – escorted them through the airport lounge and out to the pick-up point where, taking up the space of two or three lesser vehicles, a black stretch limo awaited them. As porters loaded their luggage, Chastity, Cynthia, Roger and Bob clambered into the back of the car, feeling a little like four schoolkids in a dentist's waiting room – only this room was opulently furnished, with white kid leather from wall to wall and spotlights set into the ceiling. It was cool, too, the air-conditioning blasting out from discreet vents.

'I need a drink,' Roger began, reaching over to what he clearly assumed was a mobile bar, but Cynthia reached out and unceremoniously slapped his hand away.

'No chance,' she said, narrowing her eyes and glaring at him. 'It's black coffee or nothing. You want to ruin it for us all?'

Roger sat back sulkily. He glared back at Cynthia, but clearly the message had got across.

As Manley slipped into the front passenger seat, he turned and looked back at them through the glass partition that separated them from the front seats.

'Everyone okay?'

Cynthia smiled back at him sweetly. 'We wondered if there was any chance of getting coffee?'

'Just behind you,' Manley said, gesturing towards what Chastity had assumed was a kind of mini-bar. 'Mr Eastman's a regular caffeine addict. Can't get enough of the stuff. And there's me thinking you Brits drank nothing but tea!'

Cynthia opened the compartment. Inside was a large glass pot of freshly brewed coffee, half a dozen muglike cups and cartons of cream and sugar.

'Starbuck's,' Manley said. 'Best coffee on the whole

West Coast. There's milk and sugar there too if you need it.'

'Thanks,' Cynthia said, taking one of the delicate ceramic mugs and pouring a cup. She looked up, meeting Roger's eyes. 'Sugar, Rog?'

San Francisco, Chastity decided, was a sequence of air-conditioned environments separated by short stretches of baking sunlight. No wonder no one walked.

The ride had been the smoothest she could remember, more as if they were gliding along on ice than driving along a road. Not a drop of coffee was spilt, not a single jolt was registered.

As Manley saluted them goodbye in the hotel lobby, Chastity turned to look at her companions. Both Rog and Bob had sobered up considerably, and, though neither looked particularly presentable, they were at least no longer a visible disgrace to Virt-E-Go.

As Cynthia dealt with their bookings, Roger looked about him at their surroundings, a lascivious look waking in his eyes.

'Well, we've really fallen on our feet here, haven't we?' he said, his eyes following the scantily clad form of a young Californian woman.

'We're here to work,' Cynthia said without looking up from where she was signing the registration from. 'And that's what we're going to do.'

She smiled at the receptionist, then turned. 'That is, unless you really want to be a permanent member of the P45 club, Rog?'

He smiled back at her, all of his earlier aggressiveness apparently gone.

'Whatever you say, Cyn. Whatever you say.'

Chastity was in her room, unpacking, when the phone rang. It was Roger.

'You better come and meet us in the lobby. Old Chum Tobe and his backer are waiting for us down there. And don't forget your notepad.'

Chastity put the phone down, then sat on the edge of the bed, a sudden attack of nerves making her feel like running to the loo. What do I wear? What should I say? Should I smile a lot or play it cool?

For a whole minute she sat there, her eyes closed, letting the panic attack wash over her. Then, knowing she had to do something, she stood up, shrugged her way out of her dress and walked through into the shower.

It was no good worrying now. She was here and they were downstairs waiting for her. All she could do was be herself.

She reached out for the tiny bar of soap, and peeled off its cardboard wrapping, then, adjusting the controls so it was not too hot, switched on the shower.

As she came out onto the balcony above the spacious lobby, Chastity could see them on the far side of the massive room, beside the bar. Roger and Bob were sitting together on a long, low sofa, like Tweedledum and Tweedledee, Cynthia to one side of them in a single armchair. Facing the three, seated on a matching sofa to Bob and Roger's, were Toby Eastman and his backer.

Chastity raised an eyebrow, surprised. Their prospective backer was a woman.

She made her way down, crossing the lobby slowly,

uncertainty rising in her by the moment. It was only when she was eight or ten feet away that Roger noticed her.

'Ah, talk of the devil, here she is right now! Toby, Kirsty, meet Chastity.'

Chastity turned to face their hosts as both Toby Eastman and the mystery woman rose from their chairs to greet her.

Toby was a plumpish, slightly balding man in his mid-twenties. Surprisingly he was wearing cricket flannels and a flamboyantly coloured waistcoat. But it was his companion to whom Chastity's eyes were drawn.

'Hello,' Toby said, shaking her hand. 'It's very nice to meet you, Chastity. Charles has told me a great deal about you. And this is Kirsty. Kirsty McDonald, President of Ubik Inc.'

Kirsty McDonald was a tall, elegant-looking woman with neat-cut blonde hair. She looked, if anything, Scandinavian, but her clothes were most definitely American. The light-blue suit she wore, while feminine enough, was cut in a way that gave her an almost battle-hardened appearance, as if years of vying with men in the office – of mimicking men's manners and fashions – had resulted in this look, this hybrid of business suit and fuck-me frock. Her face and arms were tanned, as was what was visible of her narrow, almost flat chest, and her eyes were a quite startling blue. When she smiled she showed a perfect set of capped teeth.

'Chastity,' she said, taking Chastity's hand lingeringly. 'What a delightful name. And what a delightful dress.'

Chastity looked down at herself. She had worn the simplest thing she'd packed – a short, sleeveless dress of deep blue.

She blushed, finding the warmth of Kirsty's hand holding her own just the slightest bit disconcerting.

'Thanks,' she murmured softly.

'And that accent!' Kirsty exclaimed, her smile widening. 'Why, it's a peach! Is that cock-e-ney?'

'Cockney,' Toby corrected her, taking his seat.

'Of course,' Kirsty said, winking at him. Then, gesturing to Toby that he should move up, she put a hand out. 'There, Chastity. You sit between Toby and me, while we talk about what we've got planned.'

An hour later they were back in the stretch limo, Kirsty and Toby sitting across from them as they headed south down the Interstate towards Santa Clara and the legendary Silicon Valley.

Roger, who had briefly come alive in the hotel lobby, had now resumed his former comatose state and sat slumped by the window, to the right of Bob Guppy, his eyes closed, his mouth fallen open.

Guppy, though equally tired, had the look of someone who has just come from a serious session of aerobics, he was sweating so much. But it wasn't exercise that had made Bob Guppy sweat, it was the news – cheerfully announced by Kirsty even as they got up from their seats in the lobby – that they could make their presentation that very afternoon and not, as previously arranged, the day after their arrival. Cynthia had tried to protest, but – short of packing up and flying home without a presentation of any kind – it seemed they had no option.

'It's the only window, I'm afraid,' Kirsty said, smiling her broad gleamingly white smile. 'I want my key men to see what you've got, and it's the only time I can get

all five of them there in the same room at the same time.
You know how it is.'

Cynthia did indeed know how it was. They were being
steamrollered. But she merely smiled and shrugged, and
sent Bob back up to his rooms to bring down the travel
cases containing the material for the presentation.

As they drove, Toby gave them an account of who
was currently who in the Valley, ending with a brief
overview of Ubik itself. Kirsty, owner and President of
Ubik, seemed content to listen, nodding from time to time,
as if in confirmation, but it was noticeable that her eyes
rarely left Chastity.

Chastity, for her part, was unaware of the older
woman's attention as she stared out of the window,
mesmerised by the view of the Bay.

It was a crisp clear day, and in its light, the drive
down through Palo Alto and Sunnyvale seemed strangely
dreamlike. Part of that, she knew, was to do with the
fact that, in her head, she was eight hours adrift and
severely jet-lagged, but also it was to do with the exotic
strangeness of the setting. It was as if they had been
suddenly transported to the Mediterranean, there were so
many palm trees. England seemed a million miles away.

Ubik Enterprises proved to be a big complex of white
stucco buildings, none of them taller than three storeys.
Black-glass windows gave them a look of anonymity
which reminded Chastity of various American cop movies
she'd seen over the years. It was the kind of place where
they'd have the final shoot-out. A place full of hidden
secrets and ultimate revelations. But inside it was all
open-plan and airy and there were lots of tropical plants
everywhere and even little fountains, so that Chastity

found herself changing her first impressions. It seemed a pleasant place to work, after all.

Toby led them through into a central conference chamber – a huge room three or four times the size of their own labs back in London – while Kirsty went off to round up her 'boys'. As Bob nervously unpacked the presentation material, Chastity looked about her, then wandered over to where Toby lounged against the wall.

'How long have you known Charles, Toby?'

Toby grinned. 'Oh, Charles and I go back a long, long way. We were at prep together.'

'Prep?'

'Preparatory school. Junior public school, if you like. We both joined the same day. Five, we must have been. I hated the little bugger at first. He was always so goody-goody. And then – oh, when I was nine or ten and we were playing rugger together – I realised that he was actually rather nice. All that goody-goody stuff wasn't some kind of strategy for coping with life, it was just how Charles *was*.' Toby laughed. 'I guess we've been friends ever since.'

Chastity looked away a moment, thoughtfully, then looked back at Toby and smiled. 'He *is* nice, isn't he?'

Clearing his throat, Bob Guppy began the presentation. On the desk beside him were his handwritten notes, on the easel behind him the diagrans Chastity had had made up from Bill and Ben's design. Kirsty had offered Bob the use of the overhead viewer, but, seeing how Bob had stared back at her blankly, she had let him get on with it.

She sat now amidst her 'boys', as Guppy stumbled through his introductory words, her head tilted back slightly, her chin raised, not unlike a rather severe headmistress awaiting some kind of explanation for bad behaviour in one of her pupils.

Her 'boys' were a motley crew, or so Chastity felt, looking on. If she hadn't been told these were Ubik's top computer researchers she would never have guessed, for they looked like ordinary workmen in their faded jeans and lumber-jack-style shirts. And they were also so . . . *big*. She had expected something along the lines of Bill and Ben — nervous, weedy types with bizarre senses of humour — but these five seemed simply dull. Introduced to their British guests, they had merely grunted, ignoring Roger's and Bob's outstretched hands, as if a welcoming handshake was something one did on another planet.

Poor old Bob Guppy — who would have been nervous even in the best of circumstances — was thus at his trembling, stuttering worst as, with the courage of a dying man, he began to detail the intricacies of Virt-E-Go's revolutionary machine.

'. . . b-but unlike other machines on the market which, er, simulate a s-s-simple activity, our, ahem, machine is designed to—'

Bob Guppy stopped dead, staring at his notes blankly. He turned the page, and his eyes widened. It was clear to everyone that he had either lost his place or lost a page — and as he looked up again he had the look of a startled cat the moment before the car hits.

'What my colleague is trying to say,' Cynthia stepped in suavely, standing and walking around the desk to place herself beside the dumbstruck Guppy who was now busily searching his notes, 'is that we have decided to go for a more complex response to the question of sex simulation.'

'Meaning precisely *what*?' Kirsty McDonald asked, her expression no indication of what she was thinking at that moment.

'Meaning,' Bob Guppy said gamely, before Cynthia could speak again, 'that we are moving away from the typical glove-and-helmet solution.'

Looking to Chastity and Roger, he gave a big grin.

'I see . . .' Kirsty nodded thoughtfully, then, leaning forward a little, fixed Bob Guppy in her keen gaze. 'So, Bob . . . what about the problem of proprioception?'

Guppy swallowed. A new sheen of sweat appeared on his well-mopped brow. He looked to Cynthia. 'I think my colleague here can answer that,' he said, praying that she, at least, knew what the hell the woman was talking about.

Fortunately, Cynthia seemed to have things in hand.

'We don't think proprioception *is* a problem,' she answered, leaning toward Kirsty aggressively. 'Indeed, with our system, it's a great big plus.'

'How do you mean?'

'I mean that, mimicking the inner machinery of the human body, our machine will have its own system of internal sensors to detect changes of pressure, movement and so on. It will even register subtle changes of temperature – an important factor when you're dealing with something as . . . *atmospheric* as sex.'

Kirsty's eyes widened as if she understood. 'You're talking about a suit, I take it?'

'Not as such. More like a sheath.'

'So what's the difference?'

'The problem with body-suits,' Cynthia said know-ingly, 'is that you need two to tango. What we intend is to create the ultimate solipsistic play-tool.'

'A masturbator?'

Cynthia shook her head. 'That's too narrow a term for it. It focuses things too much on the sex organs. No, what we're building is a full-body experience. Our machine doesn't just jerk you off, it makes love to you!'

Kirsty shook her head. 'My people tell me that's a good five years off.'

Cynthia met her eyes provocatively. 'Maybe it is – *here*. But we already have it. Or will have, given the funding.'

'Why should I believe you?'

'Come and see,' Cynthia said, a half-smile forming on her lips. 'Seeing is believing, as they say.'

'Maybe I will,' Kirsty answered. 'But first I wanna know a hell of a lot more about this machine of yours.'

In the car on the way back, Bob Guppy unfastened his top shirt button and loosened his tie, heaving a massive sigh of relief.

'Thank Christ that's over!'

'Yes,' Chastity said, watching from the seat opposite. 'And thank God for Cynthia, eh?'

'Oh, Bob was okay,' Roger said, smiling at her. 'But it's all down to you now, eh, my beauty?'

Chastity looked down, embarrassed by his familiarity and a touch irritated by the way he was looking at her. 'It's only dinner,' she said quietly.

'Right,' Roger said, unmeasured depths of irony evident in that single word.

'I think she's rather canny, actually,' Cynthia said, staring out of the window.

'Canny?' Guppy looked bemused.

'Yes. Getting us out here straight away. Putting us under pressure like she did. It was a test.'

'A test?' Roger huffed. 'What bloody nonsense!'

'No,' Chastity said, nodding in agreement. 'I know what Cyn means. It's like she was seeing if we were worth investing in.'

'Not just that,' Cynthia continued, 'but also whether we could *cope* with the pressure. We need her more than she needs us, and she knows it. That's why she played it like she did. Taking the whip hand from the outset.'

'Nonsense!' Roger said again. 'It's like she said. She wanted all her best men in on it, that's all.'

'Then she would have had us fly in a day earlier than we did, wouldn't she?' Cynthia said emphatically. 'And inviting Chastity out to dinner tonight is part of it, too. Don't you see?'

'Oh, I *see* all right,' Roger said, a touch unpleasantly.

'No, you miss the point. By getting one of us on our own – from her viewpoint, and no offence intended Chastity, the group member with the least corporate muscle – she hopes to find out a little more than she would through simple presentations.'

Chastity frowned. 'D'you think I should't go, then?'

'No,' Cynthia answered, reaching across and patting her arm. 'I think you're the perfect one to go. Just take care what you say, that's all. And don't drink too much.'

'And don't let Dame Kirsty get her hands in your knickers!' Roger said, grinning lasciviously.

Cynthia glared at him, then returned her attention to Chastity. 'Just be natural with her, Chastity. You know how good Bill and Ben are at what they do, and I think you've a fair idea just how good our machine is going to be, so just tell her that. It's all a matter of confidence.'

'Ask Bob here,' Roger said, continuing to snipe.

'Why don't you just button it, Rog,' Cynthia said, turning on him. 'If this fails, then we'll know whose big mouth we'll have to thank for it.'

'Now hold on . . .'

But even as things threatened to boil over into a full-blooded row, Bob Guppy let out a long, low fart.

'Oh, Christ, I'm sorry . . .'

There was a moment's silence and then exclamations of disgust.

'Jesus, Bob, what the fuck have you been eating!'

Even Cynthia was laughing now. 'Whatever it was, it was well dead even before he put it through his digestive tract!'

And all four of them began to giggle helplessly, the tension and tiredness each of them felt dissolving into laughter.

Manley, the bodyguard, glancing back through the glass from his seat in the front of the limo, frowned to himself and thought how strange these Brits were — at one another's throats one moment, and the next doubled up with laughter. Maybe they were all on drugs or something.

Turning back to face the freeway, he gave a little shake of his head, wondering which of them he'd be driving back to the hotel later on that night. His mistress was a strange one, too, and who knew which way the wind blew with her? As for himself, he'd take the young one any day. Charity? Was that her name? For a moment he closed his eyes, picturing her with nothing on, imagining her going down on him. Then, a faint smile on his lips, he glanced across at the driver and winked.

'Twenty it's the young girl.'

The driver, Carlos, considered that a moment, then gave the slightest shake of his head. 'Fifty it's the dyke.'

'The dyke?'

Manley looked up at the mirror, studying Cynthia briefly.

'You sure?'

Carlos turned to look at him and nodded once, a faint smile on his lips, before resuming his fixed stare on the Interstate. 'Trust Carlos. He knows these things.'

'Then make it twenty, Carlos. I've bills to pay.'

Chastity blew lightly across the white frothy bathwater, sending a spray of bubbles skimming over the surface into obliteration. Warm water gently lapped against her chin as she sank further into the deep warmth of the scented water, strands of her dark hair floating about her face like tangled weeds.

It had been a long day and all she wanted to do was sleep, but with jet lag threatening to overcome her, she knew that if she closed her eyes now she wouldn't wake up for hours. Lifting her hands from the water, she shook the clinging bubbles from her wet fingers before rubbing at her tired eyes.

The sudden knock at the outer door was irritating

but timely as Chastity began to drift once again towards sleep's welcoming embrace. Reluctantly, she raised herself and stepped out of the bath. Reaching across, she grabbed a thick white towel from the rack and wrapped it around her, fixing it above her bust like a sarong. A second, more insistent tap sent her scurrying out into the bedroom and across the thick-pile carpet, the dark imprint of her wet feet forming a telltale trail to the door.

Opening it a few inches, she peeped round, to see Roger Appleyard smiling in at her.

'Can I come in?'

'I was in the bath,' she said. 'What's up?'

'Nothing's up,' he said, smiling, unable to prevent his gaze from lingering on the bare wet flesh above and below the edges of the towel. 'It's just that I thought we should talk before you meet up with Kirsty this evening. You know, tactics.'

'Well, I *am* a bit worried . . .' Chastity began.

Requiring no further encouragement, Roger exerted a gentle pressure on the door so that as it moved backwards he slipped through, pushing it closed behind him.

Walking across to stand by the end of the enormous double bed, he looked back at Chastity with barely concealed lust. Self-consciously she hitched up the towel so that it was almost wrapped about her neck.

'I'll just go and put a dressing gown on,' she said, making her way over to the bathroom.

'Don't bother on my account,' Roger called after her, a false joviality to his voice, but from where he stood he could not see the look of utter revulsion on the young woman's face as she sank her teeth into the polythene bag containing the hotel bathrobe, ripping it apart like an animal tearing at its prey. She put on the oversized garment, pulled the belt tightly about her tiny waist and tied it in a double knot.

Roger was sitting on the bed when Chastity returned. Ignoring his hopeful smile and his hand patting the space beside him, Chastity walked over to one of the twin armchairs by the window and sat, carefully crossing her legs and folding the hem of the bathrobe across her bare knees.

'So!' Roger exclaimed, walking across to sit in the chair opposite. 'What exactly is it that you're worried about?'

Chastity shrugged. 'Well, it's just that I'm not used to this kind of thing. I mean, it's not really my place to be talking to this Kirsty woman, is it? It's you and Bob who should be chatting her up, not me. I'm *bound* to say all the wrong things.'

'Listen! Just agree with everything she says. Keep telling her how wonderful the machine is, and sound confident. As long as you *sound* as though you know what you're talking about, you'll be fine. Look at Bob!' And with that Roger leaned across and gave Chastity a reassuring pat on the knee.

'Anyway,' he said, his voice a little huskier than before, 'she's obviously taken a bit of a shine to you. And who can blame her?'

The movement of her knee was so abrupt that, when Roger's hand lost its means of support, he only just prevented himself from toppling to the floor.

Recovering his composure, he leaned back in the chair, his arms dangling casually over the sides.

'How about fixing us a drink, then? A bit of Dutch courage.'

Reluctantly, Chastity rose to her feet and made her way out to the tiny kitchenette around the corner where the contents of the mini-bar remained untouched.

'Mine's a Scotch and soda,' he called after her.

Having fixed Roger's drink, Chastity poured herself a diet Coke. 'You having dinner with Bob tonight?' she called, crouching down to tick the boxes on the mini-bar list before she dropped the empty bottles in the waste bin.

There was no reply.

As Chastity walked back through, she repeated the question, her voice trailing away as she realised that Roger was not where she had left him. The chair where he had been sitting was empty; so too, thankfully, was the bed.

'Roger?' she called. 'Roger?'

Receiving no response, her first instinct was to check behind the curtains, but the only thing hidden by the drapes was the ugly Interstate three floors below. Chastity felt suddenly rather foolish. Turning her attention from the room, she called his name a third time, then walked over to the bathroom where the door stood ajar. As she cautiously pushed it open, her jaw dropped. She found herself looking down at Roger Appleyard's hairy torso rising from a drift of deflated bath bubbles that only minutes before had caressed her own young body.

'Why don't you come and join me?' he offered. 'There's plenty of room,' and with that his knees rose through the froth like the giant humps of some great sea monster and he spread them wide so that each leg rested against the side of the bath.

Chastity was barely conscious of what he said. She

was fighting to come to terms with the shock of finding Roger in his birthday suit. She had known about him and Louise, of course, and was aware that he was a bit of a lech – even so, this little trick left her well and truly gob smacked.

'Come on,' he coaxed. 'You know I fancy you something rotten.'

In spite of herself Chastity couldn't help noticing the pink funnel-shaped object between his legs that had floated towards the surface like a rubber periscope, and with the mesmerised fascination of an innocent child she could not avert her eyes from that peculiar object as it swayed from side to side.

Roger followed her astonished gaze with a great beam of pride, silently willing his manhood to break the surface like a triumphant submarine searching for a place to dock.

'Come on, sweetheart. Don't be shy.'

The sound of Roger's voice broke into Chastity's consciousness so that suddenly she was brought back to reality, the look of bewilderment that had distorted her features turning to out-and-out anger as she contemplated the arrogance and sheer presumptuousness of the man.

The stupid expression he wore infuriated her. It made her want to go across and slap it off his face. She watched him a moment as he all but swaggered in the bath, her eyes following the dark line of curls that formed a kite shape across his chest and disappeared into the watery depths. And, bobbing just beneath the surface, Roger's penis lurked like a predatory shark.

Pushing the sleeves of her robe up above her elbows,

Chastity slowly walked towards him, a curious, unfathomable look on her face. Roger's smile broadened as she knelt down on the floor beside him, his eyes closing as her slender white fingers reached into the well of water between his legs.

Yanking the chain as hard as she could, she drew the plug out of its hole, the hard circle of plastic threatening to do Roger some serious damage as Chastity pulled it up between his thighs. But even as Roger cried out in pain, Chastity was halfway out the door, rolling down her sleeves as she went.

'You should be ashamed of your bleedin' self, Roger Appleyard! I've a good mind to tell your wife what a little shit you are!'

'You wouldn't be the first, sweetheart,' he croaked, nursing his injured manhood as he watched her walk through into the bedroom.

Huh! Women! he thought. They're all the bloody same. Play hard to get when all the while they're gagging for it. Yet even as he ran damp fingers through his dishevelled hair in preparation for his second – and, he was convinced, successful – assault, he heard the sound of the outer door being slammed shut.

'Chastity? Chastity are you there?'

But this time it was *his* voice that echoed through into an empty room.

As the white stretch limo pulled up at the sidewalk, Chastity peered out through tinted glass at the understated elegance of the restaurant. Everything she had seen so far in this city had been big and brash and overwhelming, so that the restrained minimalism of the building's façade came as a welcome surprise. Before the car had even stopped a doorman stepped forward and took hold of the handle, and, as the handbrake was applied, pulled open the door, inviting her out onto the narrow sidewalk. Walking across the car's interior with as many strides as it took to cross her bedroom floor back home, Chastity finally reached the open door and carefully stepped out. Almost immediately the car glided out into the stream of traffic and was gone, leaving Chastity stranded like an orphan.

The doorman smiled kindly as she caught his eye, but feeling foolish and conspicuous she quickly looked away, anxiously glancing up and down the sidewalk.

The doorman chanced another sideways glance before speaking. ''Scuse me, ma'am, but you're not from around here are you?' Chastity shook her head. 'Thought not,' he said triumphantly, his mouth spreading into a broad smile that showed off a perfect set of large white teeth that gleamed against his black skin.

'I'm from London,' she muttered apologetically. 'England.' And to his foreign ear the unfamiliar accent took on the sound of British royalty.

'Well, if you're waiting for someone, ma'am, they sure won't be coming along the sidewalk.'

Chastity looked first one way and then the other along the empty streets.

'It'll be by car, ma'am. Or cab.' Chastity nodded and forced a smile. 'Perhaps you'd be better waiting for your friend inside?' he said, flourishing a white-gloved hand towards the building behind them.

Chastity turned to look through the restaurant's glass-panelled doors. Beneath the subtle glow of the lights the women looked glamorous and the men overconfident, and she inwardly groaned. She was not aware of the limousine as it purred to a halt at the curb, nor of Kirsty McDonald stepping self-assuredly from the gleaming black car to stand behind her.

'Hi,' she breathed huskily into Chastity's ear, making her jump.

'Hi,' Chastity responded quickly, taking a step back as she turned to face the woman.

Kirsty McDonald towered above Chastity, her elegance accentuated by a simple but obviously expensive black silk cocktail dress. Her hair looked different from the way she had worn it earlier, the style less formal, more casual, to befit the occasion.

'You just got here?' Kirsty said, her broad smile almost splitting her face. Chastity nodded, aware of the doorman standing in mute attendance behind her. 'Good!' the older woman said, placing a hand on Chastity's arm and guiding her towards the door of the restaurant. 'Then let's go eat.'

The women had been seated at a table in a secluded corner of the busy restaurant and lavished with the kind of attention afforded those wealthy, regular clientele oblivious to its exorbitant prices. A half-empty glass was automatically filled, a half-gesture immediately acknowledged so that throughout the meal the two women had their every need unobtrusively but effectively catered for. Or almost.

Chastity looked up at Kirsty McDonald through wide green eyes. Much had been said throughout the meal, but there was one thing that had not, until now, been said — only implied. Something that even Chastity, in her naivety, could not help noticing. Biting her bottom lip now, she inhaled deeply through her nose before she spoke.

'I should tell you. I don't sleep with women.'

The moment the words left her lips, Chastity was filled with a feeling of dread. It had had to be said; she had had to say it. But she knew that this could signal Virt-E-Go's failure to secure the financial backing they so desperately needed, and the responsibility weighed heavy on her.

Kirsty sat back in her chair but did not remove her foot from where it rested beside Chastity's beneath the table. She looked across at her a moment, openly appreciative of the younger woman's physical beauty.

Chastity blushed, adding quickly, 'Not that I sleep with men, either.'

Kirsty laughed loudly. 'At least we have that in common,' she said, reaching across for her glass. Holding it to her lips she scrutinised Chastity a moment longer before sipping at the chilled wine.

'So you don't sleep with women and you don't sleep with men. You're not seriously trying to tell me that you're a virgin?'

Chastity looked down into her hands, embarrassed by the woman's bluntness.

'You *are*! How *sweet*!' Kirsty exclaimed, unable to hide her genuine amazement.

'You needn't sound *so* surprised,' Chastity responded sharply, angry at being made to feel so defensive. 'Not *everyone* sleeps around, y'know.'

'I guess not,' Kirsty answered, seemingly unaware of the personal slight and slowly shaking her head in continued bemusement. 'But it sure beats me how you've managed it, honey. And what a waste!'

Chastity forced herself to meet the other's eyes. 'This won't affect your funding our project, will it? I mean, you won't turn us down just because of . . .'

Kirsty sighed deeply, on her face an unmistakable look of regret at missing out on this rare opportunity, her eyes barely able to conceal both her lust and her disappointment.

'I guess what you're asking is whether I'm prepared to buy the cake if it hasn't got a cherry on the top?'

Chastity was conscious of Kirsty's foot edging away.

'I never let pleasure – or lack of it – get in the way of business. If we'd gotten it on, that would've been cool, but hey, it's not the end of the world. You're cute but you're not *that* cute that I'd miss out on a good deal.' Kirsty leaned forward and reached across the table, placing her hand over Chastity's. 'Honey, you just keep that little cherry of yours till you find the right guy, and I tell you, you're just gonna knock his socks off, the lucky mother!' She let out a hearty laugh and Chastity managed to force a grateful smile in return.

'Okay!' Kirsty said, signalling for the waiter to bring them another bottle of wine. 'So tell me about this sex machine of yours.'

At the sight of Chastity stepping into a section of the hotel's huge revolving doors, Bob Guppy jumped to his feet with the air of an anxious father awaiting his daughter's return from a date.

Rushing across he grabbed hold of Chastity's arm and unceremoniously marched her over to the Starlight Bar, where Roger sat at a table nursing a tumbler of Scotch. Seating her between the two of them, Bob Guppy leaned forward so that she could feel the specks of saliva that sprang from his lips as he spoke.

'*Well*?'

'Well what?' Chastity teased, leaning back in her chair, avoiding eye contact with Roger.

'Don't play silly buggers, Chastity. What happened?'

'Do you mean is she interested in funding the project?'

'Yes, yes, of course I bloody well do!' Bob said irritably, almost beside himself in his anxiety so that his eyes seemed to bulge in his head.

Chastity's mouth broke into a broad smile that seemed to light up her face.

'We got a deal. Twenty million dollars.'

'Twenty . . .' Bob's mouth fell open. 'What? No co-backer?' Chastity's smile remained fixed. 'You mean she's coming up with the full quota? The full twenty million?' Bob could barely contain his growing excitement.

Chastity nodded. 'She *loves* the idea.'

Bob Guppy jumped to his feet and, taking her face between his hands, kissed Chastity full on the lips. 'You little beauty!' he shouted, so that the other late-night drinkers looked around with vague curiosity. 'You bloody little beauty!'

The kiss had been filled with such gratitude, was so sexless, that Chastity could not take offence, and indeed took a great deal of pleasure in bringing such happiness to a fellow human being, even if it *was* Bob Guppy.

'Why don't you order some champagne?' Roger said, his voice showing none of the excitement of his colleague.

'And get Cynthia down here, while you're at it. We could do with a *real* woman to talk to.'

Too excited for Roger's comment to register, Bob smacked his hands together loudly and made his way to the telephone, calling over his shoulder as he did, 'Right! Champagne it is!'

As soon as Bob was out of earshot, Roger leaned across to Chastity. 'So what did she want in return for signing on the dotted line?'

'Nothing,' Chastity replied, staring across the room.

'Huh! Don't give me that! The woman's a bloody dyke! Why else d'you think she invited *you* out? All she wanted was to get inside your knickers!'

'Well, she wasn't the only one, was she?'

'So, go on, tell me. What did the two of you get up to? What did she *do* to you?'

'You're drunk, Roger,' she said, willing Bob Guppy to come back and rescue her.

'Too bloody right I am,' he slurred. 'But I wanna know. Did she kiss you? Did she push her tongue in your mouth?'

Chastity looked hopefully towards the lift for sign of Cynthia.

'Come on you little prick-teaser, tell me. I know! I bet you let her fondle your tits.' And with that he lurched over and grabbed awkwardly at Chastity's breast so that she squealed out in pain and surprise.

Before Roger knew what had hit him, the remainder of his Scotch splashed over his contorted face and Chastity stood over him with the menace of a soccer hooligan.

'Be honest, Rog. All you wanna know is if she had more success than you. Well she didn't. But I tell you

226

this much, given the choice I know which one I'd go for, and it wouldn't be a balding, paunchy old git who kept his brains in his trousers!'

Returning to the table, Bob Guppy just caught sight of Chastity's retreating back as she entered the lift and the doors closed behind her.

'Where's she off to?' he said, dropping down into his seat. 'Gone to freshen up or something?'

'Bloody women!' Roger hissed, wiping his handkerchief across his face. 'She's not feeling well. PMT or something.'

Bob nodded slowly, his brow furrowed in concentration as he fought to piece together the jigsaw.

'Where's Cynthia?' Roger demanded, like a disgruntled customer whose meal has not yet been served.

'No answer from her room. She must be asleep.'

'Just my fucking luck,' Roger mumbled.

'What?'

'Never mind. Forget the fucking champagne. Let's get out of here. I need a shag.'

Walking through from her luxurious kitchen into the airy opulence of her penthouse living room, Kirsty McDonald carried two chunky tumblers full of Scotch. The thin black stilettoes she wore dragged on the thick-pile carpet as she made her way across to the huge white sofa, setting the drinks down on the glass-topped table in front of her. The black rubber bodysuit she wore squeaked against the sofa's leather surface as she relaxed into its embrace, lifting her legs to stretch down its length.

Reaching up, she took the zip between thumb and forefinger and slowly slid it down to her waist, the whiteness of her breasts emerging in stark contrast to the dark synthetic garment encasing them. Stretching across, she lifted one of the glasses and held it to her lips, sipping at the amber liquid and wincing as it burned at the back of her throat. Returning the glass to the table, she turned on her side, allowing her breasts to fall from her suit provocatively.

As she leaned forward, she dipped a finger into the cooled Scotch, slowly circling it beneath the surface like a cocktail stirrer. Then, removing it, she reached beneath the tabletop, the liquid trickling slowly between her fingers and into the palm of her hand.

'Here,' she whispered, 'taste this,' and she pushed her finger between a pair of parted lips.

Kirsty felt the warm softness of the mouth close over her finger of moistened flesh and gently groaned. Through the sheet of glass she watched the young woman's naked body growing restless with arousal. The woman was resting on all fours, her back supporting the glass tabletop, and her breasts hung invitingly towards the floor. Kirsty slowly pulled her fingers away from the girl's mouth and ran them down the length of her neck to caress the softness of her breast with such painful, unbearable delicacy that the drinks rattled precariously on the glass surface and spilled onto the floor. Taking hold of an erect nipple between her thumb and forefinger, Kirsty squeezed until the woman cried out in painful ecstasy, the glass slipping from her back onto the thick carpet. She pushed it aside.

Slipping onto the floor beside her and wrapping her legs around the woman's naked body, Kirsty took her face between her hands, her breathing heavy as she pulled the girl's mouth over her own hardened nipple. Then she released her momentarily, and fought to free herself from the rubber garment, her words barely audible as she groaned her instructions.

'The whip, Cynthia. Get the whip.'

Charles stared out of his study window across the rainsoaked grounds that opened out before his view, listening with vague interest to the test match report on the radio. The long lawn, laid in his great-grandfather's time, stretched down to the river, but right now its well-kept green disappeared into the drizzling mist that clung to the ground and swallowed up the surrounding woods.

His horse, Jester, had gone lame the day before, missing his footing on the slippery hillside, and was now resting in the stables. Charles had been down to check on him earlier but even a gentle exercise was out of the question for at least a day or two.

Turning back to the room, he aimlessly wandered over to his desk, on which the fax machine stood in silent idleness. As he depressed the red button the machine switched off, and he pushed it once again to reinstate the power, tapping the top of it absent-mindedly with his fingertips. Slumping into his chair he looked over at the telephone, willing it to ring, desperate for a diversion from this hopeless, endless pining.

He had had two whole days to dwell on what a complete hash he had made of things, how he'd managed to bungle a heaven-sent opportunity to spend a couple of days away with Chastity. When they had originally chosen who would fly off to the States, he had made some excuse as to why he shouldn't go. He'd felt rather proud of himself for engineering it so that, with Patricia out of the way, he could enlist Chastity as her temporary replacement. But by the time Patricia dropped the bombshell that she did not fly – full stop – and had therefore asked Chastity to go to the States in her place, it was impossible for him to include himself amongst the team without making it perfectly obvious why he'd had a change of heart.

Charles reached over and lifted the solitary sheet of fax paper from his in-tray, stroking it between his finger and thumb as he held it up to read the short message for the twentieth time.

After the initial hiccup of the presentation, everything had gone well and things were now looking immensely promising. But the fate of their little expedition wasn't the reason why Charles now stared with loving intensity at the paper. The fax had been signed by Chastity, her flamboyant signature scrawled across the width of the page, and, tucked beneath the tail of the final letter, was a single cross. A kiss. Charles held the paper to his lips, oblivious to its foul odour, and kissed the spot where hours before she had placed this sign, this secret message to him.

The sudden noise of the study door being pushed open and banging against the wood-panelled wall surprised Charles, catching him unawares so that, in his haste to destroy the evidence of his hopeless infatuation, he shoved the piece of paper in his mouth and was only saved from swallowing it whole by the onset of a coughing fit which sent the crumpled ball shooting across the room like a giant pea from a pea shooter. As he spluttered into his hand, Davina strode across the room, her Labrador

puppy yapping at her heels, and impatiently slapped
Charles hard between the shoulder blades.

Fearing a second blow, Charles held up his hand and
fought to suppress further coughing fits. He found himself
speaking in short sharp spurts as he tried, with partial
success, to regain his breath.

'I say, Dee . . . Steady on . . . Be fine in a minute . . .'

'Oh do stop fooling around, Charlie,' she barked,
walking back to close the door before placing her back
against it. She looked across at Charles, a hint of a smile
playing on her lips.

'I've something very important to tell you,' she said,
dropping her eyelids in a failed attempt at coyness.

Charles nodded furiously, his chest expanding with
air as his lips remained firmly closed. At that moment
the puppy jumped up against his leg. Surprised, Charles
tapped it away with his toe, sending the ball of black
fur tumbling across the rug.

Davina seemed hardly to notice. Breathing deeply
through her nostrils, she filled her lungs before making
the surprise announcement. 'Charles, I'm pregnant.'

Involuntarily, Charles's mouth sprang open as his
jaw dropped, and the final resounding splutter made
its escape, forcing him to spend a full minute regaining
his composure.

'Bloody hell, Dee!' he said finally, walking across and
placing a protective arm around her broad shoulders.
'Come and sit down.'

Ushering her across to his chair, he sat on the edge
of the desk looking down on her, at a loss for what to
say.

'You're not cross then, Charlie?'

Charles gave a brief, jolly laugh. 'Cross? Why should I be cross?'

'Well, you know,' she said. 'Parents and all that.'

'I'm sure they'll be fine, Dee. They'll rally round, you'll see.'

Davina smiled up at Charles gratefully and in a way he was not used to so that suddenly he felt a pang of guilt at the immediate feeling of relief he had experienced at the first mention of Davina's unfortunate predicament.

'Now listen, Davina . . .' Charles hesitated. 'Do tell me if I'm overstepping the mark, won't you, old thing?' Again, he stopped, then, bracing himself, asked the unavoidable. 'I guess what I'm really trying to ask you, Dee, is . . . well, do you know who the father is?'

Davina's face clouded a moment, like someone trying to work out the punchline of a joke.

'You're not serious?' she said hopefully.

Charles held up his hand. 'Now if you don't want to tell me, that's perfectly all right. That's your prerogative. All I'm thinking about – and I know your pa will share my concern – is that this chap lives up to his responsibilities. I mean . . .'

Davina was no longer listening. She glared up at him. 'It's you, you bloody great chump!'

'Beg pardon?' Charles responded, not sure he had heard her correctly.

'It's *you*! You're the bloody father, God help me! Who else did you think it could be?'

Charles's brow furrowed in concentration as he ploughed the depths of his memory.

'But I *can't* be,' he protested finally, flushing a bright

scarlet. 'I mean we've never, you know . . . never actually . . . *done* it, have we?'

'Oh, Charlie!' she wailed, rising threateningly to her feet. 'How can you say that? It was the most passionate night of my life!'

Once again the muscles in Charles's cheeks chewed his face up so that his eyes narrowed in consternation. Walking across the room, he mentally turned the pages of his diary in what he knew to be the hopeless task of coming upon an occasion that might, just might — even loosely — have warranted such a description.

'But when *was* this, Davina?'

Davina puffed out her fleshy cheeks in exasperation, allowing the air to escape noisily as she followed him across the room.

'The night those people from your office stayed over. The tart and that odious little man, Guppy.'

Knowing with painful certainty that he would be bound to recall that particular occasion, Davina felt there was hardly any need for further clarification. However, looking upon Charles's vacant expression, she decided upon one last, conclusive detail.

'You came to my room when everyone else had gone to bed and made love to me all night long. Don't you remember?' Feeling suddenly aroused by the memory of their relentless lovemaking, she stretched up to whisper in Charles's ear, despite there being nobody else around to hear what she had to say.

'You were a *very* naughty boy, Charlie,' she breathed. 'The way you wanted to do it doggie fashion.'

Charles pulled away as though someone had just yelled at him point-blank through a loud hailer, the total lack of comprehension on his face giving him the appearance of an imbecile.

'But I *didn't* go to your room that night.'

A muscle in Davina's cheek twitched visibly. 'What are you talking about, Charles? Of *course* you did. Do you really think I'd let anyone else do all of those things to me?'

'Davina, I can assure you that I went straight to my room and went to bed alone.'

'Charlie! How can you say that?' she screeched.

He turned to her, jutting out his chin determinedly. 'I'm sorry, Dee, but it's the truth.'

'You bastard!' she wailed, striding towards him with her fist raised in the air. 'You're just saying that to get out of your responsibilities!'

Catching hold of Davina's wrist, Charles quickly reached down to take hold of her other arm lest she launch an attack from the other side.

'But what would be the point?' he asked, struggling to hold on to the lethal weapons. 'If it *were* my baby you'd be able to prove it easily enough, what with these newfangled blood tests and all the rest.'

Slowly the tension eased from Davina's hands as, reluctantly, she accepted the logic of his argument.

'Well, if it wasn't you . . .'

The full horror of it struck Davina in an instant. Falling onto her hands and knees, she began to wretch all over the antique Persian rug. As she looked up again, her eyes were two saucers of unutterable misery.

'Guppy!' she wailed. 'Oh my God! I spent the night with Guppy!'

* * *

Bundling Roger to one side, Bob Guppy grabbed at the handle of Chastity's suitcase and, mustering all his strength, lifted it from the moving conveyer belt.

'There you are, my lovely,' he said, triumphantly depositing it at his young assistant's feet.

'Thanks, Bob,' she said, reaching down to lift it onto her luggage trolley.

'No, no, no. Allow me,' Bob insisted, taking hold of the handle once again.

'Yours has gone round again,' Chastity observed, nodding towards the conveyer belt. Bob turned just in time to see his own suitcase disappear through the parted plastic flaps.

'Right!' Roger exclaimed, swinging his own suitcase up onto the trolley, landing it beside Cynthia's with such force that the bottles of duty-free booze he'd placed there earlier rattled dangerously against the wire basket. 'We ready then?'

'I'm ready,' Cynthia replied, weary of Roger's group mentality.

Manoeuvring the trolley to face in the direction of the exit, he leaned against the handle to set it in motion.

'Okay, then, let's go.'

'Hang on a minute!' Bob Guppy cried, blindly reaching up to catch hold of Roger's sleeve as he fought to keep track of his elusive baggage. 'I haven't got mine yet!'

Roger smiled urbanely as he accelerated the trolley away. 'It's all right, Bob. I'll go ahead with the girls and we'll meet you in the arrivals hall. All right?' And, without waiting for an answer, Roger turned his attention to guiding the trolley through the press of bodies surrounding the baggage collection belts.

Only Chastity caught the look of hurt on Bob Guppy's face and in that moment she saw through the macho bluster to the pathetically sad, downtrodden person he really was, finding herself overcome by an unexpected feeling of compassion towards him.

'You go on!' she called after Roger. 'I'll wait for Bob.'

Roger hesitated for a split second, then pushed with even greater determination through the crowded hall, Cynthia at his heels.

Hearing her words, Bob Guppy swivelled his head round, the initial look of surprise quickly replaced by a grateful smile.

'You wanna keep your eyes open for that case,' Chastity said kindly.

Obediently Bob Guppy turned back to the conveyer belt. But he was no longer in a hurry for the battered old brown leatherette case to put in an appearance.

Bob and Chastity were laughing at a shared joke as they came out into the arrivals hall. Unused to travelling, Chastity had been thrown into a state of confusion upon finding herself confronted with the question of whether she had anything to declare. Not wanting to act dishonestly she had walked through to the red channel where she was asked what it was she actually had to declare. She then proceeded to itemise everything she had bought over the past four days, most of it chocolate and most of it already consumed. Fortunately, the young customs officer had a sense of humour and waved her through.

Surprised by the number of people lining the walkway

leading out into the hall, Chastity hastily scanned the rows of faces for some sign of Roger and Cynthia, her eyes moving up and down the line as she walked along. Among the crowd at the barrier, many were holding up signs with a person's name on it, or the name of a company, and Chastity was struck by the sudden thought that Patricia had in all probability organised transport to take them back to Virt-E-Go.

'Here, Bob,' she said, nudging him in the side, 'can you see our name up there anywhere?'

They both peered along the lines of people, three-deep in places, who waited on the other side of the metal barrier, until finally Chastity tugged Bob Guppy's sleeve in her excitement.

'Look! Over there!'

As he followed the line of Chastity's pointed finger, he could see a large white placard with the name 'Guppy' scrawled across it in red.

'Come on,' she said, pulling him and the trolley after her. 'That must be our driver. I reckon Pat's organised two cars, 'cos of the luggage and all!'

Chastity waited with the trolley while Bob went off to locate the driver. She watched him as he fought his way against the flow of travellers making their way to the exit, losing sight of him as a rugby team headed towards her, his bald head re-emerging for only a moment before he was swallowed up by a further wave of returning sports stars. Standing on tiptoe, Chastity strained to relocate him, moving from side to side to gain a better view.

'Er, hello Chastity.' She jumped and swung around in one movement to find her face only inches away from that of Charles Grant.

'Um, I'm waiting for Bob,' she explained, taken aback by his unexpected presence. 'We just got back.'

Charles grinned, charmed by her awkwardness.

'He's just gone to find our driver,' she went on, nodding along the barrier. At that moment a spine-chilling scream filled the air, followed by a partially indecipherable litany of abuse. The area in front of Chastity cleared as people ran for cover, mothers grabbing hold of their children and rushing them away from the danger. As they did, Chastity saw suddenly the prostrate figure of Bob Guppy pinned to the airport floor, the considerable bulk of a demented woman astride him, her head shaking from side to side as her hands went round his throat.

'I'm going to kill him!' she screeched. 'I'm going to kill the bastard!'

Chastity made to rush across, her face white with terror, but Charles caught hold of her arm.

'Leave it, Chastity. Let *them* deal with it,' he said, nodding at the converging security guards.

It took four burly men to prise her from his body, her substantial thighs gripping him like a vice, so that the paramedics had to pump in a supply of oxygen as soon as they were able.

As they dragged the woman away to an interview room she threw back her head and wailed like an injured animal. It was only then that Chastity could see the barely recognisable face of Davina Bottomley-Crewe. She turned to Charles, a look of complete mystification on her face.

'Come,' Charles said, his hand still resting on her arm. 'I'll explain everything on the way home.'

*   *   *

Louise breezed into Roger's office, the file containing her typing under one arm.

'So how did it—?'

She stopped dead, blinking in surprise. It was Cynthia who was sitting in Roger's chair, leaning forward over the desk, writing something onto a pad. She looked up at Louise and smiled.

'Hi! Rog phoned in sick, so I thought I'd use his desk to write up the report on the trip. Mine's simply covered in things. Hope you don't mind.'

Louise's disappointment was like a great weight falling on her from on high. '*Sick*?'

Cynthia was concentrating on the report again, her head down, her hand moving furiously across the page. 'Seems so. Jet lag, probably. Or alcoholic poisoning. Difficult to tell which one got to him first, really. McTaggart's off ill, too, I'm told. And *he* stayed on terra firma.'

Louise swallowed. She made to turn away, then, hesitantly went back over to the desk. 'You were busy while you were out there?'

Cynthia glanced up. 'Never stopped. Work, work, work. You know how it is when you're under the lash!'

Louise nodded. 'Yeah . . .'

Cynthia waited, then, relenting, said, 'We were busy, Louise. And I'm sure Roger *is* sick. Is there anything urgent?'

'Nah . . .' All of the elation Louise had been feeling at the thought of Roger's return had drained from her. 'Nah, nothing urgent.'

*   *   *

239

Patricia stood beside the fax machine reading the latest communication from the States. Everyone was thrilled by the trip's success and the securing of a new financial backer had given the project a new lease of life, firing the whole company's enthusiasm for the machine.

'I'm looking forward to meeting this Kirsty McDonald,' Patricia said, turning to Chastity. 'She must be an extraordinary woman to be so successful in Silicon Valley.'

'She's extraordinary all right,' Chastity giggled.

'Why do you say it like that?'

'No reason,' Chastity said seriously. 'No, you're right. She is extraordinary.'

Patricia walked across to her desk and wrote in her diary, copying information from the sheet of flimsy paper.

'Well, I shall be able to judge for myself shortly,' she announced, closing the diary and dropping the fax into her wire tray. 'She's coming over next week. She plans to spend a couple of days with us.'

'Blimey! Lock up your daughters!' Chastity muttered to herself.

'What was that, dear?'

'I said, these plants need more water.'

'So.' Patricia said, perching on the edge of the desk and watching Chastity as she watered the plants along the window sill. 'How did you enjoy America?'

'It was great!' Chastity replied enthusiastically. 'Really great. I just loved the flight. Those little video screens they give you. We watched all the latest movies.'

'And did the men behave themselves?'

Chastity gave a brief laugh as she recalled Roger's bathroom antics. 'They were all right, I s'pose.'

Patricia stared at her. '*Really*? You know Roger's called in sick today?'

Chastity shrugged. 'Jet lag, I guess. Like my mum says, they got it wrong when they called women the weaker sex.'

Patricia gave a brief laugh.

Chastity continued watering the plants. 'You heard about Bob, I s'pose?'

'Mmm. Cynthia caught sight of him being carried into the ambulance. What a business!'

'Poor Bob,' Chastity sighed.

'Well, you get what you deserve, that's my belief. There's no such thing as a freebie, especially when it comes to sex. You *always* have to pay for your pleasure. Always.'

'But Charles said . . .' Chastity began, hesitating as she saw Patricia's questioning look. 'When he gave me a lift from the airport. Charles said—'

'Charles gave you a lift from the airport?'

Chastity nodded uncertainly.

'*Our* Charles?'

Chastity nodded again.

'I see,' Patricia said, her face breaking into a smile as sudden understanding dawned. 'I'm sorry,' she added quickly, 'I didn't mean to interrupt. What precisely *did* Charles say?'

'Well,' Chastity began slowly, wondering whether she had already said too much, 'he said that something had happened between Bob and Davina when me and Bob stayed at his house that time. Apparently they spent the night together.'

'So I've heard,' Patricia mused, slowly shaking her

head in disbelief as an image of the unlikely coupling flashed through her mind. 'Amazing.'

'But the thing is,' Chastity reasoned, 'I didn't think they even *liked* one another. I mean, how can you do it with someone when you don't even *like* them?'

Yes, well, Patricia thought, that's not a luxury we can all afford.

'Was Charles *really* engaged to her?'

'Sorry?' Patricia answered distractedly.

'I mean, do you think they were really boyfriend and girlfriend?'

'As far as I know. What are you getting at?'

'Well it's just that if they were they won't be now, will they? Not after all this business with Bob.'

Patricia smiled. 'Didn't you ask *Charles* when you were alone in the car?' she teased.

'No. It's none of my business, is it? I mean, it's up to him who he goes out with.'

Patricia's smirk was not intended to appear unkind. 'Mmm,' she said, not quite able to keep the hint of amusement from her voice. 'So you're not interested in the details of Charles's love life then?'

'No. Why should I be?'

'Indeed,' Patricia said quietly, noting how quickly Chastity had turned her attention once again to the moisture-starved plants.

Two floors up, Cynthia was pushing her way between the plastic flaps and into the labs.

Looking up from the prototype, Bill and Ben saw her at precisely the same moment and, as one, straightened up, grinning broadly.

'Cyn!' they said.

'Hi, boys,' she answered, smiling as she came across. 'You heard the news?'

'Yeah,' they said together. 'Twenty million. Cool, huh?'

'Marvellous,' she said, grinning now. 'Problem is, our new benefactor wants to come and see our toy.'

Bill looked to Ben, then back to Cynthia. 'That could be a problem, Cyn. We've hit a coupla new snags.'

'Snags?'

'Yeah,' said Ben. 'That new material we're using just won't stay erect long enough.'

'Added to which,' Bill said, 'we've a problem with grip.'

'Grip.' She nodded thoughtfully. 'Has McTaggart any ideas?'

'No disrespect,' Ben answered her, 'but does Brian know where his fanny is?'

She smiled. 'What about the sheath. Is *that* working?'

'Sort of,' Ben said, a growing tone of apology in his voice.

Cynthia sighed. 'What do you mean?'

'He means we had a short,' Bill said. 'McTaggart spilled coffee all over it.'

'He wasn't paying attention and stumbled over a loose wire.'

Cynthia groaned inwardly. 'I thought he was supposed to be on sick leave.'

'He was. But, with you guys in the States, he came in for a couple of days to see if he was ready to come back.'

Oh shit, she thought. That's all we need.

'Did Charles know he'd come in?'

The twins nodded. 'When he heard what happened, Chazza came down himself and sent McTaggart home again. Got quite stroppy with him, actually. I didn't know he had it in him.'

Cynthia raised an eyebrow in surprise. 'And the sheath? When will it be ready again?'

Bill shrugged. 'Two weeks?' Ben suggested.

'Then you've got one week,' Cynthia said.

'A week?' The twins groaned.

'That's right. Drop everything else you're doing and concentrate on getting it ready. That's the area our friend Kirsty McDonald was interested in, so that's what we've got to show her, even if it isn't working at full capacity. I want her to get at least a hint of its potential.'

Bill looked to Ben. 'I guess it could be done . . .'

'. . . if we stripped down the experimental pad . . .'

'. . . and half-wired it, so that there were less nodes . . .'

'. . . yeah and we could . . .'

She left them to it and made her way back to her office.

They had one week before Kirsty McDonald flew over. One week to get things into shape. And herself?

With her back against her office door, Cynthia closed her eyes, her right hand slowly travelling down her flank until it lay over the soft swell of her pubis.

The sex had been astonishing. Oh, she had had other women before now, but never in *that* way. It was as if Kirsty had been there inside her head half the time, knowing exactly what she wanted and just how hard she wanted it. If you could make a machine that did *that* . . .

Cynthia's eyes popped open. Of course! Why not? After all, they had tailored the machine to suit Fukuada's tastes. Why not one that suited Kirsty McDonald's?

Not waiting to discuss the matter with anyone else, she turned and opened the door again, hurrying out and up the stairs, heading back to the labs. Four days. Maybe it wasn't possible to do what she had in mind in four days, but they could try.

After all, all it took was a little . . . *imagination*.

There was no particular reason why Chastity decided to walk down the stairs that evening, rather than travel down by lift. Accumulated tiredness had perhaps made her uncharacteristically impatient as she saw the lift indicator descend to the ground floor, and in a moment of irrational annoyance, she decided to go under her own steam out of the building and home to the comfort of her bed.

Charles had been tied up for most of the day trying to deal with the airport authorities, a hysterical Davina and increasing curiosity on the part of his parents about what exactly was going on, so that when he finally drove into London it was against the flow of the evening rush-hour traffic. It was only after experiencing the acute disappointment of discovering that Chastity had already left the building that he finally had to admit to himself that the only reason for dragging himself into town had been the possibility of seeing her.

By the time Patricia came upon her young chairman, he had downed several shots of neat whisky and was finding it even more difficult than usual to form a coherent sentence. Slumped in his chair, his cheek resting on his shoulder, he looked even younger than his twenty-five years. Looking at him, Patricia felt her breasts fill with a maternal desire to *nurture* him.

Walking over, she peeled back his fingers one by one from around the empty glass tumbler. With its anchor removed, Charles's arm slipped heavily into his lap. Reaching up, Patricia pushed a lock of dark hair away from his eyes, running her palm over his smooth forehead and down his cheek, the roughness of his unshaven jaw a sudden reminder that beneath her touch lay a man, not a child.

'Charles,' she whispered. 'Charles, it's me, Patricia.'

The young man's eye flickered and there was a half-smile, perhaps of recognition, before Charles resumed his comatose state. Patricia shook his shoulder gently, but to no avail, and a more insistent attempt served only to dislodge his head from the shoulder serving as its pillow so that his chin came to rest over the middle of his chest.

'Oh, dear,' she muttered. 'How *am* I going to get you home?'

It did not take too long for her to decide that this was a clear impossibility. Indeed, there was more chance of her flying loop-the-loops in a spitfire than there was of getting Charles into a fit state to get behind the wheel of a car that night.

Having fetched a couple of cushions from her chair, she placed them at one end of the ancient Chesterfield on the far side of Charles's office, and with another glance at his sleeping form decided it would be easier on this occasion to take the mountain to Mohammed. The sofa slid effortlessly across the parquet floor and, placing it

alongside Charles's desk, she was able to push the chair
beside it and literally tip him onto his makeshift bed.

Covering him with the woollen wrap she kept at the
office, she sat beside him a moment, lightly stroking
his face and listening to his gentle groans, fascinated
by the way his eyelids twitched and the smile that
played upon his lips.

Bending down she kissed him on the corner of his
mouth, her senses alive to the smell of the whisky on
his breath and the feel of his stubble against her cheek.
She closed her eyes, allowing her lips to dwell there and
drink in these wonderful, almost forgotten, pleasures.

Then, with the sudden abruptness of a guilty child
caught doing something naughty, she pulled away.

Don't even *think* of it, she warned herself, jumping to
her feet.

Charles groaned and wriggled onto his side, pulling the
wrap up about him. And, even as Patricia closed the office
door and walked down the corridor towards the lift, he
stirred and moaned again, murmuring a single word.

'Chastity . . .'

Charles had woken several times in the night, on each
occasion at the climactic end to one of his many erotic
dreams. He'd never known dreams like them! They had
brought to vivid life so precisely his own desires and
fantasies that they had been more like daydreams than
the deeper, often unpredictable dreams of the unconscious
mind. So exactly had they mirrored the kind of sex he
had always hoped for, that in his drunken stupor he
thought he'd been transported to an earthly paradise,
they'd seemed so real.

But the harsh daylight pouring through the penthouse windows brought an altogether more cruel reality, as Charles forced open his eyes and squinted across the office past the bulbous legs of his own mahogany desk. Forcing himself to sit upright, he clasped his hands to his head. It throbbed mercilessly, as though someone were trying to break out from the inside.

A faint, vaguely familiar fragrance filled his sensitive nostrils. He bent forward to inhale it more deeply from his jacket and shirt, where it clung so hauntingly. He knew the smell – he *knew* that he knew it – but he just could not place it.

The unusual position of the sofa against the desk suddenly struck him, and he puzzled over how it had actually got there, realising, with a sudden attack of guilt and dread, that he had absolutely no recollection whatsoever of anything that happened the night before. His only memory was of vivid dreams of rampant sex with faceless women and he shook his head as if to dislodge it from his mind, at least temporarily, while he dealt with the reality of this morning.

Charles rubbed at his eyes and stretched his arms into the air, gradually relaxing so that they dropped to his chest and slowly drifted down the length of his fine cotton shirt. It wasn't until they came to rest at his waistband that he felt a hard round lump beneath the fabric. Pushing his fingers through the gap between his shirt buttons he fumbled to retrieve the alien object. Surprise, followed by bewilderment and then alarm registered on his features as he recognised it as a woman's earring.

At the sound of the door opening he guiltily stuffed the earring into his pocket.

'Ah, good. You're awake,' Patricia said loudly and with, thought Charles, a trace of smugness in her voice. 'Did you sleep well?' she asked, placing a mug of coffee on the edge of the desk beside him.

'Yes . . . thank you,' he muttered, trying to ignore the pounding in his head. 'Why do you ask?'

Patricia looked across at him a moment and wondered whether he might actually still be drunk. Certainly her ex-husband's binges used to see him through the following day in a state of blissful but more amiable inebriation. She smiled and slowly walked towards him.

'Here,' she said, reaching down and taking hold of the woollen wrap. 'Let me take this away for you.'

And as she leaned down, Charles's nostrils suddenly woke, his brain catching on an instant later as he suddenly recalled just why he recognised the fragrance he had smelled earlier. As Patricia leaned even closer her perfume invaded his senses, overwhelming him.

'Pat . . . do you always wear that perfume?' he asked shakily.

Patricia beamed. 'Do you like it? It's called Joy. Terribly expensive. Your father gave it to me when he retired.'

Charles forced a polite smile.

'Well,' she said, placing the folded wrap upon the desktop, 'you were a naughty boy last night, weren't you?'

A shiver passed through Charles's body making the tiny hairs on the back of his neck stand on end. Inside, his stomach had risen up and kick-started his heart so that it pounded furiously in his chest.

'I don't think I've ever seen anything like it,' she went

on, and in spite of himself Charles allowed a momentary flicker of pride to pass through him. 'It was like you just couldn't stop. You just wanted to have more and more.'

'Look, Pat——'

'Now don't get me wrong, Charles, I like it too. But everything in moderation. And this really is the voice of experience, you know. I remember when I was your age my husband used to be at it two days at a time, but it really doesn't do you any good in the long run, you know.'

'But——'

Patricia held up her hand to forestall any interruption. She felt she owed it to Sir James to keep Charles on the straight and narrow and he was, after all, the nearest she would get to having a son of her own.

'A little and often is fine, or a couple now and then, but sessions like the one last night just destroy you in the end, you know.'

Patricia smiled kindly at the sight of Charles's open-mouthed innocence.

'Right!' she said, striding towards the door. 'I'll organise some fresh clothes and you get that coffee down you.'

Charles stared after her, his mind still trying to comprehend the meaning of her words as he played them over and over again through the alcohol-induced fog in his mind.

Patricia had almost passed through the open doorway into the corridor when the door swung open again and she leaned round the frame, calling to Charles across the office.

'Oh, and if you find an earring, Charles, it belongs to me.'

*　　*　　*

Louise twisted the dark nylon stockings round and round over the bathroom basin, squeezing out the last few remaining drops of water, then, shaking them loose, draped them over the tiny heated towel rail behind the door, kicking the bath mat beneath to catch the drips.

Pulling a cosmetics bag and an emery board from the bathroom cabinet, she walked through to the tiny living room next door and slumped down into the armchair, tucking her legs beneath her and placing the bag on the broad chintz-covered arm of the chair. Opening it up, she lifted out a selection of false nails, which she proceeded to arrange, in order of size, along its length, presenting the bizarre image of a pair of hands clawing their way out of the chair.

The gradual transformation – from the nail-bitten, cuticle-chewed specimens that had emerged from the wash basin, to the elegant painted and polished hands she presented to the world – was carried out with expert ease and required little concentration. Besides, Louise's thoughts were some miles away, in a suburban area of Kent where she imagined, as she did every weekend, Roger Appleyard at home with his family.

Due to the time difference, she knew it had been difficult for him to contact her whilst he was in the States, and he wasn't to know that she had stayed up until two o'clock in the morning just in case he'd found time to phone. And now that he was back he was no doubt suffering from jet lag or was sound asleep. That was, if his bitch of a wife hadn't dragged him round the bloody garden centre, as she usually did, by all accounts.

When they had first started their relationship, Louise

hadn't wanted to know anything at all about Roger's home life. She had deliberately shut out the details of his other existence, not wanting to spoil the delicious excitement of the affair with stray mental pictures of those they were deceiving. Yet, as time went on, things changed and once Louise was sure that it was she that Roger loved, and not his wife, she began to feel nothing but resentment towards the woman. Jane Appleyard, she was certain, was the only thing standing in the way of their shared happiness, and Louise had little pity for the frigid cow who prevented them from being together.

With great delicacy Louise took the television remote control between thumb and finger and switched on the TV, then sat there, staring blankly at the screen as a panel of pundits gave their opinions on matters of current sporting importance. Louise had no interest in sport, yet the impassioned, laughing voices were briefly welcome in her tiny flat, if only for the fact that they kept the silence at bay.

Silence. She hated silence, just as she hated being on her own.

Standing again, Louise walked through to the bedroom, consciously avoiding even the briefest glance towards the telephone that sat upon the bedside table: that same, pastel-coloured telephone whose presence had taunted her on so many occasions, through so many lonely nights when her imagination — stimulated by empti-ness and jealousy — had conjured up endless painful images of Roger's marital idyll. Countless times she had wanted to phone him in the middle of the night as she tossed and turned, unable to sleep, wanting to hear his voice, to have him reassure her that he loved her and that, one day soon, they would live together as man and wife.

She lay on the bed, watching the net curtain flutter back and forth on the afternoon breeze. Outside in the street she could hear the voices of children playing and the occasional sound of a passing car. Turning on her side she closed her eyes, longing for the escape of sleep, but knowing that sleep was impossible. Then, suddenly, her eyes flicked open.

Scrabbling across the bed, Louise lifted the handset from its cradle and placed it to her ear. The purr of the dialling tone immediately disillusioned her. For one brief moment she had thought her phone might be out of order and that that would explain why Roger hadn't phoned, but that wasn't it! She sighed with disappointment, letting the handpiece fall back onto the cradle. Then, unable to resist the temptation any longer, she snatched it up and punched in the familiar sequence of digits that formed Roger's number. Her heart was pounding as she listened to the ringing tone. And as it rang she spoke to him across the distance, willing him to answer it.

'Come on, Roger. Answer it. Speak to me.'

'Hello?'

Disappointment jabbed through her like a spear as she recognised Jane Appleyard's clipped but undeniably pleasant voice. She was about to put the phone down, when, from somewhere in the Appleyard household, she heard the deeper, huskier sound of Roger's voice as he called to his wife, 'Darling? Why don't you come to the garden centre with me? We could get those roses you wanted, then go on to the pub for lunch.'

Clasping her hand across her mouth, Louise fought to

contain the anguished wail that threatened to escape her, and, pressing her face into the soft pillow, she dropped the handset onto the floor.

There was a click as Jane Appleyard hung up.

'You bastard! You bloody bastard!' Louise screamed into the empty bedroom.

Tears welled in her eyes, clinging briefly to her bottom lashes before they tumbled down her cheeks. Reaching down, she blindly searched the drawer beside her for a handkerchief, then stopped, her hand closing on something small and flat and hard.

The disk.

With a shuddering sigh, she sat back, looking at the tiny blue and silver floppy disk that lay in her hand. While Roger had been in America, she had decided to make a copy of those files he had been so anxious not to show her. And very interesting reading they made, too.

Roses, eh? He was buying roses for his wife and taking her down the pub, and never a single thought for her.

'Well, Roger Appleyard,' she said, with a determination born of that moment, 'it's time you made your mind up. If you think you can play around with me you've got another think coming . . .'

Charles sat at his study window, nursing a glass of fizzing Alka-Seltzer, as the aftereffects of his excesses the night before dragged interminably on. His head seemed to weigh at least a stone more than usual, and it felt as though someone had tightened a metal strap around it, perhaps to keep it from splitting open. It didn't help that he could barely remember anything from that long evening, and what little recall he *seemed* to have wasn't good and was confused to say the least. He could still smell Patricia's faded fragrance in his nostrils, and winced as an image of a depraved sexual act flashed before his eyes. *Had* he dreamed all of that – or had he actually *done* it? And, if so, how could he ever look Pat in the eyes again?

If there was one person Charles was not up to seeing that afternoon it was Davina. But, insistent that she should go straight in without being announced, she had ensured that Charles was unable to avoid her, and he felt himself visibly shrinking at the sound of her voice as it invaded the study, like the sound of fingernails being scraped down a blackboard.

'Charles! We *must* talk!'

Charles smiled weakly, his head sinking into his neck so that it appeared to rest directly on his shoulders.

'Hello, Dee.'

She strode across the room and came to attention beside the window so that she stood directly over Charles's crumpled body.

'Look, Charlie,' she said, matter-of-factly, glancing wistfully out over the estate, 'there's something I have to say.'

In spite of overwhelming tiredness, Charles found himself straightening in his seat, conscious of the serious tone in Davina's voice.

'Charles,' she began, 'I realise that it must've been a great shock to you when I announced that I was . . . well . . . that I was . . .'

'Pregnant?'

'Yes, pregnant,' she said tightly. 'And I know that you had always hoped that you would be the first—'

'Listen Dee—'

'No, no, Charles, hear me out. I know you thought that we'd get married and that we'd consummate the marriage on our wedding night . . .'

'Did I?' he said quietly, more to himself than to Davina, who had carried on speaking.

'Well, I realise that my current condition must be an enormous disappointment to you . . .'

'Well, I don't—'

'. . . and I realise that I can no longer expect you to honour our engagement.'

'But, Dee—'

'No, Charlie, really. It has to be said. It doesn't matter that I didn't *know* it was Bob Guppy I was having sex with. I feel duty-bound to set you free to find somebody . . . *pure*.' She hesitated a moment, then spoke again very softly, quietly. 'No, Charles, I'm sorry it has to end like this, but you of all people don't deserve second-hand goods.'

Davina stopped and hung her head, her self-humiliation complete.

Charles stared up at her, dumbfounded. 'Davina . . . I don't know what to say.'

She turned her head, unable even to look at him. 'No, Charles, you mustn't try to talk me out of it. My mind's made up. I shall go up to Yorkshire to stay with Aunt Celia until the family decides what should be done.'

'Well, if you're really sure . . .' he said, perhaps a touch too eagerly so that there was a look of genuine hurt on Davina's flushed face. Standing up, he wrapped his arms around her in a brotherly embrace. Now that there was no threat of romantic involvement, he felt a genuine affection for his childhood friend.

'You know you can always count on me, don't you Dee? You know, if you *need* anything.'

Davina nodded so that her nose rubbed up and down Charles's chest and the top of her head bumped against his chin. And, if Charles hadn't known better, he could have sworn he heard the muffled sound of a whimper.

'What did Bob say about the baby?' Charles ventured innocently.

'Don't talk to me about that *disgusting* little man,' she growled, the moment of vulnerability passing as the fire returned to her narrow piggy eyes.

Bob Guppy cautiously raised one eyelid, the white glare of the overhead lights squeezing through the narrow slit so that he was forced to close it again almost immediately, shutting out the dazzling brightness. He lay on the hard, narrow bed listening to a cacophony of noise as trolleys rattled past, cubicle curtains jangled along metal rails, telephones rang and patients fought for the attention of the casualty receptionist, the sounds washing over him as he struggled to recall the events that had brought him to this place.

The moment of surprise when Davina had revealed herself at the airport had been quickly replaced by a feeling of total terror as the woman turned into a demon, attacking him with the ferocity of a pit bull on speed. She had taken him completely unawares and her rantings had done nothing to enlighten him, nor any of the growing audience surrounding them as they grappled on the floor. Mind, Bob had been completely at her mercy. The strap of the holdall he was carrying across his chest had become entangled with the wire luggage trolley as he fell to the ground, rendering him helpless as he fought to defend himself against Davina's impressive forearm smash.

The physical assault had been bad enough, but it was the penultimate ear-piercing yell of 'I'm pregnant, you bastard!' from those mighty lungs that brought sudden, unwelcome clarification to Bob Guppy's shattered eardrums. However, he had barely had time to take in the meaning of her words, let alone formulate a response, when her final haunting screech of 'Rapist!' had rung out and, with a kick that had taken his breath, she finished him off. There was an instant of excruciating pain and then everything had gone mercifully black.

The appearance of a police car outside Maxine Guppy's home filled her at once with dread and an almost obscene excitement as she turned past it and up the short crazy-paved drive to her neat, semi-detached, suburban house. She barely had time to step from the car and cast her eyes along the row of houses opposite, already certain of the prying eyes that lay behind the twitching net curtains, when two young police officers were beside her, informing her that her husband had been the victim of a serious physical attack.

The news, as it turned out, came as something of an anticlimax. In the thirty seconds between first spotting the vehicle and discovering the reason for its presence, Maxine had mentally combed her wardrobe for something black, appropriate for a funeral and, finding it lacking, decided on a shopping expedition at the earliest opportunity. For a split-second she had felt a pang of remorse for perhaps dwelling overlong outside the Co-operative Society funeral parlour earlier that week, and for assuming with obscene enthusiasm that her husband would – without a doubt – be the first to shuffle off this earthly coil. However, there was still the mystery of the deranged woman. Who was she? And why should she pick on Bob, for God's sake?

As he lay inert in the casualty cubicle, Maxine Guppy tapped her husband's hand in a gesture as close to affection as she could manage, before absent-mindedly rubbing her fingers against her thigh. Looking down on his battered face – one eye swollen and purple, his bottom lip split open and a nose that looked considerably flatter than when she had last seen it – Maxine almost felt moved to giggle and was prevented from doing so only by the sudden emergence of Bob Guppy's good eye in its bloodshot socket.

'How long have you been there?' he whispered hoarsely, struggling to raise himself up in the bed.

'Only a couple of minutes,' she answered, propping up the head rest. 'You look a right bloody mess. What happened?'

'Pass us that water, will you?' he said, gesturing towards a tumbler on the side. 'I keep tasting blood in my mouth.'

'Who was she, this woman?' Maxine handed her husband the glass, taking the opportunity to look more closely at his damaged eye. 'She certainly had a good punch on her, whoever she was.'

'Stupid bloody bitch,' he hissed, wincing as the water stung his split lip. 'I thought she was going to bleedin' kill me.'

Maxine Guppy almost smiled. 'But why did she pick on you?'

Bob Guppy shrugged. Handing back the glass of water, he allowed his head to flop back against the pillows.

'Christ knows. Guess I was just unlucky.' He sighed, and, as his eye slowly closed, an image of Davina's pit-bull face flashed into his mind.

In fact, he decided, I couldn't have been any more unlucky if I was a dick caught in a trouser zip. And with that gruesome thought in mind his hand instinctively reached down to his bruised and swollen crotch where Davina had aimed her final passing shot.

– *August* –

'Tomorrow? She's coming tomorrow? But I thought—'
'It's okay,' Patricia said, giving Charles her most reassuring smile. 'I'll arrange everything. Leave it all to me.'

Within thirty minutes, news of Kirsty McDonald's impending arrival was announced at a staff meeting hastily organised by Patricia on Charles's behalf. Nevertheless, Charles felt it incumbent upon him to make an official announcement.

'As you all know,' he began, the faintest blush at his neck, 'the clock is ticking. The International Media Communications Fair is only four months away now and the machine must be ready. If we miss out on this opportunity, we could miss the boat altogether, and we can't afford to do that, especially now we've such a prestigious backer as Ubik Enterprises.'

Charles looked about him at the packed room and nervously smiled. 'Four months isn't much, I realise, but we *can* do it, and with Ubik's financial and technical backing we shall. It's going to mean a lot of late nights and a great deal of pressure, I know, but

I promise you that no one will go unrewarded for their efforts.'

There was a satisfied murmur at that. A dozen faces beamed back at Charles, proud and determined – or, at least, it seemed that way. All, that was, except Bob Guppy's. Guppy, only two days out of hospital, still found it hard to smile. His injuries were far too recent.

A certain amount of rumour had circulated following the team's return from America. The colourful saga of Bob and Davina had by now reached almost mythological status, yet even his very visible injuries had failed to elicit sympathy from any quarter other than Roger Appleyard, who had found it quite disgraceful that the wretched Davina should have washed her laundry in quite so public a fashion. In his opinion, she had a damn cheek kicking up a fuss at all! After all, it was the woman's job to make sure she wasn't going to end up with a balloon up the jumper, wasn't it?

To Chastity's embarrassment, Roger had made endless jibes about her dinner date with Kirsty McDonald. It had been obvious from the start, he'd said, that the woman was a dyke, and he teased Chastity about how impressed he was that she had been prepared to sacrifice herself for the good of the firm. She had ignored him, and had even been tempted on a couple of occasions to retaliate with the revelation of his little exploit in the hotel bathroom, but had held back for Louise's sake. Chastity guessed that Louise knew Roger was a shit, but nobody wanted to have their nose rubbed in it.

Call it sixth sense, call it woman's intuition, call it knowing your run is up, but Louise had felt that all was not well ever since Roger's return. She couldn't quite forgive him for not bothering to contact her when he got back, even though she said she had. But it wasn't that. It was silly little things she'd picked up on: a look – sometimes just a quick glance, sometimes a longer, lingering appraisal that barely concealed his lust – or a gesture, the kind she recalled from their early days together. Nothing she could even articulate. She had no reason to believe that Chastity welcomed Roger's attentions, nor craved them – indeed, she had no reason to think that Chastity was even aware of them. Even so, her misdirected hatred issued forth, like a faulty Exocet that mistakenly targets the hospital instead of the army barracks, and her young colleague was the unsuspecting victim.

Cynthia had kept very quiet about the evening she enjoyed in Kirsty McDonald's company. When Kirsty had phoned her in her hotel it had been wholly unexpected, and the night of sexual humiliation that followed so unutterably pleasurable that the only regret on both their parts had been that Cynthia's visit could not have been prolonged.

And now, as Charles spoke on, something he said seemed to touch upon the matter perfectly.

'As you all know,' he said, 'it is extremely important that we do our best to impress Miss McDonald whilst she's here. I think we are all aware just how much is riding on her . . .'

Cynthia spluttered into her hand then cleared her throat noisily.

'Perhaps we might start by providing her with a detailed update on any recent developments on the machine,' Patricia suggested.

'Yes,' Charles agreed, nodding enthusiastically. 'Yes, let's hear about any new developments.'

All eyes turned to William and Benjamin who – turn and turn about – proceeded to explain their most recent refinements to the machine. As they did, their nominal boss, Brian McTaggart, looked on, his chin resting on his crooked finger as he listened intently, trying to appear far better informed than he was.

'And will we have time to give this a test run before she arrives?' Roger asked, a note of scepticism in his voice.

'You volunteering, Roger?' Bob Guppy laughed, then winced as a sudden pain shot through his busted lip where the cut had been stretched too far, reopening the wound.

'No, I thought I'd leave that to you,' he replied, pulling a handkerchief from his trouser pocket and handing it across. 'At least then you could have sex without running the risk of getting your face smashed in.'

Bob Guppy's eyes narrowed as he looked at Roger over the top of the crumpled hankie he held to his bloodied mouth. He thought of retaliating but could sense Charles's eyes on him and maintained his guilty silence. This was their first meeting since the unfortunate airport episode and Bob had anticipated it with dread. But he considered it a measure of Charles's breeding that the young Chairman had not reacted violently or abusively towards him; rather he had been taken aback by Charles's unexpectedly cheery greeting and surprisingly hearty handshake.

'Perhaps we could move on,' Patricia suggested in a manner that left little doubt she would tolerate no more bickering.

'Roger is correct to some degree, though,' said McTaggart,

straightening up. 'I'm sure that Miss McDonald will expect to watch a demonstration whilst she's here. Which will, of course, necessitate our providing a test pilot, as it were.'

'I think you'll find that *Ms* McDonald will want to test the machine herself, actually,' Cynthia observed.

McTaggart's response was calm but incredulous: 'Surely not? I feel confident that a demonstration using—'

'Please, take it from me,' Cynthia insisted. 'I've absolutely no doubts on this score. Ms McDonald will want to put it through its paces personally. She almost said as much. And, bearing this in mind, I feel we might be well advised to look at our current programming and perhaps consider . . . well, beefing it up a little.'

'*Beefing it up*? What do you—'

'Brian,' Patricia interrupted, 'do you think you could possibly open the windows to let in a little air?'

The rest of the room watched in embarrassed silence as McTaggart scraped his chair back from the table like a naughty schoolboy being dismissed from class and, shoulders hunched, walked over to the windows.

'Now, Cynthia, what exactly do you have in mind?' Patricia asked.

'Well, my own feeling is that we should perhaps develop further on the lines suggested by our Japanese friends.'

'That was pretty much S and M, wasn't it?' Roger Appleyard said, a look of distaste on his face. 'Whips and chains and all that palaver!'

'That's right,' Cynthia replied, nodding enthusiastically before meeting his gaze with a challenging look. 'What I suggest is . . .'

Charles shifted uncomfortably in his chair as Cynthia presented her thoughts in a clinical, matter-of-fact fashion. Throughout the discussion he had risked several sideways glances at Chastity, and on a couple of occasions their eyes had briefly met, both looking away quickly with embarrassment. For his part, he was conscious of Patricia at his elbow all the while, her haunting fragrance forever in his nostrils as a grim reminder of that night of passion. Part of him wished he could remember exactly what had taken place between them that night, while the other part was content to remain in blissful ignorance.

Sometimes it was best *not* to know.

'Er, might I suggest that you have further discussions on this theme with William and Benjamin?' he said, picking an opportune moment to interrupt as Cynthia paused for breath at the end of her lecture on the importance of proper ankle restraints. 'And, er, with Brian too, of course,' he added kindly. 'Now perhaps we should move on.'

There was a collective murmur of agreement from the men around the table. Supposedly taking notes, each of them had nervously doodled throughout Cynthia's speech; doodles which a trained psychologist might have found most illuminating.

Roger's was perhaps the most straightforward of these, for on his notepad, between the underlined words 'Pleasure' and 'Retraint' he had drawn the matchstick figure of a man – quite clearly a man – between two other stick figures whose tiny triangular dresses revealed their sex. So much might have been read for normal, except that the central – male – figure had what looked like two nooses about his neck, the ends of which were in the hands of the two female figures.

Bob Guppy had drawn what looked like two large swollen testicles, while both Bill and Ben had drawn the same doodle, which, for all the world resembled nothing so much as a spiked dog-collar, from which all manner of electrical wiring came off.

McTaggart's doodle alone might have stumped the expert, for it showed what appeared to be a man in a bath, except the bath had wheels and the man was wearing what looked like a fireman's helmet.

The women, on the other hand, had listened with seemingly detached fascination to Cynthia's proposals. If any of them were aroused by the kind of sado-masochistic sex she described it was not apparent, but, noting the keen interest of at least one of her female colleagues, Cynthia mused that there could well be another convert in her midst.

'But how would one actually *feel* the pain through the bodysuit?' Patricia asked. 'I mean, would it *really* hurt?'

Cynthia opened her mouth to answer Patricia's keen enquiry but, with a crimson flush rising over the edge of his starched white collar and a vision (or was it a memory?) of his faithful secretary flashing through his head, Charles's voice – an octave higher than usual – interrupted shakily.

'Tea!' he said, standing, then quickly making for the door. 'I think we could all do with a nice cup of tea!'

'Well, Inspector Holly, what have you to say for yourself?'

Holly sat forward a little and – in his imagination – loosened the collar of his shirt. 'Say, sir?'

Commissioner Robertson looked up at him from the letter that lay on his great oak desk and repeated the word. '*Say*.'

'I . . . I don't understand, sir. I was just doing my job.'

The Commissioner nodded slowly to himself for a moment as if he understood, then, with an ironic smile, began to shake his head. 'No, Inspector, one thing you were *not* doing when you raided Virt-E-Go's premises was "doing your job". Indeed, I would say that you exceeded your authority by some considerable degree. We are not yet a police state, and God pray we never shall be, and while I am Commissioner of this force I shall insist on all of my officers acting within the limits of the law.'

Holly swallowed deeply.

'Put simply, Detective Inspector, if I find you pulling this kind of stunt again you'll find yourself out walking the beat quicker than you can say Rubber Truncheon. *You understand me*?'

The last three words came in the form of a small gale, directed straight into Holly's face. Holly gave an awkward nod and, through dry lips, formed a barely audible, 'Yes, sir.'

'Not only that, but you will return every last item you took from their offices by tomorrow morning.'

'Sir––'

'And one last thing: you will write a personal apology to the Chairman, young Charles Grant.'

Holly blinked, opened his mouth to speak, then nodded mutely. His humiliation was complete.

'Oh, and Inspector . . . ?'

'Sir?'

'Get yourself a decent suit, man. You look like you've just crawled out of a cardboard box!'

Hidden from view, Chastity stood behind the tall plaster pillar at the turn in the penthouse corridor leading to the staircase. She glanced at her watch, noting that she had already been there for more than ten minutes, but comforted by the fact that by now most people would have left the building for the day.

From inside Charles's office Chastity could detect the faint murmur of voices locked in a conversation that seemed interminable. At the same moment that she looked down at her watch once again, a wave of panic swept over her as Patricia's voice became suddenly loud. Peeping around the pillar, Chastity could see the other woman's back as she stood framed in the doorway looking into the office, the fingers of one hand curled around the door handle and the other hand clutching a small black leather handbag.

Her heart thumping in her chest, Chastity leaned back out of sight.

'Are you *sure* there's nothing else I can do for you?' Patricia asked.

Charles's reply sounded strangely distorted and shaky. 'No . . . No, nothing . . . thank you.'

'Goodnight, then,' Patricia called, and, as she closed the door behind her, it sounded for all the world like a long, pained groan echoing in the room beyond.

Chastity watched Patricia take her jacket from the coat stand and step across to the lift. It arrived quickly, but only when Patricia was finally being transported to the ground floor did Chastity allow herself to relax a little.

She waited. Some minutes later the handle rattled and the door squeaked on its hinges. Once again Chastity experienced an overwhelming feeling of terror. From her hiding place she watched Charles lift his jacket from the stand and, hooking it over his finger, swing it round to drape casually over his shoulder. With his other hand he reached up and loosened the tie knot at his neck, undoing the top button and rubbing his finger along the skin inside his collar. He had taken two steps towards the lift and had pressed the call button when Chastity took courage and seized her moment.

'Hello,' she said quietly, but even so he jumped at the sudden, unexpected sound of her voice. Turning round, he could not hide his surprise nor his delight in the discovery.

'Where did *you* come from?' he laughed.

Chastity nodded towards the staircase, hoping that she could control the blush that threatened to colour her face. It was how her mother knew that she was telling a lie.

'I was . . . looking for Patricia.'

Charles was transfixed by the way her mouth moved as she spoke and by the way her nose wrinkled a little now and then. A couple of moments passed before he realised that she had finished speaking.

'Patricia? Er, she's gone I'm afraid. Gone home.' He could not take his eyes off her, and inside his chest he could literally feel his heart beating, pumping the blood up to his head so that he began to feel quite dizzy, intoxicated almost. 'Anything I can do?' he asked dreamily.

Chastity smiled across at him. 'It's all right. It can wait.'

The bell sounding the lift's arrival broke the spell of the moment, and as the doors slid open they both looked into it, resenting its brutal intrusion. The doors slid partially closed again before Charles pressed hard on the button, forcing them apart.

'Can I give you a lift?' he laughed nervously, unaware of the joke he had made.

Chastity did not answer but walked past him into the small vestibule, resting her back against its cold metal side. He came and stood in front of her, so close that when he raised his arm towards the control panel it almost brushed against her breast. She could not know how reluctantly he pressed the button that would transport them all too quickly to the ground floor, bringing an end to this long-awaited intimacy; how the apparent casualness of the gesture denied his every wish, his every inclination to keep her there with him until their eventual discovery by the office cleaner the next morning. When the doors failed to close Charles's hand reached for the button once again, but Chastity's was there first and as their fingers touched it was like an electric current shooting through them both so that each jerked away from the other's touch, she giggling nervously while he cleared his throat.

'It's a bit temperamental,' Chastity said, smiling up at him as finally the doors closed and the lift jerked erratically towards its destination. She looked away as he smiled back, convinced that her feelings must be only too apparent and feeling suddenly very foolish. He was so close to her now that she had only to take a deep breath and her breasts would glance against his chest; she had only to inch forward a little for her thighs to touch his. A shiver ran through her.

In the next moment Charles, a confirmed agnostic, came close to believing that there really was a God, for somewhere between the second and first floors the lift juddered to a halt and the light inside began to flicker and fade. At the final jolt, Charles had not attempted to steady himself as he was thrown off-balance and into Chastity's open arms. He did not try to right himself, nor did she appear in any hurry for him to do so as their bodies pressed together in that dimly lit space. The sound of their breathing filling the heavy silence.

Chastity loved the smell of him, the light citrus fragrance tingling her nostrils and swimming through her veins like a drug so that she was unable to stop herself from nuzzling closer, pressing her face into the soft, warm crook of his neck to drink it in. The weight of his body as it pressed on her, pushing her against the unrelenting metal wall, was a powerful reminder of their positions in the scheme of things. But any fleeting reservation she may have had quickly dissolved as she felt her body respond. Instinctively, almost telepathically, their faces turned towards each other and, eyes closed, their lips met — briefly, sweetly — before they were thrown apart by the sudden, jerking motion of the lift as it juddered back to life.

Chastity barely had time to compose herself and to collect her thoughts before she found herself stepping out into the brightly lit reception area, Charles following a couple of steps behind. She stopped abruptly and inadvertently he brushed against her arm, pulling away quickly as if the touch had been red-hot, their intimacy of only moments before a distant flashing memory.

Chastity looked up at him, her hands clasped in front of her, with no inkling of the turmoil raging within Charles's becalmed exterior; she had no idea of the doors she had unlocked with that brief, passionate kiss, no sense of the desire behind the eyes that gazed down on her with apparent innocence, and certainly no inkling of the fact that the only thing Charles wanted to do at that moment was to rip off all her clothes and make love to her there on the floor.

'Well,' Charles said finally.

Chastity forced a brief smile, glancing down self-consciously to see whether her erect nipples showed through the thin teeshirt fabric that clung so lovingly to her body.

Thoughts raced through Charles's mind so that he felt his head might burst open. What should he do? What should he say? What was she thinking? What did she expect him to do now?

'I'd better be going, actually,' he heard himself say, his mouth moving with a will of its own as the words tumbled out, spilling irretrievably before the angel standing in front of him.

Mustering every ounce of self-control she possessed, Chastity managed to maintain her composure, determined that the intense disappointment she felt be suppressed until some later, private moment.

'Me too,' she said, her voice sounding strange as she fought to keep the shakiness from her falsely cheerful reply. But she did not move, and neither did he, as each silently willed the other to say something, to do something, so that what happened in the lift would not become a source of regret.

'Chastity, I . . .'

'Yes?' she said eagerly, her eyes wide with expectation.

Charles hesitated then swallowed hard. 'I'd better be going.'

'Yes,' she muttered, her disappointment almost complete. But, as he turned to go, Charles gently, briefly, touched her arm, the tiny gesture so innocent yet so intense that it felt like a foil passing through her body, so that a physical pain rose to fill her chest, taking her breath away. And as she watched him leave the building, her heart racing, Chastity was filled with one absolute certainty: she was in love – hopelessly, irredeemably in love with Charles Grant.

Cynthia had not been home ten minutes when the phone rang. She was in her kitchen, crouched in front of the fridge, trying to decide whether to open a bottle of Sauvignon or the Chardonnay, when the answering machine activated. She closed the fridge door, then stood, listening as the bleep sounded and the message began. It was a sensuous American voice. The voice of Kirsty McDonald.

'Cyn? Hi . . . it's Kirsty. I was hoping I'd catch you in. I got an early flight. Hoped we might meet up before things get too hectic. I . . .'

Rushing into the living room, Cynthia picked up the phone and, calming herself, spoke.

'Kirsty? Hi . . . It's great to hear from you again.'

'Great to speak to you, babe. Better still—'

Cynthia smiled broadly. 'You want to come round?'

'You want to try to stop me?'

'Could I?'

Kirsty's laugh was deeply sexual. 'No, sirree, honey. Not a hope in hell.'

That night, after he'd packed up the chests containing all of the material he had taken from the offices of Virt-E-Go, ready for delivery the next morning, Detective Inspector Richard Holly walked slowly back to his digs, feeling a despair that was, at that moment, close to suicidal.

Walking through the neon-lit seedy streets of Soho, he felt his life was at its lowest ebb. It wasn't just that his career was up shit creek without the proverbial paddle, it was everything else. *Everything*. If there'd been someone in his life with whom he could share his troubles it might have been okay, but there was no one, and there had been no one since his wife had walked out on him five years back.

Holly stopped in a doorway, looking up at the red-lit sign in the door. 'Model,' it read. Some days he was sorely tempted to find some solace there – or, at least, relief – but that wasn't really him. At heart, Dick Holly was a romantic. That was why he'd never fitted in in Vice, because Vice officers were supposed to be hardbitten and cynical, and he could find neither of those qualities within himself. He was forever hopeful of meeting the right woman and spending his twilight years in domestic bliss.

Or had been.

Sighing, he walked on, through the Sodom and Gomorrah of London's red-light district and on into the darker, narrower streets that led through to Theobalds Road, where he had his flat over a newsagent's shop.

But tonight he didn't really want to go home. At least, not yet.

Coming out into the great open junction of Southampton Row and Theobalds Road, Holly looked about him at the late-night streets. Empty taxis whizzed past him, their For Hire signs dark, their drivers on their way back to their homes in Essex.

It was all so bleak. All so damn bleak.

A pint, he told himself, his eyes alighting on the front of the White Hart. I need a pint.

And, with the desperation of a drowning man spying a life raft, Holly launched out into the road, making a beeline for the pub, unaware, it seemed, of the frantic hooting of the drivers who were forced to swerve to avoid hitting him.

'Nobushi!'

'Cee-fee-a, how are you?' Nobushi Fukuada asked cheerily, his feet planted firmly upon the mat outside Cynthia's flat. 'You have good day at work?' he asked, giving her a brief bow before he walked past her into the hallway, depositing his neatly rolled black umbrella in the bamboo container by the black lacquer coat stand.

Cynthia smiled weakly as Fukuada proceeded to make his way along to the bedroom. She had completely forgotten about him. Glancing anxiously at her watch, she dashed after him, immediately scooping up the jacket he had already discarded on the bed and bundling it into his hands, which had been busily fumbling over the tiny buttons on his crisp white shirt.

'Nobi, I'm afraid I'm busy tonight,' she apologised, smoothing a hand across the white appliqué bedcover. She laid her hand gently on his shoulder. 'I've got a friend coming over any minute. It's . . . rather personal.'

'Ah . . .' Fukuada said. 'I unner-stan'. You play game of har'-an'-sof'.'

Cynthia smiled. 'No hard-and-soft tonight, Nobi. She's a client of ours. An American lady.'

'Ahhh . . . Merican rady. Maybe I stay. We ha' free-some.'

Cynthia giggled. 'You're absolutely incorrigible, you randy little man. This is my friend.'

'Well?' Fukuada said, wide-eyed. 'Am I no fren'?'

'Yes, but not tonight Nobi. Stay out late, eh?'

Walking across, she picked up her bag and took out her purse, meaning to give him some money, but Fukuada shook his head.

'No, Cee-fee-a. I sit in park. Contemplate fate.'

'Contemplate. That's good, Nobi. You've been pra-ctising, haven't you?'

'Prenty practice,' he answered, grinning. 'But now I go. Give you good caning tomorrow, eh? On Cee-fee-a's naughty bum.'

Cynthia gave a brief laugh. 'Tomorrow. And I promise it'll be worth waiting for.' She leaned forward to whisper softly in his ear as she reached over his shoulder for the latch on the front door. 'Oh, and Nobi . . . I have some interesting new equipment I think you'll like.'

Excitement clearly showed on Fukuada's face. He was

about to make one last-ditch plea for a quickie when the doorbell rang again. Cynthia's hand twitched on the lock and in a split second the door was open, the two of them guiltily looking into the face of Kirsty McDonald.

The woman's smile was fixed, as though her mouth had been stretched wide and pegged at the corners, and even as her calculating brain ticked over, attempting to assess the situation, the smile never sagged to make her appear anything less than a gullible friend coming upon a completely innocent situation.

'Kirsty!' she exclaimed, with a surprising degree of surprise in her voice.

'Cynthia,' the older woman replied, leaning over Nobushi Fukuada to plant a kiss in the air either side of Cynthia's face. Leaning back, she looked down, openly scrutinising the man who stood between them, awaiting an introduction.

'I'm sorry,' Cynthia said, picking up the signal. 'Kirsty, this is my friend, Nobushi. Nobi, Kirsty.'

Nobushi Fukuada made a slight bow of the head and placed his hand round Kirsty's extended hand.

'My preasure,' he said.

'Likewise,' she replied, pulling her hand from his grasp whilst maintaining the smile. And almost imperceptibly her body inched one way and his the other until eventually they had swapped places and it was Fukuada who stood, isolated, on the doorstep.

Smiling nervously from one to the other, Cynthia finally turned to Kirsty, extending her arm along the corridor.

'Why don't you go to the living room and fix yourself a drink? It's second on the left.'

Kirsty forced a brief smile and turned to follow her direction.

'Velly nice meet you, Miss—'

'Please,' she said, smiling at Fukuada over her shoulder. 'Call me Kirsty.'

But, as he watched her disappear off the corridor, Nobushi Fukuada couldn't help thinking that he had met this 'Merican rady' somewhere before.

Patricia was feeling rather tipsy, to say the least, as she tottered down Cosmo Place and into Queen Square. She hadn't meant to stay in the pub all evening, but it had been so nice to talk with Louise for once, that she had quite overstayed her time. Making her way home down Boswell Street she smiled broadly to herself, thinking of some of the things Louise had confided.

'You dirty devil, Roger Appleyard,' she murmured, then gave a tiny drunken giggle. Why, in her present state she could almost fancy him herself.

It was as she made her way past the White Hart that, glancing in, she saw a familiar figure seated alone at a table in the corner, head down, nursing a pint between his hands.

Holly?

For a moment she leaned against the window, her hand to her brow, almost as if she was staring out to sea.

As she looked, she saw him raise his head and – unmistakably – sigh, then, lifting his glass to his mouth, drain the rest of his pint.

Pat frowned. It was Holly. No one else wore a suit that badly cut. But it was Holly as she had never seen him before. He looked so sad. So . . . well, so bloody

pathetic. Watching him struggle up and go across to the
bar to order in another pint, she wondered for the first
time just what kind of man Detective Inspector Holly
was when he was off duty. She knew what they said
– that a copper was a copper was a copper – but was
that always true? The poor sod looked like he'd suffered
a bereavement.

For a moment she felt like going in and joining him,
but then a sudden awkwardness came over her. It wasn't
as if they were friends, after all. And what if he simply
told her to bugger off?

Moving back from the window, she staggered a little,
then turned.

A man was watching her from the pavement on the
other side of the road. Scowling at him, Patricia walked
on, struggling to maintain her dignity as she half walked,
half staggered, out into Theobald's Road.

Poor bastard, she thought. Poor lonely bastard.

Nobushi Fukuada stepped down from the bus and looked
about him. It was late evening now and the West End
streets were packed with sightseers and those out for a
good time. Normally he would have joined them, but
tonight he had something important to do.

Making his way carefully and politely through the
crowd, he ducked down a narrow side street and out into
a square. In a street on the far side was his destination, a
pawn shop.

Standing outside the shop, Fukuada smiled, recalling
his original mistake. On his first visit to London he had
bashfully asked a native Londoner for the directions to
one of the famous 'porn shops' he had read about – one of

those that London's Soho was famous for worldwide. Not knowing that the round white collar and black shirt of the man were anything other than a strange new fashion, Fukuada had therefore been surprised when he had been led to this shop. Pointing up to the three golden balls that hung over the doorway, the vicar had smiled, said, 'There you are, old chap,' and left him to it.

What had been embarrassing then now proved surprisingly useful, for in his hour of need this answer – born of desperation – had occurred to him. His watch. He would pawn his watch.

Fukuada pushed at the door, expecting it to swing open, but it did not give. He frowned, then looked at his watch. It couldn't be closed, surely? After all, it was only twenty to nine. In Tokyo *nothing* closed before midnight.

Peering through the protective glass, Fukuada raised his hand, then knocked loudly on the door's wooden frame. He waited a moment, listening, trying to see if there was any movement within. Nothing. He knocked again.

This time there was a scuffling noise. The sound of a door being opened and then closed. A shadow approached the glass.

'We're closed!'

'No,' Fukuada said. 'You must open. Need money. Des-prat.'

'You 'eard, we're closed!'

'Have go' watch. Prenty spensif. Re' go'. See. Got TV an' fax.'

There was a hesitation, then the sound of a latch being drawn. The door opened slightly on the chain.

'Show me,' the voice demanded. 'Put your arm inside.'

Fukuada did as he was told. He felt the watch being taken from his wrist.

'Okay,' the voice said after a moment. 'Let me look at this a moment. I have to shut the door. Wait there.'

Fukuada withdrew his hand and waited as the door slammed shut again. And as he waited he counted in his head. One ere-fant. Two ere-fants. Free ere-fants. He had got to free hun-red an' ten ere-fants when the door opened again.

'I'll give you a hundred.'

'A hun-red? It wor' fou-san dorrar!'

'One fifty tops.' A hand appeared, offering the watch back.

'Okay,' Fukuada said. 'We ha' deal!'

The hand disappeared. A moment later it reappeared, holding a piece of paper and a pen. 'Sign that,' the voice said.

Fukuada signed and handed the pen and paper back. Clearly the man had decided on one hundred and fifty right from the start. There was no way he could have prepared the paper that quickly.

'Good,' the voice said. 'Here . . .' The hand popped out, holding three crisp red fifty-pound notes. 'Now bugger off!'

'Thank you!' Fukuada said, bowing to his unseen benefactor. 'I bugger off!'

Slipping two of the fifties into his suit pocket, he took the third over to a nearby newsagent's stand, where he purchased five ten-pound phonecards. It was almost nine now in London, so in Tokyo it would be nearly six o'clock. Matsushito would be climbing the stairs to his office even now, as he did every morning. He would stop at the machine to make himself a coffee, then walk down the corridor. At five past six he would be at his desk.

Fukuada smiled, then walked across the square towards the line of telephone boxes on the far side. The middle two were being used. He took the one on the far left, idly studying the prostitutes' cards for a moment, admiring the curvaceous Western models, all the while counting elephants in his head. At three hundred elephants he lifted the handset, slipped the first of the phonecards into the slot, and – from memory – dialled the long number that would put him in contact with his cousin Matsushito in Tokyo.

Charles had tossed and turned all night. Lost in the fog of half-sleep he had replayed *that kiss* over and over again in his mind, more often than not in a strange, almost cinematic slow motion, his senses lingering over that moment when his lips found Chastity's and he was consumed by an almost overwhelming desire. But each time he had almost drifted off, seduced by the cherished memory of their brief moment of passion, he recalled with anguish and despair the disastrous balls-up that had followed – that fateful missed opportunity when he had allowed her to slip away.

As he turned the wheel to take the car into the Square, Charles shook his head in silent disbelief as he relived the moment once again, mouthing the words as the picture of their parting flashed through his head, torturing himself with thoughts of what might have been, and chastising himself for being so unbelievably gauche.

The building was locked. Glancing at his watch

Charles was surprised that it was still so early. From the moment he had woken that morning, his eyes heavy with tiredness, he had been desperate to get back to the office; drunk with the heady, obsessive infatuation that is the prerogative of the young, his only thought was to see Chastity.

Using his own personal set of keys he let himself in, walking across the empty lobby to the waiting lift. For a moment he stood outside it, looking dreamily into the dreary grey metal box with as much tender reverence as if he were revisiting some romantic moonlit enclave, or a fondly remembered childhood scene. Sighing deeply, he stepped inside and pushed the button for the penthouse, slumping against the wall where hours before Chastity's body had rested. He sniffed the air, trying to get the faintest scent of her, then reached up and touched the spot where she had been, like a worshipper at a religious shrine. Bringing those same fingertips to his mouth, he kissed them lightly, closing his eyes as he imagined her there beside him.

'Chastity,' he whispered to the wall. 'My darling Chastity.'

The thought of what might have been flooded his mind. He closed his eyes, indulging in the 'what-if' fantasy he had indulged in a dozen times already. What if the lift really had stuck? What if he had had to spend a whole hour there in the half-light with her. Or, just maybe, the whole night? Surely – *surely?*—they would have made love.

The very thought of it sent a strange shudder up his spine and raised the hairs on the back of his neck, and, by the time the lift arrived at the penthouse, Charles Grant had the most enormous erection!

Self-consciously he hurried across the corridor and unlocked the door to his office.

Love. He'd always thought love a little soppy . . . a little . . . *girlish* until now, all soft lights and candles and violins.

Charles closed the door and leaned his back against it, conscious of the hard swelling at his groin. Almost against his will, his hand went down and touched himself there, while in his mind he imagined it was her hand. And as he closed his eyes he groaned – a groan of sweet torment.

'Oh, Chastity . . .'

'King's Cross!'

The bus conductor's voice rose above the noise of the engine as he moved towards the platform at the rear of the vehicle.

A procession of grim-faced commuters shuffled along the gangway and stepped off the bus, jostling past Chastity as she clung to the overhead bar.

She barely noticed.

'Move down the bus, please,' the conductor yelled from his strategic position, feet placed territorially upon the footplate, his arms outstretched to bar the way of commuters and tourists as they fought for a place, their hands grasping for the bus's upright pole. The conductor's grey Brylcreemed head moved from side to side as he counted up the number of available seats.

'D'you wanna take a seat, love?' he called impatiently.

Chastity turned and gazed dreamily down the length of the gangway.

'C'mon, love, I ain't got all day you know,' he added, shaking his head exaggeratedly as he watched her move to the front of the bus and slide into an empty seat.

Moments later the bus was filled with a new wave of travellers, each jostling for a place. Chastity eased her way over to the window seat in order to accommodate an elderly lady, umbrella in hand, who had obviously managed to elbow her way to the front of the queue. They exchanged a brief smile and Chastity turned her face to the window, resting the side of her head against the cold, damp glass.

Her mind had not had a moment's peace since *that kiss*. Sometimes she wondered whether it had actually happened at all, whether she had, in fact, dreamed it, it seemed so unreal. Yet every detail of those precious moments they had spent together was etched on her memory so clearly, every movement, every sound recalled so vividly, that she felt certain it must have happened. She closed her eyes and immediately she was back there, feeling the weight of Charles's body as it pressed against hers, the warmth of his mouth as it closed over hers. Instinctively her lips parted.

Chastity shook her head as though to dislodge the memory, banging her forehead against the unforgiving window. She caught sight of the old woman looking at her out of the corner of her eye and shifted uncomfortably in her seat.

But along with those tantalising, precious memories, Chastity's sleepless night had been filled with self-recrimination. She felt sure he must have realised she had ambushed him, that she had lain in wait for him, maybe even tried to ensnare him. And what about that kiss? She just knew he wouldn't have expected her to allow him to kiss her, to be so *forward*. So what must he think of her now? Chastity bit her lip, a sudden nausea, born of shame, rising in her throat at the thought of having to face him at the office.

She felt the old woman's sharp elbow dig into her side and rubbed distractedly over her ribs.

'Got your fare, dear?' the woman whispered into her ear, the faint scent of lavender filling Chastity's nostrils as she leaned into her.

Chastity glanced up to see the bus conductor looking down at her, one hand on his ticket machine, the other outstretched as it awaited her money. She reached into the outside pocket of her shoulder bag and flashed her bus pass at him.

''Bout time,' he said gruffly, acknowledging the pass with a brief, dismissive nod. Then, in a somewhat friendlier tone, he added, 'You wanna get some sleep when you go to bed, love. Tell that boyfriend of yours I said to give you a night off.' And giving her a wink he moved down the bus.

Chastity could feel the heat passing up her neck and into her cheeks as several people looked across at her and sniggered, including one repulsive middle-aged man with centre-parted hair and a pork-sausage complexion. She wanted to curl up and die. But even as that wave of self-consciousness swept over her, she felt another, this time gentler, dig in her ribs from the old woman's elbow.

The old dear leaned close, then whispered conspiratorially into Chastity's ear, 'He's only jealous, love. Take it from me, you get it while you can!'

*   *   *

Cynthia switched on the computer and stared bleary-eyed into the depths of the bright blue screen, thankful for Brian's absence in her delicate condition. Reaching into the bottom drawer of her desk, she fumbled amongst tampons, deodorant, toothbrush, mouthwash and an assortment of packets and jars for the plastic container of paracetamol, her head pounding even harder against her skull as she sat upright, clutching it in her trembling hand. Opening the container was more difficult than she'd anticipated – the idea of pushing and twisting the cap at the same time proving almost too much to cope with – until, with a really concentrated effort, she finally managed to pull it off. Pushing two tablets to the back of her tongue, she rinsed them down with a mouthful of sparkling water, wincing at the bitter aftertaste.

She had been relieved not to have Nobushi Fukuada to cope with that morning. Whether out of consideration or embarrassment – though she doubted it was the latter – he had phoned just before midnight to say he wouldn't be back that night and that he was staying with friends. Cynthia had not asked who they were, nor, at that moment, did she care; by then her thoughts were elsewhere, with someone else.

With her back to the door, Cynthia was able to sit with her eyes closed, undetected, as she quietly indulged herself. The thought of Kirsty McDonald brought a smile to her lips and almost immediately her body became aroused by the memory of the night they had spent together. She could feel Kirsty's mouth on her breast, could feel her fingers on her skin, parting the lips of her vulva, she could taste the saltiness of the other woman's sweat as it had run between her breasts and onto her eager lips. Cynthia reached beneath the folds of her skirt and lightly stroked the inside of her thighs, aware of a faint soreness there, and further up, between her legs, of a dull but not unpleasant ache that dragged at her insides.

A shudder passed through her body and slowly, gently, her fingers inched beneath the elastic of her panties.

Tonight, she thought. I wonder if she'll stay again tonight.

The rattle of the tea trolley in the corridor outside brought her sharply out of her reverie. Even so, it was with regret that she removed her hand and turned to face the door as Carol, the receptionist, popped her tightly permed head around it.

'Something hot and warm, Cynthia?'

'Please,' she said, stifling the laugh that almost spilled from her. 'And make it two lumps, Carol. I need the energy!'

An hour back, Kirsty McDonald had parted the thin wooden slats of the blind and watched Cynthia as she emerged from the building three floors below, pulling on her jacket as she hurriedly crossed the street on her way to the tube station. Kirsty had offered her the use of her chauffeur-driven car, which had arrived just after dawn and was parked outside, but Cynthia had declined. Kirsty's gaze had followed her new young friend until she disappeared round the corner and out of sight.

Now, as she walked about the room, it was as though she were seeing it properly for the first time. Without the polite, unspoken restraints of being in the presence of her host, Kirsty felt at liberty now to roam freely through

Cynthia's apartment, poking into nooks and crannies, dipping into drawers and jars, fitting together the jigsaw pieces of Cynthia's life to make up the whole picture.

The decor was minimalist, austere almost, and the influence definitely Eastern. There was little clutter and few of the kind of intimate, personal items from which one could guess at a person's history or invent a past.

Kirsty walked through to the bedroom, her naked body wrapped in the silk kimono Cynthia had draped across the bed as she'd bent to kiss her goodbye. Sitting on the edge of the bed, she idly opened the drawer to the cabinet beside her, reaching in to rummage amongst its contents, smiling as her fingers closed over the familiar shape of a dildo. She brought it out, and held it up before her, running her hand up and down the smooth dark shaft. Closing her eyes she placed the bulbous tip into her mouth, and as her tongue played over it she was convinced that she could taste Cynthia.

A shiver passed through her body.

The contents of Cynthia's wardrobe also bore testimony to her sexual preference: the umbrella stand tucked in the corner at the back contained an impressive collection of whips and other corrective paraphernalia, whilst a range of five rubber outfits stiffly dangled from brass hooks screwed to the back panel of the cupboard, camouflaged by Cynthia's more sober daywear from the likes of Laura Ashley and Marks & Spencer. Kirsty flicked her way along the row of hangers, amused by the contrast, slowing only as she neared the end and her hand touched upon the first of Nobushi Fukuada's business suits. The six Savile Row suits – in different shades of grey – gave the American pause for thought and added yet another dimension to her young British friend, who had already turned out to be so surprising.

The small bamboo and cane table in the corner of the room served as a desk, and strewn across it, in no particular order, were pieces of paper and piles of paperbacks. Kirsty ran a manicured finger down the row of book spines, noting with interest the unusual range of subjects – from works on cybernetics and state-of-the-art technology, to slush romantic novels, books on the Tao, a Japanese Manga comic book and a tiny, leather-bound edition of the essays of William Hazlitt, a man she'd never even heard of. Randomly selecting pieces of paper she sifted lazily through snippets of Cynthia's life, trying to make sense of the seemingly contradictory elements she had so far discovered.

She was used to people being not quite what they seemed. In the States everyone appeared so damn happy, but half of them were on Prozac and most of them had analysts, they were so fucked up. The Brits were supposed to be different. With the Brits she thought it was supposed to be what you saw was what you got. Well, not with Cynthia.

With Cynthia what you got on the surface was Miss Prim and Proper. But under the frilly floral skirts was a sexual adventuress with a predilection for pain. Here was someone whose home reflected a neat, tidy persona, yet whose desk was a total contradiction as it swam with disorder. Kirsty shook her head and smiled, squatting down to retrieve a scrap of paper that had drifted to the floor. With vague interest she read its sparse contents: 'Nobushi' followed by a telephone number. Her brow creased as she fought to recall where she had heard that word before and suddenly remembered the little Japanese man she had met the previous night. Yes, Cynthia had introduced him as Nobushi.

Kirsty sat in the chair, her eyes focused on the piece of paper, her face set in concentration. After a couple of minutes, and, with the look of someone who has not completed a crossword or has almost reached the end of a puzzle only to discover there are pieces missing, she placed the note back on the table. Then, frowning a little, she reached across and picked up the handset of the telephone, punching in the code for Seattle.

Chastity rushed into Patricia's office and, holding onto the edge of the desk, said breathlessly, 'Pat! Pat! You'll never guess what!'

Patricia stared up at Chastity, her mouth fallen open. 'He hasn't!'

'He has!' Chastity answered. 'He's downstairs in reception right now! They've brought all the boxes back!'

'*Boxes*?'

'Inspector Holly!' Chastity said. 'He's brought everything back. And he's handed over a letter for Charles.' And now she held it out, so that Patricia could take it.

'But I thought—'

'What?' Chastity said, confused. 'What did you think?'

Patricia's mouth slowly closed. She looked down. 'Nothing. I just misunderstood you, that's all.' And, having slit the letter open with her thumbnail, she unfolded the single sheet and read it.

'It's an apology,' she said, looking back up at Chastity after a moment. 'And a promise not to bother us any more.'

'Great!' Chastity said. Then, seeing the strange expression on Patricia's face, she asked, 'What's up?'

Patricia laid the letter down, then stood, coming round her desk. 'Is he still down there?'

'Yeah. Roger's dealing with him.'

'Poor man.'

'Oh, I don't know,' Chastity said perkily. 'Roger's actually being very decent to him for once.'

'I don't mean for having Roger deal with him. I mean . . .'

'What?'

'It's just that I saw him last night, sitting in a pub I was passing on my way home. All alone. He looked so . . . sad.'

'Sad?' Chastity looked at Patricia as if she'd gone mad. 'But I thought you said—'

'I know what I said,' Patricia interjected, 'but you have to feel sorry for the man.'

'Why?'

Patricia smiled at her, then went over to the door. 'You wouldn't understand, my dear. You wouldn't understand at all.'

Patricia saw Inspector Holly at once – or, rather, what she took to be Holly from his shabby suit, for he was bending down over one of the boxes, checking on something.

'Inspector!' she called, walking smartly towards him across the lobby.

Holly stood bolt upright, the look of consternation he
had been wearing changing instantly to an expression of
sheer terror. He turned, half raising his hands as if to
fend off some oncoming horror.

'It's all right, Patricia,' Roger began, sauntering across.
'I've got everything in hand.'

But Patricia waved Roger Appleyard aside. She went
over and stood before Holly, shaking her head. 'This
really is too much, Inspector! We've a delivery of important machine parts within the hour, and here you are
cluttering up our lobby with your boxes!'

'*My* boxes?' Holly blinked. 'But, but—'

But Patricia was not about to let him get a word
in. 'So if you and your men' – she glanced at the two
plain-clothes detectives who stood nearby, visibly wincing
as she tongue-lashed their boss – 'would shift these boxes
into the lift, I'm sure Chastity here will show you where
they should be stacked.'

'But, but—'

But Patricia was adamant, uncompromising. 'The
delivery will be here any minute, Inspector!'

Holly swallowed, then, with a look partly of resentment, partly of admiration for the woman, began to
turn away.

'And Inspector . . .' Patricia added, her eyes narrowed
slightly as she watched him.

'Yes?' Holly said, hunching one shoulder, clearly
expecting another broadside.

'Thank you. I appreciate your cooperation.'

And with that Patricia turned on her heel and marched
over to the stairs, leaving Holly looking after her,
blinking with shock. For a moment he did not move,

then, coming to himself again, he turned and looked at his men, scowling at them.

'You heard 'er. Shift 'em! Now!'

With scarcely a glance at the receptionist, Kirsty McDonald swept through the glass doors and across the lobby of Virt-E-Go's office.

Even as Carol hastily punched in the number of Charles's extension, the lift doors closed and, with a whining hum, the car began to ascend towards the penthouse.

As Carol connected with the number, there was the beep-beep-beep of an engaged signal.

So it was that Charles put down the phone and turned, unprepared, to find Kirsty McDonald standing in his doorway, Chastity and Patricia hovering just behind her.

'You must be Charles,' Kirsty said, walking across to him and extending her hand. 'Toby's told me a lot about you.'

Charles cleared his throat nervously, then put out his hand, his face registering surprise at the strength of the woman's grip.

'I . . . I've been expecting you,' he said.

It was a ridiculous thing to say really. Of course he'd been expecting her. All morning he'd been expecting her, until, worn out from nervous anticipation, he had taken to phoning her hotel to find out whether she really *had* arrived in London, after all.

'So?' Kirsty said, relinquishing his hand, then moving past him to look at the view from his window. 'Where is this machine of yours?'

'I . . .' Charles clicked his mouth shut, internally counting to ten. Now was not the time to go into stammer mode. A lot was hanging on this meeting. They had to impress Kirsty McDonald.

'It's in the laboratory,' he said, as she turned, smiling, to face him again. 'That's two floors down from here.'

'Right,' Kirsty said brusquely, the smile never wavering for a second. 'Then let's not waste time. I want to try it out for myself.'

As Kirsty McDonald slipped off her jacket and began to undress, Charles turned away, horrified.

'But I thought . . .'

He looked to Patricia, his eyes willing her to do something. Patricia, noting that look of panic, took control.

'Roger! Bob! Out of here, *now*. Miss McDonald would like some privacy while she's testing the machine.'

But Kirsty merely smiled and began to unbutton her blouse. 'Don't worry about me. We sure as hell ain't making no baby-comforter here, are we? So let's not be uptight about things.'

'Even so,' Patricia said, her eyes drawn — despite herself — to Kirsty's small but impressively firm breasts as she slipped off her bra, 'I'm not sure . . .'

'Christ!' Roger Appleyard murmured under his breath. 'Talk about Silicon Valley!'

Bob merely groaned.

Even Bill and Ben seemed somewhat shocked by their new backer's behaviour, and, as she finally slipped from her thong and stood there stark naked before them, they merely stared at her goggle-eyed as she held up her arms and said, 'Okay, boys. Wire me up!'

298

Bill looked to Ben, then stammered his reply. 'B-but the p-program's wrong.'

'Wrong?'

Ben nodded his agreement. 'You see it's . . .' He swallowed deeply. 'It's meant for a man.'

'Oh, shit, is that all?' Kirsty took another step towards them, holding up her arms, as if about to be fitted for a new dress. 'Well, get on with it, boys. I'm only going to wear the damn thing, I ain't gonna marry it!'

With considerable embarrassment, the twins fitted the body suit, adjusting it by means of a number of long leather straps that joined together the sensory panels. These panels were stippled on the inside, like the back of a table tennis bat, each stipple wired up to register the pressure exerted upon it and feed that information back into the computer.

The suit, therefore, was a crude recording device; and what it recorded was how the body that wore it was touched and brushed and stroked – and penetrated.

But it was also a playback machine, and, just as the stipples could register pressure, they could also exert it, moving in accordance with a prerecorded program that existed on a series of CD-ROMS.

Other elements were also involved in the process. There was a special mask, for instance, that went fully over the head, a pair of liquid-crystal-display lenses – LCDs – feeding back an image into the eyes, so that, just as the suit gave its wearer the illusion of being touched, the lenses gave an illusion of just who (in this case, a rather stunning blonde they had hired from a model agency a month or so back) was doing the touching.

Bill and Ben had other plans, too, involving taste and

scent, but as yet they had not incorporated them into the program. But there was sound. The noise of someone vigorously enjoying what was being done to them!

Looking on, Cynthia felt herself becoming excited once again. In the full-body suit and mask, Kirsty McDonald took on a whole new dimension. The straps and wires, and especially the mask, triggered something deep in Cynthia's psyche so that, as Kirsty was guided onto the VR lounger, Cynthia felt she wanted to climb on with her and simply rub herself against her.

'Seems all a bit complicated to me,' Roger Appleyard murmured from where he stood just behind her, but, even as Cynthia made to turn and hush him, she heard a grunt of pain. Patricia had clearly elbowed Roger hard in the solar plexus.

For the next ten minutes they all stood in embarrassed but fascinated silence as Kirsty squirmed about, clearly in the throes of acute pleasure. 'Jesus!' Bob Guppy murmured, at least a dozen times. And, looking round, Cynthia could see that, beneath the tightly stretched cloth of their trousers, both he and Roger sported huge erections.

As the program came to its climax, everyone in the room seemed to lean toward the lounger as Kirsty McDonald climbed that final peak, panting all the way, as if short of breath, then threw herself off the edge in a long ecstatic cry of pained pleasure.

Cynthia shuddered. Her body ached to be touched. As Bill and Ben sheepishly stepped forward to remove the mask and help Kirsty from the lounger, Cynthia turned and looked about her.

Charles was bright red with embarrassment. Beside

him, Patricia was looking down, thoughtfully. Chastity, standing by the door, also had a flush at her neck. Roger was grinning. Even as she looked, he turned to Bob Guppy and gave a conspiratorial wink. Louise, like Patricia, was also looking down, yet she seemed angry rather than thoughtful. Or distracted, rather.

As the mask was removed, Kirsty's face emerged. She looked about her coolly for a moment, then gave a huge grin.

'It's great!' she said. 'It has real potential!'

'Oh, wonderful!' Charles said, expressing their general relief. 'Then we have a deal?'

Kirsty stepped out from the tank, then stood there as Bill and Ben began to unstrap her.

'Oh, most certainly. But I have one or two conditions.'

'Ah . . .' Charles nodded, as if he had expected this.

'First, I want to bring in some professionals.'

'Professionals?'

'Actors. People I know from the LA scene. And a director pal. I've worked with him before, years ago.'

Charles still seemed to be missing the point. 'I'm sorry, I—'

But Kirsty was not to be interrupted now. 'You see, what you've got here is fine, to a point, but, if we're going to get the big money to support us, we need something a bit slicker, a bit more professional to show. Oh, I can give you the computer power to do the job, but you need something more. You need an edge. And these people can help you get that edge.'

Cynthia spoke up. 'You're talking porn-movie actors, right?'

'Right!' Kirsty said, turning – as much as she was permitted by the harness – towards Cynthia. 'As I see it, if we're going to deal in fantasy, let's give the customer what they want. Let's give them the best fantasy screw they've ever had. And then – God willing – they'll keep coming!'

And she laughed, as if it were the most original joke ever cracked.

There was some laughter, but mostly there was a stunned silence about the laboratory. Porn-movie actors? Was that really the direction they were headed in?

'I—' Charles began, but Patricia touched his arm.

'Not now Charles,' she whispered to him.

'Yeah,' Kirsty went on, as her breasts reappeared into general view, the nipples still erect with excitement. 'But we need to get moving. We need to have something ready for the International Computer Show in December.'

Charles looked to the twins. 'William? Benjamin? Can it be done?'

The twins looked up as one and, after a brief glance at Kirsty, nodded. 'Give us the tools . . .' Bill began, '. . . and we'll finish the job,' Ben ended.

'Great!' Kirsty said. She shrugged off the last vestiges of the body suit, and, without a shred of self-consciousness, walked over to where her business clothes lay in a neat pile on the chair. 'Then I'll get my legal department to draft a contract. We're gonna change the world, boys and girls. We're going to change the fucking world!'

Half an hour later, up in Charles's penthouse office, Kirsty McDonald handed over a cheque for a half a million pounds sterling, drawn on the London branch of her bank.

'Time's short,' she said, sitting back in her chair, 'so, whatever you need to speed things up, you tell your boys to get. And send me the bill, okay? As far as the actors are concerned, leave that to me. I'll organise everything.'

'Good . . . erm, yes, very good. I'll—'

'Hey, don't let it worry you, Charlie boy. We're not doing anything illegal, right? Just filling a gap in the market. This is the future. And there's no stopping the future. Sex when you want it and with whomsoever you want it – that's how we're going to sell this. And I tell you, everyone is going to want a bit of this action. *Everyone.*'

Charles stared at her a moment, as if he was going to argue with her, then, looking back at the cheque in his hand, he gave a single nod.

'Look, erm . . . are you staying over?'

Kirsty narrowed her eyes slightly. 'I might be. Why?'

'I . . .' Charles took a breath. 'I thought we might celebrate, that's all. Have dinner.'

It was not that Charles particularly wanted to have dinner with the woman, but Patricia had suggested to him earlier that it might seem awfully 'off' if he didn't entertain her while she was here. No. Personally, he would rather have asked Chastity out, but business was business and this once it made sense to follow his head, not his heart.

'That'd be nice,' Kirsty answered, with the beginnings of a grin. 'Anywhere special?'

'No,' Charles said, having no intention to impress her. 'I thought the Ritz, perhaps. I have a table there.'

'The Ritz?' She nodded, impressed even so. 'And afterwards?'

But Charles barely heard what she said. He was thinking about Chastity, and wondering what she would be doing that evening.

The overhead strip of fluorescent light shone unkindly onto Patricia's upturned face as she pouted into the mirror above the washbasin. A regiment of tiny lines gathered about her lips, a fine dusting of face powder falling into each tiny crevice. Staring at her reflection – at an alien image that had more to do with her mother than with the person she felt she was – Patricia raised a hand to her face, delicately patting the fine lines around her eyes. As she looked into those dark, deep pools it was hard to imagine that so many years of her life had passed; that she was no longer considered young except by those who were themselves waiting to die, and whose opinions were therefore of no consequence to her.

The sudden appearance of Louise through the doorway drew her from this morose train of thought and she smiled into the mirror at the younger woman as she came to stand beside her at the adjoining basin.

'All right, Patricia?'

'Yes, thank you, Louise.'

Patricia watched with fascination as Louise reached into her handbag, producing a voluminous toiletries hold-all from which she drew an assortment of make-up items which she proceeded to apply with expert ease. The skin became suddenly silkier, the eyes bigger and darker, the cheekbones more defined, and the lips daringly red and provocatively pouting. Patricia was mesmerised.

Pushing her fingers into the tangled curls of her hair, Louise fluffed out her long tresses and, when finally she had finished, allowed herself a brief smile of satisfaction into the mirror.

'Are you out, tonight?' Patricia asked, taking her own ancient-looking lipstick from the inside pocket of her handbag. Opening her mouth, she guided it over her upper lip with little attention to detail, before stretching her bottom lip taut across her teeth and covering the thin, wrinkled strip with pale pink colouring.

'Nah,' Louise replied distractedly, unable to take her eyes from Patricia's reflection. Reaching into her bag she produced a tube of lipstick, removed the lid, and twisted the base until a capsule of rose red emerged above the shining silver case. 'Here,' she said, proffering it to Patricia, 'try this.'

Patricia shook her head. 'No thank you, dear. I don't think it's really me.'

'Go on,' Louise urged, thrusting the lipstick towards her once more. 'It'll take ten years off you.'

Reluctantly Patricia accepted it and, after removing the coat of lipstick she had just applied, began to run it over her thin lips.

'Nah, not like that,' Louise said, taking it from her hand and gently turning Patricia to face her. 'Let me do it.'

It was with a degree of trepidation that Patricia faced her reflection in the mirror, but there was no getting away from it: the girl was right! She definitely looked younger.

'Goodness!'

'See, told you, didn't I?' Louise said with satisfaction,

pushing the tube of lipstick back inside its casing. 'Here,' she said, handing it to Patricia, 'a present for you.'

Patricia gave a broad smile into the mirror, admiring the way her fleshily pouting lips seemed to light up her face.

'So. No Roger tonight, then?'

'Nah. I reckon he's got other fish to fry.'

'Roger?' Patricia's brow furrowed as she struggled to think which other poor unsuspecting female might be Roger Appleyard's next victim. 'Like who?'

'Well, who do you think? I mean, I think it's really obvious.'

'I really have absolutely no idea.'

Louise raised her eyes towards the ceiling. 'Chastity of course,' she spat. 'Huh! That's the wrong bloody name for *that* one!'

'Chastity?' Patricia's voice was incredulous. 'Well,' she added after a moment's consideration, 'that may be true about Roger, but I feel sure the feeling is not reciprocated. No, I think it's safe to say that Chastity's interests lie elsewhere.'

Louise looked almost close to tears and Patricia was moved by the girl's misplaced affections. Men like Roger Appleyard needed to have their balls bashed together between two bricks, she decided; and girls like Louise – well, there was no helping girls like Louise.

'Please, don't say anything to anyone,' Patricia began, 'but I think it's safe to say that Chastity is very much enamoured with our young Chairman.'

'*Charles?*' Louise said, with a disproportionate degree of incredulity. 'You think Chastity fancies Charles?' Louise laughed. 'He's a bit wet, don't you think?'

'A bit shy, maybe, but . . .'

'But what?' Turning from the mirror, Louise made her way over to the door. Before she left, however, she turned, one hand holding the door open. 'Mind you, he's rich enough. And that's a nice car he drives.'

Patricia frowned. 'Meaning what?'

'Just that our *Chastity* might not be quite as innocent as she looks.' Louise smiled tartly, all of her bitterness transferred suddenly from Roger to this new target. 'There's no way someone of Charles's breeding would end up with a little tramp like Chastity Lloyd. Nah, she's only after his money. And good luck to her. But don't give me any of this love lark. The only love our Chastity has is for that bulge in his jacket pocket!'

Patricia went to answer, but Louise had gone, the door swinging closed behind her. Sighing heavily, Patricia took one final look at herself in the mirror, then, with a shake of her head, turned and left the restroom.

It wasn't until the outer door of the ladies' closed and all was silent within that the lock to one of the cubicles was pushed back and the door rattled in its flimsy frame. Gingerly stepping out into the washroom, Chastity looked stunned, her pale young face a mask of pain and distress as tears gathered on her bottom eyelashes and began to trickle over her flushed cheeks.

Charles slipped his gold American Express card into the inside breast pocket of his jacket and, folding the receipt in two, slipped the square of flimsy paper in beside it. A moment later Kirsty McDonald was inching her slim hips through the gap between their table and the next.

Charles raised himself out of his chair, resuming his seat only when his dinner guest was once again seated opposite, looking perfectly coiffured. Not a hair of her neat, cropped head was out of place, not a microscopic morsel of food had disturbed those perfectly drawn lips, and barely a crease lined her elegant, shoulder-padded Armani suit.

'Hey, that's one helluva powder room, Charlie,' she said, leaning forward to rest her elbows on the starched white tablecloth.

'I'm afraid I shall have to take your word for it,' he smiled.

She laughed aloud and openly studied him, the flickering candlelight throwing a cast of dancing shadows across his face.

'You got a girlfriend, Charlie?'

Charles fidgeted in his seat, averting his eyes from her probing gaze. 'Er, no. Not at the moment.' He forced the kind of smile that a more sensitive soul would have accepted as a signal that the matter was closed.

'So what's the score? What're you looking for?' she persisted unabashed. 'I mean, a good looking guy like you, well-to-do, you should have the chicks flocking.'

Charles placed a hand over his chin and began nervously rubbing first one cheek and then the other, his eyes darting anxiously round the room. He opened his mouth to speak but, before any sound was made, Kirsty suddenly reached across and laid a hand over his.

'Hey, you're not gay, are you?'

Charles's eyes narrowed as he struggled to follow her train of thought.

'If you are, that's cool. No problem. It's just that when

you meet a good-looking single guy, you gotta wonder. Leastways, you do where I come from.'

Charles's face was a mask of incomprehension. A faint smile played on Kirsty's lips as she tried to gauge whether this guy was an Oscar-standard actor or was really as naive as he would have her believe. At the thought of the latter possibility her mind raced way ahead and her tongue turned lasciviously over her top lip so that it glistened in the candlelight, a sudden hunger in her piercing blue eyes.

Charles's thoughts were a million miles away, with poor Davina and then in the lift, wrapped in Chastity's glorious arms. He had not been aware of the eagerness with which Kirsty had left her seat and slipped between the tables, and was surprised by the huskiness in her voice as she bent to whisper in his ear.

'Let's go back to my hotel for a nightcap.'

'Roger?'

Louise slipped the catch and stood back, surprised to see her lover standing there. Yet as Roger stepped past her into the flat, she caught the faintest trace of perfume on him and instantly her delight at seeing him transmuted into suspicion.

'Where've you been?'

Roger turned, surprised. 'Been?' His voice seemed slightly slurred. 'I've been out, if you must know. Out.'

'Yes, but who with? Chastity, I bet,' Louise spat, unable to keep the acid from her voice. Her face had crumpled into a mass of bitter jealousy, and Roger, staring into it, felt it made her look a good twenty years older.

A bit too much like his wife, in fact.

'*Chastity*?' He shook his head in bewilderment. 'That frigid little bitch?'

'She turn you down then?' Louise said, taking a step towards him threateningly. 'She lead you up the garden path, then dump you in the cold? And is that why you're here now? 'Cos she made you horny and then wouldn't let you have your way?'

Roger swallowed, a genuine indignation now filling his voice. 'You think Her Ladyship would spare a second glance for me?'

'So she's better than me, is that it?'

Roger frowned, trying to follow this convolution, then shook his head to try to clear it. 'No . . . look, no . . . I don't mean she's any better than you. *You're* my girl,' he said, reaching out to take her shoulders, 'you know you are, it's just that Chastity has bigger fish to fry than just the Finance Director . . .'

Louise was still glaring at him, but something in her face softened as she considered that. Then, with a little shrug, she dropped her eyes, the harshness leaving her face. Even so, there was still the matter of the perfume.

'So who *have* you been with?'

Roger blinked, then, as if conscious of his own smell for the first time, said, 'Oh, that! That was an accident?'

Louise looked up again. 'Accident?'

'Yeah,' Roger said, his fingers beginning to smooth and stroke Louise's shoulders. 'The bulb went in the bathroom at home, and there weren't any spares. In the dark I mistook Jane's perfume for my aftershave.'

Louise flinched slightly. She hated it when he used *her*

name. Even so, the explanation soothed her. 'You went home, then?'

Roger nodded, then laughed. 'Yes. I told her we were all having dinner with the American before she flew back to the States. Said I had to be there. So here I am.'

'You took your time.'

'What?' Once again, Roger looked flummoxed. 'But you weren't expecting me!'

'Maybe. But you didn't come straight here. We could have spent the whole evening together.'

'Yes, but—'

'So where were you?'

Jesus, Roger thought, this is worse than the Spanish bleeding Inquisition.

'If you must know,' he said patiently, 'I went for a drink with Bob Guppy.'

'Guppy?' And now Louise stared at him in total disbelief. 'You really expect me to believe that? When did you start going drinking with Bob Guppy, when you could have been round here with me?'

Roger raised his hands defensively. 'Look, Lulu, I know how it sounds, but it's true. I was about to set off from home when Guppy phoned. He sounded really pissed off. Something about having a ding-dong of a row with his wife. I couldn't say no, now could I, sweetheart?'

Louise stared at him hard a moment or two more, as if to try to catch him out, then, seeing the look of genuine appeal in his eyes, relented and let him take her in his arms.

'I s'pose not,' she said. 'Poor sod. Mind, I guess he deserves it, what with shagging that Davina woman. I wouldn't put up with it!'

Roger nodded, but in his eyes was a look of relief that Louise had bought his story. He had, indeed, had a drink or two with Bob Guppy, but that had been an hour back. Between times he had paid a visit to another old friend. It was *her* perfume Louise had smelled.

'So?' Louise said, nibbling his neck. 'What do you fancy? A nice hot bath? A session in the shower? Or would you like one of my specials?'

Despite his slight drunkenness and the fact that he had already had sex that evening, the mention of one of Louise's 'specials' did the trick. Roger's prick immediately sprang to attention.

'That sounds . . . wonderful.' Then, chancing his luck, he said, 'What about a shower *and* a special?'

'To get that perfume off you, you mean?' Louise said, looking at him playfully, one hand reaching down to feel just how firm he was, clearly pleased with the result of her suggestion.

'I just thought it might put you off, that's all,' he said casually.

'Okay,' she said, her face – now that it was free of all bitterness and jealousy – much more the face of a young mistress than that of a potential wife. 'And if you're really good I'll let you play that little game again . . .'

Charles had good reason to be feeling pleased with himself as he accelerated down Tottenham Court Road, skipping through on amber and gliding onto the Euston Road.

Kirsty McDonald had been terrifyingly insistent that he should join her in her room for a nightcap, her invitation issued with the assurance of someone used to getting what she wanted and offering no possibility of polite refusal. Anticipating the experience with something akin to Daniel's reservations as he approached the lion's den, Charles's brain had been spurred into a state of high mental activity. With a surprising degree of authenticity, he proffered the gippy-tum excuse that had served him so well and on so many occasions with Davina. His face had screwed up like an old apricot, his hands spread across his abdomen as he groaned convincingly, apparently in the grip of some nasty gastric thingummy.

Luckily for Charles, becoming intimate with someone who was likely to be relieving their bowels at frequent intervals, was not appealing even to Kirsty McDonald (though she knew a couple of guys who paid money for that kind of thing), so, in spite of feeling incredibly horny, she kissed Charles on the cheek and stepped into the lift alone.

The A–Z lay open on the seat beside Charles, a small white Rotadex card marking the page. Charles pulled up at the traffic lights outside King's Cross, reached over for the book and, finding the station on the map, ran his finger up along the route to his next destination, which he had marked earlier with a red circle.

There was no moon that night. As Charles pulled over to the curb, a black expanse stretched away to his right, the far edge of the Hackney Downs, skirted by a row of amber street lamps, while to his left a trio of tower blocks rose towards the dark cloud-filled sky. Shifting across to the front passenger seat, Charles pressed his cheek to the side window, his gaze following the ugly lines of the buildings as they rose threateningly above him, their starkness bearing cruel testimony to the age from which they were born. He stared up at it, finding it almost impossible to imagine the lives that were being lived behind those endless rows of small, square windows, and it was difficult for him to understand just why people stayed in so awful a place.

Reaching up above the dashboard, Charles slipped the Rotadex card from inside the book and read aloud Chastity's address as Pat had typed it, repeating her name, savouring the sound of it upon his lips. He could just make out the name painted on the large wooden notice board at the entrance to the group of buildings: beneath the green and red graffiti visitors were welcomed to the oh so inappropriately named Paradise Park Estate. Sitting there, checking once again the address on the card, Charles was a little more than surprised by what he had found. He hadn't imagined Chastity living anywhere, but, now he had seen where she *did* actually live, he felt sure this was not what he would have thought of.

He leaned forward, and looked up through the windscreen, resting his chin on his hands as he gazed out with hopeless expectation. In desperation he began to count the number of floors, with the vague hope of being able to ascertain which window was Chastity's. He raised his finger towards the building and counted off each row of windows until, finally, he was convinced he had found it. And, as if it were a sign, a light appeared at the window and moments later the figure of a woman, her arms outstretched as if she were being crucified as she reached for the curtains and pulled them together, plunging the window once more into darkness.

But Charles's gaze never left that window, his eyes focused on the tiny chink of light that poked through the gap where the curtains met, until finally, exhausted by emotional stress and overcome with tiredness, he was forced to drive off into the night.

Chastity's mother stood outside her daughter's bedroom, biting her lip as she listened to the pitiful sound of crying coming from within. Earlier that evening she had looked on with concern as Chastity moved her food around her dinner plate, unable to eat; she had ignored her when she'd lost her temper for no apparent reason, screeching unpleasantly before stomping off to her bedroom and slamming the door behind her. And now she listened helplessly as her precious, beautiful child sobbed into her pillow.

Unable to contain herself any longer, Faith Lloyd reached for the door handle, but in that instant her husband's hand covered hers, his fingers closing firmly over her own.

'Leave her be, Faith,' he said kindly, bending forward to kiss his wife softly on the cheek, the taste of her tears salty on his lips. 'She knows you're here if she needs you.'

Faith allowed her hand to fall to her side and rested her head on her husband's shoulder. Placing an arm around her, he squeezed the soft fleshiness over her waist and turned her away from Chastity's door.

'Come on, love,' he said. 'Whatever it is, she'll work it out for herself.'

Patricia sat in the corner of the saloon bar, nursing her third gin and tonic and staring into space, unaware of the other people who stood between her and the bar, crowding the tiny back street pub. In an hour or so they would be gone – returned home to their loved ones or to their lonely one-bedroom flats – this transitional part of the day, between work and home life, over for the evening.

Patricia had never been a great after-work socialiser. Oh, she enjoyed it occasionally, but generally she preferred to go straight home, drawing a stark line between office and home, but recently she had come to wish somehow to blur that division.

It wasn't that she hated going home: no, she rather liked the privacy and cosiness of her tiny flat. Indeed, after years of living with her slob of a husband, it was nice to have a place which was solely hers – but lately she had found herself more and more reluctant to leave the office. Nor was it that Virt-E-Go's offices were so attractive. It was the people. Or, to be more specific, the girls.

Sitting there, Patricia realised just how small and circumscribed her social life had become these past few years. Once – a long, long time ago, it seemed – she had had friends; now she only had the people she worked with, and, when the day was ended, they went their separate ways.

Leaving her here, alone, nursing a gin and tonic.

Patricia, she said, addressing herself in her head as if she were talking to one of the more junior secretaries, *you are in serious danger of becoming a sad old bag*.

Maybe, but what was she going to do about it?

To be honest, until Sir James had gone, she had not even thought there *was* a problem. While he was still there, she had been content to live in her daydreams, remembering that one heavenly night in Amsterdam –

back in the days when Virt-E-Go had been plain old English Electrical Goods — when Sir James had come to her room and made love to her.

It had been a mistake, of course, and they had both been quick to re-establish their old, more distant relationship, yet it had been enough to give her a romantic glow over the coming years and enough for her to imagine that, after the demise of Lady Grant, she might once again find herself in Sir James's bed.

Patricia sighed, then, lifting her glass to her lips, downed the remainder of her drink in one. Now that Sir James was gone, she saw how futile that dream had been. No, she had to get on with her life. It was no good living in the past and dreaming about what might have been.

She looked up, studying the drinkers all around her. There were few obvious couples, but one never knew — the office was a breeding ground for illicit relationships: a regular hothouse of adultery. Like Louise and Roger.

The thought of them reminded Patricia of what Louise had said about Chastity, earlier on. The venom in Louise's voice had surprised her at the time, but, looking back on it, she thought she understood. Louise was feeling insecure, and insecurity bred jealousy. And what better target for her jealousy than Chastity? Even so, it had been unfair on the poor girl. Whatever anyone said, Patricia could not believe Chastity was a gold-digger. No, her interest in Charles was quite pure. She had seen how wistfully young Chastity looked at her young Chairman and — with a pang of recognition that at the same time both hurt her and made her smile fondly — she understood.

Chastity was in love.

And Charles? He too was in love. In love with Chastity.

And if she could see it, why couldn't they? Why didn't they just throw themselves at each other, as she and Sir James had done that evening in Amsterdam?

Patricia closed her eyes and shuddered, remembering once more how he had taken her, there against the wall, too impatient to take her to the bed, and how afterwards he had carried her across and laid her down, his eyes watching her all the while as he undressed.

Again she sighed. One brief night, that was all it had been. One brief night, and then a lifetime's wistful longing.

Patricia set her glass down heavily, then, reaching behind her chair for her handbag, stood up.

The dream had not come true for her. But that didn't mean it couldn't come true for someone. And what better someones than Chastity and Charles? She could see them now, stepping down the aisle, the perfect couple.

Patricia stepped out into the warm night air and smiled, picturing it vividly in her mind as she walked along. She could see the little country church, the white Rolls waiting beside the lych-gate, the vicar standing on the top step smiling fondly as the two he had just joined in holy matrimony walked slowly, joyfully, down the grass-bordered pathway, pink and white confetti being scattered in the air by smiling onlookers. Why, she could even see the kind of floral arrangement Chastity was carrying.

She stopped suddenly, looking about her. She was in Boswell Street again. Her feet, unwittingly, had brought her back here, where she had been only the other night. To her right, just across the narrow road, was the White Hart.

Like a sleepwalker, she crossed to the opposite pavement and, putting her forehead against the glass, looked in through the window of the pub.

There, in the same corner, at the same table, sat Detective Inspector Holly, nursing what looked like the same half-full pint mug of beer, the same sad – defeated? – expression on his face.

For a moment, Patricia toyed with the idea of going in and sitting down across from him, maybe even buying him a drink. Then, thinking that, as the architect of his humiliation before the Commissioner, she was probably the very last person that Holly wanted to see, she moved back away from the window, then turned, walking on.

But, as she stepped out into Theobalds Road, Patricia could not shake from her mind the picture of Holly's miserable expression.

Maybe you're not such a bastard after all, she thought. Maybe you're just lonely, that's all. Lonely. Just like me.

From where he sat, naked on the end of the bed, Roger could almost see Louise's tonsils – or would have, had there not have been something else blocking the view. As her little-girl eyes stared up at him, he groaned.

Louise's specials, he had to admit, were really special. Some women had this talent, others didn't, and Louise had it in spades. Indeed, if this were all there was to it, then he would quite willingly have stayed here for evermore and never have seen his wife again.

Cupping his balls tenderly, Louise eased back a trifle,

her mouth moving away from his rigid penis. As Roger made a small sound of disappointment, she smiled and reached once more for the bright red lipstick.

It had been rather late in their relationship before Louise had discovered that Roger had this fetish, but it had proved handy from time to time, and it was about to prove handy now.

'Is that nice?' she asked, in a husky little voice that was guaranteed to provoke him.

'Fucking wonderful,' he murmured, his fingers caressing her neck, then reaching down to rub against her stiffly erect nipples.

'And you'll speak to her about it soon?'

Roger, who had edged forward a little, trying to push his penis back into Louise's mouth, merely grunted at this non sequitur.

'About us I mean?' And she gave the tip of his cock the gentlest little lick.

Roger groaned. 'Yes,' he said. 'Oh God, yes.'

'You promise?'

And as she said it she gave his balls the most delicate stroke, which she knew was guaranteed to make him shiver.

Roger shivered. 'Whatever you want, Lulu, just put it back in, for God's sake!'

She gave the bulbous end another delicate little lick, then, making sure he was watching what she did, applied another coat of glossy red lipstick to her lips, pouting them sensuously at him.

'First you must promise.'

Roger groaned, in real pain now. 'I promise. God help me, I promise. Now—'

His words were cut short by a little gasp of ecstasy, as Louise's glistening red lips closed once more about Roger's stiff and aching manhood. He closed his eyes, a long, animal sigh escaping him.

It was thus that he did not see Louise's little smirk of triumph.

There! she thought, as he shuddered and came explosively. That's got the frigid bitch!

Nobushi Fukuada was waiting for Cynthia in her living room when she got home from the office.

'You velly late,' he said, getting up out of his chair, a tentative smile on his fixed Oriental features. 'You work hard rately.'

'Yes,' she said, not quite sure whether she liked or didn't like the fact that he was there. 'Where did you stay the other night?'

'Fren's,' he answered.

Only then did she realise that he was wearing his raincoat, and that his executive leather suitcase was beside the chair.

'Look, Cee-fee-a. Nobushi need favour. Big big favour. Need get Tokyo. But no money.'

'Ah,' she said. Then, understanding his predicament – and the loss of face such a question meant for him – she gave a little bow. 'It would be my great pleasure, Nobushi, and my duty to a friend.'

She saw how that lifted him. Fukuada smiled broadly. 'You good woman, Cee-fee-a. You unner-stan' Nippon, neh? Nobushi no forget.'

'No,' she smiled. 'I know you won't, Nobushi. But even if you did, I'd help you.'

And, seating herself by the phone, Cynthia phoned Heathrow and booked a ticket on the first flight to Tokyo, paying for it with her credit card.

'There,' she said, putting the phone down. 'The ticket will be waiting for you at the Air Nippon desk. All you have to do is show your passport.'

To her surprise, Fukuada knelt and, reaching out, took her hand and kissed the back of it. Then, looking up at her, he smiled.

'I be back, Cee-fee-a. You see. I be back.'

After Fukuada had gone, Cynthia walked about the apartment, feeling strangely empty and at a loose end. She had hoped that Kirsty might phone and invite her over to her hotel, but there had been no messages on the answerphone. Indeed, even a session with Nobushi Fukuada might have lifted her spirits, but that was out of the question now.

A club? she asked herself. But the bother of getting dressed up and phoning for a car was all somehow too much for her. But bed? Alone? Feeling the way she was feeling?

For the truth was, Kirsty McDonald had awoken something in her. Something a bit more than the usual cravings. Indeed, if she was honest with herself, she was almost a touch in love with the American woman.

Silly, she told herself. Now you're being silly.

But there was no doubting it. She missed Kirsty. Was upset that she hadn't rung.

Walking back to the phone, she flicked through her black leather phone index until she came to the M section. There, at the bottom of the page, in Kirsty McDonald's own handwriting, were three phone numbers — one for her at Ubik, one for her at her home in San José, and a third for her hotel in London.

Nervous suddenly, she lifted the phone and rang the last number. After three rings someone answered it.

'Room twenty-eight, please,' she asked.

There was a moment's pause, then the phone began to ring again. It rang, and rang, and rang. Cynthia was just about to put it down, when the ringing stopped and Kirsty's voice answered.

'Room twenty-eight . . .'

But, even as she went to answer, Cynthia heard, unmistakable in the background, a man's voice call from the next room.

'Hey, leave that. Come back to bed, honey. We've some unfinished business here!'

Cynthia caught her breath, then, as Kirsty said, 'Hello? Who is that?' slammed down the phone.

Just another notch, eh? Just another damn notch on your bedpost?

Without even admitting to himself that he was doing it, Charles Grant drove past the front of King's Cross station and, instead of taking his usual route home, retraced the journey he had made the night before, relentlessly, almost helplessly drawn through the unfamiliar streets of East London to the place where Chastity lived.

Pulling up in the same spot he'd occupied before, Charles switched off the engine and sat back in his seat, taking a moment to gather his thoughts. He was surprised by his own impulsiveness, and his pleasure in this uncharacteristic boldness was tempered by a fear of discovery; yet at the same time the possibility of a chance meeting was, he knew, the reason for this pilgrimage of the heart.

Almost imperceptibly, a small group of young boys had gathered round the front of the car, eyeing Charles with a mixture of mistrust and curiosity, their grubby hands stroking the gleaming chrome over the expansive bonnet, leaving it smudged and smeared. His concentration broken, and seized by a moment of panic, Charles looked about him and realised for the first time just how conspicuous he must be. The road was lined with unremarkable saloons, most of them old, some with mismatched and oddly coloured doors, and a few mounted on small piles of bricks where the wheels had been removed. The group of boys had swelled in number so that they now stood two-deep from one wheel, along the front of the car and round to the other wheel. Charles was beginning to feel like the leading horseman in the Charge of the Light Brigade.

'Nice car, mister!' called a particularly surly specimen, who seemed to stand a good foot or so taller than the others, his shaven head accentuating the natural belligerence of his features.

Charles forced a weak smile. He reached out, meaning to activate the central locking and drive away, then changed his mind. At times like this one had to play a straight bat or take a walk back to the pavilion. Bracing himself, Charles took his wallet from his jacket pocket, then stepped from the car and beckoned the youth towards him, filling his voice with a confidence he did not feel.

'Excuse me, my young friend, but would you like to earn yourself a bit of pocket money?'

*　　*　　*

Chastity lay on the sofa, staring uninterestedly at the television screen. It had been a hard day, much of it spent avoiding her Chairman and coming up with half-baked excuses to keep herself out of his presence. In the end it had all become too much and she had asked Bob Guppy's permission to leave early, telling him she didn't feel well.

Try as hard as she might, she couldn't get Louise's conversation with Patricia out of her head; the damning phrase played over and over again in her head, haunting her, causing her real physical pain.

There's no way someone of Charles's breeding could end up with a little tramp like Chastity Lloyd. Nah, she's only after his money.

Chastity winced at the memory of it.

'I bet they're up to no bloody good,' Chastity's mother muttered as she looked through the window onto the street below, her words spoken with the unmistakable voice of experience. She'd lived on estates all her life and knew mischief when she saw it. 'Mind you,' she went on, to no one in particular, 'some people have got no bloody sense, have they? I mean, fancy parking a car like that round here. Them lot'll have it stripped down as quick as bloody look at you!'

Chastity's dad discarded his newspaper on the floor beside him and joined his wife at the window.

'Where?'

Faith Lloyd nodded to where Charles Grant's Bughatti was now entirely surrounded by curious youngsters, their hands stroking the shining turquoise bodywork with an almost reverential awe.

'Is there anybody in it?' he said, stubbing out his cigarette in the ashtray on the sideboard.

'Yeah. Look! You can see his head. He's only a young fella, an' all.'

'Daft bugger!'

Faith tilted her head to one side, considering for a moment.

'Nice colour though, turquoise,' she said.

'Turquoise?' her husband scoffed. 'Bloody pansy colour for a car, if you ask me. He's probably got little flowery cushions inside.'

Chastity was not even aware that she was listening to her parents' conversation until that moment. In a split second she was by their side, peering out through the window upon an image that set her heart racing and her head thumping as blood pumped through her veins.

'Oh, no!' she gasped in disbelief.

'What?' her mother said, turning to steady her. 'What is it?'

'It can't be,' Chastity wailed.

'What can't be?' her mother asked, a tone of exasperation entering her voice.

But Chastity just stood there shaking her head.

'Chastity! Can't be what?' her mother persisted. 'What *are* you talking about?'

'Leave her alone a minute, woman, will you?' Her father placed a hand reassuringly on her shoulder, his voice coaxing when he spoke. 'Chastity, what is it? What's the matter, love?'

His daughter turned to face him, her body a battlefield of such emotion, her face racked with such confusion and pain, that he felt a lump rise to his throat and a burning sensation in his chest.

'In the car, it's Charles.'

Her father stared at her blankly, then turned to his wife. 'Charles?'

Faith shrugged and turned to Chastity, her voice calmer now. 'Charles who? Prince Charles?'

'Don't be silly, woman,' Tony Lloyd said to his wife.

But Chastity was barely aware of them. Placing her palms against the cold pane she pressed her face to the window, her warm breath clouding the glass as she gazed at the figure stepping out from his car five floors below.

'Oh, Charles . . .' she whispered.

Chastity's mother stood on one side of Charles and her father on the other as they waited in awkward silence outside the lift shaft.

Charles looked over his shoulder at the car, gleaming beneath the street lamp, a worried expression on his face.

Following his gaze, Faith patted his arm comfortingly. 'Now don't you worry, Mr Grant,' she reassured him. 'Tony's had a word with the boys and they're gonna keep an eye on it for you. No harm'll come to it, I promise.'

Charles nodded, not wanting to spoil their good deed by telling them that he'd already taken care of the matter.

'Bloody lift,' Tony Lloyd grumbled, pressing the call button once again, in spite of its already being alight, indicating that the lift was on its way. 'The other one's out of use – as usual. Bloody council!'

'*Tony*!' Faith said, her eyes bulging in their sockets

as a signal to her husband to curb his language. Understanding her perfectly, he buttoned it at once.

A long, awkward minute later, the lift arrived and as the three of them stepped inside. Charles was immediately struck by the overpowering stench of stale urine. If the others noticed, it was not apparent – any more than was the source of the unpleasant odour. A cursory look to the floor revealed it to be puddle-free, and, beneath the flickering glow of the covered light, Charles judged the walls to be grimy but basically as dry as a bone. But the smell seemed to go deeper than that: it had penetrated every atom of the lift, emanating from its every pore, so that Charles was forced to close his mouth and hold his breath for the short journey to the fifth floor.

'Chastity?' Faith Lloyd turned in the hallway to smile at Charles, then called again. '*Chastity*?'

'Come through,' Tony Lloyd said, in a half fatherly, half 'mates' fashion, indicating the plushly decorated living room. ''Ave a seat a minute.'

'Chastity?' Faith Lloyd called again, going to the end of the corridor and knocking on a door – Chastity's door, Charles realised, his mouth suddenly dry. 'You in there, love?'

As Chastity's mother pushed back the door, Charles hesitated, his heart thudding in his chest. But the room was empty.

'Now that's strange . . .' Janet Lloyd said, frowning. 'She was here only a minute ago.'

But Charles was barely conscious of her words. He was staring open-mouthed at the sight of Chastity's room – a young girl's room, unlike anything he had ever imagined for her.

'Charles?' Tony Lloyd said, a touch of concern in his voice now. 'You okay, mate?'

'What?' Charles said, turning abruptly to face him again. 'Erm . . . yes. Yes, fine, thanks.' And without another word he stepped into the living room and sat in the red velour armchair beside the imitation gas fire.

'Well . . .' Janet Lloyd said, coming back into the room. 'That's a mystery. She *was* here, but now she's gone.'

'Ah . . .' Charles's disappointment was massive. He placed his hands on the arms of the chair, meaning to get up, but Faith Lloyd stepped in front of him, and with a smile asked.

'Cup of tea, Mr Grant?'

As it turned out, the next two hours were among the most pleasant – outside of Chastity's company – that Charles Grant could remember for a long while. Both Faith and Tony Lloyd were kind, friendly people, and Charles could see where Chastity got her own 'niceness' from. Moreover, he got to see a real treasure trove: the family photograph albums, with endless pictures of Chastity covering the past eighteen years.

Looking through those pages, Charles found himself mesmerised. That smile; it was unchanged throughout the years, and those eyes . . .

It was gone eleven when, finally, Charles ventured into the lift again and, escorted by Chastity's father, held his breath for the journey down.

Stepping out on the ground floor, he looked across to see his car – intact, it seemed – gleaming beneath the amber lamplight, its custodian leaning jauntily on the bonnet.

'Look, thanks awfully,' Charles said, turning to shake Tony Lloyd's hand for the umpteenth time. 'I had a smashing time. And please give Mrs Lloyd my thanks, too, for making me feel very much at home.'

'I'm glad,' Tony Lloyd said, his smile so much like Chastity's that Charles almost felt as if he wanted to kiss the man for the resemblance. 'I'm only sorry our Chastity did a runner like that. It's not like her, you know.'

'Oh, I'm sure she had her reasons,' Charles said diplomatically. But the reminder brought with it a fresh wave of disappointment. 'I guess I'd better be off. Got a long drive.'

'Sure,' Tony Lloyd said. 'Look, I'll walk you to your car.'

'No,' Charles said hastily, recalling his arrangement with the youth. 'I'm okay. Really!' And, turning, he hastened across.

'Thanks,' he said to the shaven-headed youth, taking the tenner from his pocket and handing it across. Twenty pounds was a stiff car-parking charge, but it was a lot better than losing his wheels.

The youth held the note up, as if to check it was real, then, pocketing it, handed Charles a slip of paper on which was scrawled a phone number.

'Next time you come 'ere, you ring me first, eh?'

'Yes,' Charles mumbled. 'Yes, of course.'

And with that he slipped the key into the lock and slid into the driver's seat. Yet, in his preoccupation with putting the key into the ignition, Charles did not notice a slender figure slip across the paved courtyard in front of the block of flats and duck in through the doorway.

Gunning the engine – something he did not normally do – Charles put the car in first and roared away.

Behind him Chastity turned, looking on silently, then, as the car disappeared around the bend at the top of the road, she turned and made her way across to the lift, her heart heavy, knowing she had some explaining to do when she got home.

Despite the early hour, the terminal building was crowded. Several flights had been delayed, owing to severe weather over Northern France and the Netherlands, and a host of tired and fed-up-looking travellers filled the chairs around the gates.

Standing on the moving walkway, her bag beside her right leg, Kirsty McDonald yawned and then smiled to herself. Talk about screwing the Brits! A boy, a girl and a machine – now *there* was something to brag about!

In a slender attaché case under her left arm, she carried the papers Charles had given her last night. She looked down at the brown leather case and smiled fondly at it.

Half a million, it had cost. 'Goodwill money', as she had called it. And for that she had brought away what she couldn't have purchased for a hundred times the price!

She almost laughed. Poor Tobe! Once he knew what he'd done, he'd be mortified, but by then it would be too late. Too late for him to *do* anything, anyway.

Kirsty looked up, still smiling, her eyes travelling idly over the anonymous faces of her fellow travellers, until, with something like a shock, she saw one face that she recognised, standing among a whole host of other Japanese.

Nobushi!

She turned slightly, looking back over her shoulder; then, sensing that he had noticed her interest, quickly turned her back so that he'd not recognise her.

It was! The Jap from Cynthia's apartment. Now what in hell's name was *he* doing here?

Coincidence, she told herself. It's just coincidence. Yet it felt as though a shadow had passed over her.

Clutching the attaché case tighter, she picked up her bag and began to hurry along the moving walkway, heading for the far gate and the Seattle flight.

That next day was very strange. Chastity had wanted to phone in and plead illness once again, but her mother, after Chastity's confession, had insisted that she go in.

'You can't keep running away from things, my girl,' she had told her, but that was exactly what Chastity did. Yet far from being pursued by Charles – as had been the case throughout the previous day – it seemed almost as if he too were suddenly avoiding her.

Did he feel snubbed by her disappearance? If so, then why had he not simply walked out? Why had he stayed so long in her flat, drinking tea and looking at the old photograph albums?

That last, now that she knew of it, made her wince with embarrassment. Had he seen that awful picture of her at thirteen with plaits in her hair? Of her at Bognor when she'd been six, mooning at the camera?

At five o'clock, she grabbed her coat and hurried out, heading for the lift, then, fearing that he might already

be in it, and that there might be an awkward and less
romantic rerun of that earlier scene, she turned and
hurried down the stairs, safe for another day, her pride,
if not her heart, intact.

At that same moment, Charles stood at his penthouse
window, staring out across the square and sighing. He
had tried hard all day not to impose himself upon her, but
it was no good – he wanted her. Yes, but she quite clearly
didn't want him. And who could blame her, after all? If
she knew what he had done with Pat that night . . .

The thought made him stop dead, his mouth falling
open. What if she *did* know? What if, in that intimate
way that women had with one another, Patricia had told
Chastity everything?

'Oh God,' he groaned. Yes, that was it. *That* was why
she was avoiding him as if he had the Black Death; why,
earlier, she had seen him coming down the corridor and
had turned tail and run.

She knew!

Again Charles groaned. The more he thought about it,
the more certain he was of it. What else could possibly
have made her change so quickly?

At first he had thought, perhaps, that he might have
gone too far with that kiss. That, taken by surprise, she
had permitted him, not necessarily because she liked him,
but because . . .

And there it got complex. Why *had* she let him kiss
her? And why – or had he imagined it? – had she kissed
him back? Why had her body seemed so welcoming, so
unrestrained as it pressed back against his own?

No, it had to be that Patricia had told her everything.

Charles sat and, burying his head in his hands, groaned a third time.

It was thus that Patricia found him.

'Charles?'

Charles went rigid. Oh God! Oh Jesus Christ! He peeked through his hands at his secretary, as if at the Gorgon.

'Yes?' he croaked.

'Are you all right, Charles?'

Charles nodded, but kept his head down. 'Migraine,' he said, telegraphically. 'Taken something. Leave me. Be all right.'

'Ah . . . Right.' Patricia nodded. 'I'm off, then. See you tomorrow . . .'

He grunted a reply. But, when he glanced through his fingers a moment later, she was still standing there.

'Are you sure you'll be okay?'

'Hmm. Just need rest. Bye.'

He saw her frown, then, thankfully, turn and leave, but a moment later she was back.

'We need to talk sometime, Charles. About Chastity . . .'

'No!' Charles stood and, coming round his desk, he rushed past her and out of the room, as if pursued. 'No!'

As she walked through the green channel and out into the main lobby area of Seattle airport, Kirsty McDonald yawned and gently stretched her shoulders, but she felt good. In fact, she felt very good indeed. It had been a good trip, and hopefully, it would be at even better homecoming.

Her travelling bag was in her right hand, the attaché

case in her left. As she emerged from the little crowd at the barrier, she raised the attaché case to signal a greeting to a big man in a white suit and sunglasses who lounged casually beside one of the car-hire desks on the far side of the lobby.

'Good trip?' he asked, in a Southern States drawl, the faintest hint of a smile on his well-tanned face.

'As good as they get,' she answered chirpily, setting down her travel bag and hugging him in greeting. 'Those Brits certainly know how to look after a gal.'

He studied her a moment, his eyes travelling down to the attaché case. 'Well?' he said finally.

'Very well, thanks,' she said teasingly, then, winking at him, handed him the case. 'It's all there. Plans. Operation programs. Development schedules. Costings.'

This time the smile was much more than a hint. 'That's my girl,' he said, taking it from her. Then, with a slight tilt of his head, he produced a cheque from his jacket pocket and offered it to her, taking it back a couple of times, teasing her with it, until, at the third attempt, he let her keep it.

Kirsty took it, looked at the figure on it – ten million dollars – kissed it, and then, folding it in half, slipped it into the pocket of her jacket.

'There'll be more if it works,' he said.

Kirsty smiled. 'Oh, it'll work.'

He stared at her again, then nodded. 'So what's it to be? Your hotel or mine?'

Kirsty turned, looking about her, then gestured towards one of the restrooms. 'I don't know about you, but I just can't wait that long. You know how it is. Money *always* makes me feel horny.

He smiled, then removed his sunglasses, revealing ice-blue eyes.

'You know I never like to keep a lady waiting.' And, picking up her case, he walked towards the restroom.

Kirsty grinned, watching the way the big man's shoulders moved, the way the cheek bones of his arse rippled as he walked, then hurried after him, like a cat about to get the cream.

— *September* —

The sudden ringing of the phone jolted Charles's attention away from the window, through which he'd stared sightlessly these past twenty minutes, thinking of Chastity.

He went over to the desk and, clearing his throat, picked up the handset. 'Yes?' he asked tentatively.

'Hi!' a female voice boomed at him through the ether. 'Are they there yet?'

'Pardon?' he said. 'Are you sure you have the right number?'

'Charles?'

He stared blankly at the desk, then, abruptly and belatedly, recognised who it was. 'Kirsty . . . Miss McDonald, I mean . . . How are you? I'm terribly sorry, I was miles away.'

'Miles away?' Kirsty McDonald clearly didn't understand the colloquialism. 'Look, Charles, I was just checking to see if my guys have arrived there yet.'

'Your . . . guys?' Charles looked perplexed. He had no idea what she was talking about.

'You know . . . the actors. They were supposed to

fly in last night from LA. They're the best, Charlie, I promise you.'

'Oh, right . . . I . . . I don't know, actually. If they have, I've not been told about it.'

'Well, expect them any minute. And remember, I'm picking up the tab for this. Ciao!'

Charles went to reply, but the line was already dead. There was something he'd been meant to ask her. He thought a moment, then cursed. The contract! That's what it was!

It was a full month now since Kirsty McDonald's visit and, though they had had that first 'goodwill' payment of half a million, they had not yet received the promised draft contract.

Ah well, Charles thought, sitting down in his leather-backed chair, I'm sure it'll arrive soon.

He reached across, picking up the phone again, meaning to ring Patricia, but, even as he began to tap out the extension number, Patricia herself appeared in the doorway, a strange look on her face.

'What is it?' Charles asked, replacing the handset.

Patricia opened her mouth, as if about to explain, then shook her head and said, 'I think you'd better come and see.'

It seemed as if the whole of Virt-E-Go's staff had made their way to the labs to greet their guests, and Charles, making his way through the little throng at the door, wasn't quite sure what or who to expect, but the sight that greeted his eyes was wholly unanticipated.

There, standing by the machine, examining the straps and various fastenings with what seemed an expert interest, were two of the most stunning-looking human beings Charles Grant had ever seen. For the briefest moment he wondered – seriously – if they were real, but as they turned and smiled at him, showing perfect pearled teeth, he quickly dismissed the thought.

The man was all of six foot eight and built like an Adonis, with muscles in places Charles did not even suspect one ought to have muscles. He had long, crinkled, blond hair and a tan that one could only develop by way of obsessional worship of the sun. It might have been nice, perhaps – reassuring to the male egos of those looking on? – if this young god's face had been a disappointment, but it wasn't. He looked like a hippyfied version of a young Paul Newman – Butch Cassidy with flower power.

As for the woman, she was every bit as breathtaking. Six foot two in her stockinged feet, she had long, wavy, blonde hair and the kind of looks – and bust – that one saw only in the kind of classy soft-porn magazines his father kept behind the cistern in the downstairs toilet back home. Even fully clothed she had a predatory, erotic look and a face that, in other times, might have launched a thousand ships across the Aegean.

Together, they looked like they'd stepped from the set of *Super-Gladiators*.

Charles, standing between Bob Guppy and Roger Appleyard, stared at the two open-mouthed, unaware how his expression mirrored perfectly those of his two associates.

'Hi!' the man said, putting out a hand the size of a tennis racket, his soft Texan drawl making Louise, who stood just behind Roger, visibly shudder. 'I'm Tom Dupont. I understand we'll be working together.'

Charles swallowed. 'Well, not exactly working together . . .'

He stopped dead, not wanting to get in any deeper, then extricating his hand from inside that massive, muscled paw, turned to the woman.

'And you are . . . ?'

'Jerry Michelle.' The woman had an East Coast accent, softened by her years in California. A voice that, like her looks, was designed to give a man an instant erection. Charles, despite himself, was aware that that was exactly what he had. Embarrassed, he took her hand briefly, nodding to her.

'Tom and Jerry . . .' Louise said suddenly, and gave a short embarrassed laugh. 'They're called Tom and Jerry!'

Tom Dupont heard this and smiled. 'Yeah. Neat, huh?' And, taking a card from his pocket, he handed it to Charles.

Charles read it. 'Tom and Jerry. Cat and Mouse games our speciality.'

'That's us!' Jerry said, beaming, and looking to each of the men in turn, as if unaware of the effect she was having on them. 'The Hindus say that there are over a thousand ways of making love, and Tom and I have probably tried every last one of 'em!'

'Oh, twice!' Tom said, grinning, as if they were talking about skiing or some other harmless activity.

Charles cleared his throat. 'So you're our . . . *actors*.'

'That's right!' the two said as one, then laughed.

'Yeah,' Tom took up, 'and we're sure as hell looking forward to working on this project of yours. Kirsty's told us a lot about it. It's real cutting-edge stuff, huh? And it's real nice to be part of the vanguard, so to speak. Fucking our way into the future!'

There was an embarrassed moment. Tom looked about him, then, with an apologetic expression, said, 'Hey, sorry. I forgot. Just that we're used to calling a spade a spade where we come from.'

'No, no,' Charles said, hurriedly. 'That's okay. It's just—'

At that moment he saw – for the first time – a third figure, bobbing up and down behind the machine. A short, fat, rather swarthy figure, with what looked like an artificial thatch of jet-black hair stuck on his head.

Tom turned, looking in the direction of Charles's gaze, then said, 'Oh, this is Sam . . . Sam Heifitz, our director. Sam, come and meet Charles.'

Sam came round the machine and, with a smile that was as much a sneer as anything resembling delight, nodded at Charles.

Charles, taking in the sight of Sam Heifitz standing next to Tom Dupont – and was that *really* the name he'd been given at birth? – suddenly had a vision of the human race as existing somewhere between these two poles of ugliness and beauty.

'Um . . . hi!' Charles said, at a total loss for words.

'We got a script?' Sam said, his Brooklyn accent unmistakable.

'A script?' Charles hadn't the vaguest idea what he was talking about.

'A scenario. You know . . . something that links the action. We gonna do our job, we gonna need a script. It ain't just fucking you know. Gotta have a story.'

'Ah, yes . . . of course.' Charles turned, looking about him. 'Roger?'

'Not my department, I'm afraid,' Roger said, hastily passing the buck. 'That's McTaggart's line, but he's off sick . . .'

Charles looked to Cynthia. 'You wouldn't, by any chance . . . ?'

'Sure.' Cynthia smiled at Charles, then, looking to Heifitz, said, 'We'll sit down, Sam, and work out what you need. I thought it'd be best to wait until you were here before we got as far as a script. After all, we don't want to go shooting off in the wrong direction, do we?'

An hour later, Cynthia marched into Roger's office.

'Okay,' she said, seating herself across from Roger as Louise hovered in the doorway, 'we've got to come up with something, and fast.'

'What's that?' Roger asked, pointing to the video that rested on top of Cynthia's notepad.

'Homework,' Cynthia said, noting Roger's unhealthy interest. 'A tape of our actors in action. Heifitz wants to get to work straight away. So we need to come up with some kind of story.'

'You mean, girl-meets-boy kind of stuff?'

'If you like,' Cynthia said. 'But nothing too fancy. Nothing that causes us any programming difficulties, anyway.'

'What kind of programming difficulties?' Louise asked, coming over from the doorway. 'I thought you just, like, got into the machine and . . . well, did it.'

Cynthia shook her head. 'It seems that that's where we've been going wrong. According to Sam Heifitz, you gotta build the customer's interest. Get them ripe and ready for it before you deliver the goods. So we need an outline. Any suggestions?'

Roger leaned forward, nodding towards the video. 'D'you think we could see that first? Maybe it'll give us a few ideas.'

Cynthia raised an eyebrow, then. 'Okay. There's a machine in the boardroom. Shall we go and watch?'

'Don't you think we should get a few more people involved?' Roger queried. 'It's fairly important, after all.'

Cynthia smiled broadly. 'Oh, I've already consulted Patricia. It seems our Chairman's happy to leave it to us. It's only a prototype, after all. As long as we can come up with *something*.' She paused, then, looking pointedly at Roger, said, 'I thought that maybe an office scenario might be worth exploring. You know what I mean . . . adultery in the office. The boss and his secretary getting it on. There ought to be a big audience for that kind of thing.'

If Roger sensed that this was a dig at him, he didn't show it. 'Great idea!' he said. 'But let's have a gander at that tape first. You never know, something might pop up!'

Yes, Cynthia thought, and we all know what!

There was a knock on Chastity's bedroom door.

'Chastity?'

'Yes, Mum?'

'Are you sure you won't come shopping?'

'No, Mum.'

Sitting on the edge of her bed, Chastity closed her

eyes. She could almost hear her mother's sigh through the thickness of the wall.

'You certain?'

'Yes, Mum. Now go. I'll be okay.'

'All right. But phone Auntie Kay if you need anything, okay?'

'Mum, I'm eighteen now. I can look after myself.'

'I know, but—'

'Mum, just go, will you?'

The last was said with a good-humoured exasperation that finally had the desired result. Chastity listened a moment, then heard the front door close.

Chastity's eyes popped open. 'Thank God.'

She didn't know which was worse, avoiding Charles at work, or avoiding her mother's endless questioning at home. By taking a week's holiday, she had hoped to get over the awkwardness of the situation, but she hadn't reckoned on her mother's persistence.

After that first visit, Charles had come again another three times, and every time she had quietly slipped away, leaving him to the tender mercies — and the endless stories — of her mum and dad. But, after that fourth time, Charles had come no more.

'He's such a nice boy,' her mother had said at least a thousand times. 'I don't know why you keep avoiding him, Chastity. Such nice manners, and well off, too.'

It was that last comment that had had the greatest effect on Chastity, restoring her flagging determination. She would *not* be seen as a gold-digger. Even if it meant spending the rest of her life alone — for how could she marry anyone if it was not Charles? — she would not have the world think *that* of her!

Yes, yet when Charles had stopped his visits, far from being relieved she had found herself devastated. She had not wanted him to come – indeed, she had been embarrassed by his visits – yet their cessation brought nothing but torment.

Chastity let her head drop slightly. 'Oh, Chas,' she said, looking at her reflection in the dressing-table mirror, 'you are a bloody mess, ain't you?'

Her image gave a sad smile back, but then she recalled her father's words last night and the smile faded.

'You shouldn't be so bloody high and mighty, Chastity,' he had told her. 'A well-to-do bloke like Charles Grant – you should think yourself lucky.'

But that was just it. She didn't want to think of herself as 'lucky', even if she was. She didn't want to be in anyone's debt. And that was really the nub of it, because if – and this 'if' was the biggest 'if' she dared let herself imagine – *if* she were ever to marry Charles Grant, then she would always be in his debt, for she had nothing and he had . . . well, *everything*.

It was impossible. Absolutely impossible.

Chastity sighed, then, wiping away the tears that had formed at the corners of her eyes, stood up and went over to the wardrobe in the corner of the room, staring out of the window at the ground five floors below, willing his car to be there; willing him to come and take her, to brush away all her silly fears as one might brush away cobwebs. But the street was empty and Charles, she knew, was not coming. Four times was enough for any man to get the message.

*   *   *

'Oh my God! *Look* at the size of it! Oh no! That *can't* be natural!'

Louise was staring at the TV screen with one hand almost covering her mouth, unable to believe what she was seeing. Cynthia, sitting beside her, looked on in amazement, while Roger, standing just behind them, was shaking his head, conscious no doubt of his own inadequacies.

'It *is* huge,' Cynthia conceded after a moment, mentally applying a measuring tape to the giant phallus that was thrusting up out of the neat tangle of Tom's pubic hair.

'Paint it green and call it a cucumber,' Louise said and giggled.

'What *I* can't understand,' Roger said, his head tilted at ninety degrees as he studied the TV screen, 'is how she can get all of that into her mouth at one go! What did she use to be, a sword-swallower or something!'

'God!' Louise said again, a look of awe in her eyes. 'Fancy having that up you. You wouldn't be able to sit down for a week!'

'Louise!' Roger said, a bit discomfited by the look on his lover's face.

'Well . . .' Louise said. 'It's only fantasy after all!'

'It looks real enough to me,' Cynthia said, imagining just what it *would* be like to have Tom Dupont thrusting away at one's insides. 'But come on, this isn't helping any. We're supposed to be coming up with a storyline.'

'Bugger the storyline,' Roger said, his eyes hungrily staring at Jerry Michelle's doorstop nipples. 'Let's watch this through to the end.'

But Cynthia felt they'd seen enough. Leaning across she ejected the video.

'Oh!' Louise said. 'It was just getting going.'

'Right . . . well . . .' Cynthia said, opening her notebook and taking out her ballpoint pen. 'We've now got an idea what our actor friends are capable of.'

'Practically anything, by the look of it!' Roger said admiringly. 'I wouldn't have thought she was double-jointed, but there you are . . .'

'Yes, well the problem now is to find a simple setting. Ideally we don't want to have to change scene at all.'

'Then let's do what you suggested,' Roger said, winking at Louise. 'Let's set it in an office. That way it can all happen in the same room. The boss can be working late, perhaps, putting some figures together for a meeting, say.'

'And maybe there's a new secretary,' Louise said, getting into the swing of things. 'And maybe she's had a bad day and got things wrong and when she comes to say goodnight, she suddenly bursts into tears and he has to comfort her and—'

'Wo-ah! Hold on!' Cynthia said, unable to keep up with what Louise was saying. 'One thing at a time. So these two don't really know each other before this. It's their first day together, right?'

'Right!' Louise and Roger said as one, their eyes meeting.

'And she's a bit fearful and upset?'

'And he's noticed her,' Roger said.

'And she's noticed him . . .' Louise added.

Cynthia looked up and saw them staring at each other,

a strange wistful look in both their eyes. Oh shit, she thought, this really, actually happened.

She looked down again. 'So there's an immediate attraction, right?'

'Right!' Both of them said again, then laughed.

Cynthia felt that laughter ripple down her spine. Suddenly she felt as if she was eavesdropping on an intimate moment. 'Look,' she said, 'I think I've got enough. I'll work at it overnight and show you in the morning.'

'And the tape?' Roger said, his eyes never leaving Louise's.

Cynthia smiled tightly. 'I'd better keep hold of the tape. After all, I might need to refer to it.'

Patricia was just sorting out her handbag, preparing to lock her desk and go home, when a call came through for her.

'Yes?' she answered, rummaging through her bag, looking for her travel pass.

'Patricia?'

It took her a moment to recognise that voice, but, when she did, her stomach did a complete flip-flop. 'Sir James?'

'Yes, my dear. Sorry to be phoning you so late in the day, but I wondered if you would do me a bit of a favour?'

Patricia swallowed, wondering what he was going to ask. 'Of course,' she said, her voice softer suddenly. 'You know I'd do anything for you.'

'That's really kind,' he said, then, 'Look, it's like this, Patricia. I'm having this do for my seventieth in a couple of weeks' time. A bit of a bash, here at the house, and I thought . . . well, I wanted to invite the staff along.'

'That's . . . really thoughtful, Sir James. I'm sure they'll be delighted.'

'Yes. It was Charles's idea, actually. He thought it might be good for morale. Anyway, I've got some printed invitations and I wondered if you would organise to send them out. I can have them biked over to you in the morning. You know the ropes, old girl.'

'Just leave it to me, Sir James.'

'I knew I could count on you, Pat. Thanks awfully.'

'Any time, Sir James. Any time.'

After he'd rung off, Patricia sat there for a long time, staring into the air. Just the sound of his voice had brought it all back to her – the strength of his arms, the smell of him.

Seventy, eh? Well, contrary to what these youngsters thought, one could still play the goat at seventy.

'Any time, Sir James,' Patricia murmured, staring at the phone. 'You know I'd do *anything* for you.'

Next day they got down to work in earnest.

Cynthia had been up most of the night, writing and rewriting the script, taking breaks to watch the video antics of Tom and Jerry, her anticipation of watching the real thing rising with each viewing.

And now she sat there, in the lab, looking on as Sam Heifitz and his cameraman, Jurgen, set things up.

They had locked the lab doors from inside and, just as a precaution against a possible police raid, had switched off the lift and positioned Patricia in the lobby to ward off any unwelcome visitors.

Soft music played. Mood music. Black seventies soul, mainly. To get the actors 'in the mood'.

Their two principal actors sat in a corner of the lab, talking to Bill and Ben, Tom Dupont in a bright red silk robe, Jerry Michelle in a flimsier robe of blue, so that the two of them looked a little like heavyweight boxers about to enter the ring.

In the session with Heifitz the previous day, Cynthia had agreed a crude working method. First off they were to make a thirty-minute video with both actors working in normal clothes and – of course – naked. Then they would do it all over again, but this time in full-body suits. To achieve a good match between what was seen by the camera and what was recorded by the pick-ups on the suits would probably need a good few takes, Heifitz reckoned, but Bill and Ben were confident they could get the two to fit – eventually. All it needed was good choreography: 'Sex as dance', as Sam Heifitz put it.

'Okay,' Sam said, snapping his fingers. 'You ready, guys?'

With no more self-consciousness than two salmon swimming upstream, Tom and Jerry shed their robes and, buck naked, came out into the set, which had been hastily put together using furniture from nearby offices.

'But I thought—' Cynthia began.

Sam Heifitz turned and hushed her noisily. 'You want me to direct or not?'

Cynthia looked down, chastened.

'Good,' Heifitz said, and turned his attention back to

the two actors. 'Okay. You've read the script. I want you to start from the top of page five, where Roger's giving it to Louise from behind . . .'

Bill and Ben looked to her, eyes wide. *You didn't?* they mimed.

I did, she mimed back. And they slapped each other's hands in a high five.

'Okay,' Tom said, getting himself into position. 'You ready, Jel?'

'Ready and willing!' Jerry answered, pushing out her buttocks welcomingly, then reaching down behind her to begin, slowly, to manipulate her co-star.

In a moment Tom's manhood was stretched out at its full, glorious length. Cynthia swallowed, her mouth suddenly dry, then glanced at Bill and Ben. The twins, who were meant to be checking their machinery, were both staring goggle-eyed at Tom, as if they couldn't quite believe what they were seeing.

Cynthia looked back. Before her eyes – right there in Virt-E-Go's laboratories, where she had spent many an evening discussing technical problems with the twins – Tom began to give Jerry what for, Jerry's cries of passionate enjoyment making Cynthia's nipples stiffen beneath her blue floral shirt.

'Yeah . . .' Sam was murmuring, half crouched alongside them. 'That's right, baby. That's nice . . .'

Jurgen, the cameraman, was one moment on his back on the floor beneath them, then the next he was alongside, Tom's balls almost knocking the lens of the camera as he thrust and thrust.

God! Cynthia thought, enviously. It's like watching some kind of machine. That man isn't human! The last time she'd seen a movement like that it was on the front wheels of an old steam train!

'Jerry, get your head down,' Sam said. 'Lay it flat on the table, sweetie, right cheek pressed against the leather. That's it! Great! Now stretch out and cover her, Tom. That's it. Dig deep now. Deeper, man. Yeah, that's cool . . .'

Oh God, Cynthia thought, wishing it was her there beneath Tom's heaving body. Oh, Jesus Christ! She had to fight to stop herself from rubbing against the edge of the desktop that dug tantalisingly into her thigh. Yet Sam Heifitz seemed not to notice what was going on.

'Yeah!' he was going, and 'Great!' But there was not the least flicker of excitement on his face.

Jurgen was now kneeling in front of the table, getting a close-up shot of Tom's and Jerry's faces. A moment later he slid under the table and lay on his back again, like a car mechanic checking the clutch.

'Okay,' Sam said, his voice oozing encouragement. 'I want a come shot. Now!'

And, on order, Tom's face convulsed, his hands gripping Jerry's haunches. At the same moment she seemed to shudder right through from the tips of her toes to the follicles of her sun-bleached hair, her buttocks pushing back into Tom's groin as if they wanted to become a part of it. And the sound they made! Hearing that great groan of pleasure, Cynthia herself groaned, a little shudder running through her. If the VR version was as good as this, then they had a sure-fire winner!

'Great!' Sam Heifitz was saying. 'Let's call that a wrap!'

To Cynthia's amazement, Tom and Jerry straightened

up, as if nothing had just happened between them, Tom's penis springing up into full view again, as stiff as an Olympic springboard.

'You wanna do that again?' Tom asked, his face earnest, professional.

But Sam was now looking at the script. 'No,' he said. 'Let's move on to the mouth shot, page seven. Tom, you're in the chair there, Jerry . . .'

And so it went on, for the best part of three hours, and never once did Tom's manhood flag, until Cynthia, exhausted and frustrated, began to believe that he'd had some kind of silicon implant to achieve that kind of rigidity for that period of time.

It was astonishing. Moreover, she had begun to wonder whether a night with Tom Dupont would be such a good idea. I mean, how did you make this guy come? What *was* the trigger?

Strangely, the last take was the most affecting. Watching Tom and Jerry — now fully clothed — acting out the parts of Roger and Louise, Tom sympathetic, Jerry fearful, vulnerable, Cynthia found herself genuinely admiring the two. They weren't just a pair of sex studs: they actually could act, and at the end of it, Cynthia found herself wiping away a tear.

Standing, she went across to Heifitz. 'That was great, Sam. Just what we wanted.'

'Yeah?' He acted as if he didn't much care whether it was what she wanted or not. 'Well, we gotta do it all again, in the suits this time. Now *that's* when we gonna get problems!'

'Well?' Patricia asked, coming into the restroom and

standing beside Cynthia at the mirror. 'What was it like?'

Cynthia shook her head. 'The man's like a steam train.'

'The Flying Texan?'

Both women laughed. Then, more seriously, Patricia asked, 'Do you think it's right, what we're doing?'

Cynthia frowned. It was the first time anyone had asked her that. 'Why, don't you think it is?'

'I don't know,' Patricia said, a faintly puzzled look on her face. 'I guess it was all rather theoretical until now. But now we've a couple of real porn actors and so on and it feels . . . well, *different*, somehow.'

'Hmmm.' Cynthia considered a moment, then. 'Look, the way I see it is that providing we're not hurting anyone – not molesting anyone or making anyone do what they don't want to do – then where's the harm in it? In fact, if, in the future, one of our machines prevents some pervert from going out and doing damage to someone because they're sexually frustrated, then we'll have done society a damn good service!'

'You think so?'

'Oh, I know so, Patricia. Nothing's so destructive as sexual frustration. Look at the whole history of Christianity in this country. All those religious wars, and why? Because the monks needed a damn good screw!'

Patricia giggled, then she saw that Cynthia was being serious. 'Is that what you think? You think war is pent-up sexual frustration?'

'What else is it? It doesn't make sense otherwise.'

'And you think our machine might be the solution to that?'

'I think it might help. I mean, if it reduces the incidents of rape and sexual violence, then I'd say we'd have achieved a great and noble thing.'

Patricia nodded, then smiled, seeing herself suddenly as a crusader for moral good, and not — as she'd begun to worry — a seedy peddler of filth.

Cynthia turned to face her. 'In fact, if there was any justice in the world, we'd be getting a government grant for this work. Imagine it, Patricia! A cheerful, enthusiastic workforce. And why? Because they'd all had a good time in our machines the night before!'

'Making love to Tom . . .'

'. . . or Jerry.'

And the two women looked at each other and smiled.

'Oh well,' Cynthia said, 'work calls,' and, giving Patricia an affectionate squeeze on the shoulder, she left the rest room.

Patricia watched her go, then turned back to the mirror, looking at herself. Frustration. Yes, she knew just how corrosive frustration could be in one's life. She reached down and touched herself, there, where she did not often touch herself these days, and felt a tiny tingle of need.

'You ought to get your life sorted out, Patricia,' she said softly to her image. 'And you ought to do it now, before it's too late.'

If the morning session went well, the afternoon session was a total disaster.

The first little snag was discovered only minutes into the first take. Tom and Jerry had just started to re-enact the over-the-desk scene, when Bill called a halt.

'What the fuck . . . ?' Sam Heifitz said, storming round to confront the twins.

'There's no signal . . .' Ben said sheepishly.

'No *what*?'

'No signal,' Bill repeated, 'from Jerry's . . . you know . . .'

'No,' Heifitz said, putting his hands on his hips. 'I *don't* fucking know. So tell me and we can put it right!'

It had already taken them two and a half hours to get to this stage, what with the amount of wiring and strapping-in that had had to be done, and for things to go wrong this early on was clearly too much for the little director.

Bill and Ben looked to Cynthia for help. She came over and, after much whispering, turned to face Heifitz. 'It seems that one of Jerry's pressure pads isn't registering anything. A rather crucial one, actually . . .'

'What? The pussy-pad ain't working?'

Bill, Ben and Cynthia cringed as one.

Jerry smiled. 'Well, *I* sure as hell was getting the signal . . .'

'It's probably only a connection,' Cynthia said, hastening over and, edging around Tom's heavily wired yet still prominent member, knelt beside Jerry, beginning to check the wiring around her groin, trying not to feel embarrassed by what she was doing.

'Hey,' Jerry said quietly, as Cynthia's fingers tugged at one of the wires. 'You ever want to do this in private sometime, just say.'

Cynthia did not look up, but Jerry's words had registered. As if she hadn't heard, however, she called across to Bill and Ben, her voice all businesslike: '*That* make any difference?'

'Nothing!' Came the duplicated answer.

'That?' she asked, adjusting another wire, and feeling Jerry push gently against her fingers.

'Yeah . . . No . . . yeah, that's it!'

'It was just loose,' Cynthia said, looking up Jerry's voluptuous body and meeting her eyes.

'I'll be as loose as you like, honey,' Jerry said, and winked.

Tom, who must have overheard everything, said nothing.

Cynthia walked back across. 'Okay,' she said to Heifitz. 'Something just worked its way loose, that's all.'

'Okay,' he said grumpily. 'But I don't want us having to stop every time Tom jerks his ass!'

Then, just when things seemed to be going swimmingly, Tom came.

'Tom?' Jerry looked back over her shoulder at her partner as if she couldn't understand quite what was going on. They were supposed to keep going for a good four or five more minutes yet.

'Oh, Jeeze, I'm sorry,' Tom said. 'It must be these restraints. I couldn't help it!'

'Cut!' Heifitz yelled, that same belligerent look returning to his scrunched-up face. He walked round the now separated couple, then bent down, as if trying to work out just what went wrong. Tom's manhood had shrivelled up forlornly, as if ashamed.

'Oh shit,' Heifitz said, staring at it and shaking his head. 'That's all we fucking need!'

'I'll be okay,' Tom said, half turning to him, the wires of the suit making movement awkward. 'I can take something to delay me.'

Even so, it was a good hour before Tom's libido had been restored to the point where he could sport a stiffy again. And then came the third and definitely worst of the afternoon's accidents.

Patricia stood in the doorway, looking on aghast as the two ambulancemen edged past her and into the corridor, the huddled figure beneath the blanket on the stretcher groaning in agony.

There was the smell of burning in the air.

On the far side of the lab Bill and Ben were crouched over an empty body-suit, examining its smouldering wires while Sam Heifitz stood over them, bellowing obscenities.

Oh God, Patricia thought. Here we go again!

As the ambulancemen squeezed out, Patricia slipped inside, hurrying across to where Cynthia stood, looking on.

'What's happened now?'

'There was a sudden surge,' Cynthia said, turning to meet Patricia's eyes. 'I'm afraid our Jerry got a great jolt of electricity straight up her fanny!'

Patricia winced.

Tom Dupont, standing nearby, shrugged and said, 'It was strange. I didn't feel a thing!'

'No wonder,' Patricia murmured. 'He's got his own built-in lightning rod!'

Even so, it was bad news. Jerry had received quite a shock and would clearly not be able to perform for several days.

'You know, it burned every last hair off her minge!' Cynthia confided, making Patricia blush. 'It wouldn't surprise me if she sued.'

'I think not,' Patricia said, glad to be able to convey some good news.

'Why's that?'

'Because I made sure they both signed release forms beforehand.' Patricia smiled. 'After what happened to poor Mr Fukuada, I thought we ought to make sure this time round.'

'And good job, too!' Roger Appleyard said, breezing into the room. 'Has big boy here put his playmate in hospital, then?'

'It was the machine,' Cynthia said, casting a sympathetic look at Tom, who had yet to shed his body-suit. 'We don't know quite what happened yet, but—'

At that moment, with a final obscene yell, Sam Heifitz stormed past them, the plastic flaps whup-whupping behind him.

'Oh, shit . . .' Cynthia said, making to go after him, but Patricia caught her arm.

'Let the man calm down. It's a hitch, that's all. If I know Kirsty McDonald, he won't get paid unless he gets the job finished. He'll be back.'

'You think so?' Cynthia said, only half believing Patricia.

'Of course. He's a professional.'

'And what if he doesn't?'

Roger Appleyard came up with the answer. 'Then our Cyn will have to step in and direct.' He winked lasciviously. 'I bet you always wanted to be a hands-on director!'

'Why don't you go fuck yourself,' Cynthia said, her face hardening; yet deep down Roger's idea had taken root. She'd seen what Sam did, and it wasn't so hard, really. And she did rather fancy taking Tom through his paces. Maybe even help him with a bit of private coaching.

'Well,' Patricia said, looking across at Tom with a clear interest in what was dangling down inside his leather cod-piece. 'I guess there's nothing much we can do right now except wait and see how badly injured Ms Michelle is.'

'Unless we hire a stand-in . . .'

The two women looked to Roger, who had made the suggestion. Both, it was clear in that instant, would love to volunteer for the part, but both were far too embarrassed even to suggest it.

'Maybe . . .' Cynthia said. 'But first we ought to notify Ms McDonald. Let her know what's happened. Patricia . . . ?'

'I'll do it straight away.'

'And Roger?'

Roger turned, a smirking smile on his face. 'Yes, Cynthia?'

'Why don't you bugger off back to your office and leave us to clear up down here!'

A fax from Kirsty McDonald arrived back within the hour. It was brief and to the point. Sam Heifitz had quit. Cynthia was to take charge of the shoot until a replacement director could be found. As for a replacement for Jerry, Kirsty McDonald gave a London phone number of an agency who 'might be able to help fill the gap'.

Charles, handing Cynthia the fax, asked her if she really wanted the job.

'How do you mean?'

'Well . . .' Charles began awkwardly. 'I felt you might think it a bit . . . delicate.'

'It's only temporary,' Cynthia said, smiling in her best Mary-of-the-Fourth-Form manner. 'I'm sure I'll cope until Ms McDonald finds someone else to do the job.'

'Okay, then,' Charles said. 'That's good. If there's anything you need' – he nodded towards Pat – 'Patricia here will help you.'

Cynthia smiled at Patricia, then, keen to get back to things, turned and hurried away.

Outside, alone in the corridor, Cynthia stopped, feeling a little surge of exultation sweep through her. In charge! Kirsty – and Charles – had put her in charge!

Returning to her office, she closed the door, sat down at her desk and, spreading the fax out before her, picked up the phone, beginning to dial the number of the agency.

She had decided she would not wait until the morning, but would begin at once. If she could sort out a partner for Tom tonight, then they could get back to work tomorrow with little time lost. Bill and Ben, she knew, would not go home until they'd worked out a solution to the problem – they never did – so she did not have to worry about that end of it. The only other problem was making sure Tom Dupont was kept happy.

As she sat back, listening to the ringing tone, she pondered the question. What if he only got it up for Jerry?

Cynthia shook her head, dismissing the idea. She'd never met a man yet – or a woman, come to that – who was turned on by only a single partner. They were all animals, every last one of them, and try to disguise it as they might, when the sexual chips were down, they rutted like animals.

That was why, ultimately, the machine was going to be a success, because it was an avoidance of the old issue of monogamy versus polygamy. With the machine, a man – or a woman – could have sexual adventures *without* being adulterous. Could do what every last one of them wanted to do, without ever once stepping outside the confines of the happy home.

It was a licence to be free. And that was what excited her most about it, for she had lived all her life in a world where one had to hide what one was – to keep it all tucked away in grubby little cupboards.

But in the future it would be different. In the future one could buy a nice, sparkling clean CD-ROM and take it home. And voilà! Out would come all of the old, old dirt! That four-million-year-old inheritance of the apes that was still deep inside them all.

She shivered at the thought, even as a cultured man's voice answered on the other end of the phone line.

'Geoffrey DeBerry here. Can I help you?'

Cynthia leaned forward and, adopting her most efficient phone manner, smiled into the handset. 'Geoffrey, you don't know me, but a mutual friend has given me your number . . .'

Geoffrey DeBerry's offices were in a small news in South Kensington – all cobbles and white-painted walls. Stepping from the taxi, Cynthia looked about her, impressed. At least the man had taste.

As for Geoffrey himself, Cynthia found herself far less

impressed. His hair was unfashionably shoulder-length
– no ponytail, thank God – and the bushy moustache
and sideburns – sideburns! – made him look like a less
swarthy version of Jason King. His dress sense was also
frozen – like Adam Adamant – in the early seventies.

A narrow stairway led up into his offices. Entering
them, she began to have second thoughts about the man.
The place was done out like an Edwardian boudoir, with
plush red velvet everywhere. It was like being on the set
of a Hammer horror movie.

'I understand you're looking for a girl?' Geoffrey
began, handing Cynthia a large brandy in a cut-crystal
tumbler before taking a seat across from her.

'Yes,' Cynthia answered, smiling, then taking a small
sip of the excellent Chivas.

'Can I ask why?'

Cynthia blinked. She thought she had made it perfectly clear on the phone.

'Pardon?'

'Forgive me,' Geoffrey said, with an urbane charm,
'but from where I'm sitting I see an absolutely stunning
young woman who simply *oozes* sexuality. It should be
me who's offering *you* a job, not you seeking to hire a
girl from me!'

Cynthia looked down. For a moment she didn't know
what to say. Then she met his eyes again.

'Are you saying that I ought to be in porn movies?'

Geoffrey smiled disarmingly. 'You'd be a star, my dear.
I knew it the moment you walked through the door.'

Cynthia laughed. If this was a chat-up line then it
was the strangest she'd ever heard.

'Ye-es,' he said, elongating the word in a peculiarly

upper-class fashion, 'there's something *boyish* about you that a lot of my clients would really like.'

'This girl,' Cynthia began again.

'Are you *sure* I can't persuade you?' Geoffrey asked, raising an eyebrow at the same time he raised his glass.

'Absolutely not. Now this girl . . .'

Geoffrey stood and, setting his glass down, walked over to the bookshelves just to the side of where they were sitting. Taking a photograph album down, he came back and handed it to Cynthia.

'There. Those are my girls. I can show you video if you like.'

Cynthia nodded distractedly, then opened the album. At once the stunning, full-colour photographs seemed to leap out at her. All of the girls were naked and posing provocatively for the camera. Cynthia swallowed then turned the page.

'See anyone who interests you?' Geoffrey asked.

To be honest, every single one of them *interested* her.

'They're . . . good.'

Geoffrey leaned across, taking the album from her a moment, leafing through it; then he handed it back, tapping one of the photos with his fingertip.

'There!' he said. 'Bubbles. She's the one for you.'

'Bubbles?'

'It's her nickname. Her real name's a real mouthful. She's the daughter of a duke, actually, but you're not supposed to know that. But I tell you . . .'

Geoffrey stopped, then raised a hand. 'No. Sit there, Cynthia. I'll put the tape on. Then *you* decide.'

Having seen the tape, Cynthia not only wanted to meet

Bubbles, she wanted to keep her in a cupboard at home and bring her out whenever she felt lonely!

Yes, and that's exactly what this VR thing's about, isn't it? she thought.

Her hand trembled slightly as she dialled the number, then waited.

'Hell-o-oh!'

'Hello?' Cynthia frowned. The voice on the other end sounded at least two hundred and fifty years old. 'Is that Bubbles?'

'Oh . . . goodness no!' There was a peal of high-pitched laughter. 'I take it you want Dorinda?'

'Dor—' Cynthia took a mental step back. 'Yes . . . yes, if you wouldn't mind.'

Again she waited.

'Hello?'

'Hello . . . is that Bubbles?'

The accent was cut-glass. 'I'm sorry, but do I know you?'

No, Cynthia thought, but it's only a matter of time.

It was thus that, two hours later, Cynthia, Bubbles and Tom could be found sitting in the Safari Bar of the DeGroot Hotel. Bubbles was even more stunning clothed and in the flesh than she'd been unclothed on the video, yet Tom had seemed relatively unimpressed by her. Certainly his eyes hadn't popped out the way Bubbles' eyes had on seeing Tom.

Maybe he's just jaded, Cynthia thought as she looked from one to the other, conscious that she had butterflies in her stomach at the thought of what she was doing here. Maybe he's seen it all, and she's just another piece of fanny for him to perform with. It must be hard to form real relationships, doing what they do.

It also quickly became clear where Bubbles had got her nickname, for within five minutes she was ordering champagne for everyone.

Tom, professional that he was, shook his head. 'Just a juice for me,' he said. 'Don't want to impair my performance.'

Bubbles giggled. She was an absolute vision in her tight, royal-blue dress. Her breasts, her shoulders, her neck, her legs – everything about her seemed in perfect proportion. But the crowning glory was her face, surrounded as it was by a cascade of long, jet-black curls. What Cynthia couldn't understand was what she was doing messing about in the porno movie business.

The drinks arrived. With a resounding pop the champagne was opened, Bubbles holding out her empty glass to be filled. Clinking her glass against Tom's tumbler of chilled freshly squeezed orange juice, Bubbles winked at him, then looked to Cynthia. 'Bottoms up!' she said with a giggle, then downed her drink in one.

While Cynthia explained what it was she wanted, Bubbles slowly drank her way through two whole bottles. By the time the hotel porter came across to say that their cab was there, she was well on the way to being very merry indeed.

Walking down the front steps of the hotel between the two, Cynthia once again felt how strange it was. Only a day ago she had been little more than the assistant to the Director of R and D at Virt-E-Go.

Now she was about to become a porno film director, and as such she could make these two quite stunningly beautiful human beings do whatever she asked them to do.

As they climbed into the cab, she made sure she was the second one in, squeezing in between Tom and Bubbles, her skin tingling with anticipation.

It was gone ten when they arrived back at the labs, but Cynthia was not worried about the time. Her concern was to get this done before Kirsty could appoint another director. This was her big chance and she was sure as hell not going to throw it away!

The lobby was in darkness. Unlocking the glass front door, Cynthia ushered Tom and a very giggly Bubbles inside, then locked the door behind her. By the light of the street lamp outside they crossed the reception area and summoned the lift.

Travelling up in that small, brightly lit box, Cynthia felt her legs go weak. This was it! Tom stood to her right, his body touching hers, his shoulder on her eye level. She could smell his heavy masculine scent, while to her left Bubbles leaned against her half drunkenly, all warm and curvaceous, the smell of her as delicious as strawberries in summertime.

Coming out into the corridor outside the lab, Cynthia could sense how unsteady Bubbles had become. Bubbles leaned against her, steadying herself, then giggled again.

'Coffee,' Cynthia said. 'You need coffee.'

Bubbles giggled. 'What *I* need,' she said huskily, 'is *not* coffee.'

Cynthia glanced at Tom, but he seemed barely conscious that Bubbles was there. He was mumbling something that sounded like a mantra of some kind, psyching himself up, perhaps, for the session ahead.

Unlocking the laboratory doors, Cynthia ushered them inside. Bubbles made to turn on the lights, but Cynthia beat her hand away gently.

'Not yet. Let me pull the blinds first.'

She went round quickly, pulling them down, then came back and switched on two of the four switches. 'There,' she said, 'that should be enough.'

Tom walked across, then threw his jacket down over the back of a chair. 'Right,' he said, all businesslike, 'you want to go through the moves first, or shall we put on the suits?'

It was clear Tom hadn't quite understood what she'd been saying back at the hotel.

'No, Tom,' she said, watching him slowly unbutton his shirt, unable to look away as that mountainous chest appeared once more, 'we're going to do a kind of compromise. It'd take too long to get the full suits on, so I'm just going to wire up the important bits.'

'Right,' Tom said, giving her a beaming smile that made her want to cross her legs, 'Got you.'

'Bubbles?' Cynthia turned. 'Oh shit . . .'

Bubbles had put down her bag, slipped off her thin silk jacket, sat down, and . . . promptly fallen asleep.

Cynthia went across and shook her. Nothing. Again she shook her, anger and frustration making her far from gentle. But Bubbles was sleeping the sleep of the dead and the inebriate.

Cynthia turned, looking at Tom. 'Look, Tom, I . . .'

She stopped, an idea coming to her. 'Look,' she began again, this time more hesitantly, 'we've got to do this, so . . .'

'Suits me,' Tom said. 'You're the boss.' And without a further word he began to strip off.

'We'll rehearse it first,' Cynthia said, nervous now, peeling off her top then fumbling at the catch to her bra.

'Good idea,' Tom said, slipping out of his jeans so that only his briefs remained.

God! Cynthia thought, unable to tear her eyes from that bulge beneath the thin fabric. This is just like the first time all over again.

Tom reached down and slipped off his briefs. As he did, his penis sprang up to its full, magnificent length.

Christ, that cock! She almost swooned at the thought of actually touching it!

Tom turned to her, his eyes narrowing momentarily. 'Cyn?'

'Yes?' The word was inaudible. She tried again. 'Yes?'

'You are clean, right?'

'Clean?' She stared at him, then understood. 'AIDS, you mean?'

'Right. Because Jerry and I have check-ups every month. You can't be too sure in our line of business.'

'No . . .' It was the first time she had even considered it. 'I . . .' She nodded. 'Yes, I'm clean.'

'Good,' Tom said, beaming at her. 'So where d'you wanna start? You want me in the chair, or do you want me to do you over the desk?'

Patricia had just finished addressing the last of the

envelopes containing the invitations to Sir James's seventieth birthday party, when she had heard the lift start up. Creeping out into the corridor, she had listened, thinking that maybe Bill and Ben had returned. She saw the light above the door stop on the third floor where the labs were, and tiptoed down the stairs to try to see who it was, arriving there just in time to see Tom, Cynthia and an unfamiliar but stunning dark-haired woman step into the lab.

For a moment Patricia stood there, outside, listening and wondering whether she ought to announce to Cynthia that she was there; whether she might . . . *help* in some way.

There was some talking. She could hear Tom's Texan drawl and Cynthia's clipped English replies, then there was silence. Placing her left hand flat against the door she pushed it gently, just a fraction, so that she could peek inside.

Cynthia and Tom were in the centre of the lab, where the mock office had been set up. Both were stark naked, and the sight of Tom's massive erection made Patricia's mouth fall open.

So where was the other one? The stunning, dark-haired girl?

As if in answer, Patricia heard a snorting snore just to her left, behind the door. But her eyes were glued on what Cynthia and Tom were doing.

She can't . . . Surely she . . .

The noise Cynthia made – half pain, half pure delight – sent a strange ripple shooting through Patricia's nerves.

'Oh, slowly, Tom . . . slowly . . . yes, that's it. Oh yes, that's *it*.'

Patricia watched, open-mouthed; and as she watched her free hand drifted down, over her breast and down the curve of her ample hip, until it nestled tight between her legs, moving back and forth, slowly at first and then, matching the rhythm of the couple she was watching, faster and faster, until, with a cry that came from three mouths all at once, the point of ecstasy was reached.

In the centre of the lab, Tom was stroking Cynthia's back tenderly, then bent over to kiss her shoulder, murmuring, 'That was great, honey, really great.'

Patricia, watching the strange tenderness of that moment, shivered. They hadn't even noticed her, not even when she'd cried out! Moving back, she let the door close silently, then, taking quick but quiet steps, she hurried away, the image of what she'd seen burning in her mind.

Patricia caught a taxi at the corner of the Square, meaning to go straight home, but, as it cruised along Southampton Row, she suddenly leaned forward and, tapping on the glass panel between her and the driver, told him to pull over at the side of the road.

Paying him off, she turned, looking down Theobald's Road. In all likelihood he had gone home now. It was late – almost eleven – and the pub would be closing any minute. Even so . . .

She stopped outside the White Hart, peering through the window, then felt her heart begin to thud in her chest. He was there, at his usual table, just to the left of where she was standing!

You're being silly, Patricia, she told herself. But that was the old Patricia. The one who was afraid to do what her heart commanded her to do. The old, cautious Patricia.

He'll just tell you to go away, that's all, the voice in her head persisted, but she wasn't listening. She had stopped listening the moment she had crouched by the door, watching Tom and Cynthia.

Grab what happiness you can now, another, new voice answered. Go on. It really doesn't matter if you make a fool of yourself!

Patricia pushed the door open and stepped inside. There was a faint murmur of conversation, the smell of beer and bodies. A jukebox played an old country-and-western song, the sound unobtrusive.

She walked over to his table, then stopped, waiting for him to look up. At first he didn't notice her. Then, conscious that someone was hovering nearby, he glanced up, bleary-eyed.

'Oh,' he groaned, seeing who it was. 'It's you.'

Patricia sat, placing her handbag on the table by her elbow. 'Would you like a drink, Inspector?'

He hushed her. 'Holly. Call me Holly.'

'So, Mr Holly. Would you like a drink?'

He held his glass up and stared at it, then downed the remaining contents. Then he burped. 'No,' he said, shaking his head, his voice slurred. 'I've had enough.'

'Then perhaps I should take you home.'

She could hardly believe she had said it. Holly, who had been looking away across the bar, slowly looked back at her.

'Pardon?'

Patricia leaned toward him slightly. 'You look lonely. You look like you need company. So . . .'

He looked down, a strange, bitter expression on his face. 'You're taking the piss.'

'No, I . . .' She reached across and covered his hand, noticing the ring for the first time. 'You're married.'

Holly gave a kind of shrug. 'Was.'

'So you're divorced?'

He nodded.

'Me too. Bastard left me. Ran off with another woman.'

'Probably my wife,' and, realising what he'd said, Holly gave a brief laugh.

He looked up. Patricia was smiling at him. 'Well?'

'Well what?'

'Would you like to come home with me? For a coffee. I'm lonely, you're lonely. Maybe we could be lonely together.'

Holly huffed. 'I'm pissed.'

'So?'

He shrugged, then: 'All right . . .'

'Good,' she said, the faintest tingle running through her. His dress sense was appalling, but he wasn't such a bad-looking man, and it would be nice simply to know that someone was there. 'Come on, then,' she said, standing up, 'before I change my mind.'

Holly stood, unsteadily, then looked at her frowning. 'You sure you ain't taking the piss?'

'You want me to?'

Holly gave a little shuddering sigh, then shook his head. 'No.'

'Good, then give me your arm. It's not far.'

Louise had been right: it *was* hard to sit down. Standing

naked beside the bath as the water tumbled in, Cynthia stared at the window, watching the dawn light grow while she recalled what had happened.

That first time with Tom, she had been so wet she had barely noticed just how big he was. Or rather, she had *noticed* – that first full thrust of his had taken her breath away – but it had not *hurt* her. Indeed, she had been rather proud that she could stretch to accommodate him; but, after that first rather hurried session, she had begun to develop a healthy respect for Jerry Michelle.

Turning off the flow, Cynthia gingerly climbed into the tub, wincing slightly as she lowered her buttocks below the water level.

From a technical point of view it had been most useful. Not only did she have one remarkable and two relatively good female orgasms on tape, she also had a fair understanding now of just what was needed for the machine. Tom was a good thing – there was no doubting that – and he would be a big seller for them if this ever got onto the market. But you could have just a bit too much of Tom. Being shagged senseless was one thing – being shagged senseless by a massively hung superstud was another, and, while most women might dream of it, the reality was somewhat different. One might call it the law of diminishing returns, but ten minutes of Tom Dupont was quite enough. As for the rest, one might as well take up aerobics, and it had the advantage of being considerably less painful.

They had finished the session just after four. Bubbles had slept straight through and was still beyond recall when they'd packed up, so Tom had picked her up and carried her down, placing her between them in the taxi; then, at the other end, he had carried her up into Cynthia's apartment and laid her on her bed, undressing her and tucking her under the sheet before he blew Cynthia a kiss and vanished into the night.

Lying back, Cynthia rested her head against the back edge of the steeply sloping bath and sighed, tired suddenly. If the session had taught her one thing, it was that she didn't have what it took to be a porn-movie star. You had to be detached, and she didn't have that kind of detachment. For her sex was too important. It had to be spontaneous and passionate – cruel, even – or it was nothing. Oh, that didn't mean that she hadn't enjoyed it after the first time – it was just that she hadn't enjoyed it *enough*. And the 'enough' was absolutely crucial to her.

Cynthia closed her eyes, recalling the moment when, kneeling down before Tom, she had prepared to take him in her mouth. The *thought* of sucking him off – of doing something that was, to be frank, quite extraordinary considering his proportions – had proved more thrilling than the act itself. Indeed, after the first minute or so it had been quite dull, and, though she was able to take Tom's full length into herself down below, there was no way she had Jerry's sword-swallowing abilities. She had had to content herself with licking up and down it like a painter giving a barber's pole a quick coat of gloss, and after a while it had seemed no more exciting than licking a warm piece of gristle.

Not that you'd have thought that by the way Tom had groaned and writhed about. Indeed, there was no doubting Tom's acting abilities. He was able to fake it with the best of them, without a doubt.

Not that that first time had been faked . . .

She had wondered about that all the way home in the taxi. Was it just the excitement of someone new, or had Tom actually fancied her? To be honest, after what she'd seen that morning, she was surprised Tom *could* come, and even more surprised that he'd come inside *her*!

Unfortunately normal service had been quickly resumed, and the Flying Texan had been back in action for the rest of the session, pistons pounding, his well-trimmed buttocks moving like the treadle of her grandmother's old sewing machine.

And that was it. After that one brief experience she had decided that enough was enough. With Tom, anyway. As for Bubbles . . .

Despite the soreness and the dull ache, Cynthia felt something stir in her at the thought of the delightful Dorinda. Climbing up out of the water, she grabbed a towel, wrapped it round her and tiptoed through into the bedroom, stopping in the doorway to look.

Bubbles lay in her bed, naked, dead to the world, lying on her back with her mouth open and her legs apart, the sheet kicked off.

Slowly Cynthia walked across, towelling herself as she went, then, standing over her naked guest, she let the towel fall away and, sitting on the bed beside her, reached out to touch and then cup one of those gorgeous pert breasts.

Bubbles stirred slightly and murmured something inaudible. The nipple had hardened in Cynthia's embrace.

Cynthia's body was in no shape for this, but she knew she would regret it if she didn't take this golden opportunity. Leaning over her supine guest, Cynthia placed her lips gently to the other nipple and began to suck at it, teasing at it gently with her teeth, while her other hand moved softly, slowly down the length of Dorinda's flank, barely touching the soft, warm flesh until it nestled between the other's legs like a strange chick in a soft brown nest.

Bubbles smiled lasciviously in her sleep, then reached up sleepily and pulled Cynthia down onto her. Cynthia winced slightly, then, placing her lips against the other woman's, surrendered herself to the moment.

Inspector Holly woke with a big smile on his face. He had been dreaming, but now he was awake and the sun was shining pleasantly on his naked back. There was a faint, refreshing breeze in the room and, somewhere in the near distance, he could hear the rattle of a train.

Holly blinked, surprised, then sniffed the air. Was that fresh coffee he could smell?

He turned, realising as he did that, far from feeling his usual like-shit hungover self, he actually felt rather good. His muscles felt relaxed, his head clear.

'Morning.'

Holly stared at the figure framed in the doorway in amazement, his lips slowly parting until his mouth gaped. It was that woman from Virt-E-Go! How the fuck had *she* got in here?

Then, in a moment of blinding realisation, he understood. This wasn't his flat, it was *hers*. And then he remembered. It hadn't been a dream after all – he had actually just spent half the bloody night humping like a good 'un!

'It's all right, love,' Patricia said, smiling tenderly at him. 'You lay there a while. I'll bring you in some breakfast.'

'What . . . ?' Holly started, then, clearing his throat, he began again. 'What time is it?'

'Gone eleven.'

'*Eleven*?' He sat bolt upright, only then realising that he was wearing no underwear.

'Don't worry,' Pat said, coming over, her smile knowing. 'I've phoned your office and told them you won't be coming in. They didn't seem to mind.'

'You did *what*?'

Patricia came across and sat beside him on the bed, her dressing gown falling open slightly so that he could see her breasts. 'I phoned your office. Then I phoned mine. I've taken the day off.'

'I . . .' Now that he'd noticed them, he could not take his eyes off Patricia's breasts. Her nipples were unexpectedly stiff. He swallowed, images from last night flitting across his mind.

'Would you rather wait for breakfast?' Patricia asked softly, reaching out to lay her hand over the telltale bulge in the sheet.

'I . . .'

Patricia's fingers closed over the sheet around Holly's penis, enclosing it in a little tunnel of cloth. Holly groaned. Without letting go of him, Patricia untied the cord to her gown and, with a little movement of her shoulders, shrugged it off. She sat there now, naked on the bed beside him.

'Can I . . . ?' Holly stopped, not quite knowing what to say next.

But Patricia knew the answer anyway. 'You can do anything you want, my love. Absolutely anything.'

When the large white envelope – addressed to Mr and Mrs R. Appleyard, and containing an embossed invitation to Sir James Grant's seventieth birthday party – arrived at his home, Roger was careful to intercept it. Slipping it into his jacket pocket, he later stashed it in the top drawer of his office desk, so that Jane Appleyard remained in blissful ignorance of its existence.

All of Virt-E-Go's workforce had been invited to what promised to be a most lavish occasion, and, though Roger had never had much time for the old man, he did admire his ability to throw a good bash and so was rather looking forward to it. He had even suggested to Louise that they book a room at a nearby pub, planning to slip back there after the party for a quick one. But the best-laid schemes often go astray. Only two days later, Roger walked into his office to find his young Chairman standing beside his desk, replacing the handset to his telephone.

'Ah, Roger!' Charles said cheerfully. 'You've just missed your wife, I'm afraid. I said you'd phone her back.'

'Oh . . . Right . . . Thanks,' Roger replied warily. He did not encourage Jane Appleyard to call him at the office.

'She sounded absolutely charming!' Roger smiled, nodding agreeably. 'I told her to be sure to get you to introduce us at Sir James's party.'

Roger's smile fixed like quick-drying concrete. 'You did? What did she say?'

'Um, she asked me to remind her when it was.'

Between his clenched teeth Roger groaned. 'Er, then she said there was someone at the door and that she would be sure to speak to you about the party.'

Roger nodded, his smile slowly cracking.

Charles walked past him towards the door, only turning when he was almost out in the corridor.

'Oh, yes, I almost forgot the reason why I came in here. I've had a memo from Brian which I need to discuss with you. I'll leave you to phone your wife, but I'll see you in my office when you've a minute. Okay?'

Roger nodded mutely, then looked towards the phone. With a sigh he lifted the handset, then tapped in the number, cursing his bloody awful luck.

For one to whom lying had become an almost habitual pastime, coming up with an excuse for why he had not mentioned the party invitation presented Roger with few problems. He had become so adept at thinking on his feet and wriggling out of tight corners that coming up with something convincing proved a complete doddle. Jane Appleyard accepted without a murmur his explanation that he'd thought she wouldn't want to go to the party; that it was bound to be boring and full of stuffy people.

He'd thought he would surprise her, he said; take her away for the night to a little hotel he'd been told about, just the two of them. But if she *really* wanted to go to the party, after all . . .

To his surprise, and total horror, Jane Appleyard announced that that was *exactly* what she wanted to do.

A horrific image of his wife and mistress under one

roof flashed through Roger's mind. A cold shiver ran down his increasingly weakening spine. But, never one to confront a problem if he could possibly run away from it, Roger Appleyard pushed his head firmly into the sand and prayed to God for divine intervention.

A pathetic attempt to persuade Louise that he had so much work on that the party was beginning to look like a non-starter received short shrift and was abandoned in its early stages. He then tried to convince her that it would be full of old farts from Sir James's golf club and that they shouldn't bother, attempting to entice her instead with the promise of a whole weekend away sometime before Christmas. Displaying an unexpected degree of stubbornness, Louise announced that her mind was made up. Besides, she'd bought an expensive new frock and had made the booking at the pub. There was no getting out of it, she said. They *were* going to the party.

Displaying a high degree of misguided generosity, the Almighty did, indeed, appear to look favourably upon Roger Appleyard when, the morning of Sir James's party, Louise woke early with awful stomach cramps and a bout of vomiting. Every attempt to prepare herself for the office resulted in failure as, doubled up with pain, she staggered to the bathroom, positioning the appropriate orifice over the toilet bowl until that particular bout had ended, leaving her drained and feeling terribly sorry for herself. But relief was temporary and, finally, reluctantly, the wretched Louise was forced to take to her bed, mustering just enough strength to phone in sick.

In fact, she sounded so terrible that, even in his euphoria, Roger Appleyard was moved to pity the poor girl, and so grateful was he for this minor miracle that he readily agreed to call by on his way home that evening. By the time Roger had finished rubbing his hands together and had written himself a note to order some flowers, Louise was once again staring into the foaming lavender-scented bowl of the flushing lavatory.

Chastity listened with barely concealed contempt as Roger Appleyard explained over the telephone to his wife that he would be a little late arriving home – something to see to at the office – before reassuring her that they would be in good time for the party. Just moments before, he had handed Chastity a twenty-pound note with instructions to arrange for a bouquet to be delivered to the office before the end of the day. When she had asked if he had any preference for flowers he'd told her to choose – whatever she thought Louise might like.

'Right!' he said, placing the handset onto the telephone. 'Where were we? Ah, yes,' he said, tapping the note in front of him on the desk. 'Your little friend, Kirsty McDonald.'

Chastity refused to rise to the bait, or to look up into Roger's leering face.

'Send another fax, will you?' he said, his voice suddenly businesslike. 'I think we're going to have to start getting a bit heavy. That bitch is just pissing us around. Right, take this down: Due to your unexplained silence following our last four faxes, the matter of the contract is now extremely urgent and we are most anxious that the matter be concluded as soon as possible. Stop. Ideally we should prefer it if you were here in person to enable us to discuss any areas of concern. We are, of course, very much looking forward to working with you . . . blah, blah, blah . . . etcetera, etcetera. Bloody fucking cow!'

Chastity closed her notebook, uncrossed her legs and rested the pad on the edge of her knees.

'Will that be all? Only I'd better get back and do some of Bob's work.'

Roger eyed her up and down, with no attempt to conceal his lust. 'Yes, that'll be all,' he sighed, sinking back in his chair and pushing himself back from his desk, watching her appreciatively as she stood up and moved across the room. 'Unless you fancy . . .'

'Don't even *think* it,' she called over her shoulder, not knowing who she pitied most – Louise, Roger's wife . . . or Roger.

It wasn't until he was actually turning the key in Louise's front door that Roger realised he had forgotten the flowers.

'Shit!' he said under his breath, annoyed not only by the waste of money but because Louise was bound to think he was lying when he tried to explain that in rushing to see her he had left the carefully chosen bouquet on the office desk.

Quietly closing the door behind him, he made his way along the hall to the bedroom where the door lay slightly ajar. He poked his head round the side of it and was a little surprised and, indeed, disappointed, to see Louise, propped up on pillows, gazing gratefully across at him, her arms folded across her chest. He had half hoped to creep in and find her fast asleep, scribble a note to prove that he'd been there – and the flowers, damn it! – and scoot home to change for the party.

'Hello dar-ling,' he said, his face all pity as he came to sit beside her on the edge of the bed.

Louise smiled weakly, on the verge of tears as she at last gave way to the self-pity that had threatened to consume her all day long.

'My poor little Lulu,' Roger oozed, taking her hot clammy hand in his and smoothing her burning brow with the other. 'I've been thinking of you all day. I bought you a beautiful bouquet . . .'

Louise opened one eye, surveying Roger's empty hands.

'. . . but I was in such a rush to see you I left them at the office.'

Louise closed her eye again without saying a word.

'Honest Lulu—'

'Save it, Rog. I feel like shit.'

'Poor baby,' he said, pushing his fingers through the damp hair around her face. 'Poor, poor baby.' And as Louise visibly relaxed beneath his touch he risked a quick glance at his watch.

'I think you need to get some sleep,' he announced authoritatively, after what he considered a respectable period of time – respectable only in that it wasn't quite indecent, for it amounted to no more than three minutes. 'I'm gonna leave you alone now to get some peace, sweetie pie.' And removing his hand he wiped his palm across the duvet cover.

'Oh, don't go yet, Rog,' she said, grabbing hold of his arm. 'Stay for a bit longer. Please.' And, pulling him towards her, she deposited Roger's head face down upon her ample bosom so that the thinnest layer of fine cotton lay between him and Louise's bare flesh.

There was something about Louise's laboured breathing that Roger found strangely exciting; the rapid rise and fall of those soft pendulous breasts enticing him as they glanced against his cheek so that, without thinking, his mouth opened instinctively, his tongue sliding beneath the edge of her nightie in search of her nipple.

'Oh, Roger, no,' she whined, a pathetic disappointment in her voice. 'I'm not in the mood. *Really*.'

'Sorry, Lulu,' he panted without looking up. 'You know I can't keep my hands off you.'

'But I feel so hot and sweaty . . .'

Roger snatched a quick look at his watch as he brought his arm up, the expandable silver strap disappearing as his hand dipped beneath the edge of the duvet cover.

'Oooh, Lulu,' he groaned. 'No knickers . . .'

'Please, Rog . . .'

'You'll be all right,' he soothed, shifting his leg so that it lay between Louise's, pushing them apart.

'You'll be late for the party,' she ventured, mopping her face with the back of her hand.

'Party? What party?' he said, with a conviction that almost fooled himself. 'I couldn't go without you, could I?'

'You're not going, Rog? *Really*?' Louise said, her voice cracking with emotion as a solitary teardrop slid from the outer corner of each eye.

'Really,' Roger croaked, his face disappearing into Louise's damp, dark cleavage, while with one hand he fumbled to undo his belt.

* * *

Despite taking the stairs two at a time, Chastity was not quick enough to catch Roger Appleyard before he disappeared round the Square in his bright red Rover and out of sight. In her hand she held the flowers she'd purchased earlier for Louise, which Roger had absent-mindedly left on his desk. Dipping her nose into the sweet bouquet, Chastity inhaled deeply, closing her eyes as she drank in the intoxicating smell. Poor Louise, she thought, turning to walk back towards the lift.

All day there had been an undercurrent of excitement among the rest of the staff in anticipation of the party that evening. But the very thought of it made Chastity's stomach turn over. As if to taunt her, the party dress she had collected from the dry cleaners earlier that day hung on the outside of the stationery cupboard, its thin cellophane covering rippling in the early-evening breeze blowing in through the window.

The one good thing about the party had been Charles's absence from the office that day. The strain of avoiding him was becoming too much and on numerous occasions she found herself close to tears – but, each time, Louise's taunting, hurtful words ran through her head invoking fresh determination not to succumb to the desire that pulled at every fibre of her body; not to give in to this hopeless, unrealistic love she felt for Charles Grant.

Chastity's gaze fell on the bouquet of flowers, which she had placed in a small glass vase of water on her desk. For a minute or more she studied them, her eyes glazed, before suddenly grabbing at them, reaching for her handbag and rushing from the room, the cellophane wrapping over her dress billowing as she swept past it.

*　　*　　*

There was no sign of Roger's car when Chastity pulled up in the cab outside Louise's flat. She stood for some time with her thumb poised over the entryphone button before finally summoning the courage to press it. After waiting for more than a minute, she decided, with a mixture of relief and disappointment, that Louise must be either out or asleep. She turned away, meaning to go, when the intercom crackled into barely decipherable life.

'Who . . . it?' came Louise's muffled voice through the speaker.

'Louise?' Chastity shouted in a falsely cheerful voice. 'It's me, Chastity. Can I come in?'

'Who?'

'Chastity. It's Chastity. Can I come in?'

'. . . the door,' came the distant reply, followed by a loud buzzing sound.

Chastity pushed the unresisting door, which banged shut behind her, and walked the two flights up to the first floor.

Louise was standing in the open doorway, resting against the frame, her eyes as red as the thick towelling robe wrapped around her body.

Ignoring the weary 'what the hell do you want?' look on Louise's face, Chastity smiled sympathetically. 'Hi,' she said sweetly.

'To what do I owe this pleasure?' Louise asked sarcastically, making a point of not looking at the bunch of flowers in the younger woman's hand.

'Roger forgot these,' she said, proffering the bouquet and forcing another smile.

The sound of Roger's name on Chastity's pouting lips sent a pain of raw jealousy shooting through

Louise's aching body. Forcing her hand to reach out, she ungraciously snatched the flowers from Chastity, petals scattering at her feet as she dropped them to her side, smashing the blooms against her leg.

'Can I come in, Louise?' Chastity asked quietly. 'I think we need to talk.'

Roger was whistling as he stepped from the shower and stood before the steamed-up mirror, towelling himself down.

Things could not have gone better, considering. Indeed, had Charles Grant called him to his office to announce he was giving him a two-hundred-per-cent pay rise, he could not have felt so good. Not only could he take his wife to the party without fear of her bumping into Louise — with all the dangers that *that* entailed — but he had also managed to wangle his way into Louise's bed.

Oh, it hadn't been as good as usual, not by any means. Louise had been an irritable and unsympathetic lover, but a shag was a shag after all, and even a bad shag with Louise was better than nothing.

Throwing the towel aside, Roger turned, meaning to reach out for his bathrobe, only to find it gone.

'Now what the—?'

'Are you looking for this, sweetheart?'

He turned, to find Jane in the doorway, wearing his bathrobe. And nothing else.

'*Jane*? What are you doing?'

Jane Appleyard smiled. 'You used to like me joining you in the shower. Remember?'

'Yes,' he said, surprised by this sudden turn in events.

'But we really ought to be getting ready, you know. The party will be starting in an hour.'

'That's all right,' she said, walking slowly over to him. 'There'll be plenty of time to get there. Besides, it doesn't matter if we're just a teensy weensy bit late, does it?' And, letting the robe fall from her shoulders, Jane Appleyard stepped closer, pressing her body against her husband's.

'Jane? This really is—'

Roger swallowed as she closed the fingers of her right hand over his steadily swelling penis.

'I just wanted to thank you, that's all . . .'

'*Thank* me?' Roger almost squeaked.

'Yes,' she said, her fingers stroking gently up and down his now fully aroused shaft. 'I was beginning to think you didn't *want* me to meet the people you work with.'

Roger caught his breath, then closed his eyes. He had forgotten just how light – how pleasant – a touch his wife had. 'Hmmm,' he said, as if in answer to her. 'Hh-hmm.'

'Come on,' she said, leading him by the penis back into the shower. 'You know you want to.'

Roger groaned, then, succumbing to the inevitable, reached over and switched on the water again before turning his wife and pushing her gently back against the white tile wall.

'You know, Janie,' he said, meeting her eyes as he pushed up into her, 'I could quite get to like this . . .'

'Louise, I need to know if I've done something to you,' Chastity said, the words blurted out almost before Louise had closed the front door behind them.

'Well only *you* know that,' the other woman replied,

brushing past her and walking along the hallway towards the living room.

Chastity followed at her heels, a note of desperation in her voice. 'But you seem so . . . so, *angry* with me. And I don't know why,' she persisted.

'Don't you?' Louise slumped into the chair, folding her arms across her aching stomach. 'You *do* surprise me.'

Chastity sat on the small sofa facing her. The flowers lay between them on the coffee table, their petals reflected in its glass surface.

'Is it something to do with Roger?'

'Huh! Don't play the innocent with me. You know bloody well it's got *everything* to do with Roger!'

'Well, what exactly is it you think we've been up to?' Chastity challenged, her voice gaining a little edge now. 'I mean, what has he said to you?'

'He hasn't *had* to say anything.'

'Well, what's this all about, then?'

'I've got eyes, you know.'

'Well what is it you think you've seen, Louise? ''Cos whatever it is, I can tell you you're mistaken. I'd be more likely to be interested in a tub of bleedin' lard than in Roger Appleyard. I think he's an arrogant, male chauvinist pig with as much sex appeal as Sooty, and if you'd half a brain you'd see him for the lying, cheating bastard he really is!'

Her tirade finished, Chastity sat in shocked silence as Louise gazed across in open-mouthed astonishment.

Watching Louise crumble before her eyes, Chastity felt suddenly ashamed, angry with herself and with Roger Appleyard for bringing this poor, pathetic creature to this.

'Louise, I—'

Louise held up her hand to stop her saying any more as she struggled to keep back the tears that sat precariously on her lower lashes.

'Louise, I'm sorry. I shouldn't have said that. It's none of my business.'

'No. No, it's all right,' she replied shakily, sniffing loudly and wiping her nose on the cuff of her dressing gown. 'I deserved it.'

'No you didn't. I was just cross because of what you said about me and Charles.'

Louise looked across at her, genuine bewilderment clouding her already distorted features. 'I don't know what you mean,' she said, sniffing again and this time wiping her nose across the other cuff.

Chastity reached into her bag and pulled out a tissue, handing it across to her. 'It was when you were talking to Patricia. In the loo. You said . . . No, it doesn't matter. Forget it.'

'Yes it does matter,' Louise said, blowing her nose into the crumpled ball of soggy tissue. 'What did I say?'

Chastity took a deep breath. 'You said . . . that I was a little tart who was only after Charles's money.' And she looked down into her hands, which sat clasped together in her lap.

Louise smacked a hand across her open mouth. 'Oh my God,' she gasped through her fingers as recollection began to dawn. 'Me and my bloody big mouth!'

Having brought it out into the open, Chastity felt a sudden lightening of the load she had carried ever since that fateful eavesdropping, so that suddenly she felt foolish for even mentioning it.

But Louise was mortified. 'Oh, Chastity, you must know I didn't mean it . . .' It was the first time she had called her by name since the team had returned from America. 'I was just, well, jealous I suppose.'

'What of?'

'Oh, I don't know. You and Roger being away together, I guess, and him being all distant when you got back.' She shook her head in disbelief at her own stupidity and sighed deeply. 'It's just that Roger . . . oh, *sod* him!'

Chastity couldn't help smiling.

'I know what he's like,' Louise said, and seeing the doubting look on Chastity's face went on: 'No, really I do. It's just that he can be so . . . so affectionate and so loving, and I know he really does care for me. Like this evening. He came round on his way home to make sure I was all right. And he said he wouldn't be going to Sir James's party because I wouldn't be there.'

'But I heard him tell his wife—'

The words had left Chastity's lips before her brain had caught up with the possible ramifications of what she was about to say.

Louise was on the edge of her seat in an instant, all pain and discomfort momentarily forgotten. '*What*? What did he tell his wife?'

Chastity smiled and shook her head. 'Nothing. I must've got it wrong.' She reached forward and lifted up the bunch of flowers. 'Look, let me put these in water for you?'

'Fuck the flowers!' Louise said, leaning forward and catching hold of Chastity's wrist. 'Tell me. *What* did Roger tell his wife?'

'I've probably got it wrong . . .' Chastity began.

'Go on.'

Chastity could not meet Louise's eyes and stared across the room at a painting of a clown – a teardrop on his cheek – that hung lopsided on the far wall. 'I thought I heard him promise his wife . . . that they wouldn't be late for Sir James's party.'

'He did *what*?'

'Like I said, I've probably got it wrong.'

'The two-faced slimy bastard!' Louise was on her feet now, her fists clenched at her side. 'I'll kill him!'

'Louise . . .'

'Right!' she said, fired with renewed energy and determination. 'Come with me!'

Chastity rushed after her along the hallway and into the bedroom, where Louise was already flicking hangers along the rail in her wardrobe as though searching through a filing cabinet for the right document.

'Louise, what are you doing?'

'Here!' she said, slipping a dress from its hanger and throwing it to Chastity. 'We're going to a party!'

While Bill and Ben tucked into the smoked salmon and caviar canapés, Patricia looked about her at the elegance of the massive room. Though she had worked for Sir James for more than twenty years, she had never once in all that time been invited to Maltby Hall. Indeed, to be here now was, for her, somewhat strange, for in those twenty years – and especially after the Amsterdam incident – she had often daydreamed not merely of visiting the place, but of coming here as the second Lady Grant – after the current Lady's demise, of course – to live here in splendid luxury for the rest of her days. But now, seeing it in all its sophisticated glory, she knew that she would never have fitted in. A night in a hotel room in Amsterdam was one thing but sharing a life of such regal elegance was quite another.

As Cynthia brought their drinks across, Patricia smiled, then, leaning towards her, whispered, 'Do you think that's *real*?'

Cynthia looked up at the Whistler painting hanging on the wall above the huge open fireplace and, after a moment's contemplation, nodded. 'I'd say so. I mean, he'd hardly hang a copy, would he?'

'No . . . no, of course,' Patricia said. She took a large swig of her champagne, then looked about her again at the other guests who, in their perfectly cut dresses and beautifully tailored suits, seemed perfectly at ease in these surroundings.

'You know what?' she said, leaning towards Cynthia again. 'I've got butterflies in my tummy.'

Cynthia looked at her, puzzled. 'Butterflies?'

Patricia shrugged, then: 'It's just . . .' But how *did* she explain. Amsterdam. The daydreams. The inner void she'd felt since Sir James had left the company. No, it was best not to say a word, but the truth was that she, who was usually so unflappable, felt suddenly like a schoolgirl out on her first date, and all at the thought of seeing Sir James again.

Handing Cynthia her empty glass, Patricia mumbled her apologies, then hurried across the room, skirting various small knots of guests as she sought the refuge of the ladies'.

Leaving Bill and Ben to work their way stendily along the buffet, Cynthia wandered slowly across the room until she stood at the massive leaded window that looked out onto the great lawn.

Here, she was thinking. We ought to set our next VRE here.

Yes, the more she thought about it, the stronger was her instinct for it. They could set it in Napoleonic times; after all, people loved costume dramas. Only this would be more of a *lack-*of-costume drama.

There was the sound of someone clearing her throat just behind her. She turned, to find Mrs Webb, Sir James's housekeeper, standing there.

'Forgive me, Miss Harding,' she said, clearly ill at ease, 'but I have three guests at the door. They say they have lost their invitations.'

Cynthia raised an eyebrow. 'And?'

'And they say that *you* know something about the matter.'

Cynthia smiled politely. 'And you want me to come and verify that they are bona fide guests, is that right?'

Mrs Webb lowered her head the tiniest fraction, a little embarrassed. 'If you wouldn't mind, Miss.'

'Then lead the way.'

Patricia was just emerging from the ladies' when she heard the sudden babble of noise coming from the entrance hall. Some new guests were arriving at the front steps and, by the sound of it, they were attracting an immense amount of interest.

Standing on tiptoe, Patricia strained to see just who it was – a film star, maybe, or a Cabinet minister – then gasped as she saw not merely who it was, but what they were wearing.

'Oh my god . . .'

Tom Dupont handed Mrs Webb his stetson, then looked back at Lady Grant, smiling his most charming smile before he bowed low, his chest muscles rippling as he did so. Big Tom was wearing a tuxedo, but he had omitted to wear a shirt. Flanking him, like goddesses just down from Olympus, were Jerry and Bubbles, both attired in diaphanous, light-blue gowns that left little to the imagination.

For one brief moment, as heads moved aside, giving Patricia a clear view, she glimpsed Sir James's face and saw the broad, lustful grin that lit his features.

She shivered, knowing that look. *Remembering* it. So he had once looked at her, in the dawn's first light.

Confused now, not knowing really what she felt, she turned, to find Sir James's son, Charles, facing her. He seemed incredibly agitated.

'Patricia. Oh God. Look . . . we've, erm . . . well, we've got to talk.'

'Of course, Charles,' she said, mystified by his behaviour.

With an endearing awkwardness, Charles led Patricia into a side room, not merely closing but locking the door behind them.

'Charles?'

Charles turned, then looked down, blushing. 'Patricia . . .' he began, unable to look at her. 'Pat . . . I've . . . well, I've known you since . . .'

'Since you were a young boy.'

'Yes . . .' Charles groaned. 'Look, this is difficult. I . . .'

'Is it about Chastity?'

Charles glanced up, a look of pure fear in his eyes, then tucked his head back down again. 'In a way. I . . .' Then, wringing his hands. 'Oh God . . .'

'Charles?'

'I'm sorry, I . . .' Again he groaned. Then, clearly steeling himself, he forced himself to look at her, his expression set into a grimace. 'Something happened, didn't it? I mean, between you and . . .'

Patricia shuddered. So he knew. She swallowed, then answered Charles.

'Yes.'

'Oh, God!'

'I didn't mean it to. I mean, I *wanted* it to, but . . . well, when your father came to my room . . .'

Charles looked up, startled. 'Pardon?'

'I shouldn't have, I know, but I simply couldn't help myself. Your father's such a passionate man, Charles. So . . . *forceful*.'

Charles was staring at her now, open-mouthed. 'Then I didn't . . .'

Patricia frowned. 'Didn't what?'

But Charles was beaming now. He turned, fumbling with the lock, then laughed; a laugh of pure relief. 'Thank God!'

'Charles?'

But he was gone.

As they turned in through the broad iron gates to the estate, Chastity glanced anxiously at the taxi's clock.

They had managed to chalk up over thirty-eight pounds in taxi fare, and she was only too well aware that all she had in her wallet was the five pounds change she had been given at the dry cleaners that afternoon.

Her own simple but elegant black dress, which still hung over the stationery cupboard door was but a wistful memory as she glanced down apprehensively at the creation Louise had insisted she borrow. The figure-hugging scarlet silk dress stretched across her thighs, the hem barely concealing the dark strips of her sheer black stockings. On her feet were a pair of thin-heeled, strappy patent sandals. Chastity shifted uncomfortably in the seat, lifting her neckline and pulling at her hemline, feeling suddenly horrified as she caught sight of her reflection in the side window of the cab. This was not the image of sophisticated elegance she had had in mind.

'Louise, I haven't got enough money for this,' she whispered.

'Don't worry, it's on account. I've charged it to Roger,' Louise answered efficiently, edging forward on her seat and holding onto the handbar by the window, her face set in concentration as they journeyed ever closer to the house.

As the taxi crunched its way back down the gravel drive, Chastity and Louise stood side by side before the imposing building, a row of steps leading up on either side to the illuminated entrance where Sir James and Lady Grant stood, greeting their guests, their voices drifting out on the crisp night air.

'Alex! Elizabeth! How are you? And this must be Camilla . . .'

'Right!' said Louise, taking one of her breasts in each hand and rearranging them within her Wonderbra, gaining at least two more inches of cleavage. 'Let's go find the little toe-rag!'

To say that Charles had been disappointed when he'd learned that Chastity might not be coming to the party was an almighty understatement. He had been devastated.

Patricia had sensed the girl's reservations about the evening much earlier when Chastity had remained silent while the other members of staff had been talking excitedly, looking forward to the party. And, when Pat had called by to collect her travelling companion, there had been no sign of Chastity. What's more, her dress had been left hanging in the darkened office in its cellophane wrapping.

It was then that Patricia had phoned to report the fact to Charles – to prepare him.

Up until that point Charles had eagerly anticipated his father's party, welcoming it as an ideal opportunity to meet with Chastity in a purely social situation, to talk with her and hear her laugh, to dance with her, perhaps, to feel the warmth of her body against his own. In his imagination he had hoped for more, of course. In the dark, silent hours in the middle of the night, when he lay awake, restless with desire, he could taste her on his lips, the memory of the kiss that had sealed his fate still so keen, so fresh in his mind. In those private, intimate moments he allowed himself to think of more.

Now the sparkle had gone. The absence of just this one person had turned what had promised to be a glittering event into a trial to be suffered, indeed to be endured, surrounded by people who did not matter to him in the slightest, with his next visit to the office the only thing worth looking forward to.

The only patch of blue sky amidst the grey was the fact that he'd finally resolved just what had happened that night in the office.

Charles looked across to where his parents stood welcoming the latest group of guests, the odious Sir Alex Littlejohn, Virt-E-Go's absentee director, his third wife, Lavinia, and his frightful daughter, Camilla, whose voice could shatter a pint mug at twenty paces. Sensing his mother trying to catch his eye, Charles turned on his heels, snatched a drink from the tray of a passing waiter and made for the ballroom, not noticing the two young women, who, even at that moment, climbed the front steps with a strange determination.

Bob Guppy stood alone in a corner of the ballroom, a half-empty glass of champagne in each hand. His head bobbed up and down as he sipped first from one and then the other until, spotting an approaching wine waiter, he drained both glasses and swung them round onto the tray, swapping them for full ones.

Across the other side of the room Bob could see Roger Appleyard sucking up to some of Sir James's old cronies. His mouth curled into a disdainful sneer as he listened to their hearty laughter, bile rising to his throat as he watched them slap each other's back.

'Toffee-nosed bastards!' he hissed, taking two more gulps of champagne.

What he hadn't noticed the first time he'd looked

was the woman standing at Roger's side, all elegance
and quiet sophistication. So when he glanced across, over
the rim of his glass, and saw her stretch up to whisper
in Roger's ear, her touch on his shoulder unmistakably
intimate, he almost exploded with pent-up frustration,
caught somewhere between admiration and loathing for
the jammy bastard.

In the act of gazing after the woman, watching
her walk across the room and leave by the far door,
Bob Guppy was totally unaware of Roger Appleyard's
approach.

'Bob, my old mucker!' he said, slapping the shorter
man on the back. 'What are you doing over here all by
yourself?'

Bob Guppy jerked forward, spilling the remainder of
the champagne over his feet, squirming as he felt the cold
liquid trickle over his shoes and soak into his socks.

'Eyeing up the talent, no doubt!' Roger laughed. 'Tell,
you what, Bob. I clocked a very tasty bit of stuff just
now. Your cup of tea — young, long legs.' He sighed
whimsically, 'If I didn't have the missus with me . . .'

There was a moment's pause before understanding
appeared to dawn within Bob's skull. 'The missus.'

'Yeah. Jane. She's just gone off to the little girls'
room.' Roger's eye wandered round the crowded ballroom. Then, as though struck by a sudden thought, he
turned abruptly. 'Oh, and, keep quiet about Louise, eh,
Bob. Don't want to set the cat among the pigeons, eh?'

Bob nodded slowly, still apparently confused. 'She's
not quite what I expected,' he said.

'Who?'

'Your wife. Jane.'

'Oh? How d'you mean?'

'She's quite attractive really.'

'Course she's attractive,' Roger said, with a trace of irritation. 'I wouldn't marry a bleedin' dog, would I?'

'No, no, course not. It's just, well, from what you've said in the past, I just thought she wouldn't be much cop, you know. She's actually quite, well . . . *sophisticated*, I suppose.'

'Too bloody right she is. I tell you, Jane comes into her own at bashes like this. She can hold her end up with the knobs, can Jane. I tell you, I think that lot over there were quite impressed, which is no bad thing for the old networking.' And, smiling broadly, Roger raised his glass in a toast to Sir James's city cronies across the room.

Bob Guppy gave a heavy sigh.

Taking the empty glasses from Bob's hands, Roger placed them on the table beside them, signalling across the room for a waiter to bring them fresh drinks.

'What's up, Bob? You look like you swallowed a pound and pissed a penny.'

Bob Guppy eagerly accepted the glass of champagne Roger handed him, downing it in one go. As he handed it back empty there was a sort of hurt innocence in his eyes.

'It's Maxine,' he said. 'She's left me.'

'Left you?' Roger seemed to have difficulty with the concept.

Bob Guppy stared blankly ahead, nodding moronically.

'When?'

'Yesterday. I didn't think she was serious.'

'Fucking hell. You need a drink. Hang on mate!' He

signalled to the waiter, who immediately brought two fresh glasses.

'Here. Drink this,' he said, handing one across. 'Fucking bitch! So what happened?'

Bob Guppy slowly shook his head as though he couldn't quite believe it himself. 'I went home after work to pick her up for the party. You know, thinking it would have all blown over.' Bob glanced up at Roger like some pathetic spaniel. 'And she was gone.'

'What d'you mean, *gone*?'

Bob Guppy shrugged. 'Gone. Left. Taken all her gear and buggered off out of it.'

'Take no notice, mate. She'll be at her mother's. That's where they all hole up. Give it a couple of days . . .'

'Not this time,' Guppy said, staring vacantly across the room. He sniffed loudly and wiped his hand across his nose. 'She left a note. She's only gone and left me for another bloke!'

'No!'

Bob Guppy nodded and Roger grabbed two more glasses of champagne from a passing waiter, pushing one into his friend's hand.

'What a bitch! Who is he?'

Bob threw his head back and drained the glass. 'Some bloke she works with.' He gave a small sardonic laugh. 'I should've guessed. All those nights working late.'

'Fucking cow!' Roger sympathised, grabbing his friend round the shoulders and swaying, off balance, knocking into the table so that a row of empty glasses fell noisily to the floor.

Whilst he nodded in agreement, Bob Guppy felt a

momentary amazement at Roger Appleyard's hypocritical condemnation of his wife.

'Mind you,' Bob began, with a surprising degree of reasoning, 'I probably wouldn't be feeling so bad if I'd managed to get in first.'

'What, if you'd managed to shag that frigid little bitch in your office, you mean?'

Bob Guppy nodded. 'But then I s'pose that would've made me as bad as her.'

'No!' Roger responded emphatically. 'No, that's where you're totally wrong, old mate. You see, men are not *meant* to be monogamous. It's just the way we're made. It's impossible. Whereas women are, you see. They want to be with one man all their life.'

'But Maxine obviously didn't.'

Ignoring him, Roger continued expounding his theory. 'It's their job to be at home looking after the kids and the house, just like their mums did. That's where they're happy. Forget all this feminism shit. *That's* what they really want.'

Even in his inebriated state, Bob Guppy detected a flaw in Roger's reasoning. 'If that's the case,' he began tentatively, 'then who are we supposed to shag? I mean, if women are gonna be at home cooking and cleaning, where are the birds to have a good time with?'

'Well, of course, you've gotta have your bit of fluff, an' all, haven't you?'

Had Roger Appleyard's eyes been focused in the other direction, he might at that moment have thought twice about voicing his concluding argument. Approaching at speed, her stilettoes clicking on the wooden floor, like a

First World War destroyer powering its way across the waves, came Roger's own bit of fluff!

Relieved that Louise had wanted to confront Roger alone, Chastity hovered self-consciously in the ballroom doorway. If she was aware of her effect on the male population of that room, it was not apparent, nor did she appear conscious of the irrational antipathy of the majority of the female contingent, who viewed this fresh young newcomer as a challenge to their very femininity.

Her silk dress clung relentlessly to every curve, the thin fabric leaving little to the imagination as it moulded around her breasts and over the gentle rise of her buttocks. She stood there, a vision to behold, and, had she had FUCK ME emblazoned across her chest in burning letters, she could not have felt more embarrassed. Stretching up onto her toes, Chastity strained to follow Louise's progress as she wound her way through the press of bodies.

They saw each other simultaneously. Even at a distance Chastity could see Charles's eyes widen and almost hear his breath catch in his throat at the sight of her. Her heart began to thump in her chest so that she felt sure it must be visible through the painfully thin material of her dress.

But 'Knock him dead,' Louise had told her, and so, as Charles pushed through the crowd to reach her, Chastity allowed herself to give a brief smile of encouragement.

Fate also held its breath, yet, even before Charles could reach her, a pained cry rose up from the far side of the room, followed by a hysterical screeching. As Charles hesitated, then turned towards the noise, Lady Grant's voice could be heard from somewhere in the crowd as it closed in on the area of commotion.

'Charles! *Charles!* Do something, for God's sake!'

Roger Appleyard lay on the floor, curled up like a hedgehog, fending off Louise's relentless blows. She knelt beside him, her fists pounding his body, a different line of abuse accompanying each fresh attack.

'You lying, gutless swine!' she yelled. *Punch.*

'You two-timing, no-good bastard!' she cried. *Wallop.*

'You're gonna wish your dick had dropped off!' she hissed. *Swipe.*

With his arms raised to protect his head and his knees brought up to provide some kind of defence of the obvious target area between his legs, Roger listened with a detached interest as Louise's hysterical outburst swept over him, thankful for the mildly anaesthetic effect of the alcohol. It was a bit like waiting for a heavy shower to end, and on a couple of occasions Roger stuck his neck out, attempting to make a dash for it, only to be caught in another downpour.

From amongst the almost silent crowd, the familiar hands of Patricia and Cynthia had attempted to lift Louise to her feet, to lead her away and save her any further embarrassment, but, each time, she had shrugged them off, oblivious to the thoughts of those surrounding her.

'Charles, we have to do something,' Patricia whispered to her Chairman, who had pushed his way to the front of the crowd. 'She's making a complete fool of herself.'

Charles looked on anxiously at the pitiful sight of Louise attempting to straddle Roger Appleyard, her dress riding up her voluptuous thighs as she spread them either side of his cowering torso. As she leaned over him, Louise's breasts threatened to tumble from her low-cut dress, the soft white flesh rippling mesmerically as she continued to pummel the body beneath her.

Feeling hopelessly ill-equipped to intervene, Charles simply shrugged his shoulders, his eyes drawn irresistibly to the strip of white flesh between Louise's stocking tops and the hem of her dress.

'I hate you, I hate you, I *hate* you!' Louise screamed, like a naughty child having a temper tantrum. *Thump.*

'Excuse me.'

All eyes turned to the woman whose calm but authoritative voice had pierced the barrier of silent onlookers.

Louise threw her head back, her eyes blazing with anger, like a wild animal interrupted as it enjoyed its prey. She wiped a hand across her sweating brow, pushing her thick dark mane of hair back, away from her face, so that she could see the woman properly. In that split second she recognised the newcomer as Jane Appleyard. She opened her mouth to speak, but the calm voice of Roger's wife stopped her in her tracks.

'You must be Louise,' Jane said, smiling sweetly at her. 'I've been wondering when we'd meet.'

Having instructed the waiters to keep the champagne flowing, with Patricia's help Charles ushered the reluctant trio onto the terrace where they could settle matters unheard and unobserved, much to the chagrin of several of the older guests who had quite enjoyed the spirited display by the 'young filly'.

'You'll have to do something about them, you know,

Charles,' Patricia said, looking out through the french windows at the unlikely threesome.

'I know, I know. But not tonight.'

Patricia turned to see him looking anxiously round the room, his head moving this way and that to see past the groups of people huddled in conversation. She smiled.

'So you've seen her then?'

Charles's head whipped round, a questioning look on his face.

'You might just catch her if you hurry. I saw her going downstairs.'

Charles was already several strides away by the time Patricia finished her sentence, apologising profusely as he pushed his way past people who had not yet finished discussing the earlier entertainment.

Rushing to the balustrade that ran along the broad stone landing, Charles leaned over, desperately searching for Chastity amongst the crowd gathered in the reception area below as guests continued to arrive and leave in equal numbers. She was nowhere to be seen. Taking the stairs two at a time, he swung round the carved mahogany handrail at the bottom and rushed along the corridor, heading for the library.

Three more rooms had been searched when Charles emerged once again into the reception area, panting, desperate now. His arm resting on the handrail, he stood for a moment, trying to collect his thoughts and be logical. But each time he closed his eyes he saw an image of Chastity and all reason, all possibility of rational thought, became impossible.

He was almost clinging to the wooden post for support when out of the corner of his eye he glimpsed a flash of scarlet and, looking up, saw Chastity heading towards the front door. He tried to call her name but the word would not form on his lips. Rushing across, he caught hold of her by the shoulder, more roughly than he'd intended, so that when she turned she had a hurt look in her eyes.

'Where are you going?' Charles demanded.

Chastity's brow furrowed. She wasn't sure what was happening.

'You *can't* go!' he insisted, rather too forcefully. 'It's early yet.'

'I have to,' Chastity said, a quiet resignation in her voice. 'I have to get Louise home.'

'No. No, you don't,' he said desperately. 'She's with Roger . . .'

'Yeah, I know!'

'No, what I mean is, she's with both of them, sorting things out.'

'Yes, but we both know that Louise will come out of this the loser. She has no chance.'

'But I *need* you to stay,' he said, the words blurted out so that only afterwards did his features register surprise at what he'd said.

'*Do* you?' she said quietly.

Charles silently nodded, unable to take his eyes from her face, fearful yet excited by this long-overdue declaration.

As they faced one another, each body all but trembling at the thought of the other's touch, neither was aware of the arrival of the Lady Davina until her voice assaulted their consciousness, the sound of it shrill and offensive even to Charles's over-accustomed ears.

'Charles! Charlie, I'm back!' she squealed, taking hold

of his upper arm and pulling him towards her so that she could plant a kiss on both cheeks.

'Davina!'

'Oh, Charles, we've got *so* much to talk about!'

'Have we?'

'Yes! I've got some wonderful news.'

'Have you, Dee? Jolly good.' Charles forced a smile for Davina and risked a quick glance towards Chastity, who had begun to edge away. 'Go and get yourself some champers, old thing. Perhaps we'll have a chat later. Then you can tell me all your news.' Charles gave her a friendly pat on the back and took a tentative step in Chastity's direction.

Davina appeared to see Chastity for the first time, acknowledging her presence with a disdainful sneer.

'It can't wait, Charles. And anyway, I would've thought you'd be only too pleased to see your fiancée!' Davina glanced at Chastity, delighted to see the shocked look on the young girl's face.

'My *fiancée*?' In spite of the words being directed at Davina, Charles looked helplessly at Chastity, immediately aware of the change in her body language, the distance that had grown between them, even though she stood no more than an arm's length away.

'Yes, Charles, your fiancée. That's what I want to talk to you about.'

Charles's heart lurched as he witnessed the pain on Chastity's face, the reproach in her eyes.

'I don't know what you're talking about, Davina. We're *not* engaged.'

'Look, Charles, the plain fact is that I'm not pregnant. It was a false alarm, thank God. So you see,

Charlie, nothing's *changed* between us. We can still get married.'

'Oh, my God!' Charles wailed, looking at her in horror. 'No! We can't!'

Davina's beaming smile turned to a threatening glower. '*Can't*? What d'you mean, *can't*? You're my bloody fiancé, aren't you? And we're damn well getting married!'

Charles looked round anxiously at Chastity but she had already turned away, making her way towards the front door. Hastening after her, Charles grabbed hold of her arm, then gently pulled her to him so that her face came to rest before his own.

'We can't,' he said slowly, speaking to Davina even as he gazed into Chastity's downcast face, 'because . . . well, because I don't love you. I'm in love with someone else.'

Through tear-filled eyes, Chastity looked up, unable to believe her ears, her eyes pleading for confirmation; wanting Charles to say it once again so that there could be absolutely no misunderstanding. Giving her a brief, uncertain smile, Charles took a deep breath before, half turning to look back at his long-time companion, he spoke again.

'I'm sorry, old thing, but the fact of the matter is, I'm in love with Chastity.'

Davina blanched. 'You're *what*? Are you *mad*, Charles?'

But Charles was no longer listening. In fact, neither Charles nor Chastity was paying the least attention to the demented woman as she screamed and stamped her feet, nor were they aware of the abuse she hurled at them as a smiling Mrs Webb led her away, arms thrashing, into the garden.

No, for they stood motionless, spellbound, their hearts pounding, their eyes, their ears, every fibre of their aching bodies aware only of each other. As shriek after shriek went up into the heavens, the young lovers clung together, a thousand questions on their lips.

The empty champagne bottle clunked noisily down the stone garden steps before finally splashing into the ornamental fish pond, sending Sir James's collection of koi carp flickering off in all directions. Bob Guppy gave a loud, triumphant burp from his position on the top step and, placing a fresh bottle of champagne between his knees, loosened the wire casing over its neck and pushed out the cork, sending it flying off into the darkness.

In exchange for a crisp ten-pound note, the wine waiter had been persuaded to furnish him with two bottles of bubbly to aid Bob Guppy's attempt to wallow, if not drown, in solitary self-pity. A fiver's worth later, he felt well on the way and mumbled incoherently to himself about the treachery of women.

His senses now completely dulled to the delicate sounds of nature coming from the surrounding trees and bushes, he was only vaguely aware of the more intrusively vulgar noise of a near-hysterical Louise, a determined Jane Appleyard and a seriously lumbered Roger, issuing from the nearby terrace.

'What d'you mean, you've known about us for ages?' Louise shrieked.

'Oh, don't flatter yourself that you're the first, my dear,' Jane Appleyard replied patronisingly. 'In fact, if I drew up a list of Roger's little indiscretions you probably wouldn't even make it into the top ten.'

Bob Guppy winced.

'Jane . . .' came Roger's voice, pathetically feeble.

'Shut up, Roger!' his wife commanded. 'You see, Louise, I *know* my husband. I understand his little — what shall we call it? — his little *weakness*.'

'*Weakness*?' Louise fought to keep control, her voice quivering with emotion.

'*Mmm*. 'Fraid so. You see, Roger's like most men his age. Suddenly afraid of responsibility. Thinks he's missed out. Scared of getting older. Worried about dying. Girls like you help him take his mind off all that.'

'It's not like that! *Tell* her! It's *not*, is it Rog?' Louise wailed.

There was a moment's silence and then a piercing scream filled the cool night air.

Bob Guppy sat shaking his head, still amazed by his own wife's little *weakness*. If she had told him she'd taken up nude bungee jumping he wouldn't have been more surprised than he was by the revelation of her affair. In all the years they had been married he had never thought of her as a passionate woman.

He wondered vaguely about the feasibility of turning a blind eye, wondering whether he was capable of turning the other cheek, like Roger's wife. But the answer came quickly and unequivocally. Paradoxically, he couldn't pretend it wasn't happening because, when it came down to it, he didn't care enough. He just didn't love his wife enough to fight for her. That sudden realisation was like a bolt from the blue, filling him with a peculiar sense of inner peace.

The hollow mouth of the champagne bottle had

barely kissed Bob Guppy's pouting lips when he felt a blow to the back of his head, sending his teeth chinking against the thick green glass, and himself into a cowering foetal position, his hands covering his bollocks.

'You, bastard!' Davina screamed, her fists pummelling his arched back. 'It's all your fault! It's *all* your fault!'

The voice was unmistakable and the onslaught, too, was frighteningly reminiscent of the attack at the airport. Feeling hopelessly inadequate to defend himself, he was grateful for the distancing effects of the alcohol as he curled his body into an even tighter ball.

An impressive blow to his upper arm jerked the champagne from his grasp and, in his desperation to save it, Guppy blindly grabbed at it the very moment the bottle shattered against the stone step. A slither of glass spiked through his finger sending blood spouting from both holes so that when he held it up he sat mesmerised by the symmetry of its emissions.

'Oh my God!' Davina shrieked. 'Blood! Oh my God!' And with that she promptly took hold of Bob Guppy's finger, pulled out the shard of glass, and shoved the bloody flesh into her mouth. Guppy's eyes rolled as Davina's tongue played over his fingertip, its warm moistness slowly drawing off his defences until, with some pride, he felt his penis stir inside his trousers.

Emboldened, he slowly pulled his finger out a fraction, through the rouged chasm of Davina's lips, and then, with equal slowness, pushed it in again, the moist pad of her tongue quick to embrace it. Again, he teased it away until he could feel the hard angles of her teeth with his fingernail, running the soft flesh of his fingertip across her bottom lip before easing the finger back into her eager hole.

Davina groaned, the sound coming from deep within, causing Bob Guppy's stiff willy to jerk against his fly, like a prisoner tapping at a window, begging to be let out. Within seconds his prayer was answered as Davina's hands reached down and with surprising deftness undid the zip of Bob's trousers, pulling his straining member through the gap in his Y-fronts.

With equal desperation Bob Guppy reached up and unceremoniously pulled apart the bodice to Davina's evening dress, so that she gasped with anticipation as her voluptuous breasts spilled out, her nipples hard as unripe grapes, standing proudly erect, caressed by both the cool breeze and Bob Guppy's eager fingers.

At the sound of approaching footsteps the panting bodies tumbled sideways into the pitch-black shrubbery, the only evidence of their presence a pair of white monogrammed panties hanging from the tangled hedge.

It was late now. Most of the guests had gone home. Servants moved about the now empty rooms, clearing up, but Patricia had one last thing to do before she too made her way home. She had to explain to Sir James about the incident earlier on with Charles. Had to warn him that his son knew now about that night in Amsterdam.

Coming into the billiard room, she hovered on the fringe of the group surrounding Sir James. The old man stood beside the brightly lit green-baize table, listening with a barely concealed amusement as Tom – his blond locks flowing incongruously down over the shoulders

of his smart dinner jacket – sounded off in his broad
Texan drawl.

'Gee, you guys have just got so much *history*. I mean,
this house, it's so *old*. And the paintings and everything,
man, I tell you, it just blows me away.' And Tom's
perfect white smile spread from ear to ear as he gazed
around the walls of the room, slowly shaking his head
in wonderment.

'Mmm. I just love it here in England. It's so *quaint*,'
Jerry added with a pout and a wiggle.

'Quaint?' Sir James gawped unashamedly at the young
woman's breasts as they rose and fell before his eyes. 'Yes,
I can see how you might think so. I'm afraid we probably
seem a bit stuffy to you young Americans.'

'No, not at all,' Jerry went on, oblivious to his
attentions, wrinkling her nose as though she were talking
about a cute little puppy. 'The way you take tea. Those
little sandwiches. I just *love* it. It's so, so . . . *civilised*.'
And she wrinkled her nose as though cooing over a tiny
baby in a pram.

Sir James smiled indulgently.

'And English men are just *so* reserved,' Jerry added.

'A national trait, I'm afraid,' Cynthia said, smiling,
her hand, Patricia noted, planted firmly on Bubbles' right
buttock.

'No, I love it!' Jerry squealed. 'It's real sexy. All those
inhibitions boiling beneath the surface. Wow!'

Mesmerised, Sir James watched her thick red lips
pout as she pushed out each word, her body wriggling involuntarily within her dress as she listed every
notable Englishman she knew from Prince Charles to
Jeremy Irons.

Patricia knew every intonation of Sir James's voice; was able to understand the hidden meaning of each inflection, every nuance; was able to read the signal behind every look. She felt that now was an appropriate time to intervene.

'Tom and Jerry come from California, Sir James. They're in the film business,' she said enthusiastically, smiling encouragingly up into Tom's tanned and chiselled features.

Although he had not acknowledged her before that moment, Sir James did not seem surprised to hear Patricia's voice and to see her appear at his side.

'Really? How interesting.' Looking past Tom, he signalled to the waiter for more drinks.

'Tell me Mr, er . . .'

'Please, call me Tom.'

'Tell me, er, Tom. What have you been in?'

'Sir James is a bit of a film buff, actually, Tom,' Patricia said, eager to build up her ex-boss.

'Really? Great!' Tom said, impressed.

'Did you see *Deep Penetration*?' Jerry's voice seemed suddenly huskier.

Sir James looked up, startled, then shook his head. 'I . . . er, I'm afraid I didn't see that particular title.'

'We're real proud of that one,' Jerry said, her face utterly serious. 'I think it was some of our best work.'

Tom nodded in agreement. He too had a look of professional earnestness on his face now.

'Maybe you've seen *Sex Slaves Down Under*?' Jerry enquired eagerly. 'It had a big distribution over here. Tom played the lead.'

The old man gulped audibly. 'No, I—'

'Shame,' Jerry purred. 'I think you'd love it!'

There was a moment's awkward silence before Jerry sighed deeply. 'It sure is beautiful here,' she said and, as she tilted back her head to look at the ornately carved ceiling, Sir James was struck by the long smooth line of her neck as it plunged into the deep crevice of her cleavage.

'Perhaps you ladies would like to see round the house?' he offered. 'The upper bedrooms, er, I mean, bathrooms are *most* impressive.'

'Really?' Jerry squeaked, stepping on Patricia's toes as she grabbed hold of the old man's arm.

'Fantastic!' Bubbles said, separating herself from Cynthia and linking her slender hand through the other side.

'Good show,' Sir James croaked, his body responding with unaccustomed eagerness to the fulsome breasts pressing against his arms, an impressive erection showing beneath the baggy folds of his trousers.

Patricia, noticing it, curled her injured toes within the narrow confines of her new patent shoes, her fixed smile bravely disguising both her physical and emotional pain.

'Sir James,' she murmured, attempting unsuccessfully to catch his eye. 'I wonder if I might have a brief word?'

'Not now, Pat,' he replied as the improbable threesome walked off arm in arm. 'For God's sake, not now.'

As Cynthia turned from the hire car, she noticed the small, shadowy figure hovering outside the main entrance to her apartment block.

Not now, she thought, wondering if it was one of her regular businessmen. After all that had happened at the party, she just wanted to lie back in a hot bath with a glass of chilled white wine and relax.

As she approached the glass doors, the figure stepped out.

'Cee-fee-a?'

'Nobushi!' Cynthia stared, astonished. 'I thought you were back in Japan.'

'I was,' Fukuada said, bowing and grinning at the same time. 'Now I back. Good see you, Cee-fee-a.'

'And you,' she said, pleased to see him despite all. 'You want to come up? I'm a bit tired, but you're welcome to stay.'

Fukuada shook his head. 'I no come stay. Need meet you. In moh-nin'.'

'Tomorrow? Here?'

'No. At office. Need talk. Bout very 'poh-tant matter.'

Cynthia frowned. She had never seen Fukuada quite this serious before. 'You want to come in to see us at Virt-E-Go, is that what you mean?'

'You arrange it, Cee-fee-a. But make sure onry people you trust. Trust abso"rutery. Nobushi have 'poh-tant news.'

'Can't you tell me now, Nobushi?'

Fukuada looked about him, as if he were being followed, then shook his head. 'Must go now. I see you in moh-nin', Cee-fee-a. Ten o'clock. You arrange.'

'Sure, I . . .'

But Fukuada was gone, slipping away into the bushes like some mad ninja. Cynthia stared after him, slowly shaking her head. Weird, very weird. Then, taking her pass key from her bag, she slipped it into the lock and went inside.

What a day! she thought, then giggled, remembering how she had left the delicious Bubbles and Jerry cavorting in the jacuzzi in the presence of a quite obviously delighted Sir James. What a day!

'Cynthia, are you *sure* Mr Fukuada is coming?'

Cynthia looked across the length of the boardroom to where Charles stood, and nodded. 'If he said he'll be here he'll be here.'

But she felt less confident than she sounded. Nobushi had said he'd be here at ten, and it was now almost a quarter to eleven. He had never, in her knowledge, been more than a minute late in his life.

'Well, have you any idea what he wants?' Patricia asked, from where she sat with Bill, Ben and Chastity around the big oak table.

'None at all,' Cynthia answered, staring down the corridor toward the lift. 'But he was insistent that we have a meeting. He said it was very important.'

At that moment the bell pinged and the lift doors hissed open.

'Mr Fukuada,' she said, hurrying towards him and bowing, 'I'm so glad you've come.'

'Most sorry,' he said, returning her bow, then stepping past her to greet the rest of Virt-E-Go's senior management. 'Have to wait for fax. Wait and wait but no come. When finary come, Fukuada late.'

'It's okay, Mr Fukuada,' Charles said, crossing the room and taking his hand. 'It's awfully good to see you again. To what do we owe this pleasure?'

In answer Fukuada raised the briefcase he was carrying in his left hand and offered it to Charles. 'Aw there. In case. Erry-fing. Once you read, you unner-stan'.'

Charles took the case and, flipping open the catch, took out the file. He stared at the cover a moment, then opened it, reading a few paragraphs before he looked up at Fukuada again, startled. 'But this is—'

'Erry-fing 'bout Ubik. At reast . . . erry-fing they no want you know.' Fukuada looked about him deter-minedly. 'You been screwed, Mr Grant. Ubik try gobble up Virt-E-Go. But Fukuada no let them. Fukuada have plan. You listen now . . .'

~ December ~

It was late evening now, and, while Bill and Ben worked on inside the Virt-E-Go stand, making their final adjustments to the machine, Charles and Patricia sat outside, at the desk, sorting out the last few administrative details.

The great exhibition hall was quiet now after all the hammering and sawing that had gone on all day, and there were few people about. The lights had been turned down and there was a sense of the lull before the storm. Tomorrow, at ten, the doors would be opened to the public, when the hall would seethe with people anxious to experience the cutting edge of technology. Right now, however, it was peaceful.

'Well,' Charles said with an air of finality, sitting back and stretching out his arms behind him, 'I think that's it, Pat. The actors know where to come, I take it?'

'Cynthia has briefed them fully,' Patricia said, jotting a note in her Filofax, then closing it up and smiling at her young Chairman. 'They'll be here, don't worry, Charles.'

'So this is it,' he said, giving a brave smile. 'Make-or-break time.'

Patricia nodded. For the last ten weeks everyone in their team-within-a-team had worked like a demon, pretending to go home after their normal day's work had finished, only to sneak back secretly an hour later to work on into the small hours. They were all tired, but also they were all very proud of what they had achieved with Fukuada's help. But now, as Charles rightly said, it was make or break, put up or shut up.

'Where's your friend?' Charles asked, looking about him suddenly. 'I thought he was supposed to be here by now.'

'I said nine,' Patricia said, pulling back the sleeve of her blouse to look at her new gold watch. 'It's not ten to yet.'

As if on cue, at that very moment, Holly appeared around the corner of the end stand on their row, smiling at Patricia as he walked on, his two young assistants just behind him. It was four weeks now since he had resigned from the force, but Holly Security was going from strength to strength, thanks mainly to Patricia's organisational abilities.

'Hello, my love,' Holly said, leaning across the desk to peck her on the cheek. 'Hello, Mr Grant.'

'Hello, Richard,' Charles said, smiling amiably. 'Pat's told you what's what, I take it.'

Holly turned slightly, smiling down at Patricia and winking at her. 'Oh, she's briefed me fully, Mr Grant. We'll make sure no one goes near the machine until tomorrow morning.'

'Good,' Charles said, 'then let's call it a day, shall we, Pat? You fancy a nightcap before retiring?'

Patricia looked to Holly, who smiled and nodded, then

looked back at Charles. 'That'd be lovely. But only one. I need my beauty sleep if I'm to be bright and perky in the morning.'

'The one it is, then.' Charles turned and, stepping across, called in to the twins. 'William, Benjamin, we'll be in the Kipling Bar if you fancy a quick drink.'

'Cool!' they called back as one.

Charles turned to Patricia, offering her his arm. 'Patricia?'

They walked on down the row of stands until, coming to the end, they stopped. There, facing them at the end of the next row, was the Electronics USA stand. Or so the board on the black-painted wooden wall read. The truth was that no one had ever heard of Electronics USA, and this stand – more than any other in the exhibition hall – had been shrouded with mystery all day. Unmarked crates had been carried into the stand throughout the day. Now three muscular security guards, dressed like California motorcycle cops, complete with dark glasses, patrolled the stand, their chief glaring at Charles as he stopped to look.

Charles smiled back at the man, then, giving Patricia's arm a tiny squeeze, walked on.

Listening to the murmur of conversation amongst her colleagues, Chastity absent-mindedly tapped her fingers over the gentle swell of her breasts. Glancing along the bar she caught sight of Charles smiling at her and felt a blush rise up her neck. He winked conspiratorially and Chastity quickly dropped her hand into her lap.

Charles had insisted on buying her a ring in spite of their joint decision to postpone the announcement of their engagement until after the fair. The delicate diamond and emerald cluster had looked so perfect on her slender finger that she had been most reluctant to take it off, even though she knew it would be for only a short while. Romantically, on bended knee, Charles had asked her to marry him and since then, each night as she she'd lain alone in bed, she had taken it from the chain around her neck and placed it where it belonged, on the third finger of her left hand.

Dangling between her breasts, it was a constant reminder of Charles's intentions, its presence making her glow so that she felt sure it must be obvious to everyone that they were two people very much in love.

'Well,' Cynthia said, swallowing the remains of her whisky, 'I don't know about you guys but I'm bushed.' She tipped off the edge of her barstool, the generous folds of her skirt falling around her ankles. She reached down to the floor for her bag, swung it onto her shoulder and dipped into the outside pocket for the key to her hotel room.

'Hang on, Cyn,' William said and nudged his brother, who immediately picked up his bottle of Bud and drained its contents in one gulp, the fizzy liquid swelling his cheeks before sliding slowly down his throat.

'Yeah, we'd better turn in,' Benjamin agreed, pushing his empty bottle across the bar. 'Early start tomorrow.'

Sitting close by, Patricia smiled as she saw Dick Holly stop for a moment directly outside the huge glass doors of the bar, his eyes meeting hers, his lips curling into the briefest smile before he walked slowly away across the marble lobby towards the lift.

'Um, I think I'll be turning in, too,' Patricia said,

quickly slipping from her stool. Hurriedly retrieving her bag from the floor and adjusting the line of her skirt, she was halfway across the room before Charles and Chastity had a chance to bid goodnight, which she answered with a brief wave over her shoulder.

Charles's body slumped a little as he sighed with relief that they were finally alone. Below the counter he reached across into Chastity's lap and took hold of her hand, bringing it across to rest on his thigh beneath his own warm palm.

'At last!' he said, smiling at her.

Chastity looked up at him through thick, dark lashes, causing his heart to lurch in his chest. 'Do you think they know?'

Charles shrugged, a deep sigh blowing out through his nostrils as he contemplated the beautiful creature before him.

'It won't be long before everyone knows,' he said, lifting her hand to his lips and kissing her fingers lightly.

'I shall probably miss it. It's quite exciting really. You know, having a secret.'

'Talking of secrets,' Charles grinned, nodding towards Chastity's covered chest.

'It's still here,' she said, patting the ring through her shirt material.

Charles's smile stayed fixed as he imagined for one brief moment being in that same enviable position, nestling between the soft mounds of Chastity's breasts. A faint whimper echoed behind his tightly closed lips and inadvertently his fingers closed so that he held her hand within his clenched fist.

'I'm ready to go up,' she said, wriggling her hand from his grasp.

'Oh . . . erm . . . all right. I'll see you to your room.'

Chastity's room was at the far end of the corridor. As the two of them walked along the air was heavy and tense with the silence that hung between them. As she reached her door, Chastity turned the key in the lock before leaning back against the heavy wooden frame, one hand dropping down behind her back, encircling the large brass doorknob.

Charles found it difficult to meet her eyes, not wanting her to see what lay behind his own; not wanting her to think ill of him for wanting her so much. Every moment he spent with her like this was pure agony, her physical proximity tormenting him so much that he almost dreaded her touch. Dreading it but unable to imagine life without it.

'Well,' she whispered, 'I s'pose it's goodnight, then.'

Charles's smile was almost a grimace as he fought for control of his body. Leaning forward from the chest up, careful to maintain some distance between them, he kissed her gently on the cheek.

Chastity reached up and, pushing her fingers through his hair, turned his face so that they gazed into one another's eyes. Their noses almost touched and their lips were only a breath away. She held him there a moment, then slowly guided his mouth to hers, its warmth, its moistness filling her so that her body tingled. Slowly she ran her hand down his back, gently pulling him towards her so that she could feel finally the hardness of his desire pressing into her.

With a brief twist of the wrist, Chastity turned the door handle. At the sound of it Charles pulled away from their embrace but she held his hand in hers, her thumb stroking his.

'Would you like to come in?' she whispered.

'Chastity, of course I—'

He was not allowed to finish. Chastity placed a finger over his lips, his eyes closing at her touch. Then, pushing the door open behind her, she slowly drew him into the darkened room.

Roger Appleyard woke and stretched — or tried to, his hands thumping against the arm of the sofa. He groaned. His whole body ached and his neck felt as stiff as a board.

And that was not the only thing that was stiff. In the night he had had those awful, taunting dreams again: dreams in which he was giving Louise one over the Chairman's desk in the Virt-E-Go offices, that wonderful arse of hers lifted in the air to receive each quivering stroke of his; dreams from which he woke, pained and frustrated, having to rush to the bathroom for the relief of a quick jerk.

Oh, shit, he thought, reaching down to hold himself, I'm becoming a sad old wanker.

Scrambling up, he stumbled across the living-room carpet, heading for the bathroom, his right hand fumbling with his cock through the flies of his cotton pyjamas.

Trying the door handle, he found it closed, locked against him.

'Oh, no-ooh!' He rattled the lock. 'Jane? Is that you, Jane?'

And now he could hear the sound of the shower, of water pouring down over his wife's naked body. Roger leaned against the door and closed his eyes, his imagination going into hyperdrive. He could see her, standing there, the water running down over her breasts, soap suds gathering in the dark curls of her public hair. He groaned and gripped himself tighter, then called to her again.

'Jane? Jane . . . let me in, *please*!'

'Go away!' Jane Appleyard yelled back. The sound of falling water continued, added to now by the clear sound of someone soaping themselves loudly.

'Jane? Janie, sweetheart?'

'Don't sweetheart me, you dirty sod.'

'Jane? How long is this going to go on for, Jane?'

There was laughter – cruel, cold laughter. 'Until you've learned how to keep your fly zipped up.'

'But it's been ten weeks now,' he wheedled. 'Surely . . . ?'

But there was no surely about it. Jane Appleyard was as implacable as the Hindenburg Line and it would take more than a single footsoldier to shake her resolve. 'Go and sort yourself out in the downstairs loo!' she called back heartlessly. 'And don't make a mess. I've only just had it redecorated.'

Giving up Roger Appleyard had been like a dose of cold turkey. In her head Louise knew that the lying rat was no good for her and that he could only cause her hurt, but her heart made no such judgements, leaving her with a hopeless, unfulfilled desire that defied all rationale.

From the moment she had stepped into the cab, leaving Roger and Jane Appleyard standing side by side on the steps of Maltby House, she had known, deep down, that all was lost; that no matter how much she wanted it, there was no way Roger was ever going to leave his wife for her. That, at least, had been made perfectly clear that night.

But like thousands of women who had gone before, Louise would happily have forgiven him. He had only to come to her, to tell her he was sorry and that, of course, he loved her. She would have screamed and yelled, she probably would have hit him, but finally she would have listened to his promises as though she were hearing them for the first time and, ignoring the voice inside her head, would have welcomed his lies as eagerly as she welcomed him back into her bed.

But Roger had not come. All weekend she had waited in vain for a telephone call, rehearsing over and over again the conversation they would have so that in the end she almost convinced herself that it had happened. On Monday morning she was at her desk bright and early but had sat alone until the middle of the morning, when Patricia informed her that Roger was taking a couple of weeks' leave of absence. It was then the real tears had flowed; there in Patricia's arms that she had wept for the sheer waste of it all, drowning in the self-pity of a lover spurned, the other woman's arms bringing comfort as Louise purged herself of her pain.

The first week had been hell. Several times a day she would dial his number in the hope of hearing Roger's voice, slamming the phone down if his wife answered and listening in pathetic silence if it was him on the end of the line. He'd known it was her – he *must* have known – but not once had her name passed his lips. Not once had he given her the tiniest glint of hope.

By the middle of the second week of Roger's leave, Louise's docile acceptance of the situation had turned to vengeful anger and, imbued with renewed determination, she had offered Patricia her resignation, asking for it to take immediate effect. The two women had sat for a long time talking through the whole wretched scenario, a cathartic experience that nevertheless brought fresh floods of tears and inevitable pangs of regret. At her lowest point she had looked in danger of losing her resolve but Patricia had nursed her through it and had encouraged her to find a life of her own before it was too late.

Once she had made up her mind, it hadn't been hard for Louise to get Roger to take her call. She had simply asked the temp to tell him she wanted to discuss the special floppy disk he kept in his top left-hand drawer. Five minutes later he was on the phone and they were arranging a rendezvous.

The meeting had been brief and businesslike with Roger readily and dumbly agreeing to hand over five thousand pounds of his ill-gotten gains in exchange for the copy disk containing details of monies he had siphoned off from Virt-E-Go over the past ten years, together with a promise to put an end to it.

She folded the cheque in half, and placed it in her handbag. Looking across into Roger's ashen face – his jaw sagging, his hair looking thinner than she remembered – Louise's face broke into a gentle smile and as she shook Roger's hand the only thing she felt was the sweat passing from his clammy palm.

Eight weeks on and Louise felt like a new woman. The money had enabled her to make a fresh start, buying herself a partnership in a friend's florist's. The hours were long but she loved every minute of it, and at last she was doing something for *her*self.

It wouldn't be true to say that she never thought of Roger Appleyard, nor that she no longer ached for his touch in those lonely hours in the middle of the night. And sometimes as she travelled to work, her face pressed against the window on the top deck of the bus, she hoped that she might see him. But these were feelings that quickly passed, no longer consuming her to the exclusion of all else.

She had taken Patricia's advice. She had found a life of her own.

A damp towel was twisted into a turban around Louise's freshly washed hair as she sat at the kitchen table eating toast and marmalade and drinking tea. The newspaper was open before her and she idly flicked through, alighting upon the odd item of tabloid gossip; in the background pop music poured from the breakfast show on the radio.

The advertisement for the International Computer Show taking place at Olympia caused Louise a moment's pang of nostalgia as she imagined her ex-colleagues at Virt-E-Go excitedly preparing the Old Banger for its maiden voyage in the public arena. She gave a heavy sigh and slowly turned the page.

Glancing at her watch she quickly tugged the towel from her head and pushed her fingers through her damp hair. Then, taking one last gulp of tea, she grabbed her bag from the chair, folded the newspaper under her arm, and made for the door on her way to work.

She was late, but what the hell. She was her own boss now.

Chastity stood naked before the bathroom mirror, her wet hair lying over her shoulders in thick, dark locks. Droplets of water fell from the ends onto her back, slowly tracing their way over her tight buttocks, and as she leaned forward to examine her tired eyes more closely in the mirror, still more trickled down her neck and over her breasts. Standing back, Chastity closed her eyes a moment, her mouth slowly curving into a broad smile so that her young face was transformed into something suddenly more mature, more like the woman that she would one day become.

As she lifted her eyelids, Chastity gave a little jump on seeing Charles's reflection in the mirror. Standing against the doorframe, watching her, he was naked to the waist, below which he wore only his boxer shorts.

'Hi,' he said softly.

'Hi,' she replied, her back to him as she spoke to his reflection, suddenly self-conscious in her nudity. She reached across for a towel and made to wrap it round her but Charles had stepped forward and had taken hold of her hand.

'Don't. Please,' he said. 'You're so beautiful.'

Chastity smiled, her coyness melting away at the kindness in his voice, the gentleness of his touch. She dropped the towel to the floor, raising her eyes to watch him as he watched her through the mirror.

A shiver ran up her spine as she felt his hands

on her arms and the warmth of his mouth as he kissed her bare shoulder, his tongue licking at the water there.

'I'd love to have a painting of you,' he whispered into her ear, bringing his hands round to cup the delicate skin beneath her breasts.

'Above your desk at the office,' she giggled, bringing her hands up to cover his.

'No,' he said quickly, his voice suddenly serious. 'For me. Just for me. I don't want to share you with anyone else.'

Chastity kissed his cheek as he nuzzled into her neck. 'It seems a bit funny, standing here with no clothes on,' she said.

Charles nibbled at the soft flesh of her ear lobe, 'Ah yes, but like this we're all equal aren't we? Lord Adam and Lady Eve.'

Chastity gave him a playful dig with her elbow and he clutched his side, feigning injury.

'I love you, Chastity.'

'I love you, too,' she whispered, turning to face him, pressing her body to his and wrapping her arms about his neck. 'I just love you so much.'

In the adjoining bedroom the telephone began to ring. It rang and rang, but went unanswered.

Cynthia stood on the balcony of the stand, peeking in through the crack of the door, anxiously surveying the work.

'Are we ready?'

'Almost,' Bill answered, and there was a clunk as he hit something metallic.

'Nearly there,' Ben added, and there was a gurgle and a hiss as something hydraulic responded to his touch.

Cynthia turned, looking along the line of stands. All the others were ready, their sales reps standing alongside, neat as first-day schoolboys and girls, practising their sales patter and their welcoming smiles.

Only half an hour, Cynthia thought, at the same time wondering what in God's name Bill and Ben could still be tinkering at. Where are all the others?

'Coo-ee!'

She turned, to see Bubbles and her co-star, Matt, a real ape of a man, coming up the steps of the stand. They were both dressed respectably.

'Thank God,' she said. 'I was beginning to think I'd got the wrong day.'

'Poor Cynthia! You look so stressed, darling,' Bubbles said, and giggled. 'You could do with a massage.' And she winked.

'Inside,' Cynthia said, all stern and businesslike. 'Your costumes are hanging up at the back of the stand. And don't mind the twins. They've seen it all before.'

'Lucky them!' Bubbles said, and, giggling again, ushered Matt inside.

Cynthia turned back, scanning the long aisle between the stands. Where the hell were Charles and Patricia? They were supposed to be here half an hour back.

There was another clunk from inside the stall, a giggle, and then another hiss and gurgle.

'There!' Bill and Ben said as one. 'It's ready!'

Patricia and her new friend, Holly, were now in sight, strolling slowly between the stands. Cynthia waved to them and Patricia waved back.

Bill and Ben emerged from within, aproned and goggled, for all the world like two nineteenth-century inventors. Looking at them, no one would have guessed that they were in any way high-tech, except perhaps for their slightly nerdy look.

'He's ready,' Bill said.

'And she's willing,' Ben added, and the two grinned like mischievous schoolboys.

'Great!' Cynthia said. 'And the Old Banger?'

The 'Old Banger' was their nick-name for the VR lounger.

'All wired up and ready to run,' Bill said.

'You both know what to do?'

Two heads bobbed up and down.

'Good,' Cynthia said, taking a calming breath. 'Let's hope to God this works.'

Patricia climbed the steps, smiling. 'Everything ready?'

'Looks like it,' Cynthia answered.

'And our models?'

'They're inside, changing.'

'You've seen the other stand?'

'Electronics USA?'

Patricia nodded. 'Looks like they're waiting till the last minute.' She paused, then. 'You think Fukuada's right, then?'

'Don't you?'

Patricia shrugged. 'I suppose so.' Then, noting Charles's absence, she frowned. 'Where's our young Chairman? And where's—?'

She stopped, her mouth falling open, then turned, in time to see Chastity and Charles walking up the great aisle hand in hand, beaming smiles on both their faces.

As they approached the others they dropped their hands to their sides, but they were fooling no one.

Patricia opened her mouth to say something, then closed it again. It was none of her business. Then again . . .

'They make a nice couple, don't you think?' Cynthia said quietly, leaning close.

Patricia smiled. They did. You could see at a glance just how happy they were together. She gave a little sigh, then turned, all businesslike again.

'Okay. Where are our actors?'

Roger sat in the queue of traffic and honked his horn for the umpteenth time.

'Oh, shit!' he said, looking at the clock on the dashboard. 'Nine thirty-five and we're nowhere fucking near! If we keep on at this rate we're going to get there when the bloody thing shuts!'

'Keep your hair on, old man,' Bob Guppy said from the passenger seat. 'It isn't your fault that water main burst.'

'Yes, but if you hadn't kept me bloody waiting in the first place . . .'

Bob Guppy shrugged. Personally, he didn't give a shit whether they got there or not. As far as he was concerned, the whole sodding thing could fall into the sea and he wouldn't give a toss. Oh, he'd lose his job, but what did that matter now? All it would mean was that Maxine wouldn't be able to screw him for maintenance.

'You know what, Rog?'

'What?' Roger said irritably.

'These upper-class women . . . they're all cut glass on the surface, but down below . . .'

Roger groaned. 'Oh, fuck off Bob! Tell someone else your sordid tales, will you?'

Bob Guppy turned, looking at his colleague. All these years he'd envied Roger Appleyard – envied his easy way with women, the way he could charm the drawers off them – but now the boot was on the other foot and Roger couldn't stand it.

'When was the last time you had it, Rog? A week? Two weeks? Ten?'

Roger's hands clenched on the steering wheel and his face muscles tightened. 'Leave it, Bob. All right?'

'Last time I had it was . . . oh, two hours ago. Doggie fashion. She was hanging on to the brass bedstead and I was going at her like a train.'

Roger closed his eyes and groaned.

'God she makes a bloody racket, though, Rog? Grunts like a bleedin' stuck pig.'

Bob made a tiny, squealing noise.

Roger swallowed, then, banging his hand against the steering wheel, honked the horn again.

'It's strange. Thinking about it, I don't s'pose Maxine ever came. Never ever. Nearly thirty years we spent together, on and off, and she never once made a noise in bed. Never once. But Davina . . .'

'Oh, *Christ*! Will you shut up, Bob! Can't you just put a fucking sock in it!'

Bob raised an eyebrow. 'Still sore about Louise, eh?'

'Right . . . *out*! Get out of the fucking car!'

'But Rog, I was only—'

'Taking the piss. Now out!' And, leaning across Bob Guppy, Roger threw open the passenger door.

Unfortunately, at that very moment, a motorcycle

messenger was weaving his way between the cars. As the door flew open, he tried to break, but it was too late . . .

'Well?' Sir James asked, placing his hand on Charles's shoulder, almost making the young man jump with surprise. 'Is this ours?'

'Um . . . no, sir,' Charles said, glancing at his father, then looking back at the Electronics USA stand, which – even at this late hour – was still boarded up, 'this is—'

'Mine,' Kirsty McDonald said, stepping out from behind one of the hoardings that were being nailed up in front of the stand.

'And who are you?' Sir James said, puffing out his chest, sensing that some kind of challenge was implied by her words.

'I'm Kirsty McDonald.'

'Ah . . .' Sir James said, narrowing his eyes. 'Our erstwhile partner.'

'*Partner*, Sir James?' she said, an ironic glint in her eyes. 'Do you know something I don't know?'

Sir James turned, looking to his son, puzzled. 'But I thought you said—'

'The contract's still not signed,' Charles said quietly.

'*Still*?' Sir James stared at his son a moment longer, then turned back to face the American woman. 'So this is your company's stand, is it? And what precisely are you making?'

Kirsty's smile never faltered. 'Sex machines,' she said. 'The best damn sex machines in the world!'

Again Sir James looked to Charles. 'You knew about this?'

Charles was silent.

'You wanna take a peek?' she said, looking at Charles, a mocking amusement in her eyes.

'If you want.'

Kirsty turned, signalling to her chief of security, who immediately set about organising for the boards to come down. Within minutes the stand was revealed in its full glory. At the back, on a huge cloth banner, was Ubik's name and logo, and just beneath it, on a raised dais, were two VR loungers, exactly like those Virt-E-Go had been using, with full-body suits – again, precisely like those Virt-E-Go had developed – seated like dummies in them. Between the two, attached by a maze of wires, was a huge computer, placed on top of a great stack of Cray rendering machines.

'*Voilà*!' Kirsty said triumphantly, turning to smirk at Charles and his father.

It was at that moment that Roger Appleyard appeared, out of breath and sporting a real beauty of a shiner. After one look, he turned to Charles, astonished.

'But that's *our* machine!'

'Wrong,' Kirsty McDonald said, a sudden hardness in her face. A white-suited man was at her side now, staring at them coolly through dark glasses. 'The machine is the property of Electronics USA, of which Ubik are a subsidiary.'

'But, but . . .' Roger began.

'But nothing, Mr Appleyard,' Kirsty said. 'This proto-type is provisionally patented, and Ubik own the patent . . . *worldwide*.'

'Charles?' Sir James, now bewildered, looked to his son for some kind of explanation.

But Charles simply shrugged. 'It seems you win, Ms McDonald. As you rightly point out, we have no contract with Ubik, and you have the provisional patent for this Prototype, so . . .'

'Charles?' Sir James queried, astonished that his son should give in so easily. Then, turning on Kirsty, he thrust out an arm at her, wagging his finger threateningly. 'You're a thief, madam! No better than a common-or-garden thief! And I'm going to make sure my lawyers sue your tinpot little company until it bleeds, you hear me, woman!'

But Kirsty simply smiled. 'You can try, but personally I don't think you've got a leg to stand on – legally.'

'She's right, Father,' Charles said, as Cynthia, Chastity and Patricia came up in a group. 'We'd lose a court case hands down. No, we've been outplayed. I feel the only course is to concede defeat gracefully and retire to the pavilion.'

'Charles?' Sir James said, 'have you completely lost your senses? This is business, dammit, not some bloody cricket match!'

'Oh come now, Sir James,' Kirsty said, grinning. 'I rather admire your boy's stoicism. It's a good English trait, don't you think, knowing when you're beaten?'

Sir James looked close to apoplexy, but, before he could say another word, Charles laid a hand on his arm.

'Stoicism?' Charles said quietly. 'No, not stoicism, Ms McDonald, *realism*. You see, we Brits – as you Yanks love to call us – may look quaint and our ways might seem quaint, but there's a doggedness to us – yes, and an innate intelligence, too – that has taught us just when and where to fight.' He smiled. 'Oh, I concede you won the first battle, Ms McDonald, but wars are not won with a single battle.'

Charles paused, looking about him at his little team. Cynthia, Chastity and Patricia were all smiling broadly now. 'Come,' he said, gesturing to Kirsty to follow him. '*You* might wanna take a peek at *this*.'

'Well?' Kirsty McDonald said. 'What's new?'

In front of her, dominating the stand, was the Old Banger, trails of wire leading from it to the huge modem at the centre. It was identical, in almost every respect, to the machine on Ubik's stand.

'You were very clever,' Charles said quietly. 'I never suspected a thing. But our friend Fukuada did.'

'Fukuada?'

The tiny Japanese man appeared from behind the screen that separated off the back of the stand and bowed. Then, stepping aside, he beckoned to someone out of sight.

Kirsty was staring at Fukuada, trying to place him, realisation coming slowly to her face. Yet even as she recognised just who he was and where she had seen him before – and not just at Cynthia's – Bubbles and Matt stepped out from behind the screen.

Kirsty McDonald gasped.

'Stunning, eh?' Charles said.

The glossy blue-black VR suits the two models were wearing looked not so much like bulky wrap-around machines as pieces of designer swimwear – swimwear that had been filtered through the imagination of a high-tech fetishist. They had something of the look of lightweight samurai armour, mixed in with elements of the S and M scene. But one thing struck the eye before all else – they were beautiful. Moreover, there was no sign of any trailing wires; these suits were radio-controlled.

'But this . . .' Kirsty began, almost stammering in her surprise.

'Is impossible?' Cynthia finished for her. 'Makes your old piece of has-been technology look like shit, eh?'

'B-but . . .'

Cynthia smiled. 'Ever been *screwed*, honey?'

The words were like a dash of cold water in Kirsty McDonald's face. She turned to face Cynthia, her eyes flaring. 'That's *ours*!' she screamed. 'We paid for the R and D!'

Cynthia outstared her. 'You got a *contract*, Ms McDonald?'

Long queues were forming in front of the Ubik stand as three security guards led a screaming Kirsty McDonald away. Watching proceedings from a distance, Nobushi Fukuada turned to Charles and gave a little bow. Charles bowed back, both men smiling at the success of their little subterfuge.

'My frens be here soon,' Fukuada said. 'With their help we make new suits biggest thing since biro pens.'

'Friends?' Sir James queried, stepping up to join the conversation. 'What friends are these, Mr Fukuada?'

Fukuada smiled broadly, showing his huge white teeth. 'IBM, Microsoft, Sony. They pay big be part of this. This biggest thing since . . .'

'Tom Dupont?' Cynthia suggested, and Fukuada grinned. 'We stuff them, eh, Cee-fee-a? Give Ubik big stick up the arsehole!'

Charles spluttered, but his father roared with laughter. 'Didn't we just, Nobushi! But tell me,' he said, beginning to lead the Japanese businessman away, one arm about his shoulder, 'just how did you know what was going on?'

As Fukuada explained things to Sir James, Charles turned and looked about him at his team. Bill and Ben had come out from behind the screen now, so all six of them who had worked on the project were together. Roger, who had been kept in the dark, looked on in bemusement, still stunned by the turn and turnabout of events.

'Well . . .' Charles began after a moment, 'I think this calls for a little celebration, don't you?'

'And I've got just the thing,' Patricia said, disappearing inside the stall, then returning with two huge bottles of champagne.

'It's a bit early, don't you think?' Roger said, finding himself in the unusual role of party-pooper.

Charles looked at him, then shook his head. 'No,' he said decisively. 'In fact, as your Chairman, I order you to celebrate. Patricia, hand out the glasses. Cynthia, Chastity . . .' And he looked at her with loving eyes. 'Do the honours.'

Corks popped, the bubbly poured. A moment later, all raised their glasses. 'To us!' Charles said.

'To us!' all echoed, but, even as their voices faded, there was a blood-chilling scream from the Ubik stall. A moment later a heavy-set German staggered from the stand, clutching his groin. There was the smell of burning in the air.

'Ach! Mein balls! Mein balls!'

~ *Epilogue* ~

Following the incredible success of their new slimline VR suits – renamed the 'Cybersex Mk I' when Sony launched them worldwide twelve months on – William and Benjamin were headhunted by Microsoft to head up a new VR research facility based in San José, California, and so got to visit Silicon Valley at last.

Cynthia, too, was rewarded for her contribution to the machine's success, being promoted to Director for Research and Development with a much-increased salary commensurate with her new responsibilities. But Cynthia was an ambitious girl and soon launched her own company, Virtual Love (UK), specialising in producing software packages for the new Cybersex machines, proving that the bonds had not been made that could hold a girl like Cynthia!

Patricia remained at Virt-E-Go's helm, but rarely stayed on in the office after five and never ever took work home. These days Patricia has better things to do, like performing with a Latin American dance group, with her partner . . . Dick Holly.

Louise bought out her partner and with the proceeds

bought the first franchise in Virt-E-Go's Dream Parlours. She has since opened four more branches and was recently shortlisted for a local Business Woman of the Year award. Louise is currently having an affair with one of her keenest customers, the Personal Account Executive from her bank.

Bob Guppy leads the life of a bachelor – frozen meals for one, Sunday-morning visits to the launderette and a fondness for videos that arrive through the post in plain brown wrappings. Since Davina's marriage to Viscount Fitzgormley, that source of nookie has dried up and he can often be seen along the darkened streets behind King's Cross seeking solace between the bony legs of a stranger.

At the unexpected news that his sixteen-year-old daughter was pregnant with twins, Roger Appleyard went berserk and following an assault on the alleged father – already married with three kids – was placed on probation. Since hearing the eighteen-month-old girls utter the word '*Grandad*' Roger has undergone a course of hair-replacement therapy, bought a two-seater open-top sportscar, and discarded his Y-fronts for Calvin Klein boxers. His wife, Jane, meanwhile, carries on her long-standing and secret affair with her therapist.

As for Charles and Chastity, they were married two months after the Trade Fair, in the same small local church as Charles's father, grandfather and great-grandfather were married. They, of course, lived happily ever after, and never once had call to use the machine that had so revived the family fortunes.

As far as we know . . .

POCKET
B O O K S

REAL WOMEN

SUSAN OUDOT

Five women, three days and a wedding.

Twenty-five years on from their first meeting, five friends
reunite for a riotous hen night. The two days that follow
reveal more secrets than any of them could ever have
imagined . . .

Love, friendship, marriage, kids, affairs, sex, life; no one
said it would be easy. But REAL WOMEN battle through
. . . and survive.

'Oudot writes as though you're eavesdropping on an
intimate girls' night out conversation. It makes a refreshing
change from the norm' *Today*

'Raunchily humorous' *You Magazine*

PRICE £5.99

ISBN 0 671 01598 2